THE
SORCERER'S GUIDE

INSIDIOUS SIX

L SCOTT CLARK

PART 1:

THE FACEOFF

CHAPTER 1

All four cavern walls crept in slowly, as if a colossal monster was gripping the mountain and squeezing. A metallic and bitter taste filled Jet Black's mouth as, for the first time, every magical spell he attempted failed him and, by extension, failed the friends he was trapped with.

Blood trickled from his lips and nose from the effort. *We're going to die and it's all my fault.*

Closing his eyes, he heard a crunch from his back right and knew the corpse he had once thought was one of his best friends was being pushed toward the center of the room. He nearly vomited. His eyes flashed open, resolved to break down the stone door. What he found was alarming. His friends stood behind him, huddled, and the stone walls hadn't moved an inch.

Am I losing my mind?

"Stand back!" he bellowed, his voice apprehensive, worried that the stress was getting to him. "It'll work this time." Focusing on the space below the door, though he couldn't actually see it, he spoke "Ne—"

Arms wrapped around him so tightly, he couldn't finish the spell. A voice whispered, "Stop freaking out. This isn't your fault. Brute force isn't the answer."

He knew that voice anywhere.

Mckenzey Downs, with her golden-brown hair, soft lips, and kind face, held him close. Pulling back, he tried to free himself. Several strands of her hair fluttered down, covering her right eye, but her genuine smile halted him. "You've tried twelve spells. Either Kevin unleashed a previously unknown Brotherhood curse, or this entire cavern is protected against Elemental magic."

"I just can't understand why we're trapped in here."

"None of us can," she said. "Eric suggests we brainstorm different options to get out."

Jet suddenly stepped back, absentmindedly rubbing at his injured right shoulder. Just a few hours ago, he had fought two mythical creatures just to make it to this room. His shoulder had been dislocated, and Eric, Mckenzey's boyfriend, had put it back into place. Right now, Eric was scrutinizing the hug she had just given him.

Jayco Carter declared, "Let's look at this logically." His towering figure was less than two feet from touching the eight-foot ceiling. His cargo shorts were torn, and a layer of sand was visible in his bleached-blond, surfer-style hair. "We're trapped in a mountain in Congo. Kevin is here, and from the looks of it, he's working with Shane, and they beat us to the location of the fourth piece of the Phoenix."

Jet sighed. "Any suggestions on how to get out of this mess?"

Jayco continued, as if announcing everything that Jet had done wrong up to this point. "Somehow, even though only the Elementals can touch the golden items, promised to us by the Rivalry, they're gone. As are the black ones."

"Jayco—" mouthed Mckenzey, but he cut her off.

Jet had an idea. He walked toward the wall, closed his eyes, and concentrated.

"Seyanna, one of our best friends, has been kidnapped by her father. We all thought she was dead, but now, we have a different corpse on the floor, which happens to be Rozene's best friend. We're trapped in this magic-protected room while your four golden animals are useless in the next-door chamber. Can't you communicate with them?"

The question surprised Jet, not for what it was, but for coming from Jayco. He mumbled, "Working on it."

Iris, a golden panther, along with three other golden animals, could transform from golden pyramids at Jet's request. They protect and follow his requests, thoughts, or even his feelings. She never spoke back. He searched for her presence and found her standing in a hallway beyond a large room, hiding.

What's wrong? he asked through his connection.

He received the impression that Kevin used something to force her and the other golden animals to retreat. *Is Kevin gone?*

A feeling of relief rushed over him, and Iris stepped back into the room.

"What is she saying?" demanded Jayco.

Jet lifted a hand to silence him. *Find the three pedestals in the center of the room. Go to the middle one and knock off the box.* Iris hurried to follow his request. To the others in the room, he added, "I can talk with her. She's trying to find the latch to let us out."

"About time," said Asher, who was grouped with several Elementals and had accompanied him to Congo.

Natalia, Allison, Alivia, and Jade avoided glancing in the direction of the covered corpse. Phoebe, Keesha, Lucas, Quinn, Lydia, and Melvin were seated against a side wall, as if they had run a long race and were trying to catch their breath. They each attended Chadwick's boarding school in California. Traveling to Congo had been necessary to thwart Shane Fallon and the other Runics from finding the fourth piece of the Phoenix before them. They had failed on so many levels.

Jade stepped past the prone figure. "I can't stand another second in this room with a dead body."

Iris's reaction filled his mind, and he pounded the rock wall once.

"What's wrong?" asked Mckenzey.

"We're stuck," said Jet. "Iris can't open the door." He released the connection with her.

"This can't be happening?" Keesha gasped.

Jayco said, "Everyone, try your talents and see if we can knock down the door."

Mckenzey's eyes closed, and she tried digging into the mountain as Jayco rained down powerful strikes, after having pulled up his golden bracelets. Others tried different things, and the next thirty seconds were loud, but after the dust settled, the cavern looked exactly the same.

His anger became focused on Jet. "We're trapped here. You had better give us some answers."

"About what?" asked Jet.

"The truth about what's happening here. Who's with us, and who's against us?"

"I've told you what *The Sorcerer's Guide* has told me."

Lucas and Quinn inched closer as Natalia, Allison, and Alivia sat on the ground against the far wall. Lydia, Melvin, Maria, and Keesha remained standing.

Jet whispered, "Bookshelf," so that only he could hear. He pulled out his ancient tome, which he kept hidden with other items. The leather bindings felt smooth despite its age. It only opened to his touch, and only he could read the words on its pages. It was his mentor who taught him about magic, instructing him on how to allow magic to choose others. His inner circle of friends, the Echoes, had seen and touched it before. If chosen to become an Elemental, you would be chosen to perform a single spell from either Water, Earth, Fire, Wind, or Spirit magic.

Jet tossed the book to Asher. "Try opening it."

"With my mind or my body?" He caught it deftly.

"This should be interesting," whispered Mckenzey.

"Whichever works."

Asher pulled at the front and back covers, but it didn't budge a millimeter. After a full minute, he gave up.

"Now, lay it on the ground."

Asher did so elaborately, clearly unconvinced that anything would happen.

Bending down, Jet flipped the front cover using a single finger. He saw Jayco roll his eyes.

"No way," gasped Phoebe. "I want to try." She hurried over to make an attempt with the same result.

"This tome, *The Sorcerer's Guide*, has taught me about Goth Aritha, a time when magic was well known. A civil war followed. The Demon Prince, known as Arisol, or the Grey Panther, was captured and imprisoned. I found it in a shadow box at my home. My parents must've found it before they died. When I turned sixteen, the book opened for the first time. It turns one page at a time when it wants to teach me something." He flipped it open and riffled through a dozen pages. "These pages I can access, but the rest I can't. Additionally, only I can read the words on its pages." Jet opened the tome to "The Legendary Battle." "This describes the Rivalry, the contest to control the six pieces of the Phoenix. These pieces are why we are in Congo. We've missed out on attaining the fourth piece. Whoever controls all six pieces will control the ability to defeat or join Arisol."

"Why does the Rivalry involve only the Elementals and the Runics?" asked Alivia.

Jet stared at her dyed black hair with blond tips and smiled. Her face revealed she was both curious and fearful. "I'm not entirely sure. *The Sorcerer's Guide* teaches the Elementals, while *The Mage's Letters* instructs the Runics. Shane Fallon is the leader of the Runics. The other three types of magic still sit on the sidelines."

Jade asked, "What are they?"

"Resititual, Shaman, and Incrementum."

"Those sound stupid," said Asher. "What good are they?"

"Resititual fixes magical mistakes that can be purposeful or arise from nothing. Shaman works with spirits and those who have passed on. Incrementum is focused on nature and growth."

"Yep," added Asher. "They do sound stupid."

"How did the Runics beat us to the fourth piece?" asked Alivia's friend Natalia. She was short, fair-skinned, and had brown hair, and she seemed eager and excited.

"Julian, that boy who died in the traps, is a good friend of Shane. Only Runics can touch the black items, including weapons, and Elementals can touch the golden ones."

"Kevin locked us in here," said Eric, holding Mckenzey close. "Does that mean Kevin is working with Shane?"

"No way," said Keesha. Her dark eyes were fierce and certain. She had more confidence than almost anyone Jet knew. She had been one of the first people outside the Echoes to learn about magic and become an Elemental. She was beautiful with black hair and skin. "Don't you remember what Kevin said when he closed the door?"

Phoebe recounted, "'Death to the Mikado. The Azurites have killed the Elementals. The Runics are next in Washington, D.C.'"

Jayco hissed, "Death to the Mikado is you Jet...the rest of us are collateral damage."

"Who are the Azurites?" asked Melvin.

Jayco answered, "They are a group that broke off from the Brotherhood. A difference of opinion." His eyes focused on Jet. "It might seem like the Brotherhood is helping us, but it's clear the Azurites are trying to stop us."

Phoebe asked, "Don't you trust the Brotherhood?"

Jet thought Jayco would answer for him, but he didn't. "Sometimes, but never completely."

"Kevin is the Brotherhood's prized possession," explained Jayco. "They gave him many of his powers. I don't think even they know what he is capable of."

Lydia asked, "Where's Seyanna?"

This question stung Jet. She had been missing for the last few months, then she texted and told him she would meet him at the airport in New York before coming to Congo. Jet said, "We think that she was kidnapped by her father, Chief Charlie Eckenkeep of the Brotherhood."

"We definitely can't trust the Brotherhood," agreed Asher.

"If the golden items aren't here, then someone from the Elementals is helping Kevin and whoever he's working with," said Lucas. "Was it Seyanna?"

Jayco took an aggressive step toward Lucas, "That's the stupidest question I've ever heard. Of course she wasn't involved."

Keesha stepped in front of Jayco.

Jet said, "I have no idea who can actually touch all the golden items. That's another reason we need to get out of here." He moved to store *The Sorcerer's Guide*.

Asher asked, "Where are you going to hide that?"

Jet lifted his hand. "This ring came from Alces, the daughter of Queen Aurora. When the Chupovanas attacked the school, she helped."

"I remember her," said Phoebe. "A purple moose. Didn't she die?"

"She did. Her sister killed her. But she offered me this ring with its hidden compartment before she died."

"I want one," said Asher.

"Keep dreaming," said Eric.

Jayco added, his voice cold, "Don't you know? Only the cool things happen to Jet?"

Mckenzey mumbled, "Like getting attacked, almost dying, and being tortured nearly to death."

Jet wanted to argue with Jayco, but it would serve nothing.

Keesha said, "Jet's been nearly killed twice. He was given a tonic that caused his mind to forget magic. We've all been through hard things. Aren't you jealous?"

"Totally," said Quinn. "The pinnacle moment is being locked inside a cave box with no way to escape."

Mckenzey replied, a pleading in her voice, "When we don't show up soon, they'll send someone, right?"

Quinn's face brightened. "That guy, Seyanna's father, called Marapi's phone. Shouldn't we be able to call out?"

Everyone pulled out their phones and checked their screens.

"Mine doesn't have any bars," said Lydia.

"SOS," added Jade.

Maria asked, "What about that girl's phone?"

It lay exactly where Jet had dropped it after speaking with Charlie. No one else moved. Hesitantly, he picked it up and checked the screen. "Nope. It's dead."

"We need a better plan," argued Asher.

Jayco retorted, "Be our guest."

Only silence followed.

"What skills do you guys have?" asked Mckenzey, her voice shaky.

Asher said, "I'm not completely aware of *all* my skills, but one thing I could never do before was focus on one item or picture in my past and recall it perfectly."

"Like a photographic memory?" asked Alivia.

"Yes. It's so cool. If I read only a single page of a book, later, I can recall the meaning of the entire book, even some of the more important details."

Melvin said, "That's crazy useful for tests."

"Quite possibly," said Asher, and he winked.

Jade said, "I was left-hand dominant, and now they both work the same. My hands can do separate things at the same time."

"I have a type of night vision," noted Phobe. "It isn't the same as infrared. It's more based on inanimate objects. Every living mammal is white; reptiles are yellow, and birds are red. Plants, rocks, buildings, and other things are much clearer."

Jet asked, "Did you use it when we were fighting the Drekavac demons?"

"Yes. It was valuable."

Jayco asked, "Anyone else?"

They glanced from one person to the next. Each shook their head no.

"None of those are going to help us get—"

"Iris just heard something," interrupted Jet.

"Something what?" asked Mckenzey. "Is Kevin coming back?"

"Shush," hissed Jet, stepping toward the door. A few moments later, he said, "Looks like it was nothing."

"This is so frustrating!" screamed Jayco. "How did this happen?"

"Kevin didn't fight the Ratas and Razors? Shane must've been first, and Julian was killed."

"Why is that important?" asked Mckenzey.

Jayco hissed, "Both Shane _and_ Kevin beat us here. Getting better by the second."

Ignoring this, Jet said, "We're in Congo. Marapi must've been alive at some point. When did they kill her?" Jet moved to the body. She had been positioned carefully. Reaching out, he pulled up her sweater to reveal the skin of her abdomen. There was a huge gash on her right flank.

"Why are you touching her?" Jade shuddered. "That's the grossest thing I've ever seen."

Ignoring this, Jet lifted the back of her head. There was blood smeared into her hair and on the back of her neck. Rolling her over, he found that her left and right arms and left ankle had been severely broken. Her body was becoming stiff. The pink and white striped sweater, which he thought was Seyanna's, hid most of the injuries. "How did we miss this?"

"Miss what?" Asher asked.

"They didn't kill her. She got killed."

"What's the difference?"

Keesha answered, "We saw blood on that rotating black metal box in the passageway coming here."

"That might explain these injuries," agreed Mckenzey.

"Like you said, how did *you* miss this before?" asked Jayco.

"I thought it was Seyanna, then Kevin showed up. It wasn't like I was looking for injuries. Her face is clean." He reached out to push some hair from her face, and a jolt of pain was sent through his shoulder. He had moved it slightly wrong, and his previous dislocation flared.

Phoebe knelt closer to Marapi's body. "They used makeup to hide some of the damage to her face."

"Who cares," said Asher. "It doesn't change anything."

"Well," said Jet. "It's unlikely they left the same way we entered. Possibly a second access. If that's the case, maybe this room has a second entrance."

Before anyone moved, the main door sprang open. Everyone spun, preparing to defend.

"Don't attack," said a voice from a far distance away.

"Who's there?" asked Mckenzey.

Jet tried speaking with Iris, but there was no response. He couldn't even sense her. This alarmed him.

The voice said, "It's Rozene Bluesky. Mikey, Trinity, and Hebrew are with me. Mikey just opened the door. It's just the four of us."

Jet shared a look with his friends, his eyes landing on Jayco. "How do we know it's you?"

"Come take a look."

A broad, knowing smile formed on Jayco's face.

"What happened to the golden animals?"

"An invisible barrier traps them."

Jet wanted to rush forward.

Quinn asked, "Why are you here?"

"I asked them to come," said Jayco, stepping forward.

"When?" asked Keesha.

"Before coming here. I had no idea if Jet, Mckenzey, and Raul would meet up with us after their adventure in Canada. I wanted a backup plan."

Jet said, "The Rivalry is for Elementals and Runics, not Predilectors."

"I know. That's why they didn't come *with* us."

Lucas asked, "Bro, why didn't you tell us sooner?"

"I honestly had no idea if they'd made it to Africa. We couldn't communicate."

Jet shook his head as things fell into place. "That's why you kept dropping those breadcrumbs."

"So, they would know which way to go," he agreed.

"Who freaking cares," said Asher. "We're free."

The group stepped forward, but Jet spoke. "Wait! How can we trust them?"

Jayco ignored this. "I trust her completely." He walked to the door and picked up Rozene, only she was visible to him. Her dark hair sat frayed on her shoulders, and she gushed with excitement.

Jet said, "Can Mikey reappear?"

Rozene squealed as Jayco tickled her. "He's right here."

A short, squat boy emerged into sight. He was mute but heard perfectly. Seeing him, Jet relaxed. The boy waved enthusiastically at everyone.

"Everything good?" asked Jet.

Mikey's lopsided grin assured him.

"Don't go in there," Jayco warned.

"What's wrong?"

"I don't know how to tell you this, but Marapi is in there. She isn't alive."

Rozene's face contorted. She glanced at Jayco, then into the room. She began sobbing. "What are you saying? Where is she?"

A chill ran down Jet's spine. Marapi and Rozene were best friends.

Rozene cried, "I thought you told me that she died at Dillon Lake."

Jayco said, his voice as kind as Jet had ever heard it, "That's what we thought. We were shocked to find her here. It appears that she has been assisting the Azurites. Kevin locked us in here."

"She despised Kevin. They had a few classes together, but she always ragged on him."

Jet said, "We think Azurites, Kevin, and Chief Eckenkeep are here. They kidnapped one of our friends, and either Marapi was helping them, or they were forcing her. They killed her."

"I've heard rumors at Dillon Lake that the Azurites had spies," said Rozene after a long pause. Her look at Jayco was pleading. "I don't know how Marapi could have been one of them. Are you sure? She wanted an opportunity to get magic as much as I did."

Jayco said kindly, "We're sure."

Rozene pushed her way into the room as everyone else, including Jet, exited. A moment later, a wail echoed through the cavern.

He found Iris and the other three golden animals cornered and blocked by a protective layer with a soft green hue. She scratched energetically at the layer but couldn't penetrate it.

For the next few minutes, he tried spells and some of the items he carried with him. He had kernels of corn, arrowheads, and shark's teeth. These items were handed down to him from his grandmother, though she had no idea what they could do. He had been given black powder, multicolored stones, feathers, eagle talons, and more. He had a decent understanding of what most of these items could do. When he held up a multicolored stone, Iris and the other golden creatures began to jump in unison.

"Does that mean anything?" asked Eric.

"Seems like it," admitted Jet. He tossed the item into the air, toward the ground, and took a step back.

"Do you know what you're doing?" asked Mckenzey.

"Not a clue. But Iris seems to think it's important."

CHAPTER 2

The multicolored stone fell through the air, as if in slow motion. The others in the room all turned to watch it fall. They moved normally. A heightened sense of anticipation rose as the stone came into contact with the floor. In the blink of an eye, it grew ten times in size.

"Is that an egg?" asked Eric.

Before he answered, the hard outer covering cracked and split, and a piece broke away. A single eye peeked out of the shell. A clawing sound ensued, and the creature broke completely free.

Quinn asked, "What the heck is that?"

"No clue," said Jet.

"It better not attack us," added Lydia.

Keesha exclaimed, "It's a cross between a lizard and a salamander. Check out the elongated body, four legs, and the colorful tail."

The creature was nearly two feet long. It climbed the closest wall, reached the ceiling, and then dropped, landing as expertly as a cat. Its texture mimicked the outer peel of an orange. Liquid glistened off its back, and there were three toes on each appendage. It stared up expectantly at him.

"Don't ask me," he said, speaking to the creature. "I don't know what to do."

The creature, still the same texture, somehow shifted into a bird. The creature bristled and shook, and several feathers fell to the ground. In the next instant, the creature transformed back to the salamander.

Phoebe asked, "Do you have a feather in your bag of tricks?"

"I do." He searched through his items and pulled out a twelve-inch red and black feather. "What now?"

The salamander dove at him, bit down on the feather, and broke free. It landed, scurried to the invisible barrier, and stuck the quill of the feather into the floor. The result was instantaneous. The entire feather sizzled and melted into the stone. The salamander pounced forward, its nose touching the barrier, which melted away.

Iris and the other animals toppled out, hurrying to the salamander. All four thanked the salamander profusely with chatters and squeaks.

Jet shook his head, unsure what had just happened. From the looks of the others, they were just as confused as he was. Phoebe appeared downright delighted.

Jayco and Rozene, arm in arm, returned, looking sullen. "What did we miss?" asked Jayco.

As Mckenzey explained, Jet said, "Let's try to find a way out of here."

The salamander broke free of Phoebe and came to Jet, nipping at his hand.

Phoebe fell onto her knees. "I think he wants you to release more of him...or her."

"Really?" asked Jet. He pulled out three other multicolored stones. The salamander danced emphatically. Jet dropped them onto the ground.

Each expanded until its shell broke. Three more salamanders with different colors and sizes scurried around.

Unsure what to do with the newcomers, Jet sent Jade and Asher to check the walls and Natalia, Allison, and Alivia to the hallways. Twenty minutes later, nothing new had been discovered.

"We'll have to go back the same way we came," said Allison. "It looks clear and Rozene and her friends made it without problems."

Jet asked, "What Predilector abilities can Trinity and Hebrew do?"

Asher replied, "They can't do magic."

"We know," said Keesha. "Predilectors have abilities but no magic. Kevin gifted them, but it isn't the same."

Rozene explained, "Hebrew can cause bug hallucinations and Trinity can whisper unintelligible words."

"How can Predilectors do this?" asked Quinn.

Hebrew said, "If you want a demonstration, I can show you."

Quinn didn't back down. "Not what I meant. How were you gifted?"

Trinity replied, "We rolled the Rohart dice and received an ability. Much like after you are chosen by magic."

"It's not the same," said Asher. "Don't pretend it is."

Natalia said, "You trick people into thinking something isn't there, and they go run off."

"Pretty much," replied Hebrew, but his eyes never left Asher.

"Cool," the girl replied.

Iris moved to the center pedestal and pawed the ground. Jet lifted the lid to the box—empty. Iris swiped again, near the ground, and hit something.

Eric hunched down. "Is that metal?"

"Sounded like it." Jet knocked twice. A high-pitched sound resonated. It didn't take long to uncover a three-foot-by-three-foot metal door with a single hinge and a keyhole.

Jet said, "Melvin. We're going to need that key."

"What about Marapi's body?" asked Rozene.

Standing, Jet spoke to Iris. She converted his idea to the grizzly bear. "We'll strap her onto the golden bear."

As Melvin unlocked the door, Jayco, Jet, Rozene, and Eric tied Marapi's body to the grizzly bear and then draped her with a blanket. Everyone else prepared to leave the room.

When they were ready, Jet said, "I doubt we'll be able to bring her home. Hopefully, we can find a place to bury her."

"Okay. Whatever you think, but I can't leave her here," said Rozene.

"Are we ready?" Jet peered around the room. Reaching down, Melvin pulled open the door. Suddenly, Jet was overtaken by a desire to scratch every ounce of skin off his body. The sensation was beyond anything he'd ever imagined. He scratched his arms and his legs and began tearing at his face.

Rozene pushed past him and slammed the door closed. The desire vanished.

"What the hell was that?" asked Asher.

Rozene explained, "There's a Predilector down there, making sure we can't escape."

"Any ideas?" asked Jet.

Eric asked, "Did anyone see if Iris or the others were affected?"

"They were," said Trinity. "We all were. That's the thing about Predilectors. We can affect each other. We aren't immune."

Melvin said, "There is a small space leading downwards. A ladder is attached to the wall, and it goes down maybe twenty feet."

Hebrew said, "I bet it's Samson. He's in the inner circle with Kevin."

"He's trying to give Kevin a chance to escape," said Jet.

Asher said, "Just drop me down. I'll distract this Samson, and you guys can take him out."

"Doesn't work that way," said Rozene. "Samson doesn't need to see you. You'll be scratching off all your skin by the time we arrive."

Jet said, "But think about it. We aren't getting affected by it right now. The rock is too thick, and the metal door is stopping it. So, there are things that can block the attack."

"Do you want me to rip off the door and use it as a shield?" asked Jayco.

"Yes," said Jet. "That's exactly what I want to do." Grabbing one of the extra golden swords, he tossed it to Jayco. "Do what you do best."

After five minutes of heavy pounding, the door broke off its hinges, but it was kept in place.

Jet said, "Get behind my air shield. If the Predilector's affinity travels like a sound wave, it might help."

Jayco pulled the door free, and the sensation of scratching returned, partially blocked. Those behind Jayco felt nothing.

Jet screamed, "Mckenzey. Make the hole bigger."

She shuffled forward. Her ability caused the rocks to swirl and drop to the floor below them. Jet lightly scratched at his arms and face.

Lydia asked, "Are we getting used to it?"

"No," said Rozene. "Something else is going on."

Jayco dropped the metal door, picked up a boulder, and tossed it into the hole. Rozene used her wave aptitude, and together, she and Jayco unleashed an attack.

The scratching sensation abruptly ended, but the broken pieces of stone and clay began to rotate in a funnel cloud.

Jet spoke "Kali," and the tornado of debris blocked his firebolt. "There's a Runic as well. I've seen that Matter shield before." He pulled out Gravity and whispered "Gravitas," and pulled out his enchanted blue blade. He dove into the hole and, using the blade, he slammed into the barrier. It held for a single moment, then vanished. The sensation of wanting to scratch off his skin returned immediately. He landed hard on his back, somehow avoiding his injured shoulder. From the corner of his vision, he saw someone standing in a recess of a tunnel, ten feet away. He tried to tear off his skin and stand at the same time. A swirl of wind began to rotate at his back.

Someone else landed next to him. There was a flurry of movement, but Jet focused his next attack and spoke "Kali," and four stunning firebolts shot forward, striking the figure. The itching sensation vanished. He spun around and found someone taking flight.

"You good?" asked Jayco.

"Get him," growled Jet as blood trickled down his face and neck.

Asher landed next to Jayco, and the two of them followed after the Runic. Jet turned his attention back to the Predilector, walking forward slowly, wincing at the throbbing pain in his back and shoulder. When he reached the unconscious Predilector, Rozene and Mckenzey stepped up on each side of him.

Rozene slapped the unconscious boy until he was awake. "What have you done, Samson?"

It took him a moment to recognize her. "You betrayed us?"

She placed her foot on his chest and pulled out a black dagger, bent down, and rested it just under his chin. "Who killed Marapi?"

Samson flinched at her rage, and the tip of the dagger cut into his skin. "It was an accident," he pleaded. "We didn't see the machine in the wall."

"Why was she here?" she asked.

"You know," said Samson.

A look of confusion crossed Rozene's face. "I really don't."

"She promised me she told you."

"Told me what?"

Samson glanced at Jet, then mumbled, "The Brotherhood has been lying to all of us. Kevin was created to kill those with magic. The Brotherhood doesn't want magic to return. Kevin uncovered the truth from Chief Eckenkeep and broke away from the Brotherhood."

"Are you this stupid?" asked Jet. "You're a Predilector. Why attack us?"

His eyes found Jet again. "You're in league with the Brotherhood. If you help them, they won't take away your magic."

"How exactly was Chief Eckenkeep involved?" asked Roszene. "I barely heard anything about him?"

"He first discovered the Rohart dice. He brought it to the Brotherhood, and they created the Predilectors as an army. That's what we are...an army."

Jet said, pointing his enchanted blade at Samson. "Kevin and Charlie Eckenkeep are working for the Azurites. They're against the Brotherhood, and it seems against magic."

Samson retorted, "We're all against the Brotherhood. Without Charlie and Kevin, we would have become slaves, just like you." He focused on Rozene. "Marapi said you would understand. She said you detest the Brotherhood."

"I do," said Rozene. "But I would never work with the Azurites. They're far worse."

Behind them, the rest of the group, including the golden animals, were climbing into the tunnel.

Samson said, "That's what Dart and Elliot said. Look at what it cost them."

"What happened to them?" asked Rozene.

"Dead. Kevin made sure they no longer spied on him for the Brotherhood."

"You killed Dart and Elliot?" asked Jet. "Weren't they some of the leaders of Dire Fraternity?"

"No," Samson said sharply. "They were puppets of Principal Berry and the Brotherhood. The only one who learned the hard truth was Marlon. At least he had the good sense to see reason. He's the face of Dillon Lake now. He still has everyone's respect."

"Why this hostile takeover?" asked Rozene. "Why now?"

"We realized the Jet and Shane can't win the Rivalry. They don't get along, and both think they are superior. They want to locate the other three types of magic and set them free."

A voice above them asked, "Can the rest of us come down?"

"Yes," answered Jet.

Mckenzey said, "You just said the Brotherhood ordered Kevin to kill everyone with magic. Now you're saying Jet and Shane want to free everyone. What are you guys trying to do?"

"A little magic is good; a lot is terrible. Arisol is a fable meant to control and divide those with magic and those without. The Demon Prince will end the chaos. Magic is too unstable."

"Magic chooses who should get magic," countered Jet.

Samson laughed. "Right. Jet once had two roommates with Elemental magic, then they tried killing the Echoes and taking Seyanna."

"How do you know who Seyanna is?"

"We've had spies in all the schools for months. Chief Eckenkeep rewarded us when we found Seyanna. She'll be such an addition to our army. We have a dozen Runics and Elementals on our side, and they've proven worthy to keep the magic. Unlike you all. Your time is almost over."

"Best of luck," said Mckenzey.

Rozene added, disgust in her voice, "Your foolishness got Marapi killed."

"Nah," Samson sneered. "You lied to her about your frustrations with the Brotherhood. She wouldn't have been so lost if *you* had been on her side. Instead, you choose the side of the enemy."

Samson moved, knocking Rozene's hand away from his throat, then unleashed a force so strong that nearly everyone was thrown to the ground, scratching themselves, including those behind them. Jet tore at his ear, nearly ripping it off. Somehow, with his right arm, he swung his blade, but the aim was slightly off, and it slammed into the back of Samson's shoulder and partly into his neck. The light in his eye vanished, and he slumped over, the compulsion ending instantly.

Rozene said, having fallen to the ground, "He's dead."

Several people, including Mckenzey, were huddled together. Jet touched her shoulder and rolled her over. She had scratch marks on her neck as if she'd been trying to choke herself.

She asked, "How did you stop him?"

"I've felt compulsion like that before when *The Sorcerer Guide* demands that I open it. I suppose I've had some practice in ignoring it."

"Good thing or we would all be dead,"

He nodded. "Can you try to heal some of these injuries?"

Ten minutes later, Mckenzey returned and announced, "I've seen almost everyone and they're alive. Melvin damaged his left eye. I don't think he can see. He'll need to see a specialist. Natalia is unconscious. She dug into her armpits until she passed out. I closed the wound, but it'll take time for her."

Jet hugged Mckenzey. He was relieved she'd been there to help, and he was overwhelmed by everything they'd been through. Eric eyed him, but then went to help Allison and Alivia, both of whom had scratches, prepare Natalia to leave.

"What do we do now?" asked Keesha.

Jet said, "Jayco and Asher ran after the Runic. We need to follow them. We're leaving in five minutes."

"I'm exhausted," whispered Mckenzey.

"I'll help," said Jet. He pulled out some muddy water and passed one to her. Elemental magic required energy and lots of it. Early on, Jet discovered that the combination of earth and water helped. Grantham studied several different variations. He and Mckenzey each drank a combination of lagoon water, clay, crushed mushrooms, and black sand. The return of energy was sizable.

"Anyone see Mikey?"

Rozene answered, "He's over here. He bit a chunk out of his arm. I'm cleaning it now."

Mikey leaned back and shrugged.

"What are we doing with Samson?" asked Lucas as he and Quinn stood near the body. Both were bleeding from superficial scratches.

"Leave him and Marapi," said Rozene. "I don't have the energy to care anymore about them."

Mckenzey bent down, touched the ground, and a hole appeared. Marapi and Samson were rolled inside. A moment later, she covered the hole.

Melvin came forward, a torn shirt over his left eye. "Can we talk?"

"Sure," said Jet.

"When we came down, three of those walking fishes came down with us. One stayed behind. Iris and the other golden animals also stayed up top. There was nothing I could do."

"Not a problem," said Jet. "But interesting." He walked to the tunnel upward and yelled, "Iris. Time to go."

Iris and the other animals jumped down. A few minutes later, they began walking. It was slow going with the injured. No one said anything. The walls were rough and twisted back and forth, sometimes narrow, tall, wide, or short. Often, rocks crumbled into small clumps.

Maria whispered, "What's the plan?"

"Depends on where this leads us," said Jet. "We need to get to D.C., but we need to find Kevin."

Five minutes later, they rounded the next corner and found Asher helping Jayco wrap something around his arm. Near his feet was the Runic, dead and unseeing.

"What happened?" asked Rozene, hurrying forward to comfort the boy.

"She knew we were catching her, so she hid and attacked." Asher pointed to a crevice off the main tunnel. "She jumped out from there and cut Jayco's arm, but she wasn't fast enough to get away."

Jayco said, "She had the drop on me. Asher saved my life. Thanks, man. I never saw her coming."

Jet went to the body and checked. "No pulse." The cut had gone right across her neck. He didn't recognize her.

A large, curved blade lay on the ground a few feet away. Eric stepped over and picked it up. "This is impressive."

Jayco straightened up. "We need to keep moving."

Ten minutes later, Maria asked, "Why D.C.?"

"That's where the next piece of the Phoenix is," replied Jet.

"Will that be the fourth or fifth piece?" asked Rozene.

Jayco answered, "The fourth was supposed to be here."

"The first piece was in Silverton, Oregon, where the first disaster was, and where some of us went to school," explained Mckenzey. "The second was in Argentina, and the third was on Starbuck Island in the South Pacific."

Jet continued, "We discovered Shane found the opening near a place called Spruce Knob. We sent some Elementals there to ensure we know where to go."

"So...Shane came here, beat us, then flew directly to D.C.?" asked Asher.

"Seems like it," agreed Jet.

Hebrew said, "That disaster last August happened near New York and D.C., when the two storms collided, was caused by Spruce Knob?"

"Yep," said Jet. "The pieces of the Phoenix are related to natural disasters."

"Crap," said Quinn. "That means the sixth disaster is still going to happen. So many people are going to die!"

"Yes, they are," muttered Jayco.

CHAPTER 3

The cave began to widen slowly, and the floor dropped slightly. The first hint of sunlight crept into the cave, halting the group. Jet guessed they'd traveled around three miles. He had no way to know where they were, but if they came out on the opposite side of the mountain from where they'd entered, it might be twenty miles from any transportation.

Several large trees obscured the precise opening, and the light reaching them was filtered. He said nothing but pointed at the group, stopping them. Natalia was lowered to the ground, and Mikey practically collapsed. Jet crept forward.

"I don't want to die," echoed a soft voice to his right.

Jet's head jerked to the noise. A wide crevice, big enough to hide someone, was cut into the wall. A pool of congealing blood was at its opening.

"Who's there?" asked Jet, and he pointed to Eric and Asher to move against the same wall. He signaled for Maria and Keesha to be ready as well.

"Sarika," came a soft voice from the darkness. "I haven't chosen magic yet, but I want to be an Elemental. I'm also an Azurite."

"Are you armed?" demanded Eric. "Are you a threat to us?"

"I have a green hammer. Kevin made it so that only I can touch it."

Jet peered at Jayco and frowned.

"How injured are you?" he asked.

"I can't move my left arm. It was cut badly. I've lost a lot of blood."

Jayco said, "Toss out your hammer?"

"You won't be able to pick it up," replied the girl.

"You won't be able to attack us with it either," answered Jet.

"Fair enough." Her voice was soft and weak.

The hammer rolled end over end until it came to a stop in the middle of the tunnel.

"Come out slowly," said Jet. To Eric and Asher, he whispered, "Grab her and move her away from the hammer. Check for any other weapons."

Sarika emerged, one arm in the air, the other hung loosely at her side. She was instantly pinned to the tunnel's wall, her head facing the opposite direction. She winced in pain, and a sigh escaped her throat.

Rozene hurried forward and examined her injured arm. "She's fine. I don't think it's dislocated, but she has a large gash from her wrist to her elbow. Her elbow is swollen. It might be broken."

"No weapon," said Asher.

"Bind her hands in front of her," said Jet. "Then Mckenzey can try to heal her. Everyone else, take a break."

Eric worked quickly, turning Sarika's face forward. In seconds, both hands were bound. Mckenzey approached, and soon her skin was scabbed, the skin red.

"Can't heal the elbow right now," said Mckenzey after downing another muddy water.

Jet strode forward, wanting a quick look at where they were. Two feet from the entrance, Sarika said, "Don't take another step."

Jet froze.

"There's an alarm that will sound if you go any further. Our camp is in a clearing a quarter of a mile beyond the opening, shielded by some trees on the opposite side. No matter how strong you think you are, they're prepared for you. You'll need a solid plan to escape from here."

Jayco asked, "Why should we believe you?"

"The Azurites believe that," she paused for a moment. "I've always agreed with it until I found myself in my current predicament—don't let yourself be a prisoner. If I'm seen with you, I'll have a target on my back, and I don't want to die."

"You tried killing us," said Keesha.

"Yes. And I would've kept trying. That changed when you caught me and, more importantly, healed me. Now, I'm indebted to you."

"We can't trust you," said Keesha.

"You'll learn that you can. Where I come from, my family worked behind the scenes until they were caught. We've helped rescue slaves, the despised, and those exploited for one reason or another. I believed that was the goal of the Azurites, up until this incident. They left behind kids to make sure you were trapped and killed. They sacrificed the injured to ensure the group's escape. They left me to die."

Jet asked, "What do you mean?"

"I'm not leaving Congo alive. They never really believed you would escape, but I was forced to wait."

"Where are you from?" asked Jayco. "I've seen you before."

"Kochi. In India."

"Are you a student at Chadwick's?"

She nodded. "This is my second year. I was sent there to learn as much as I could about magic and those involved. My family has known the Azurites since I was younger. They were caught by the government smuggling people out. The Azurites freed them and many others. We were forever indebted to them. We moved to England, and I learned English. That was when we learned about the Brotherhood and the return of magic to the earth. I met Kevin five months ago. He told me to join the Elementals, but I haven't had a chance."

"You're traitors?" said Jayco.

"No," Sarika said, "Maybe infiltrators, but not traitors."

"What's the difference?" asked Mckenzey.

Keesha answered, "She's doing whatever it takes for her cause."

Sarika shifted. "What would you do if you realized your protectors had lied to you, tried to sacrifice you for their cause?"

"Is that what you think?" asked Maria.

Eric added, "Or are you doing whatever it takes to gain our trust?"

"I saved you and me from certain death," Sarika replied. "And it no longer matters what my cause was; it's over now."

"I'm not sure we believe you," said Jet.

Sarika stared at him in disbelief. "How can I prove it to you?"

"You will help us get back safely. Get her ready."

"What are you going to do?" Sarika asked.

"You are going to help us see who is out there. You could have heard us coming and set off an alarm and now you're wasting our time." He peered around at the others. "Everyone...get ready. Drink some energy and wrap your wounds."

"I'm telling you the truth."

Jet added, "Maybe." He pulled off his jacket. He wished he were wearing his cloak, but it had been destroyed. "Mckenzey. Can you wrap my shoulder so it doesn't get dislocated again?"

"I can try."

She found a shoulder strap, but it limited his motion. It wasn't a sling and fit tightly over his shoulder and upper arm. He slid it on, grimacing the entire time.

Allison and Aliva moved to Natalia and tried to wake her. She was still groggy, and when Natalia tried to stand, she was unsteady. The rest of his friends began to prepare for battle. Iris came to stand next to Jet. She growled once at Sarika. His eyebrows rose slightly.

"How can you disable the alarm?"

She pointed to a spot in the ceiling. "There is a lever up there?"

"How?" asked Jet. He placed the enchanted blade back into Gravity and used the staff to locate and turn the switch, pushing it forward.

A shimmer occurred in the air before the entrance.

"I saw it too," said Mckenzey.

Sarika said, "Beyond the trees shielding the entrance are two paths. The one to the right is more open with shrubs, smaller trees, and a pile of rocks. The one to the left is more hidden, situated in a small forest and surrounded by many trees. Between the two paths lies a large ravine or gully, which is deep. The camp is on the opposite side."

Jayco suggested, "I'll take Rozene, Mikey, Hebrew, and Trinity to the left. You and the others go right. If anyone is waiting for us, they won't be expecting both paths to be taken."

"Good idea," said Jet. "Be ready for anything."

"This is a mistake," announced Sarika.

Iris growled again.

Jade cleared her throat. Jet turned to face her. "That is the most truthful thing she's said."

"How can you tell?" asked Jet.

"My ability started when we landed in Congo. I'm just understanding it. Sarika has a way of telling the truth by telling a lie. I feel it."

"No one tells the complete truth," retorted Jayco.

"I'm learning that. It's just a feeling I have. Take it or leave it." She stepped back.

Jet asked, "Is there a trap near the cave entrance?"

"No," said Sarika.

Jade coughed.

"Just testing you," said Sarika. "We were all thinking it."

"What kind of trap?"

"It causes a mist to immobilize anything that moves through it."

"It could be an animal."

"It's possible there is a pile of stunned animals."

Rozene asked, "How?"

"It's a mist," she replied.

"Truth," said Jade.

Peering at Jade, she bowed her head.

"How were you going to escape?" asked Jet.

"After two days, Samson was to deactivate the alarm. But I overheard Charlie tell Kevin that there was no way home. Samson and I were dispensable."

"Can Rozene do it instead?"

"No," said Sarika.

Jade announced, "A lie and a truth."

"Without this," Sarika held forth a key.

"How?" asked Asher.

Her hands were no longer bound.

"I've had practice before. I'm no threat to you."

"What are we walking into?" asked Jet.

"Not sure. They could be standing in lines, waiting for you, or they could be gone."

"Both are truths," said Jade.

"How did you find this place?" Jet's hands swirled about his head to indicate the tunnel they stood in.

"Dania. A girl from Dillon Lake has echolocation as her Predilector affinity. She was shown a dozen caves. We found two more entrances, which were full of these strange creatures. This was the only safe entrance. We had no knowledge of your entrance."

"How did you know?"

"We had Quills and students following you since you set foot into these mountains. Kevin put up a barrier so you couldn't see or feel us. He said he should have done the same thing when chasing Jet, Mckenzey, and Raul in Canada."

Jet glared at her. "He tried killing me."

"Don't tell me you are surprised by his behavior?" asked Sarika.

Jet glanced at Jade; she nodded once.

"I see."

"A dead Mikado or Czaric means the Rivalry fails. Or if we can steal the items needed to stop Arisol, you'll be weakened. The Azurites believe Arisol will save them, and the real evil is the Silver Fox."

Jayco said, "We heard mention of the same thing at Dillon Lake."

"Marapi wouldn't stop talking about it," said Rozene. "I thought she was joking around."

"It's what we believe," said Sarika, her voice strained.

Jade tilted her head back and forth, and Jet thought he understood.

"Can I have the key?" asked Rozene.

Sarika stretched out her hand, but Rozene kept her distance. "Marapi always thought you would join her. I guess she was wrong."

"She wasn't wrong," said Rozene. "Just missed the mark. We were supposed to join the students at Chadwick's, not the Azurites." She took two steps forward and plucked the key from her fingers. "Tell me what I need to do."

"Outside the cave, to the right, is a box the size of a shoe box. It'll be hidden. You'll need to open it and place the key inside the console. The spot will be on the left. Don't lift the box, knock it over, or move it otherwise. Turn the key to the left, back to the center, and to the left again. You will hear the box power down. That's when we can escape."

"All truths," said Jade.

"Let's do this," said Rozene.

Trinity and Hebrew blocked her path. Trinity asked, "Are we going behind you? We need to watch out for each other."

Mikey rushed forward, and as he passed Jet by, there was a pat on his shoulder.

Rozene said, "Mikey, you need to stay behind."

Mikey nodded as if agreeing, and then he vanished, snatching the key from Rozene.

"We're talented rule followers," said Jet. "It's a miracle we get anything done."

Jayco, Rozene, Trinity, and Hebrew dashed to the cave's entrance, but said nothing and listened intently. The next few minutes passed by slowly. Mikey suddenly reappeared, a grin spanning from one side of his face to the other.

Rozene nearly smacked him. "You could have been injured."

He shrugged, then scribbled something onto his pad. Rozene read it aloud, "Trap is disabled. Packing up camp. Four vehicles. A girl is tied up under a large tree. Several guards."

Jet nearly sprinted from the cavern.

Jayco pulled up both golden bracelets, ready to attack, "We can't delay."

Everyone began to prepare. In just a few minutes, additional weapons and muddy drinks were passed out. Jet pulled a golden sword from his hidden compartment and gripped Gravity in his right hand. Anyone could use this particular golden weapon. Some of the other weapons had chosen their wielders. Along the far side, Maria held two orbs. They had once chosen him, but that had been ages ago. Mckenzey held her golden daggers at the ready.

Eric announced, "I think that everyone but Jet, Keesha, me, and Sarika should go left. We'll distract them and let you guys sneak in."

"We should try to disable the vehicles quickly," said Hebrew.

Trinity added, "It sounds like we're going to be outnumbered. The element of surprise is essential."

"Let's even the odds," a voice echoed behind them. Everyone jumped, spun, and shifted to a defensive posture.

Four figures stepped from the shadows. Jet recognized two of them. Beckham, Jocelyn, a boy, and a girl, all of them Runics.

Jocelyn refused to look at him.

Eric hissed, "What are you doing here?"

"We come in peace," said Beckham, but he didn't look at peace. "Consider it a temporary truce to what has been going on for the last several weeks. This is Derek and Victoria. They're excellent in a fight." Derek was tall, lean, and strong. Victoria, with short-cropped black hair, wore army boots, a camouflage vest, and pants. She was hiding several weapons.

"Not a chance," said Keesha, glaring daggers at Beckham. "We know all about your dirty work."

"It's called ambition, little girl. But today, we're on the same side. So, chill. Our black items are missing, and I think you might know why."

"It was Julian," said Sarika. "He was an Azurite and gave us information on Shane and Jet."

"What?" said Jet and Beckham at the exact same time.

All eyes focused intently on Sarika. She added, "He joined Runic magic to get close to Shane. He could talk with animals. He moved up quickly."

"Are you saying that Shane hasn't already been here?" asked Jet, confused.

Beckham answered. "Of course he hasn't, or why would we be here?" Turning back to Sarika, he asked, "Are there other Runics working for the Azurites?"

"Yes. But they couldn't pick up the black weapons."

"So how did they get them?" asked Jayco.

"One of his hands was missing," said Jet, picturing the image of Julain's battered body. "They must've cut it off to pick up the black pieces."

"Probably why things have been going so slowly," explained Sarika. "They should've been packed an hour ago. It takes time to load the pieces one by one."

Mckenzey said, "Just put the pieces on a sheet and carry them."

Beckham answered. "They can't. They become as heavy as an elephant if the right people don't touch them. Isn't it the same with the golden pieces?"

"Maybe," said Jet. "We haven't done that extensive research."

Sarika said, "I watched part of it. Every twenty minutes, the black pieces needed to be touched by the severed hand. It wasn't pretty."

Derek asked, "Do you have the golden items?"

Jet didn't want to answer, but Maria shook her head.

Jocelyn asked, "Who betrayed the Elementals?"

"No one," said Jayco emphatically. "They kidnapped Seyanna."

Sarika said, "We have some Elementals on our side, like Darium Fitz. He's here."

Jocelyn just shook her head. "We all have some serious problems. We need to figure this out."

"How did you find us?" asked Jet.

Beckham jeered, "Shane sent us to follow Jayco. To our surprise, we also saw Rozene. We thought there was going to be a fight. We came in, and no one from Chadwick's was dead. Too bad. It was clear you had gone down the passage, into the tunnel. It really wasn't that hard."

Rozene said, "No one likes a pretentious ass."

"I do," said Victoria, wrapping both of her arms around Beckham and kissing him with an open mouth, her tongue expertly cleaning his teeth.

Bile rose in Jet's throat, but he couldn't look away. In the next second, he was overwhelmed by a feeling of compulsion, but only slightly different than the need to scratch his own skin and far more powerful. Without consciously acting, he dropped his weapons, pulled out his tome, and slid onto the floor.

From hundreds of miles away, he heard Beckham demand, "What's happening? Is he giving up?"

A few figures moved to protect him. Mckenzey said, "No, you idiot. His book wants to show him something. Doesn't the same thing happen to Shane?"

"Maybe." Beckham inched closer. "Will someone look at what he's reading?"

"Even if you could," added Mckenzey, with her dagger in her hand. "There's no way we would allow you to get that close."

CHAPTER 4

The Syntac

A Rhoenix gives birth to a dozen offspring every year. These eggs resemble colorful, smooth rocks more than spawn. For birth to occur, there is no need for fertilization, but the seed must be planted in a sacred location, often a place associated with death. The stones have become precious, for they can elevate the poor, the defenseless, and the ambitious to an unattainable status. As a result, eggs have been an imperative commodity. The more stones you possess, the greater your prestige.

Over the years, the true nature of the eggs has become lost, especially after magic was lost. Still, they are searched for, stolen, and bartered for a king's ransom by those who have access to the den of a Rhoenix. A den is seldom discovered, but it often lies at the apex of a waterfall, hidden within a small cave. They will not be found in any lower cavern used to hide treasure, find shelter, or the birthplace of all dragons. These shells have become more valuable than gold, silver, most weapons, or any jewel obtainable. Of these eggs, only one in a hundred becomes a full-fledged Rhoenix; there hasn't been a live one in centuries. The death of Sarcoff changed their legacy forever.

Hundreds of Syntac eggs have been found, used, and hidden for a more common purpose. If a Rhoenix is not borne from the shells, it is a Syntac. These creatures will do your bidding and can never be tricked, coerced, or fooled. They become of one mind and one purpose with their owners. They are all but indestructible and can only be killed by Incrementum magic or one of the five Chalna weapons.

The limits of Syntac are well-documented and widely known. The spells initiating control can be performed by anyone with magic, even Predilectors, or those not blessed with magic. Once a spell has been performed, the Syntac may or may not accept its use. If not, the Syntac will become a salamander or a lizard and live out the rest of its days in obscurity.

Syntacs become tethered to where the spell was performed. It may travel a short distance to perform the actions required. Some will remain in the precise location for ten years after the spell is initiated, while others can only be used once. Once the ten years are finished, the Syntac will transform and disappear.

The following are the types of Syntacs and their associated spells:

A Watcher - Doreskimo

This Syntac will remain in a location, often unseen, and will act as the eyes of those who cast the spell. Use the additional spell of "In-com" to gain the foresight of a watcher.

A Fighter - Flurskina

This Syntac will transform into a Dragon's mist and can attack the enemies of those who cast the spell.

A Protector - Jabacona

This Syntac will transform into Angel's wings and will protect those who cast the spell.

A Mimic Killer - Vikooma

This Syntac will only transform for someone challenged by a Mimic. This Syntac is the rarest. Because a Mimic can isolate those not in-volved in a challenge, this Syntac is beyond valuable. It will remain in the exact location forever, as Mimics can be reborn multiple times.

A Finder - Slarspina

This Syntac will locate a lost artifact, door, cavern, or other item. However, this Syntac will vanish the instant the item is found. It can only be used once.

A Replenisher - Humsingala

This Syntac will transform into a Mending Mistress and fix the unfixable. This is nearly as rare as a Mimic Killer. Once it is used, it will be lost forever. It can be used on the cursed but may not completely fix the bane unleashed.

CHAPTER 5

Precious seconds ticked by as Jet stared blankly at the stone floor. Slamming close his tome, he tried standing as the new information gelled together in his mind. Despite his unsteadiness, he said, "Doreskimo," concentrating on the Syntac back in the upper cavern. He now understood why the salamander had remained behind.

A warmth spread across his chest, telling him he had done it correctly. He said, "Incom," and the salamander's present vision overlapped his current sight like a movie projector. Ratas and Razors approached the cavern through the long hall, then poured into it and surrounded the hole in the floor. It wasn't large enough to fit through, so they began clawing at the stone floor.

He spoke "Incom," and the vision disappeared. Everyone stared at him, perplexed. "I'll tell you the specifics later. For now, there's a horde of Ratas and Razors coming. We should go—now!"

He pulled out kernels of corn, arrowheads, and six shark teeth from his backpack.

Mckenzey asked, "What did the book tell you?"

"A change in the plan," he said. To the group, he added, "The kernels of corn will create duplicates of you if you keep one in your hand. No clue how long it will last, so be careful. Placing the tip of the shark tooth into the dirt will create a protective barrier from outside attacks. Using the arrowhead and adding water will create a huge surge in power in the direction the arrowhead is pointing. Use these if you need them."

Beckham held out his hand, and several Runic items materialized. "The ivory sticks need to be held between your teeth, giving you speed. If you swallow them, you'll get an increase in strength. The glass vial, when opened, will create a magical barrier, like a shield. You can communicate with animals when the small antler piece is pushed against your skin. None of these will last forever." These were passed out among the group quickly.

"Thanks." Jet inclined his head at the Runics. "This was more help than he could have expected."

"What now?" asked Jayco.

Weaving through the group, he reached Sarika, lifting a golden blade to her neck and staring deep into her eyes. "I suggest Sarika and I step out first. I'm going to pretend to take her hostage. We're going to the right, just the two of us. I have a few other things up my sleeve. Break into two groups, and divide the Elementals, Runics, and Predilectors as evenly as possible. One group goes to the left and the other right, but well after Sarika and I. Remember, the Quills hate water, so use it against them. Attack when I give the signal."

"What's the signal?" asked Keesha.

"You won't miss it." Jet leaned close to Sarika. "This is your only chance to make it out of here alive. Are you game?"

"Yes. But this is a terrible plan."

Scratching sounds echoed from the tunnel behind them.

"I think you'll be surprised." He dragged Sarika toward the opening. He added, "Iris and the other golden animals...stay with the group but come if called." He broke the barrier and moved to the right.

"I can walk," the girl hissed.

"How would that look if someone is watching us now?" He yanked her hard, and she stumbled onto the ground. Her knee hit a rock, and the pant leg tore. Blood flowed freely down her leg.

The path to the right bordered a natural rock wall over a dozen feet into the air. The bottom of the pit beside the path was obscured by plants, trees, and the angle looking into its depths. He continued pushing forward, dragging Sarika past the trees and rocks, heading toward the two boulders. He couldn't tell if anyone had seen him yet, but there was activity on the far side. The camp was nearly taken down. He could see where crates, tents, chairs, and other items had been placed, leaning against two vehicles.

When they reached the two large boulders, he pulled her to the ground. "You're doing great. Sorry you tripped."

She retorted, "You're very believable. Have you decided to use me as bait?"

"Wouldn't that be fun?" Scanning the area, he saw no sign of Seyanna. Two students stood behind a truck with an open bed, putting in supplies. Another two were dousing a fire. Others were cleaning or carrying items. Gear was being arranged. Two vehicles were fully loaded, while the fourth was an SUV. Each vehicle's windows were tinted, preventing him from seeing inside.

"Where's the girl?" asked Jet.

"Your people said she was tied to a tree. I need to start screaming to get everyone's attention if I'm going to sell this. It's a code word to say we're under attack."

"Do it," said Jet.

"Sparrow!" screamed Sarika.

Hoisting Sarika to her feet, he wrapped an arm around her neck and held the golden blade to the skin of her neck. He positioned her body in front of him. Four students next to the fire reacted first. They said something, and then a boy's head shot up, scanning their direction.

Jet hissed, "Darium."

The boy bound off the back of the truck with a sly smile, heading toward his weapons. Another student howled into the air, his voice echoing around the clearing. Ten students, holding weapons, exited the forest on both sides of the vehicles.

He recognized Kevin McCormick. His long, brown hair and slight beard gave him a look that suggested he was in his early twenties. He had once attended Chadwick's and had even been in elementary school with Jet in Silverton, Oregon. He'd known him for years. The contours of his face had been erased, replaced by new ones; this was no longer the same boy. He was taller and skinnier but screamed brutality.

A few months ago, Shane had attacked the school with a powder to identify those with an affinity to Elemental magic. Kevin had been identified, taken, and brought before the Brotherhood for their own purposes. He was supposed to be the Brotherhood's puppet, but something else had happened. Jet had seen Kevin for the first time since he had disappeared at Dillon Lake a few weeks ago. Now, Kevin was helping the Azurites, enemies of the Brotherhood and the same group that had killed Jet's parents.

"I shouldn't be surprised you made it out of that tomb," shouted Kevin, smirking. "In what direction are your friends hiding?"

"I killed some of your friends to get here. Samson was just not formidable. That Runic was pathetic. And this one..." Jet yanked Sarika, cutting her across the neck. He healed it immediately.

His plan might suck, but it was all he had. Kevin's face contorted into a rage, and he lifted both hands to communicate with his accomplices. On his left hand he wore a black glove, while the one on his right was green.

"What do you want?" demanded Kevin.

"You know what I want. I'll trade this girl for Seyanna."

"How do you know she's still here?" Kevin peered around. His friends laughed as they spread out.

"If she's not. Call her back."

"Or what?"

Jet shoved Sarika toward the pit, ready to shove her in.

"Jet!" screamed Seyanna from deep within the forest. "It's a trap." Jet's heartbeat quickened, worried that Sarika had double-crossed him. He pulled her back, and this time, his knife dug into her side. With each prominent movement, he pushed them closer and closer to the group.

"One way or another, I'm coming to get Seyanna. This girl is no consequence to me."

"Guess what, Black? Bring it. I'd love to see you try," said Darium.

Jet shouted back. "Shut up, traitor." He spoke "Abzu," and a large ice crystal dropped toward Darium. The boy had nowhere to hide, and he wasn't fast enough. But a square barrier extended up as much as ten feet. The ice crystal smashed into the barrier and exploded. The group of students, the vehicles, and a small portion of the forest were protected. Jet knew precisely where they were keeping Seyanna.

There was a flicker of movement as if the invisible barrier went on the fritz. One moment, he saw nothing, then two dozen Quills, five fighters of the Rufu squad, and two enormous flying vultures appeared; then, they were lost from view. Their position was to his right, above him on the ridge. The Quills and Rufu squad were just fifteen feet away. The Gorgeions hovered behind some trees near the only road exiting the open camp area. It was a dirt road, bumpy and uneven.

Sarika tensed. She must've seen them as well.

Jet whispered, "Don't look around." He took the knife and cut her shirt. He bellowed, "I'm not messing around." He continued forward.

Charlie Eckenkeep stepped from the small forest, dragging Seyanna. "No one thinks you're messing around. We just aren't convinced you're strong enough to stop fifteen students and an old man. As strong as you think you are, we know better."

Upon seeing Seyanna, red-hot anger surged in his chest. Jet spoke "Pachamama," and a massive crack appeared in the ground two dozen feet ahead of Kevin and the Azurites. Whatever protective barrier against magic they were using didn't extend into the earth. The back end of one of the vehicles crashed into the hole. The crack went from the pit and straight back into the forest, dividing the camp into two. Several people fell to their knees.

Using the hand with the green glove, Kevin made a motion toward the approaching crack, which stopped immediately. The barrier shifted to block his magical attack. But when doing so, the hidden attackers again came into view. Once he finished blocking the attack, he moved, and the attackers disappeared.

Sarika whispered, "Oh...you're good. I've never known how he does that."

Jet walked forward another dozen steps. "I'll attack you all day until the Ratas and Razors arrive. They'll attack all of us, and we'll see who the last one standing is."

Charlie Eckenkeep replied, "We will be long gone before that happens." He pulled out his own knife and pointed it at Seyanna's flank.

"You wouldn't kill your own daughter." But Jet's voice rose slightly, and he held his breath.

"I can cut her so that she suffers, and you can watch. We organized that game at Dillon Lake to know your abilities. We know that your talent is closely tied to your vision. Let's see if you can see this."

"No," Kevin roared, glaring at Seyana's father. "We don't have time. How often do I have to tell you? Finish packing, and I'll deal with Jet. Be ready to leave in ten minutes." He turned back to face Jet. "I don't think it will take me that long."

Jet took a few steps forward, coming within striking distance of the Quills. Either they were biding their time, or had something else planned. Jet slipped behind an enormous rock, and he let go of Sarika. Reaching into his backpack, he pulled out three salamander creatures. He murmured, "Jabacona," and two of them became protectors. He spoke "Flurskina," to the third, and it became a fighter. All three animals bowed their heads as if accepting his commands and slithered into the pit.

Jet gave Sarika a kernel of corn, and two more images of her appeared. He spoke "Opazo," and directed the spell outwards toward the Quills and the Azurites. They never saw it coming, but it felt like someone was watching. Some of the Quills bellowed in pain, and suddenly, there were screams from the Rufu squad and the Azurites collectively. His friends screamed, adding to the confusion. Spells shot forward, slamming into Kevin's barrier. "Someone else is here," cried an Azurite, who stumbled backward a few steps.

"What's happening?" demanded Darium, trying to put his hands over his ears.

Stepping out, Jet held an image of Sarika by the neck. She was free to remain behind the rock, and the body of her image felt present yet insufficient.

Kevin used his green glove to stop the next volley of spells.

Darium screamed back, "Jet. Was that you?"

"Whatever do you mean?" asked Jet.

Charlie answered, "I seriously thought we were about to be attacked by a platoon of soldiers. That was ingenious." He looked to his right, where Seyanna had been...but she had disappeared.

Jet called out, "Seyanna's gone. She can outrun any of you."

Charlie bellowed, his voice enraged, "Find her and kill Jet Black."

The ambush began in earnest. The concealed mass emerged, and several Quills launched a volley of arrows at Jet. The Gorgeions rose into the air, spreading out. The Rufu squad retreated several steps, repositioned, and went to protect the Azurites.

Jet hustled to the pit, focusing his mind on the two Syntac he had marked as defensive. They metamorphosized into flying four-legged purple lizards, almost like dragons, but with long tails and enormous wings. They shot skyward to confront the Gorgeions.

He unstoppered a vial given to him by the Runics, and a barrier surrounded him. Six arrows were caught in a glue-like substance. The others missed. Next, he focused on the attacking Syntac, transforming into an enormous purple Komodo dragon with formidable muscles, huge claws, and a jaw that looked like it could bite through a mountain. It took several steps along the edge, then vanished into the pit.

His focus narrowed on Kevin, Darium, and the thirteen other Azurites. Jayco, Mckenzey, and the other fighters sent spells and attacks toward the Azurites. Kevin pushed forward to meet Jet, who still held Sarika's image by the neck.

Jet thought he recognized four Azurites as students of Chadwick's. Christopher was an Earth Elemental, and Lucy was skilled in Wind magic. The other two were Runics. They used their magic on his friends. The other Azurites pulled out swords, arrows, knives, a hammer, and a wooden bat. One person brandished a gun, and it immediately exploded, severely injuring him, and his arm was gone. Iris and the golden animals bellowed angrily and launched an attack.

Flashing lights and several weird, dark shadows erupted around him. The attacks bore a resemblance to Runic magic in nature. The shield around him began to disintegrate, and he knew he only had seconds. Seyanna was gone, but Kevin stalked toward him. The instant his own barrier fell, the image of Sarika faded. He stood to meet Kevin.

Jet's vision expanded, and he watched as the Elementals and their allies launched an assault forward. Three students exited the pit, and the attacking Komodo Syntac did as well. Kevin unleashed elements of both Elemental and Runic magic at him, a mixture of flames, coldness, and confusion. The boy had talent, much of which Jet was unaware of. Kevin also used ice, gravity, and increased pressure. He didn't have great aim, and they collided with the dirt around him or the wall behind him. Sarika lay on the ground as if she'd been knocked out.

The spells Kevin created came from both his hands, positioned close to each other. Light and other materials converged into a ball.

Then Kevin threw the ball at Jet. He arrived at no other conclusion than calling it corrupted magic.

He was also a Predilector, and he used sound to blur his outline and moved quickly ten feet forward. Whenever he wasn't creating a spell, he used his gloved hands to block away spells.

Three Quills dropped down onto the path before Jet. They were taller than those who had chased him in Canada, wearing protective plates on their chest and brandishing longswords with a blackish-orange blade. Using the golden blade in his left hand, he attacked. He was still worried about the strength of his right arm. With Mckenzey's healing, it was stronger than it was a few hours ago, but it wasn't close to being good enough.

He quickly became surrounded, and they charged in unison. They were quick and agile, clearly better fighters. They blocked his attacks with rudimentary defensive tactics, but finding a clear path with three of them was hard. Using Capocea, he managed to avoid any damage. He decided to go for much smaller strikes. He stayed compact, cutting them across wrists, back of legs, and underarms, where their plates couldn't reach. Blow by blow, he gained the upper hand.

The last one finally fell to the ground, and Kevin clapped, clearly mocking him. He could've attacked, but was measuring up Jet. "That was downright pathetic." Then he waved a hand above his head and three more Quills dropped before him.

Jet spoke "Ogen," and a rain shower drenched the path, injuring them and sending them as if they were debris during a flood, crashing into the pit.

Kevin waved to another group, and six Quills with arrows drew on him from the upper rim. Having the high ground was smart. "This should be interesting." But suddenly, Kevin was forced to retreat. Jayco attacked, hurling boulders at him. The gloves and the anti-magical property couldn't block these projectiles.

With his expanded vision, Jet watched Kevin and the Quills, examining his options. He called down a deluge of water, and all but two of the Quills were washed away. The tallest Quill Jet had ever seen dropped down effortlessly, followed by another. Both were grotesque, and when the first spoke, his words chilled Jet. "Some in our clan have been gifted. I am one of five that can't be hurt by water. Now, you'll see my full ability."

The Quill produced a thin, curved, green blade and readied his feet. The second Quill pulled out a mace. Both were scarred from battle, and within three steps it was clear they knew Capocea. Jet pulled out a kernel of corn, held it in his hand, and watched as three other versions of himself appeared. This only slightly concerned the Quills, and the first attacked the one on the left as the other attacked the one on the right. Jet was the central figure, with one behind him. In an instant, he watched as the Quill leader swung at his version of Jet, and somehow, he simultaneously pulled out a dagger and threw it at the figure behind Jet.

Both duplicates disintegrated. Jet lunged and stuck his dagger into the flank of the Quill using the mace. Unable to pull it out before the leader stormed him, he backed away, only attempting to defend himself. The onslaught was quick and powerful. His shoulder buckled twice, and he was knocked down. Gravity was hammered hard, but it held firm.

Jet scrambled to get to his feet but only made it to his knees before the creature kicked out, knocking Gravity from his grip. The tall, marred Quill stood over him. "I have never been beaten. Killing the Mikado will be my greatest glory." He came in for the final blow. Blood dripped from a wound on Jet's forearm, and he barely had time to slam an arrowhead into the dirt, into a pool just below him.

An explosion of energy rocked forward, colliding with the Quill so hard that the green sword hung in the air for several seconds next to Jet's head before the creature's body was pitched backward. The sword hit the ground at the same time as his enemy did. Only one of the Quills was not so severely mangled that he would never stand again, let alone breathe. For a moment, the entire battle stopped and turned in his direction. He picked up his enemy's sword and placed it into a hidden compartment.

Kevin swore.

The Quills rushed at his friends thoughtlessly, full of rage. They came forward in two lines. Jet reacted and spoke "Aquaenaeth," and several things happened at once. A thick fog descended, full of lightning bolts, with buckets of water, and fist-sized hail plowed into the creatures. Their protective breastplates couldn't stop everything. A minute later, the creatures were lost in an epic flash flood.

A cheer erupted from his friends, and three Azurites, also drenched, dropped their weapons. Charlie Eckenkeep strode from the forest wearing orange glasses. He lifted both arms into the air just as the Gorgeions rose above the trees, gaining height, eyeing their prey in the clearing.

Kevin McCormick bellowed loudly, "Now that I've drained you of your magical strength, I'll savor this moment to kill you."

CHAPTER 6

Jet picked up Gravity, then stepped off the path and onto the washed-out road leading out of camp. The fog disappeared. The Gorgeions hovered but did not attack. Kevin stood ten feet away. Jet pulled out a make-shift tourniquet and wrapped it around his cut arm. His shoulders ached, and he was tired, but none of that mattered. He must defeat Kevin and rescue Seyanna.

Kevin tore off his green glove and brandished the silver sword with a broken tip; the same one he'd tried to use to kill Jet back in Illustina. He had fallen short then, and it would happen again today. The two flying Syntac reappeared, placing themselves between the Gorgeions and the clearing.

Jet asked, "Where's the stone you took from the Boar Chupovana?"

"In a safe place," hissed Kevin, and he swung his sword back and forth. He continued, "That was Uresk, you killed. The third in command of the Quills. They'll have something to say before this is all finished, but you'll be nothing more than a memory."

"Did you let the Quills take the birthing stone? They can't be trusted."

Kevin swung the sword again, and it became clear that he was not an expert. Jet was no swordsman, but he'd seen enough talent on the battlefield to understand Kevin had no real intention of using it during this fight.

Jet's interest shifted to the sword. He didn't know why, but something felt off. "Where did you get such a stunning weapon?" And it was. Besides the broken tip, it was exquisitely made. It hummed with power.

"When you help a friend, you get help in return."

To his surprise, Kevin slammed the sword into the ground, and a wave of white, malignant energy spread through the clearing. Jet dropped a shark's tooth, and a bubble sprang up around him before the wave hit him. Others were not as lucky. Both Azurites and his friends were knocked over, vomiting or writhing in pain. Jet thought that even his golden animals were affected.

Jayco tried to use the same tool as he had, and part of the wave was blocked, but Mckenzey, Keesha, and Hebrew weren't as lucky. They collapsed on the far side of the pit, in an open area, but far away from the Azurites.

The Gorgeions dove to attack. The Syntacs reacted, trying to put themselves between the fallen Elementals and the vultures. Cries of warning sounded, and the two sets of flying creatures collided, and the clash was epic.

Kevin closed the distance, and this time, he would use the sword. His first swing hit the protective bubble and cracked it. The second one shattered it. Jet ducked and rolled under the third swing. Kevin's outline shimmered, and he moved from behind Jet to in front of him and swung again. Jet lifted his golden blade to block the strike, and the instant it touched the blade, it shattered as quickly as his bubble.

Jet unleashed his first spell and fired one after another, trying to locate Kevin's weaknesses. He also used his defensive tactics to move and avoid making himself an easy target. It became clear that a frontal assault against Kevin was pointless, he was just too strong. His glove protected him, and it was almost like he knew which spells Jet would use. Jet remembered that some Predilectors could detect spells before they were used.

He cried out, "Can you use all the Predilector abilities?"

"I can't," Kevin laughed. "Just most of them. That's what the Father of the Dire Fraternity is all about. The stones help with my Elemental and Runic magic. I've become the perfect warrior."

Jet unleashed a spell to tear at the ground. Kevin moved away uninjured. "Why rebel against the Brotherhood? They aren't faultless, but they aren't killers."

"How are you so sure?"

Jet spoke "Neis," by one of the destroyed vehicles. Vines wrapped around the four wheels, and he nudged it toward Kevin. The move cost him a good portion of his remaining magical energy. Each spell had a cost, and he didn't have unlimited stamina. The tactic worked, and the vehicle collided with Kevin's back, knocking him off balance.

Jet tried hurling a rock as Jayco had done, but Kevin blocked it effortlessly, and he re-established his defensive stance. Jet said, "I don't know everything the Brotherhood is capable of, but I do know the Runics killed my parents. Professor Rysen killed them."

"That's one of his most celebrated kills," agreed Kevin. "Rysen is a legend. I will have the most renowned kills once you and the Czaric are no more." Kevin pointed his palm at Jet, and something wrapped around him that jostled him back and forth. It took everything he had to hold onto Gravity. "That's my favorite Runic motion spell."

Jet vomited mid-air, then was pushed back into it. He groaned, having believed he was testing Kevin, but it was the other way around. Kevin bombarded Jet's balance, and his senses became scrambled. The thought of Kevin being unbeatable began to take hold in his mind. The boy possessed Runic and Elemental abilities, as well as Predilector aptitudes. More than that, his gloves blocked every direct spell.

Kevin released Jet, and he toppled to the ground.

Behind him, Charlie was joyously celebrating. His vultures had gashed one of the Syntacs.

"You killed students with those hideous creatures," cried Jet. "You're a monster."

Charlie's eyes narrowed. "I found so many incredible objects as a searcher for the Brotherhood. I found the Fogle Horn, the Anti-Enchantment gloves, and the Gorgeion glasses. They thought I was a nobody. You were lucky to have survived Illustina, but you did us a favor letting us in."

"You're despicable!" screamed Jet. All his terrible planning had been for naught. Once he was dead, they would move on to his friends.

Seeming to read his thoughts, Charlie said, "And your life is about to end. Your flying lizards were no match. And no matter how fast my daughter can run, she can't outrun my darlings. I'll have her again soon enough."

Kevin smiled at him. "Time to die."

"Stand back," screamed Charlie. "Let my pets kill him."

"No," shouted Kevin, half turning back. "He's mine. You kill the others."

Charlie bellowed, "No! He stole my daughter and filled her mind with lies about me."

"My cleverness defeated him," retorted Kevin, turning back to Jet, lifting the silver blade. But the vultures would get him first.

Jet muttered, "Gravitas," and unleashed his enchanted blade. He focused on the large green gem at the opposite end of his staff and spoke "Vestalia," and a wall of fire sprang up, protecting him. The two vultures were forced to bank hard in opposite directions. Kevin was forced to retreat several steps.

Focusing on the one to his left, Jet spoke "Varoun," and his spell to increase gravity only partially hit one wing. It spun out of control and landed hard. The second flew off, over the trees.

The two defensive Syntacs, although injured, were still able to fly and attacked the remaining vulture.

Kevin's voice screamed, "You're dead." His outline softened, and he advanced toward Jet unpredictably, here, then there, then back again.

A trace of his body followed behind as if trying to keep up. It was like a metal coil following him. Taking up a defensive position, Jet held Gravity and his enchanted blade. Kevin didn't seem to care and came close enough for Jet to slash at him. He would have caught Kevin, except the trace sped up, and the Predilector vanished, reappearing on his left. Jet shifted with renewed energy, but he couldn't slow down Kevin and the bunch connected with the side of his head. Jet staggered.

He was forced to duck down as black arrows, sound waves, and Matter and Darkness spells came at him in succession. A bout of vomiting that nearly toppled him. Jet stumbled down the dirt road, spewing into some bushes, and put himself on the opposite side of a broken vehicle. Kevin gave chase, cackling the entire time.

He watched as Runics, golden animals, Elementals, Gorgeions, Predilectors, Syntacs, and Rufu squad were engaged in an all-out assault on each other.

Kevin sneered from across the bumper. "It's over. You and your friends are dead."

A detonation sounded back near the opening to the cave, and several dozen Ratas and Razors exploded into view. These two types of monsters were a cross between bugs and rock creatures. The Ratas were thick and could roll up into a ball. When they opened, they stood five feet in height. They killed with enormous crab pinchers. The Razors were a foot taller, with four arms and sharp claws. They were agile and quick.

Kevin was mesmerized by the new attackers, and Jet didn't know if Kevin had seen these demons before. He moved closer.

"Kevin," screamed Darium. "Jet's behind you."

The warning came just as Jet unleashed a spell. Kevin moved to block it, but was thrown back several feet, rotating in the air, and somehow landing on his feet.

The Azurites and Elementals began to retreat as Kevin bore down on Jet, his face full of rage.

The three Syntacs fell into place, prepared to battle the Ratas and Razors. Jet's eyes never wavered from Kevin. The boy gripped the silver sword and pushed it forward, intending to spear him.

"Abzu," cried Jet, and several ice crystals rained down on Kevin, but he shielded himself with his opposite hand.

"I'll kill everyone," said Kevin.

Jet lifted his enchanted blade and shouted, "Leave the gloves, take your friends, and depart! This is your only warning."

Kevin's movements sped up to a blur, and it became clear that the boy would get past his defenses. Jet recoiled, hoping to escape serious injury. A golden blur shot through the air, putting itself between the blade and Jet's chest. There was barely any room. The blade pierced the golden creature, and it was knocked from Kevin's hand, sailing past Jet.

The boy's eyes widened. Reacting without a second thought, Jet swung his enchanted blade with his injured arm with such force that he cut Kevin across the chest, with a portion of the blade slicing through his spine. Comprehension of his fate only flickered across Kevin's face before he lost all focus and toppled over dead.

Jet swiveled, fearful of what he knew he would find. Pinned to a tree, skewered and quivering, was the golden owl. Golden blood soaked the ground. The animal could neither escape nor survive, having sacrificed itself for Jet. He ambled forward as the owl's body became lifeless and hung limply. A stampede of footsteps closed in as Iris, the lion, and the grizzly bear arrived. The golden color faded as every ounce of blood drained out. Within a minute, a great horned owl with brown feathering and white feet hung from the tree, dead. The other golden creatures came near, bowing their heads as if to pay tribute to their fallen friend.

"You will pay for Kevin's death," screamed Darium Fitz from a dozen feet away, standing behind a car. He held Mckenzey in a chokehold, lifting her off the ground. Behind him, Ratas and Razors fought students and Syntacs. Everything felt out of place.

Darium was too far away and shrewd enough to know Jet's limitations.

Another blur of something golden soared through the air. This time, Jet knew it couldn't be an animal. Darium was knocked forward, releasing Mckenzey, and his eyes widened in surprise as he fell. A golden globe with spikes was partially embedded in his back, and Eric stood somberly ten feet away.

CHAPTER 7

efore anyone else made a move, Jet bellowed, "The fight is far from over. But now we have a common enemy...the Ratas and Razors. These monsters are immune to Fire, Wind, Earth, and Fear magic. They dislike water. You can slow their movement by affecting the environment around them. They'll kill us all unless we stand together!"

The number of these demon creatures was staggering. The three Syntacs held them back, but others were still pouring through the opening or exiting the pit. He couldn't imagine where these many creatures were coming from. The Quills and Rufu squad were nowhere to be seen, nor were Charlie or the Gorgeions.

Exhausted and emotionally spent, Jet knew the others were as well. Eric reached Mckenzey, and she hugged him, crying on his shoulder.

"Everyone pull in and let's see who can still fight."

Maria and Keesha leaned against each other, both injured. Phoebe walked up by herself, but she stood close to Jade and Asher. Hebrew had pulled over Sarika. Rozene stood next to Mikey and Jayco. He didn't see Lucas, Quinn, Lydia, or Melvin.

Jet asked Beckham, "Still willing to fight?"

"For now. Victoria was killed." Standing next to him was Jocelyn. She was exhausted and had a cut along her right arm from shoulder to elbow. Derek had a few scratches. Five Azurites joined the line.

Sarika said, "I want to fight." She held the silver sword that Kevin had dropped.

"Give that to me. We'll find you a different weapon."

She reluctantly handed him the weapon, and he stored it in his hidden compartment. She was given a shield and a spear. Touching the silver blade sent a shiver down his spine. A wet nose nudged his right hand, and without looking, he scratched Iris's head. It was good to feel her fur, but she was sad and angry. The bear and the lion came to stand next to her.

With less than a quarter of his energy remaining, Jet would have to be careful how he used magic. Two defensive Syntacs were forced into the air and retreated. The fighter Syntac disappeared into the pit.

The three golden animals unleashed a growl of longing and anger, lowering themselves into an attack stance. The Ratas and Razors howled in anger, answering the challenge.

Jet said, "Spread out. Work together, and we might make it out of this alive." He spoke "Abzu," and cut down the first several creatures with slender but sharp ice crystals. The surging creatures stepped unconcerned over their dead comrades. Sounds and vibrations shot forward like a volley of arrows from four Predilectors, including Rozene. They proved effective, and rain and mist showered down, slowing the oncoming surge. Echolocation by Dania the Predilector unbalanced several creatures, causing them to fall awkwardly or begin fighting each other. When one fell, another took its place.

Arrows black and golden sailed through the air and found their marks. The three golden animals broke apart and separated a Razor from the pack. Within seconds, they were tearing it apart. Once finished, they hunted for their next prey.

Maria used the golden orb with precision. It tore through the chests of several creatures. Her exactness flared a vein of jealousy within Jet, and for an instant, he longed to hold the orbs again. Occasionally, a creature would break through the lines, and Jet would hit it with Water magic.

The fighting continued for twenty minutes, maybe an hour. When someone needed a break, someone else would step up. The number of Razors and Ratas began to diminish, and fewer and fewer exited the tunnel. But that did not ease anyone. The group worked together, and several of the rock beasts were caught in a mudslide, decapitated by jets of water, and another five were trapped and cut to pieces. The flying Syntacs would fly by, dropping boulders, trees, and other debris.

Jet felt the moment the tide changed. He and the other fighters gained the advantage, and soon the Drekavac demons realized they had lost. It was their turn to retreat, and a cheer erupted when the last beast disappeared into the cavern.

A moment later, there was silence.

"What now?" asked Jayco, limping to stand next to Jet and breathing hard.

Smiling weakly, Jet said, "Those three Syntac will remain here and protect this area. We need to detonate that tunnel first. They shouldn't ever be a problem again."

"Choose me," cried Asher. "I'm sure Jade, Phoebe, and I could make that happen."

"Fine. If you think you can do it on your own."

"We can," replied Asher confidently.

"What's a Syntac?" asked Jocelyn.

Jet said, "I'll explain later."

"You killed Kevin," said Mckenzey, who came close. She reached up and hugged him. He was happy to see her alive.

"And Eric seriously injured Darium, saving your life."

"I know," she whispered. "My two heroes."

She kissed his cheek and stepped away.

"What are we going to do with him?" asked Maria.

Jet turned to find Darium face down on the ground, injured and alive. Two other Azurites were also injured and positioned near the forest's edge on the far side of the vehicles. Another Azurite, who had helped fight the demons, was bending low and cleaning out the wound on his back. It was deep and bleeding, but not life-threatening.

The Azurite said, "His back is broken. I don't think he can walk."

Trinity and Mikey hurried forward to help.

"But he'll live." Jet added, "We'll heal his most pressing injuries." Glancing back at Mckenzey, he asked, "Do you think you can, just enough to stop the bleeding and improve his pain?"

Mckenzey rolled her eyes. "I knew you were going to ask."

The healing took a minute. Darium's quick breathing and pulse slowed, and he appeared more comfortable.

Beckham asked, "What now?"

Jet touched Darium's head. "Parfit Inclusionem Revocandum."

The boy's face contorted, and he suddenly looked lost and unsure.

Into Darium's ear, he whispered, "We spared your life, but your magic is forever gone. You chose to follow the Azurites. I hope the cost was worth the price."

Standing, he announced, "Search the vehicles. Collect the golden and black weapons. Find the missing piece of the Phoenix. Nighttime is coming. We need to set up camp and prepare the food. Tomorrow, we're going home."

Keesha hobbled forward. She had a gash along her jawline and another cut on her shoulder. She asked, "What are you going to do?"

"Find Seyanna. Can you and Maria tie up Sarika and the other Azurites?"

She nodded.

Jet stepped a few feet into the trees and listened, allowing his vision to expand. The dirt road leading from their clearing disappeared into a jungle of trees, overshadowed by the cliff on his right, and continued into the valley. With any luck, it might connect with another road leading to Mutwanga or Nzenga.

"Push," yelled Jayco from behind. With his strength, he pushed a vehicle out of the small ravine it had fallen into when Jet had used one of his first spells. Belongings were being searched. Some of the Azurites had been secured.

Sarika cried, "Why me? I helped you."

"Just for the night," said Jet.

Before he had time to say anything else, Rozene exclaimed, "We've got a problem."

Jet's enhanced vision saw them before he heard the thumping of wings. Two Gorgeions were coming back for another attack. He spotted Charlie Eckenkeep sitting in a large tree at the highest point in the area.

Eric announced, "I found the piece of the Phoenix."

The information thrilled Jet, but he didn't react. The best way to stop the Gorgeions was to stop Charlie. Before he could respond,

Charlie was gripped from behind and tossed out of the tree. Landing hard, he rolled to see who it was. Seyanna stood over him, and she plucked off the glasses.

"Don't you dare! There will be serious consequences if you break those."

"I don't care, Charlie!" Seyanna's voice was enraged. "I'm not here to make things better for you."

"No, wait," cried Charlie. "The consequence will be dire for all of us."

"Not my problem."

A massive explosion rocked the ground just as Seyanna snapped the glasses in half.

"No!!" bellowed Charlie.

The two Gorgeions reacted, but not in a way that Jet anticipated. The two vultures instantly veered away from the clearing, quickly gained altitude, and, within a few minutes, disappeared into the clouds several miles away.

Seyanna gripped Charlie hard, making him stand. She led him down the small hill, to the dirt road, and back to the vehicles.

Jet sat with an open mouth the entire time.

As she came closer, she grinned fiercely. "He never saw me coming."

Charlie's face was red with anger, and he was breathing hard. "What do you think you've accomplished? This doesn't change anything."

Jayco stepped forward, whispering, "Good to see you." He handed her a piece of rope.

She nodded and began to tie his hands behind his back.

"Honestly, it does," replied Jet. "Your daughter gave you a butt-kicking, and now you're the prisoner. That was worth the price of admission right there. Kevin's dead, Darium had his magic taken away, and we stopped the Azurites from meddling in the Rivalry."

"Only temporarily. But you've done something far worse. The Gorgeions were under our control. Now they'll join Arisol's allies, and you'll see them again."

"I didn't think you believed that Arisol was the real villain. Doesn't the Azurites blame the Silver Fox?"

"Either way, not a good move."

Maria announced, "We found the gold and black weapons. We're bringing them out."

"Tie him up," said Jet.

Trinity hissed, "We welcomed you to our school; then, you were part of the reason that some of my friends were killed. I will never forget what you did."

Ignoring the possible treasure trove, Jet hurried to Seyanna. She looked exhausted, but as happy to see him as he was to see her. He felt guilty and overjoyed. She wrapped both of her arms around him, burying her face in his neck.

"What happened?"

It was several moments before she answered. "I was so worried you were never going to catch up. He sent other students after me. I recognized Christopher and Lucy from Chadwick's and thought they were with Jayco. They called me over. I didn't see Julian until it was too late, and he used a stun gun."

Jade, Phoebe, and Asher reappeared, smiling.

"That was the best explosion I've ever heard," said Jayco. "I think you guys can teach me a thing or two."

Asher said, "That was cool."

Seyanna stepped away. The back of her strawberry-red hair was plastered against her head. Her clothes were dirty, and it looked as if she hadn't been eating. "Has anyone seen my golden bow and arrows? They've got to be around here somewhere."

As she and some of the others searched, Natalia said, "The entire kidnapping and strategy is appalling. They wanted all of us to suffer."

Seyanna opened the vehicle door, found nothing, and slammed it closed. "They knew how we would react."

"They've been watching us for months," said Jayco.

"Found them," said Phoebe.

Seyanna hurried over and grabbed her backpack, her cloak, and her golden bow and arrows.

"Who are we missing?" asked Mckenzey.

Beckham and Jocelyn began packing the black items, shielding them from view. Jet had wanted to get a better look at what they had gained. Beckham said, "A vulture killed Victoria, tearing her apart. Derek barely escaped."

Jet remembered Victoria kissing Beckham, and he was visibly shaken by her death. He knew he would be if it had been Seyanna.

Keesha said, "I haven't seen Lydia, Lucas, or Quinn."

"What about Melvin?" asked Maria.

"I left him in a hiding spot farther down on the left side. It was a small gap between rocks. I'll go see if he's still there."

"Anyone else?" asked Jet.

Several heads shook.

"A few of us can continue to unpack the vehicles, but the rest of us should go looking for our fallen friends. They might be injured or worse. Bring them back here, no matter what you find."

Jade, Asher, Maria, and Phoebe searched the pit. Jet sent the golden lion with them. Seyanna joined him as he explored the trees on the far side of the vehicles. He took her by the hand.

Jayco gave additional orders, "That means that Rozene, me, Mikey, Trinity, and Hebrew will circle the pit but stay above it."

Maria said, "Can I stay here and watch the prisoners?"

"Perfect," said Jayco.

As they walked, Seyanna asked, "Is that brown-haired tallish girl Rozene?"

"Yes," said Jet.

"I overheard Kevin say that Rozene and that girl who died and was put in the cave were best friends."

"I think they were. Rozene was shocked when she saw Marapi. I don't get the feeling that Rozene knew that Marapi was part of the Azurites."

"And she's seeing Jayco?"

"Yes."

"Huh."

The forest was denser to the East, but Jet and Seyanna headed North. There were trees, but they were thicker, taller, and more spread out. They called out to find anyone, but saw no one.

"Who's Mikey?" asked Seyanna after fifteen minutes of searching.

Jet recounted everything about Dillon Lake and the Predilectors, including Mikey. The last time he and Seyanna had talked was when Jet had first laid eyes on Charlie. Seyanna was back at Chadwick's, but the instant she heard that her father was looking for her, she left town.

"I see something," said Seyanna, and she led him to a grouping of several rocks.

The bodies of Lucas and Quinn were shredded, with several wounds as if they had been defending themselves against something strong. A gasp escaped Jet's mouth, and he suddenly felt fully responsible for their deaths. He'd invited them here. He'd just been with them a few hours ago, and now they would not be returning home. He called out, and several people came over to help.

It took time to lay out all those who were dead. The golden animals quickly dug a large single hole.

Jet said, "We lost the Victoria, a Runic, and Lucas and Quinn, Elementals. Also, Kevin and five other Azurites are dead, and that doesn't include Samson, Marapi, Julian, and the Runic inside the tunnel. The battle was costly, and we'll leave here affected by what happened to us and what we've been asked to do. I truly appreciate each of you who fought with me today. May they rest in peace."

There was a moment of silence.

Jet continued, "Lydia has vanished. There's no trace of her. Leaving here without her does not sit well with me, but I'm not sure that we have another choice. We have prisoners Sarika, Darium, Christopher, Lucy, and Charlie. I've been told that the Azurite Runic prisoners are Lancaster and Farish. We also have other Predilectors. It'll be hard traveling and keeping this lot under control. Iris will search tonight to find a trace of where Lydia might have gone, but if nothing, we're heading out in the morning."

The group's ambiance was somber as they lit three fires and began preparing food. Once they'd eaten, Jet, Seyanna, Mckenzey, and Jayco approached Darium.

"What do you need?" asked Jayco.

"I'm in a ton of pain. This is not humane."

Mckenzey said, "I watched you eat. You were laughing and joking with some of the Predilector prisoners."

"That doesn't mean I'm not in pain. Look at me. I need a hospital."

"As soon as we can," replied Jet, who lifted an eyebrow before asking the next question. "We need to know how you planned on leaving Congo?"

Darium, his body battered, and his magic gone, took a moment to consider the question. As if coming to an answer, he said, "A plane is waiting for us at the Bujumbura airport. A single paved runway."

"What country is that in?"

"Burundi."

Jet checked a map and guessed it might be a difficult trip.

Darium continued, "These vehicles have all the papers to get us there. Trust me. It's a long drive, but no one would expect us to go in that direction. Our plane will fly to Spain, and another plane will await us. Trust me."

"I don't." A moment later, Jet spoke, his voice softer, "That's good."

"They're expecting Charlie Eckenkeep unharmed."

"He is," said Jet, motioning to a set of trees, deeper into the forest. You could barely make out the outline of someone tied to the tree and another keeping guard. "And by the time we've arrived, he'll be more than happy to cooperate."

"What do you plan to do with the rest of us?" asked Sarika, seated on a rock several feet away.

Jet concentrated on her and the other Azurites. "Kevin is dead. You have no one to lead you. You'll have a choice to make. Remain at Dillon Lake or Chadwick's and prove you can be trusted or remain prisoners."

"Prisoners?" asked Sarika. "After all I did."

Jet said, "Yes. Until we know you won't attack us again. You have the entire trip back to the States to show us your stance on the future." He considered leaving but thought better of it. "Your help today will go a long way in earning your release."

After a moment, Sarika bowed her head.

"What if we don't like either option?" demanded Dania, her voice firm.

Jet said, "You fought with us and against us. Your best chance of success is to be open and honest. If somehow, we fight again, or you try to cause us problems, you will not be treated so kindly."

"Just asking." But her voice had lost its anger.

Sarika pointed at the ring in the ground and her chains. "You can't keep us tied up like this."

"Was not this our outcome had we been captured?"

Sarika said nothing.

The tents were set up as dinner was cooked. There were five larger ones and several smaller ones. Eric and Mckenzey set up a tarp over the prisoners and dropped some empty cardboard boxes to cover the ground. Jet and his friends enjoyed a meal of dried meat, soup, water, and packaged snacks, including chips and cookies. Beckham, Jocelyn, and Derek patrolled the campground and the surrounding area.

Once dinner finished, Jet went to the back of one of the SUVs with Jayco, Seyanna, and Mckenzey. Inside the back hatch were two long and wide crates with latches on one end. On the right side was a smaller, more intricate box with carvings on the outside. Opening the two long crates, he found a treasure of golden weapons. These were different from the previous ones and reminded him of items he'd seen in Hawaii.

The first weapon had a slender golden wood handle at one end, and an ax at the far end. Instead of a metal blade, several enormous shark's teeth, as sharp as razors, gold in color, were embedded in the wood, facing outward. One side had three large teeth, and the opposite held five smaller ones. The second item was a spear with a half dozen golden feathers. The long golden wood fit nicely in his hands. The spear tip was a strong shark's tooth, also gold.

The next weapon was golden wood with a regular handle, like a baseball bat, but the wood thickened like a paddle with twenty smaller shark teeth arranged facing outward. He handed it to Jayco and watched as he swung it with one and two hands.

"This is impressive," said Jayco. "I could do a lot of damage with this."

Mckenzey picked up the fourth weapon, which had a handle, a long shaft, and a mace on the far end with unbreakable spines throughout the far side. These spines looked like something from an animal under the sea.

Jet pulled out two additional weapons, which were like three-sided boxing weapons. The bottom edge was a golden wooden handle that he gripped. The other two sides were sharpened shells that curved slightly inward and reached a point. If you punched someone with these, you could do some severe damage.

"Check out these swords." Jayco lifted different-length weapons with sharp shark teeth on the blades. Some were skinnier and some were fat and short. Each could be wielded expertly and used to cut or hack.

There was movement off to their left.

"Hey Jocelyn," called Jet. She had been patrolling. She strolled over to him as if uninterested in anything he would have to say. "Are your weapons similar to ours?"

Jocelyn considered the question for a full minute without saying anything. Her face appeared as if she'd come to a decision. Before she could answer, Beckham stepped up next to her. He scanned the golden weapons and said, "Those look breakable and weak. Our swords are thick with a curved blade. They would shatter anything I see here."

"We have several spears, swords, maces, and other cutting weapons," added Jocelyn. "I think it is fair to say we will be leaving with the better items."

Seyanna patted the third box, and the banter stopped. "I really don't think that'll be the case."

Jayco asked, "How did you really follow us here? Rozene would have seen you."

Beckham smirked. "Two things led us here. The Runics have a spell in motion that allows for tracking. Shane uses it all the time. He used it on Asher and Julian. As you know, Shane has paramounts who lead groups on campus. Jayco was interviewed for the position before magic made an appearance. It became clear that Julian and Asher were heading to the same spot in New York. We were nearby and followed closely behind. That was when we saw Rozene and followed us here. I tell the truth."

Jet asked, "Was Julian a protector of the Nimliaki? Is his pendant missing?"

"You remember them?" asked Jocelyn hastily.

Seyanna replied. "Hard not to since they tried knocking over our ship."

"His brioche is safe," said Jocelyn. "Can't go into specifics, but Shane keeps them all unless we're together. Beckham doesn't have his, nor do I."

"Why Asher?" asked Mckenzey. "Is he helping you?"

"Not to his knowledge. I'll have Shane remove it at once. Before he became an Elemental, he was on the fast track to becoming a paramount. Nothing more than that."

"Sure," said Jayco.

Jet said, "I guess that means you were near Spruce Knob when you got the call to come follow us."

"How do you guys know about that place?" asked Beckham, but his surprise changed to understanding. "I see what you did there. Good job. I confirmed something you didn't entirely understand."

"It's the location of the fifth piece of the Phoenix," said Jet. "Shane can't get inside without the fourth one being open."

"Hence why we decided to follow Julian and Asher." A sinister smile crossed Beckham's face. "But now you are miles and miles from the East Coast, and we have friends much closer."

Jet's head tilted. "Not all of us are here in Congo. Do you see Grantham, Latisha, and a dozen others? We might look ill-prepared, but you've miscalculated."

"We'll see," said Jocelyn. "Congrats on finding the piece of the Phoenix. Let's hope you'll be able to keep it."

Seyanna said, "We will get you guys switched out so you can eat. Give us ten minutes."

After they were gone, Jet opened the smallest box and pulled out the clear artifact. This was the fourth one they had recovered. Shane only had one, but he thought he had two. The second piece was a fake. All of the artifacts had six sides, including a front and back. Of the four other sides, one was smooth, and three were misshapen, but he knew they would fit perfectly, like a puzzle, with the other pieces. Writing unlike he'd ever seen was on the front side, and a jolt of electricity shot through him, realizing they had recovered the fourth piece.

Rozene, Derek, Trinity, Phoebe, and Eric returned an hour later after trying to find where Lydia might have gone and doing a sweep of the area. Jet, Seyanna, Mckenzey, Keesha, Maria, and Jayco sat near the fire.

"Nothing," said Rozene. "No sign of Lydia and everything appears calm."

"Help," cried a weak voice from the forest behind them. It was the opposite direction from where they had found the bodies of Lucas and Quinn.

Jet stood immediately.

"Over here. Under the leaves."

Flashlights illuminated the area. They walked into the trees, near a thicket of branches.

"Help."

The voice carried, and they went around the large bushes and found a clump of leaves and dirt.

Jayco asked, "Can you hear me?"

"Yes."

"Who's there?" asked Keeha.

"It's Melvin."

They hurried forward and moved several clumps of leaves. Melvin lay injured on the ground, unable to move on his own.

"What happened?" asked Jayco.

"Lydia and I were attacked by one of the flying vultures. I crawled under here, barely. She was taken. I'm positive she is dead."

"How?"

"Her screams abruptly ended, as if her throat had been ripped out."

CHAPTER 8

The intoxicating fresh smell and consumption of mugs of freshly brewed black coffee the next morning saved Jet and the others from a complete meltdown. The lifesaving stash was discovered in Charlie's SUV. The warm liquid brought energy, courage, and hope to the survivors. The camp was broken down in an hour, and as they were ready to depart, Charlie Eckenkeep was placed in the back seat of one of the working SUVs, and Darium in the other. He needed help, and two Azurites volunteered.

Everything that wasn't brought with them was burned. Jet spoke "Aer," and the constant wind gust prevented a trail of smoke from the campsite.

Jayco, Rozene, Melvin, Mikey, and Natalia were in the first vehicle with Charlie. Beckham, Keesha, Derek, and those severely injured were in the second. The rest, including Jet, were forced to walk.

As they left camp, Jet spoke "Urania," and a wind explosion knocked over some trees and moved around both dirt and leaves. He spoke "Oblekii," and cloud cover, and some rain covered the area. Ahead of them were blue skies and warm temperatures.

After a half mile, Seyanna said, "We can't get to the Bujumbura airport on foot."

"A bus brought us here," said Jet. "I bet the driver will take us anywhere for the right amount of money."

"Should we be concerned about Chupovanas?" asked Mckenzey. "Can't they detect our magic?"

"Let's hope there isn't one of those beasts anywhere near us," said Jet.

Jocelyn, walking alone, asked, "How do you plan on getting Chief Eckenkeep onto a plane?"

"Confusion spell," replied Jet. "We'll say he's sick. We'll have to do it for all the prisoners."

Without saying anything, Jocelyn hurried forward.

"How did Charlie find you?" asked Mckenzey from several spaces ahead.

"Kevin boasted that an Azurite Predilector, who can intercept text messages and phone calls, was smuggled into Chadwick's. He has to be within ten feet of the phone when it happens. He must've been around one of you when I texted. Julian was already in Washington. He and a few others were waiting for me when I arrived."

"Sometimes I hate magic," said Mckenzey. "It is hella useful when we use it to our advantage but not when it's used against us."

"That's true of almost anything," said Seyanna. "I never knew my father was so involved in the Azurites nor that he went to prison for them. He told me about some of his exploits. He was proud of them and proud that I'm an Elemental. He knew of my talent for speed and good hearing. He was prepared."

"How was it seeing him again after Hawaii?" asked Jet.

"What do you mean, Hawaii?" asked Eric.

Jet said, "When Seyanna and I went into the mountain, we were subject to dubious visions. Seyanna saw her father, and it was hard."

"It prepared for me to see him in real life. I've been mentally preparing for weeks."

Asher asked, "What do we do with a guy like that?"

Seyanna said without remorse, "The Brotherhood can question him. I never want to lay eyes on him again."

Each Azurite walked with their hands bound. They had no weapons, but Jet knew well enough that they could use their Predilector abilities. He spaced out the other Elementals, Predilectors, and Runics that had helped him to watch for anything.

Eric asked, "Was it a good idea to remove magic from Darium and the remaining two Azurite Elementals?"

"Do you have a better idea?" asked Jet.

"Maybe we should've waited until we got back to campus. Never know what might attack us."

Jet paused and stared at Eric. He finally said, "If we get attacked and if our combined strength isn't enough, we're in serious trouble for what's ahead."

"Whatever," said Eric, and he and Mckenzey slowed down to the back of the line.

Seyanna glanced at him but kept her distance. She had avoided him most of the morning. He didn't want to think too much of it.

After half an hour of walking, they came upon a ravine with a trickle of water that traveled northwest and back toward the foothills near Mutwanga, where they had started. Kal Beni, the town that had disappeared several years ago, was almost directly east of Mutwanga.

They stopped and drank some water. Charlie was dragged from the SUV, mumbling about death and destruction to everyone. After a short break, they resumed their travels.

Mount Stanley loomed over them, even from this distance, and the feeling of being in a jungle intensified. Two hours later, they stopped again and ate lunch. Predictably, an Azurite Predilector tried escaping. He pretended to need to use the restroom and was escorted by Jayco, Rozene, and Maria. The boy almost became a shadow, moving from one tree to the next. He wasn't running but rather morphing from one location to another. Rozene's vibration forced him to reappear a hundred feet away, clasping his ears, and he collapsed onto the ground. He was captured and chained with another Azurite Predilector. A few minutes later, the caravan began moving again.

An hour later, the Hydroelectric station came into view. Iris and the other golden animals transformed into pyramids. The vehicles halted, and it took some time for Jet to catch up. He went directly to the back window of the second SUV. It rolled down, showing Darium, who was uncomfortable and suffering.

"What was your plan?" asked Beckham.

"Depends on what Darium has to offer," replied Jet. He then took a long drink of water.

Seyanna, Mckenzey, and Jayco approached.

Darium pointed at a familiar figure pacing back and forth. "That guy is our contact. He can get us down the mountain."

Peering at Jayco, Jet said, "That's the tall man who tried convincing us we didn't need to go."

"He'll only talk with Charlie," hissed Darium.

Jet considered his options. "Sarika and I will go. We'll say that Charlie is injured. We can show him Charlie from the window."

"Are you sure?" asked Seyanna.

"We can't send Charlie."

"We could confuse him now," suggested Mckenzey.

Darium said, "It might work."

"Good enough for me," said Jet.

Sarika, who had been forced to walk, came over, and the plan was explained to her. "I must go on my own," she said. "I worked with that guy, along with Kevin and Charlie. He'll trust me."

Rozene said, "If you tell them about us, it'll feel like your heart is coming out of your chest. And it might."

Jet nodded.

Sarika walked purposefully forward, and Jet kept a few feet back, then stopped. The tall man with hiking pants, a long-sleeved shirt, and a hat, visibly relaxed when she approached. They spoke briefly, then she pointed back to the SUV. Both were too far away for Jet to hear anything more than whispers. The man nodded and pulled out a radio.

Jet asked, "Seyanna. Can you hear what they're saying?"

"Half of it. We're good. He's calling for two buses. They'll be here in twenty minutes."

"What about the SUVs?"

"They stay here. He has people who can use them."

"Okay," said Jet, returning to the others. "Let's get ready to move out."

The group moved quickly, carrying Darium and helping Melvin. Weapons, crates, and other supplies were quickly removed. Nothing was left behind. Charlie was led to sit behind a bush, unseen. Charlie said nothing, but glared at Jet. Iris and the other golden animals transformed, and he put them into his hiding spot.

Half an hour later, two buses pulled up to the far end of the parking lot. They had torn seats, large tires, and no roofs. Jet watched as Jayco and Eric carried Darium to the buses. Jayco pulled out some cash and passed it to the driver.

Seyanna said, "He's asking about the other group of Americans who went into the hills two days ago."

"What's Sarika's response?" asked Jet.

"That he doesn't need to worry," replied Seyanna. "They won't be coming out any time soon, and he should forget any Americans have ever passed through here in the last few weeks."

Jet watched as the man nodded, a broad smile on his face. "Let's go." He, Seyanna, Charlie, and the two Azurite prisoners headed for the bus. It didn't take long for everything to be packed. Within a dozen minutes, they were heading back down to Mutwanga.

They called their bus driver and were relieved to hear his voice. It was late afternoon, but the man answered, "I was leaving tonight if I didn't hear from you. Nzenga has become boring to me."

Jayco said, "We're ready to head home."

"I'm on my way."

They reached a turnoff section and were let off. The two smaller transport vehicles disappeared down a different road. Soon, the bus with green seats arrived. Charlie was put in the back and guarded by Jet, Eric, Mckenzey, and Seyanna. The Azurites were placed in three rows near the middle. The rest of the group were seated throughout the bus. Only Jayco and Rozene sat in the front. Mikey sat next to Seyanna, wrote on paper, and showed her. A sense of relief passed through the group.

They passed through Mutwanga and Nzenga and continued on the dirt road toward Bulonogo, intending to connect with the main road south. Staring out the window, Jet wanted to remember all that had happened in Congo. If he forgot, he would be letting down those who had not survived. Once they left Nzenga, the road narrowed with trees on both sides.

"Jet," cried Jayco from the front of the bus. "You need to see this!"

"You guys got this?" asked Jet as the bus began to slow.

Charlie watched Jet with razor-sharp focus. He spoke for the first time today. "Do you trust anyone to do something you aren't willing to do?"

"Whatever," retorted Jet, and he walked up the aisle. Out the front window, something looked to be blocking the road. There was a slight clearing on the left as if several trees had been removed forcefully.

"The Brotherhood will torture and kill me," shouted Charlie. "You know they are monsters."

Jet spun around and made eye contact with Charlie. "You mean because you're being an Azurite spy?"

The man smiled harshly, mocking Jet. "You know so little. You haven't even seen the bigger picture. There are things you don't understand."

"Jet," said Jayco, urgency in his voice. "Get up here now."

The bus came to a complete stop. A large tree had been cut and lay across the road, blocking them from continuing.

Rozene shouted, "People are getting up from that meadow!"

Jet's head jerked, and he saw them. Most were in the field, but others had hidden themselves in the roadside ditch.

"Drive," Jayco shouted. "Knock that tree aside and get us out of here."

Jet heard a click from somewhere outside and recognized it. He had heard the same thing during the vision of his parents right before the bus exploded.

"Everybody. Hold on." Jet sprinted the last few feet. "Open the door." The door moved slowly. Reaching outside, he spoke "Fericon." A blue spell engulfed the bus, and the green aura in his vision told him it was the right spell.

Heading toward the left side of the bus was a golden fireball. His spell protected the bus, but upon contact, it slid sideways several feet, but it didn't topple over. Two wheels left the ground, but just an inch or so. Screams erupted.

Torn between remaining inside and taking care of the tree blocking the road, Jet was paralyzed for a precious few seconds. His spell protecting the bus from the fire was still working. Turning his focus to the downed tree, he spoke "Fracterra," and the tree fragmented into five pieces, creating a path large enough to drive through.

He yelled at the bus driver, "Go! And don't stop."

"Jet!" Mckenzey screamed from several rows back. "Charlie is getting away."

Glancing out the window, he watched Charlie sprint from the bus to an area behind a tree. Stepping out from behind it was Professor Rysen as he adjusted the weapon to fire again.

"Go!" bellowed Jet. His spell might block the fire, but another direct hit could knock the bus on its side.

The wheels spun, and the bus shot forward. The second firebomb missed them by inches, exploding on the opposite side with a massive blast. Looking back, fire erupted. The bus smashed through the broken tree, and they tore down the road.

Looking back, he asked, "Is everyone okay?"

Keesha said, "Mostly. Charlie kicked Seyanna in the face, then Eric, and slipped out the window. Some of the other prisoners tried escaping. It was pandemonium for a second. Our pride is hurt by an old man getting the best of us."

"Seyanna?" Jet asked

"My darn nose is broken." She pinched her nose with her shirt to try to stop the bleeding. "I'm going to kick Charlie's ass when I see him again. That hurt."

"Was that magic?" asked the driver, looking as scared as anyone Jet had ever seen. "I've never seen anything like it."

"It was a rocket," retorted Jet. "I think we're safe. You can slow down a little."

The bus moved quickly, rounding the corner and nearly tipping. They entered the outskirts of Bulongo.

After several tense seconds, Jet said, "Please slow down. No one is following us."

The driver said, "Maybe I should just kick you guys out."

Jayco said, "That would be a mistake."

"For whom?"

"You," said Jet, as Jayco popped his knuckles menacingly. "We need to get to Entebbe Airport as soon as we can."

"No. No. Impossible. That's too far away."

Mckenzey sat next to Seyanna and began healing her nose.

Pulling out a tire iron, Jayco bent it with ease. "I would hate to do that to your femur."

"Chill," said Jet. "Keep south. Go through Bwera and Fort Portal. Don't let us get caught."

The driver punched the steering wheel, nearly crying. "You ask too much, sir."

"Someone just attacked us." Pointed out Jet. "Get us to the airport, and you'll never see us again."

"This is kidnapping," the man said softly but with resolve.

"We will compensate you beyond your dreams."

"Right. Kids like you."

Rozene pulled out dozens of American bills.

The man's eyes widened. "I can work with that."

Jet found his seat. The bleeding had stopped, but both of Seyanna's eyes were puffy. She looked miserable. From behind, Darium asked, "Why not go to Bujumbura airport as planned?"

Seyanna answered, her voice stuffy, "Charlie overheard the plans. He isn't going to let us leave without a fight."

"Let's hope we don't get caught," said Mckenzey, and she squeezed by and went to sit with Eric, who winced with rib pain.

Darium said, "We're screwed."

They turned south on A109, heading for the Uganda border, the same road they had arrived on. Using his peripheral vision, Jet watched as one of the Runics, a prisoner, tossed something out the window. His aim was perfect and unassuming. It was the same boy who had tried escaping while pretending to go to the bathroom. If Jet hadn't been looking in the exact right direction, he would've missed it. A shiny object landed on the road behind them.

The driver waved at him from the front. Jet stood and hurried forward.

"Can I give you a suggestion?" the driver asked.

Jayco and Rozene leaned forward to listen.

"You are trying to leave Congo, yes?"

"Yes," said Rozene.

"The closest airport to our location is behind us, on the outskirts of Beni. It isn't big. I think the runway is made of asphalt. Only private planes and, how do you say, cargo planes."

Jayco said, "We won't have a pilot or a plane in Beni. If we choose wrong, they might catch up."

"Not too many people know about the airport. It's the fastest way out."

Jet remembered the breadcrumbs the Azurite was leaving. "Turn the bus around, and let's go to Beni. If we get ambushed, we'll fight our way out. I'll tell the others."

The bus began to slow, and Jet walked back. As he passed the seat of the Azurite, who was beginning to stand, he punched the boy in the side of the mouth. The boy dropped unconscious into his seat. He announced to the group, "Put up all the windows. It's going to get hot in here. We're headed to a different airport. A closer one."

Mckenzey asked, "Why did you hit that guy?"

"He's been sending messages on our route. Can you believe he was picking off his own skin and dropping it out the window?"

"Nasty," said Seyanna, and she shivered.

"That's gross," said Maria.

"Please tie him up," requested Jet.

Darium said, "You saw that, huh."

"Did you?"

"Not exactly. But I know that's what he does."

"So good of you to let us know." But his eyes found Sarika sitting a few rows behind the unconscious boy. She glanced away.

The Beni Airport was positioned north of town, closer to Mavivi. The road leading to the main terminal was narrow, but paved, with a small fence on the right side. A handful of cars were parked in front of the main building. The bus driver passed it without a second thought. Glancing out the window, Jet saw two dirt paths leading travelers from the building, through some grass, to a large dirt parking lot of planes. Only three planes were at the airport, and it was doubtful that one of them could fly. There were no hangars or other structures.

The bus parked along the road, and the driver pointed to one of the cargo planes. A forklift was loading food and other supplies. Three men worked to add fuel and did other necessary preparations.

"Go wave your money in front of them. See if they'll fly you to the Bujumbura Airport. They will probably speak some French and English."

Jayco said, "If you help, we'll pay you more."

The driver stood. "Let's go."

It took a quarter of an hour to negotiate travel to Bujumbura. Soon, supplies began to be loaded onto the plane heading to Diboko Airport in southern Congo. Stopping in Bujumbura could be explained by refueling. Jayco kept the bus driver close until they taxied from the dirt lot to the runway. The seats were metal benches along the sides at the back of the plane. They used old seat belts that were nothing more than a string and a clasp.

"Miserable," said Asher.

"I'm freezing," added Jade.

"I'll warm everyone every fifteen minutes," said Jet. "We just don't want to burn down the plane. Someone needs to keep an eye on Melvin and Darium."

Melvin announced, "I'm fine. I need help with walking."

Seyanna smiled at Jet, but he was surprised at how little they had talked since yesterday. He wondered if she felt guilty or if something else was bothering her. Mikey sat beside her, as did Rozene, Trinity, and Hebrew.

Two hours later, the plane started its descent. Jet breathed a sigh of relief. The windows inside the cargo plane were small, and it was starting to get dark outside. He vaguely could see a white building with several dome-like structures on the roof and a row of windows in the center. Five or six more buildings were farther away, including a large open hangar. Several planes were spaced across from the buildings.

"Do you see the private plane you were going to use?" asked Jayco.

Darium was brought to the window, and he squinted through the glass. "Hard to tell. Maybe the third or fourth plane."

"When we land, Jayco, you, Rozene, Sarika, and Asher, go find the plane and the pilots," insisted Jet. "Those might be rooms in the buildings across the way. Convince them that Charlie is on this plane and injured. Don't attack anyone unless you have to."

"Well, that sucks," said Jayco. "My hopes and dreams were dashed."

Jet said, "The rest of us will get things ready here. It'll take them a few minutes to fuel the plane."

Allison said, "This is Burundi. We might need to show our passports."

Eric added, "Avoid the main building if you can help it. That'll make things harder when we have to leave. Watch out for soldiers or anyone else."

"What about a bathroom?" asked Keesha.

"We'll find one," said Jayco.

The plane landed, taxied to the third bend, then headed left. It halted some distance from the main building, near a few other planes that didn't appear in service. The back of the plane opened, and the four of them hurried off. Jet and a few of the others pretended to arrange the cargo in case anyone came to inspect the plane.

At the front, Beckham, Jocelyn, and Derek relocated the black items found in Kal Beni from crates into large black nylon bags. As the hatch opened, there was a minute or two of chaos. He thought he heard the Runics whispering and glance outside. Beckham lifted something to his ear.

Jet wondered, *Is that a satellite phone?*

Jocelyn noticed him watching them. She moved slightly to block his view of Beckham.

Allison, Alivia, and Natalia sat on the bench, checking over Natalia. She was better but still injured.

Allison said, "I think she has a concussion."

"I'm going to rewrap Melvin's leg," added Alivia. "His leg has been cut open, and it is starting to bleed again."

Jet checked some straps on the buttoned-down cargo items and inspected the middle side. He casually made his way to the opposite side of the plane, wanting to listen to what they said and get a look at Beckham. Jade approached to help.

"Are you okay?" she asked. "You were scratching under your arm viciously."

"I don't remember doing so," Natalia replied. "That kid really affected me. But I'm feeling better now."

"What do we do if this goes badly?" asked Allison. She was stout, with black hair that matched her skin. Like the others, she looked exhausted.

"Stay close to Jet," said Natalia. "He's the real deal."

"And he has those golden animals," added Alivia.

Natalia glanced around but didn't see anyone nearby. "I don't trust Jayco."

"Is it you don't trust Jayco," wondered Alivia, "Or don't like those kids who can do weird things with their minds? Jayco's dating one of them."

"Samson was a jerko. He deserved what he got. I just haven't seen someone die before. The fighting was more than I expected. I know Rozene and the others came and helped us, and I know they're trying to do good, but with Jayco, there's something off about him."

"He's good-looking," said Allison.

"Right?" added Alivia.

"Fine," laughed Natalia. "Forget I said anything about it."

Jet still couldn't get a good look at Beckham, but they no longer seemed to be plotting anything. He checked some additional items, then returned to his seat. Seyanna spoke with Hebrew and Trinity. Mikey was a few feet away, looking for something to eat.

Five minutes later, Seyanna whispered, "Looks like you're freaking out."

"They're not back yet." He silently worried it was a mistake to allow Sarika to go with them.

"This is a good plan. Give it some more time. I'm sure it will turn out fine."

"Do I look that stressed?"

Her eyebrows rose in disbelief. "Did you lose faith in me that fast that I can't read your face?"

Jet smiled. "This entire trip has been nerve-wracking. You were missing." His voice trailed off.

"I'm fine. Thanks to you and the rest of the gang." Her shoulders sagged.

"I'm sorry your dad escaped. How does your nose feel?"

"Smashed. I can barely breathe out of it." She stared at him. "I should have foreseen that Charlie would have a backup plan."

"What about your parents?"

"You can't tell them that Charlie kidnapped me. They'll never let me out of their sight again."

"You'll have to tell them eventually."

"Maybe. They're in Buffalo with a friend of a friend. I'll call them when we get Stateside."

It had been a few weeks since he'd seen Seyanna. She left while he was at Dillon Lake. When they'd come back to Chadwick's, she had disappeared. Then he had run off to Canada and Congo without her. There was so much he needed to say. He carefully described Dillon Lake and meeting with the students from the other boarding schools. Chadwick's, Dillon Lake, Cranbrook, San Mateo, and Valley Sun were all connected by talismans and ancient magic. She was keen to learn more about the Rohart dice, which Kevin had used to give Predilector affinity to students at Dillon Lake.

His voice dropped when he spoke about the Lagoon of Arches as he remembered the engulfing sorrow he had encountered within the purple water. He told her about nearly dying and discovering the other lost magic books. Seyanna was astounded to learn that he'd seen spirits within the water and that it had only been he, Raul, and Mckenzey who had traveled with the Myntra sisters.

"Can I see the sunflower gem?" asked Seyanna.

"I had to use an obsidian pickaxe and destroy it. That's where the three books were hidden."

"How are you going to give those to the other schools?"

"Invite some of them to Chadwick's if Principal Smuin allows it."

"And if he doesn't?" asked Seyanna.

"Then we'll be making a visit to each school."

Seyanna asked, "But when? School's out in just over a week."

"I know. It'll take time to put everything together."

Jade's voice reverberated through the plane, "Something's happening."

"Why do you say that?" asked Jet.

"Because Jayco is sprinting this way, and he's alone."

CHAPTER 9

Jayco arrived at the cargo opening, breathing hard. Nearly all the other students rushed forward to see what the commotion was.

"What's going on?" demanded Jade. "Where's Asher?"

"He's a little disoriented and maybe injured," said Jayco. "There were three Predilector Azurites in the room next to the pilots. They tried breaking in as we explained that Charlie and Darium were injured and the plane needed to leave soon. We took care of them."

"And that means?" asked Seyanna.

"They are unconscious." He added, "After that, the pilots weren't hard to convince. I don't think they wanted to stay here longer than they have to."

Mckenzey asked, "Are the pilots injured?"

"Not really," said Jayco, and he stumbled up the ramp. "Get everything brought over to the last plane. The pilots are going through their preflight checklist. Sarika and Rozene helped Asher to the plane and went back to dispose of the three incapacitated Azurites. I'll take Eric and help them. The rest of you should head to the plane."

Jet kept his voice even as he asked, "You left Sarika alone with Rozene?"

"Had no choice," said Jayco. "They'll lock up the plane in ten minutes. After that, we won't be able to board. We need to go now."

The group rushed into action, and it was pandemonium for a solid minute. People ran in all directions as Eric and Jayco left.

Jet helped several people grab their things. A hand clasped into his, and something was forced inside it. Opening his hand, he found a folded piece of paper. A door opened, and Jocelyn, Beckham, and Derek descended the ramp and disappeared, evidently not headed toward the plane. Focusing back on the paper, he unfolded it to find nine words scrawled on it.

Spruce Knob has opened. Shane has the fifth piece.

He swore under his breath. They were so far away from Washington, D.C., and there was no way to confirm this report.

"Jet, can you help?"

He hurried over to Seyanna, and together they lifted and carried Darium across the tarmac. Ahead of them, Allison and Aliva were helping Melvin as Natalia followed closely behind. Keesha, Phoebe, Mckenzey, and Maria were assisting the Azurite prisoners. Trinity and Hebrew were just ahead of them.

Jet's peripheral vision was on high alert, and he was ready to use magic if anyone tried escaping. The crossing was intense. On their left were a few buildings leading to the airport's central section. The hangar they were headed to was on the far side of the building. The plane was big enough for everyone. It took several minutes to get everyone on the plane.

Jayco, Eric, Rozene, and Sarika snuck around a corner and approached the plane.

"And?" asked Jet.

"These guys were great. Smooth sailing."

A voice spoke into the intercom, "I want to talk to Charlie Eckenkeep before we take off."

The door to the cockpit opened, and a tall man stopped anyone else from getting on the plane.

"Where is Charlie? How did he get injured?"

"We don't have time..."

Jet spoke "Opazo," and the man suddenly stiffened, his eyes rolled up into his head.

The next words out of his mouth were slightly slurred, "No time. We need to close the hatch. Departure in seven minutes. Someone is watching us. We've been seen."

Jayco insisted, "Then hurry. You can see Charlie when we get in the air. We can't get caught."

"Fine," the man said. "But I'll turn the plane around..."

Jet spoke "Vesta," and concentrated on causing pain in the back of his left shoulder.

The pilot screamed, "They're shooting at us!" He hurried back into the cabin, slamming the door closed.

Once the outer door was locked, they found their seats. Each of the prisoners had their hands bound. Using a spell, they calmly fell asleep. Five minutes later, their plane taxied out onto the asphalt and took off. He was certain the pilot had cut off two other planes waiting in line.

Much of the tension of the last few hours dissipated as they rose into the air. Seyanna sat in the row across from Jet, near the window, and closed her eyes. She looked exhausted.

He rested as well, but just before he fell asleep, a hand touched his shoulder. Jayco stood in the aisle. He motioned for him to go to the front of the plane.

"Now?"

"Can't be helped."

Standing, Jet asked, "What happened to Asher?"

"He's fine. A little banged up. Rozene has something to tell you."

They walked up and found Eric, Mckenzey, and Rozene waiting for them.

Rozene spoke. "I noticed something. One of the Predilectors who was in the other room, brought forward three white apparitions. I had no idea what it was, and it reminded me of a ghost. I practically peed my pants. A second one used cactus vines that grew from the floorboards to trap Sarika. The last one affected gravity. None of us were able to move. Sarika did a mind trick that blocked their abilities."

Jet said, "I didn't know she could do that. I thought she said she didn't have magic."

"It was very useful," said Rozene. "Then I knocked them out with my aptitudes."

A voice bellowed from the intercom. "It's time we hear from Charlie Eckenkeep," the pilot said.

Eric began speaking. Then stopped. His face contorted, and when he spoke next, it sounded exactly like Charlie Eckenkeep. "Crazy how stress brings out our abilities." Into the phone, he said, "This is Charlie Eckenkeep. Sorry I couldn't talk earlier."

Jet's mouth dropped open.

"You want to know if we should continue to Italy or another destination," Eric said.

Jet whispered, "Ask them if they would be willing to fly us to Morocco and then to New York. This is the change in our plans, but we need to be radio silent."

Eric relayed the new plans. "Thank you. That sounds wonderful. We will make it worth your while." He listened, nodded twice, and then hung up the phone.

Mckenzey asked, "Why Morocco?"

"It's close to Italy," said Jet. "The real Charlie will eventually know we escaped. Italy won't be safe."

Jayco asked, "Eric, can you do my voice?"

He did and proceeded to replicate those on the plane perfectly. It was disturbing and oddly satisfying.

"That's incredible," said Rozene. She and Jayco found seats at the front of the plane. Eric and Mckenzey hastened to the back as Jet returned to where he was before. He surveyed those who had survived, the prisoners and the injured.

Asher was at the back, across the aisle, and being tended to by Jade and Phoebe, though Phoebe seemed far less thrilled than Jade. All the prisoners slept on the right side. Natalia, Allison, and Alivia sat a few behind Jet, as did Keesha and Maria. Melvin took up an entire row and was in and out of consciousness.

Mikey came and pointed to the aisle seat in his row. He didn't say much but sat contentedly looking around. Sometime later, he passed Jet a note.

It read: Glad Jayco asked us to follow. We were worried. That was an adventure and a terrible battle. Is that what Elemental magic is like?

Jet answered, "Sometimes. But there were a lot of deaths. I never thought things would turn out as they did."

Mikey scribbled something else on a paper: Yes. Sad, so many died. Glad we are safe.

Jet nodded. "Me too."

Mikey leaned back in his chair and fell asleep.

Within minutes, he knew he had another task before sleeping. Pulling out his tome, he opened *The Sorcerer's Guide* and found a new page as if it had always been there.

Wier's voice filled his mind:

THE UNSPOKEN TRUTH OF LOST MAGIC

Queen Aurora, Queen Safamora, and Prince Proteus converged and created the Fisador Pact, which caused magic to be taken from the world in one manner or another. Some of the lost magic was siphoned to the Kindred Loop. Shaman magic became adrift first, then Incrementum, then Resititual. They did not expect Runic and Elemental to follow suit as quickly as they did. The three masters wanted to protect the land, the tribes, and the kingdom. Evil had been introduced in a terrible manner.

The Fisador Pact was crafted without guidance or approval by the 10 Kings. The twins had complete control of Runic and Elemental magic, but their powers would soon begin to fade as a result of the pact. Many tribes believed the battle at Darcoff Pass was justified and righteous, but the cost was devastating.

The six formidable artifacts and other weapons found in the cave of the Skeleton were presented to various tribesmen who helped, while the other items were given to the allies of the 10 Kings. The Skeleton had escaped, but his plan to overthrow the 10 Kings and Goth Airtha was in full swing. Elfin and Lalfin returned to Deshret as heroes. The six items were given to the Machitis tribe, the Geistes, the Khalicaans, the Coven, the Wandering Nomads, and the Narvanians. These weapons became known as the Insidious Six.

They included an eighteen-inch curved horn, an antique green necklace, a book of recipes with a spine of crushed blue amethyst, a silver-bladed sword, an opened-mouthed bull's head relic with curved horns carved from red stone, and a handleless jasper crystal dagger.

Once these items were received and used, Evil and Chaos began to spread across the land like an infection. Nearly the entire tribe of Geistes disappeared in just a few years. Only Queen Safamora and a few faes were immune to the green necklace. The king of the Machitis took the silver blade and accomplished terrible and celebrated things, but sick with Jealousy, he turned on his own people, sacrificing his soldiers as a tribute to his power. The book of recipes allowed some Narvanians to perform heinous acts.

The eighteen-inch horn promised protection against poisons, but the price was for the Khalicaans to become enslaved to the Titan imps. The bull's head relic was given to Wandering Nomads, who hid it for many moons. They soon had to seek protection against other members of their own tribe who would do anything to expose it to a full moon. It became later known as a weapon capable of unleashing fiery flames of destruction. The jasper crystal dagger helped imprison the Coven's children, and deceit rode through their ranks like a wave.

Queen Aurora, Queen Safamora, and Prince Proteus worked with Axenkind to create the Fisador Pact, temporarily denying their kin access to the next world, as magic was hidden for a time. Their spirits would roam Earth until magic was restored and the imbalance of the missing magic was made whole. The Golem had a part to play in binding magic.

Over the next several months, rumors of magic losing its potency reached the Grey Panther, his allies, the 10 Kings, and many tribesmen. Fear ran rampant through Goth Aritha. Those who had power lost it, and those without sought it. Elfin and Lalfin accompanied Faunal to Illustina to discover the missing magical books and Queen Aurora and many of her tribesmen were killed. The Silver Fox listened closely to the council of the other tribesmen, unaware of the duplicity occurring within the kingdom and in the 10 Kings themselves. Tribesmen and mankind throughout the land expressed a growing concern for civil war as cities fell and others grew. Emissaries were sent to every tribe, locality, group, and supporter to find what was causing magic to be lost.

After Incrementum, Resititual, and Shaman magic had vanished, Elfin and Lalfin traveled to the Crispor Valley, home of the Oarfish Dragons. Legend said that these Dragons caused the Earth to form even before the Five Goddesses came to being. The twins hoped to steal an egg, break the shell, and drink the yoke. They supposed this would enhance their power and prevent Elemental and Runic magic from departing them. The expedition was strenuous and unpredictable.

Vagerside was a noble fighter for the Machitis, whose brother had killed the king of Machitis to stop his rampaging attacks. His brother had succumbed to his own injuries weeks after the attack. Vagerside blamed the twins for the silver blade and its destruction and sought retribution. He set off tracking the twins across Goth Aritha. It took time, but he ambushed them, defeating both twins in the northern lands.

Upon their deaths, *The Sorcerer's Guide* and *The Mage's Letters* became adrift. It was some time before faint traces of Runic magic reemerged.

As magic was lost completely, Goth Airtha plummeted into a Civil war. The Khalicaans became a lost tribe, and much destruction was seen. The 10 Kings banded together with help from Lady Gaea to defeat many of the dissenters and appealed to those afflicted. Peace in the land was earned but only lasted for a short time.

In Crispor Valley, the Grey Panther discovered traces of the lost book of *The Mage's Letters,* and using the secrets he enticed from Atmos Geni, he became Arisol, the demon Prince, and controlled Runic magic. He brought forth hatred and rebellion among his brethren. He desired to control the 10 Kings and all five types of magic. For many years, combat ensued.

Words of a manner to rediscover Elemental magic were brought to light by the Oarfish Dragons. The Red Falcon and the White Snake were sent to distant lands and given keywords to bring back the destroyed book. The civil war intensified, forcing the remaining 9 Kings into battle. The Grey Panther was miraculously defeated, but not before 5 Kings, including the Silver Fox, perished in battle. The Grey Panther was captured and taken to his Earthly prison.

Lady Gaea and the remaining 4 Kings worked tirelessly to reestablish peace. The Insidious Six were lost or veiled, and peace reigned for a short time. Without a more advanced structure, the 4 Kings became divided, and they blamed and feared the Grey Panther. The White Snake and the Red Falcon left to find the ancient artifact, the Phoenix, to destroy Arisol once and for all. Some of their allies, the Machitis, the Coven, and the Khalicaans, gave their gifts, three of the Insidious Six, for a devious purpose. These three items bewitched the 2 Kings, and they became seduced by the consumption of power and treasures.

The 2 Kings met with Lady Gaea and discovered the location of the most essential artifact in all of Goth Airtha, the Phoenix. Lady Gaea was immensely relieved at the idea of stopping the Grey Panther for all he had done, especially the beguilement of Staka and the deaths of Queen Aurora and Atmos Geni. Her own hatred blinded her. They were transformed into Erpofalco. Their deceit was brought to light by the Axenkind, and the Black Lion and the Brown Owl were informed of the treachery. They confronted Lady Gaea and were granted the rite to become Leotyton.

Later, at the Starving Peaks, Erpofalco released Arisol, but only for a short time. Leotyton used magic keywords and created a new tome of *The Sorcerer's Guide*. Despite both books being present in the depths of the Starving Peaks, the Rivalry was chosen to allow, one day in the future, for Arisol to be unleashed on the world again. Arisol foresaw the need for the Rivalry and placed his allies and some of the Insidious Six in fortuitous locations worldwide.

These wicked weapons must be destroyed to defeat Arisol. The Kindred Loop is paramount, for it is the only weapon able to withstand this manner of Evil. The keyword to destroy—Uovu Vernietik.

CHAPTER 10

The plane ride to Morocco took eleven hours, and Jet reread and contemplated the words from his tome. It answered many questions yet brought forth new ones. The students stood, moved, and ate food when they felt restless. The prisoners just slept. Jet had no appetite and wanted to talk with anyone even less.

When they arrived at Mohammed V International Airport in Casablanca, it was 10:00 p.m. local time. Jayco expressed some concerns to the pilots, using Eric to mimic Charlie's voice, about their group being discovered. They wholeheartedly agreed. They remained on the plane. The instant they touched down, the prisoners awoke. They were brought to the restroom and given food. It was a challenge to carry Darium, but they found a way.

Jet watched carefully out the window for approaching soldiers or other unexpected individuals. Food, supplies, and fuel arrived quickly. Near a large hangar, one pilot met with two soldiers, and they exchanged some words and a briefcase. The soldiers departed without glancing back.

Their plane was never searched, and even the pilots kept their distance until it was time to leave. He guessed they got some sleep or some food inside. The plane departed at 1:17 a.m. for a ten-hour flight to Washington, D.C.

For the first hour, Jet sat, fearful the plane would turn around. When it didn't, he used the same spell as before but directed it at everyone in the cabin, including himself. He set an internal clock for eight hours from that moment, and when he awoke, an hour out of D. C., he was the first one. The others stirred over the next hour.

He called over several people, including Seyanna, Jayco, Eric, Mckenzey, Keesha, and Maria. "We need to start planning what happens next."

"What are our options?" asked Mckenzey.

"We need to split up."

"What do you mean by 'split up'?" demanded Jayco.

"Spruce Knob is the next location. You sent twenty Elementals to watch the area. It could have opened while we were in Congo. That means Shane has a big head start."

"Maybe Grantham, Latisha, and the others will beat him to the next piece of the Phoenix," noted Keesha.

"It's possible, but hard to imagine."

"Why, then, would we need to split up?" asked Seyanna.

"Darium and the prisoners, for one thing," replied Jet. "And I need Rozene and her friends to do me a favor."

"What?" cried Jayco. "What could you possibly need Rozene to do?"

"She isn't involved in the Rivalry," said Jet. "But we need her help."

"I'm game," said Rozene, stepping past Jayco. "What do you need?"

He hadn't called her, but she had been close enough to hear her name.

"That horn you won at paintball. I think it was called the Fogle Horn."

"I remember it. Why?"

"It combats poisons, and I think it'll come in handy. It would also help if you could calm down a confusing situation at Dillon Lake. Now that Kevin is dead, new leadership must be put in place. I'm convinced we'll still need the Predilectors in the upcoming battle."

Eric asked, "What about the prisoners?"

"Rozene should take the Predilector prisoners," said Jet. "We'll take the Elemental, Runic, and any others."

Jayco said, "That's a terrible decision. It's just Rozene, Mikey, Trinity, and Hebrew. They might get overpowered by the prisoners."

"You're welcome to go with her," said Jet.

"What?" demanded Jayco. "You don't think you'll need my help with Spruce Knob?"

"Oh...we will," said Jet. "But I won't tell you where I think you should go. But once we're done with Spruce Knob, we're heading to Dillon Lake. The choice is yours."

Jayco glanced back and forth between Rozene and Jet. He was clearly torn. A broad and kind smile shone on Rozene's face. She said, "Go with Jet. Met us back at Dillon Lake."

Mckenzey added, "I talked with Allison, Alivia, and Natalia. They aren't feeling great. They could go with Rozene."

"Sure. I need Melvin to go as well, and Jade, Phoebe, and Asher can help." Jet added, "I need Eric, Mckenzey, and Seyanna at Spruce Knob. Jayco will decide where he wants to go. We'll take the other prisoners with us. Thoughts?"

Jayco hesitated only slightly. "I'm with you."

"Good."

"We're in," said Mckenzey.

Seyanna was the last to say anything, but the smile on her face had already told him her answer. She said softly, "Yes."

Lastly, Jet spoke to Keesha and Maria. "We could use your abilities at both places. You've both been essential in our other quests. I want you to tell me where you want to go."

They both answered quickly, one right after the other, "Dillon Lake."

Jet glanced at them.

Maria said, "That's where I feel I need to be."

"Same," said Keesha.

"Okay. After dropping us off, we'll tell the pilots to fly to New York. Eric will have to pretend to be Charlie one last time. We'll take a train or something to Dillon Lake once we're finished."

"What about the golden items?" asked Eric.

"We'll transport them with us to Spruce Knob, along with the other gear."

Seyanna, Eric, and Mckenzey sat down and began planning how they would get a vehicle to drive them to Spruce Knob. Word got around about who was going where. Phoebe hurried over to Jet and asked, "Are you going to make me go with Asher and Jade to Dillon Lake?"

"You can do whatever you want."

"I want to come with you."

"We would love to have you."

Keesha and Maria huddled in conversation with Asher, Jade, Rozene, and the other Predilectors, formulating their own plan. It was chaotic over the next thirty minutes until they landed.

Eric went to the phone and explained Charlie's desire to leave with half of the group while the rest would return to New York. This seemed to relieve the pilots, who were planning to head there as well. They didn't want to stay behind in D.C.

It was just before 6:30 a.m. when the plane touched down. The moment they could, everyone turned on their phones. Dozens of texts and voice messages came through. Jet didn't bother checking his phone. He sat next to Seyanna, holding her hand.

Jayco announced, "Grantham texted yesterday morning. It says: 'Shane went into Spruce Knob with the other Runics. He came out with the piece of the Phoenix and their black items. The rest of the group looked like they had been beaten up. Shane gloated the entire time. We tried entering, but it looks like we can't until Jet arrives.'"

Jet said, "Tell him we're coming."

They exited the plane and collected their luggage. They weren't at the main section of the airport, but were shown a private entrance. They left the airport without passing through security or clearing customs. Two SUVs waited for them, keys in the ignition.

"How did you manage this?" asked Jet.

Jayco answered, "It's all about who you know."

"Meaning?"

"We called Latisha's aunt, and she knows someone."

"Wow," said Jet, impressed.

The drive to Spruce Knob took longer than expected. For the last few months, since learning about its location after intercepting a letter intended for the Runics, he believed it was near D.C. That proved to be inaccurate. The destination was deep in the mountains of West Virginia, and they were closing in on their destination. Phoebe drove their SUV, and Mckenzey was directly behind them. The two Elemental prisoners, Lucy and Chrisopher, along with Sarika, were with him and

Seyanna. The two Runic prisoners, Lancaster and Farish, were with Eric and Jayco.

Sarika had spent most of the drive engaging in a conversation about how helpful she had been. At the same time, Christopher and Lucy had done nothing but complain about Kevin's death and about having their abilities removed.

"Keep it up, and I'll freeze your vocal cords," hissed Jet.

"Fine," said Christopher.

Phoebe said, "I'm going to pull into this trailhead. They have restrooms."

Once everyone had finished, they waited for their next instruction from Grantham. It arrived, and they drove their vehicles to the far end of the lot, finding shady spots away from the trailhead. A few minutes later, a group of Elementals stepped from some pine trees and crossed the gravel lot to where they had parked.

"Finally," shouted Grantham, and he hugged everyone. The boy wore top-of-the-line hiking clothes with a blue parka and tan stretch pants. His dark skin glowed with excitement. Jayco bear hugged him, lifting him.

Latisha pushed past Grantham and screamed, "Seyanna!" She wrapped her arms around her and Mckenzey. "Are you guys alright? I'm so glad to see you. Tell me everything." The girl's usually frizzy hair was soaked down and less formed. She appeared exhausted and worried.

Mckenzey said, smiling, "We've had better days."

"We've been here for days," said Grantham. "We worried you weren't going to make it."

"It wasn't as smooth as we would have wanted," agreed Jayco.

Walking behind Grantham and Latisha were around ten students from Chadwick's. Some Jet recognized more than others. His old girlfriend Ariana and her brother Raul were there. Raul had been his roommate during part of his freshman year. Phillip, Raul's boyfriend, stood next to Autumn, a TA student with Jet in a Geology lab. She was easily considered the prettiest girl on campus. The rest he recognized but knew none of their names.

Jet hugged Raul, Phillip, Ariana, and Autumn.

Latisha let go of Seyanna and Mckenzey. She said, "I wish we could've stopped Shane, but the barrier fell, and no matter what we did, we couldn't enter."

"Grantham said that," said Jayco, "but I still don't understand." He pointed at the observation tower. "That doesn't feel like the right place."

"It isn't," agreed Grantham, who pointed to a forested area in the opposite direction. "Think of Coso Subtrano."

Jet asked, "A canyon under the mountain?"

"A new world within our world," said Autumn. She winked at him, her smile dazzling him as ever. He had no feelings for her as he did for Seyanna or used to have for Mckenzey, yet she had a power over the stability of his legs that he couldn't explain.

"All of us can't go," said Jet. "We have five prisoners from Congo. They are Azurites, but they are also Elementals and Runics. The fifth has no magic."

"Interesting," said Grantham.

Eric said, "We also have some new golden weapons. Maybe some of those weapons will help us today."

"Can we take a look?" asked Latisha.

"Over here," said Jayco.

They walked over to the back of Jet's SUV and presented two large duffel bags.

"These remind me of tools or weapons of Polynesia," said a boy who looked to be a Pacific Islander himself. "Look at all the teeth on the outer edges."

"What's your name?" asked Jayco.

"Tominiko," the boy said. He was as tall as Jet, with broad shoulders and long black hair. He looked like he could be both sixteen and twenty-five.

Jet stepped back and said, "See if one of the weapons chooses you."

The boy walked closer, asking, "What do I do?"

Eric answered, "Place your hand over the weapons. You'll feel the urge to pick up the weapon. It might even glow."

Tominiko's eyebrows rose, and a look of hesitation crossed his face. It quickly passed, and he moved closer, placing an outstretched hand over the duffel bags. He moved his hand back and forth hastily.

"Slower," encouraged Eric.

His hand moved slowly and stopped suddenly. Extending his fingers, he grasped a golden weapon with a carved golden paddle. A shimmer of red appeared momentarily.

"Incredible," breathed Ariana.

Tominiko stepped away and swung the weapon as if it were an extension of his own body.

Jet asked, "What Elemental magic do you have?"

"Earth magic," said Tominiko.

"Glad you're here with us. Who's next?"

Phillip was next. Within seconds, he touched the spear with several feathers at the far end. It glowed red for a few seconds as he held it. Next, a girl named Remi, with Water magic, picked up one of the swords with shark's teeth. It also glowed red upon her touch. Her sword was skinnier than the two other swords. A boy named Nolan with Fire magic, a good friend of Jayco and Grantham, clutched the thicker sword.

The next five in line came away empty-handed. Jet was introduced and watched as Grace with Wind magic picked a golden sword, and Tessa with Earth magic chose a golden mace. Drake was next, with Water magic, and he also picked a golden sword. Conner, with Spirit magic, took forever but walked away with a golden mace. Ian, also with Water magic, selected a golden mace.

A girl by the name of Ruby stepped forward hesitantly. Within seconds, a four-inch dagger with a golden handle and two enormous shark teeth selected her. The teeth were sharp and deadly. Three more of these weapons were still available, but each was a few inches or so longer. Two boys and a girl were chosen to wield these weapons. Hudson was stout, strong, but agile. Her weapon was ten inches long and had two shark teeth at the far end. She had access to Water magic. Leo was tall and skinny, and his weapon was eighteen inches long, designed like the others. Lastly, Wyatt, with Fire magic, held an eight-inch-long dagger. Somehow, the weapons matched the Elementals perfectly.

Two others who didn't bother to approach. When encouraged, they both shook their heads.

Grantham gathered everyone around. "Here's what we know. Runics entered the small pond, but nothing happened until Shane stepped foot into the water. Then...essentially, they were all sucked to the bottom and disappeared."

"Sounds like a blast," said Mckenzey sarcastically.

"They survived," continued Grantham. "A few hours later, they came out and gloated. Shane showed off the clear crystal piece and their new weapons. He was obnoxious but refused to elaborate on what had happened inside. He only said it was—a whole new world."

Raul said, "Hey, Jet. I'm sorry to say this, but I can't go in. Haven't yet recovered from Canada."

"No worries," said Jet. "We'll need a few people to stay back and watch the prisoners."

"Prisoners?" asked Autumn. "That sounds sensational."

Latisha said, "I'd pick Emmett and Zuri. They're both struggling with their Elemental magic, but they're good with their golden swords. I think that's why they didn't want to get a new weapon."

"Perfect," said Jet.

Ariana announced, "A funny thing happened to Raul and me on the flight to D.C."

Jet asked, "Like what?"

"We realized that we could communicate with each other without talking. He'll be able to tell me what's going on out here."

"It's settled," said Jet. "We're leaving in two minutes." Glancing at Phoebe, he asked, "Do you want to stay or go?"

"I would prefer to go, but I think I might be more useful out here."

"Keep a close eye on Sarika. I'm not sure what to think of her yet."

Phoebe nodded.

Glancing around, he wondered if the Quills or a Chupovana could be close. Those with magic had been in the area for a while. That could cause the Chupovanas to come running. He said, "Be careful. Report anything suspicious right away."

"Roger that."

From several feet away, he heard Jayco grumble, "Rozene could have stayed back and watched the prisoners."

Grantham punched his shoulder playfully, distracting Jayco, and the two began chatting animatedly.

A few minutes later, Grantham whistled, and they separated. Those who intended to enter strode toward the trees. They passed birch, maple, and beech trees. The landscape was night and day different from Congo. It was cool and refreshing. The air was sweet and calming.

They climbed up a slight incline and then passed the observation tower. After another one hundred feet, everything changed. The forest became overgrown, and you couldn't hear any vehicles. The rocky, uneven trail narrowed, and they had to push through some undergrowth. They gradually increased in elevation before descending into a small basin. There were walls of rock structures on each side of the small area.

Fifteen minutes later, they broke off from the trail and followed a small ravine until some water came into view. Seyanna kept looking back at him, as if wanting to be closer.

"Seems like you're enjoying yourself," he said when they came to a spot to rest.

"I missed you. This feels natural."

"I'm glad you're safe."

Seyanna held his hand and said, "After today, you and I will need to sit down and have a frank conversation."

"I'm game."

"Let's keep moving," said Grantham.

They dropped down a step set of rock boulders, then hit three steep switchbacks. The last part was twelve large steps, then the ground evened out, and the pond came fully into view. It was circular, with a few large trees on the north and south sides. Yellow and white Tuscarora quartzite rock went up thirty feet on the east side of the water. They were at the end of the path, and there was no other way out of this basin except the way they had come.

"What do you think?" asked Grantham.

"Breathtaking," said Seyanna.

Jayco asked, "Do we enter with our clothes on and our weapons ready?"

"Precisely," replied Grantham.

Ariana said, "All is clear back at the parking lot."

"The water is freezing," said Mckenzey, and she was bent over, studying the water. "It's the clearest lake I've ever seen. You can see the bottom."

A group of Elementals huddled together. Jet walked over and asked, "Tell me a little about yourselves."

A boy, slightly overweight with brown hair, came forward, shaking his hand and smiling brightly. "I'm Conner. These are my friends. Grace, Tessa, Drake, and Ian. Grace and Drake are from Arizona. Ian, Tessa, and I are from Texas. We met in the summer between eighth and ninth grade. We considered going to San Mateo in Texas. In the end, we selected Chadwick's and couldn't be happier."

"How did you all meet?" asked Jet.

"Musical Theater. That summer, we all went to the La Mirada Theatre in SoCal and put on a show. There had to be over a hundred students. Somehow, we bonded and decided to go to high school together. We've been best friends ever since."

"Nice. And welcome. Thanks for helping us."

Leo stepped forward. He was tall and lean, without many muscles. He said, "We're all excited to see you in action."

"Hope I don't disappoint."

"You won't," blurted Tessa.

The other four members rolled their eyes and continued getting things ready. Tessa kept staring at Jet uncomfortably, trying to use her physical appearance to affect him. She was attractive with her black hair, gigantic brown eyes, and olive skin.

Jet said, "Be ready for anything."

She smiled and nodded.

He announced to the others, "We're stepping into the water in five minutes. Don't get in after I do." He pulled out empty bottles and prepared some muddy drinks. This time, he added clay, grass, and some leaves. Oftentimes, the worse it looked, the more energy it provided.

Once finished, he released Iris and the golden lion and bear. The loss of the owl instantly struck him. He hadn't yet told Latisha or Grantham and wasn't sure he had the energy or willpower to do so. Seyanna, Mckenzey, Jayco, Latisha, and Grantham pull on their cloaks.

All the cloaks protected those wearing them, and each had a hood. Mckenzey's cloak was a knee-length, glossy black jacket that lay flat. Jayco's cloak was more like a biker jacket with red and black leather. There were metal rings embedded in the leather. Latisha's was red in color. At times, like now, it was darker than others, and it shimmered when she moved. Seyanna's was white and flared out at the waist. Even if you threw mud at it, it never stained. Lastly, Grantham's cloak was a light tan, almost like a trench coat. The different cloaks matched each of his friends.

Jet whispered to Iris, "Protect everyone." She came and rubbed up against his leg.

"What are we going to find inside?" asked Mckenzey to Grantham.

"I wish I knew," the boy replied.

Jayco asked, "What kind of status was their clothes?"

"Dirty," answered Latisha. "They had several scrapes and bruises."

Seyanna came close to Jet. "Are your shoulders okay?"

"They hurt. I might be limited with some movements. I'm going to need to watch myself."

"You might feel that way now, but I know you."

"What do you mean?"

"When the adrenaline kicks in, nothing will stop you. We'll be fine."

"Thanks," said Jet, and her smile was so genuine he couldn't help but return a smile.

"Would you guys knock it off," said Eric.

Seyanna strode away. A minute later, Mckenzey took her place.

She said, "She's right. You'll feel fine once the fighting starts. The problem is that sooner or later, you're going to kill yourself to save us. However, we'll be the ones that are left behind."

Mckenzey hurried off to find Eric.

Grantham asked Jet, "What was that about?"

"Not sure. We've been through a lot in the last few weeks. It's good to see you and the others. You did a great job."

"Jayco told me more about Seyanna's kidnapping and how all of you thought she was dead. Then you had to fight and kill Kevin. He let me know that the golden owl saved your life and was killed. I'd say you guys have had a rough few days."

Jet asked, "What's your gut saying about what's waiting for us?"

"Something different than anything we've seen. By the way, I asked Latisha and Autumn to come up with a game plan."

"I'm glad you did." Grantham gripped his shoulders and ran to find Autumn and Latisha. Then he called everyone over.

Jet watched with a smile on his face. It was good to have the others involved.

Latisha began speaking, "We've divided the twenty-two of us into two groups. I'll lead one, and Autumn the other. Jet will move back and forth between the two. If you hear your name, come stand near me. Jayco, Grantham, Tominiko, Remi, Nolan."

Those five went to stand near Latishia.

Autumn announced, "Mckenzey, Seyanna, Eric, Ariana, and Phillip."

Latisha continued, "Ruby, Tessa, Conner, Ian, and Drake."

"Hudson, Leo, Wyatt, and Grace," said Autumn. "Are we missing anyone?"

The groups were divided, and everyone had been accounted for.

Jayco asked, "Can you give us a minute to learn everyone's names?"

"A single minute," said Autumn.

Latisha could be heard saying, "We have no idea what to expect. Three groups of three with one in the front and back. Work together and announce anything you see."

Autumn chose to go with two groups of four, one in front and one in back.

"What happens next?" asked Nolan.

Grantham said, "You'll have to get into the water up to your waist."

Screams and shouts erupted as they sloshed forward.

"It's freezing in here," said Seyanna, glancing back at Jet. She was next to Mckenzey and Eric. The golden animals followed closely behind the two groups. Jet noticed the bear and lion went with Autumn while Iris went with Latisha.

Jet glanced back and forth between the two groups. He hoped everyone would come out of this alive.

CHAPTER 11

Marching into the water was an odd sensation. Some screamed due to frigid temperatures, while others felt it was balmy. Next to him, Seyanna's extremities began to shake, and she wasn't the only one. Her face became pale, and her lips turned a bluish hue. Jet felt torturous agony on every inch of his skin. The water was neither warm nor cold. He instinctively knew that if he stumbled, the results would be deadly. The water rose higher and higher. Within thirty seconds, it had gone from his ankles to his neck. He was sure he was about to pass out and drown.

An instant before he went underwater, several figures stepped from behind a tree not far from the Tuscarora quartzite rock wall. Faunal, a tall wolf-like creature resembling the Egyptian God Anubis, stood next to Professor Rysen, Charlie Eckenkeep, and Dr. Destiny Descartes. Jet had thought it would be Shane Fallon and other Runics.

Professor Rysen screamed, "Where's my son?"

Before he could answer, he was plunged into the water, unable to get free. He was underwater for several seconds as if being sucked into a drain. Muffled shouts and screams rose around him, but it was as if their voices were blocked out by a mouth filled with water. But as quickly as it had been there, the water and screams vanished. They passed through a layer of sand and were thrust into the largest underground room he had ever seen. They slowly descended into a chamber that was significantly larger than the training grounds back at Chadwick's. The grotto was majestic in its colors and its overall breadth and width. Jet washed over him as Iris and the other two golden animals landed nearby.

Diamond Falls was aptly named. The gemstone was heavily dispersed in each wall, more concentrated in some places. The refractory sparkling was magical. An added golden glow made the ambiance more remarkable. They descended at a steady rate as if floating down to the surface of the moon and seemed just as foreign.

Seyanna yelled, "That was Charlie, wasn't it? How did he get here so quickly?"

"I don't quite know," said Jet. "I hope he didn't put a tracker on you or one of the others?"

She shook her head

Jayco bellowed an answer, "Let's hope he did because if not, someone here told him where we were heading."

"Not necessarily," Jet said. "We've known about Spruce Knob for weeks and weeks. He had Runics helping him."

Phillip yelled, "There's a faint orange glow from below us."

All eyes shifted to a fire in the center of the room. A wave of heat burst upward.

Jet shouted, "Get ready for anything. Focus! Avoid all distractions."

The walls shimmered, and their descent slowed. That was...all except Jet. Instead of going down with the others, he was thrust toward the side wall. He rotated and lost view of the others.

A perfectly rectangular block of the wall, the size of a car, was missing. He was high up in the room and was unceremoniously placed into the gap in the wall. A clear material fell into place, preventing him from escaping, but permitting him to have a perfect view of the entire cavern. His friends landed softly, then scrambled around as if they were going to be attacked. He was too far away to hear anything.

Jet spoke "Pachamama," trying to rip a hole in the rock wall or the clear covering. The words didn't even make a sound in his ears. Closing his eyes, he attempted spell after spell without any success. He felt as helpless as a baby fox in a hole. Changing tactics, he tried removing a sword from his hiding space. Nothing he tried allowed him to access any form of magic.

Twenty-one students separated themselves into two groups, joined by the three golden animals. For the first time, Jet noticed that the floor was completely flat with pieces of metal and large diamonds, partially exposed, jutting upward.

A voice spoke from the abyss. Those below stopped moving and looked for who was speaking. "Welcome to Diamond Falls. This was once the domain for the upper magical echelon from each tribe, home of the Terra Maleficis, and where the Lexicon occurred. No magic was allowed, and no weapons were used to harm another. This was deemed to be hallowed ground. It has since been added to the Rivalry. I am Charcoit, the last desert firedrake, and I was once a commander in the army of the 10 Kings."

A light illuminated the wall directly across from Jet. In a similar but bigger space stood a four-legged animal, like a gigantic wolf, with long, flowing, white fur, white-and-silver eyes, and two six-inch horns that pointed upward. It was encased behind a glass wall of sorts.

Charcoit continued, "I am recognized by a select few. There is little chance I can be freed, removed, or taken from this location. One day, when magic is fully on the Earth, this cavern will return to its once-held glory, and I will be here to witness it. For now, it serves as the dungeon of carnage. All will be lost if the Elementals are not strong enough for the upcoming battle. Jet Black, the Mikado, can only watch and hope he has instructed you well enough to succeed. Remember, this space is not safe, and death can and will find you here if you are not careful."

Jet slammed his fists on the clear barrier, unable to contain his fear and frustration. He knew Charcoit, but only from the Averseen, a world of Decontide Trials, within *The Sorcerer's Guide*. The trials were to test the magical strength and aptitude against unknown enemies. But Charcoit was the imagination of Darvish, a genius who created five trials, one for each type of magic. It was unreal to learn that Charcoit was a living and breathing creature.

"In the course of the Legendary Battle, Leotyton overthrew Arisol, forcing him back into his earthly prison. Four Elemental sentinels and four Runic demons emerged from the ground. They were bred for this moment. The Elementals must fight two of each. The Runics have already been here and dispatched the other four beasts. Let us see if you are as worthy to enter the halls of this sacred structure."

The wall to Jet's right at the far end of the chamber moved, revealing four large recesses, within which were four formidable creatures. The beasts each unleashed a roar, shaking the entire cavern. Twenty-one students and the three golden animals pivoted in unison as if controlled by strings and forced to face their opponents. The four creatures drifted out as if standing on platforms with a rolling device beneath them.

The two on the left were Golden Elemental sentinels, and the two on the right were Black Runic demons. The creature on the farthest left was a standing tree, fifteen feet tall, with interwoven vines and bark making up its legs, torso, shoulders, back, and a portion of its arms. Ice crystal-like weapons were lodged at the knees, the hands, and the forearms. Nine crystals made up the chest plate. Its head was a glowing fireball with molten rock and obsidian meteorites as eyes.

The second creature was more incorporeal than the first, with dust and smoke creating a winged beast nearly fourteen feet tall. Its wings appeared composed of sand and dirt that swirled around the beast. The outline of the beast rotated, shifted, adjusted, and reformed as if a storm raged within. It stalked on limbs of crystalline particles that broke and renewed as quickly as the eye could behold. The head and beak were more metallic but turned to liquid, solidified, then turned to dust, then renewed. It was in a constant state of fluctuation.

The third creature was notably different from the first two. It had matted black fur and stood on four legs but was nearly eighteen feet tall. It was made of charcoal and had a horse's body with thicker and more muscular legs. It had two large horns on the top of its head. The front two legs had metal protections, and three mini claws connected to both hooves. The back legs were longer, with only a single, extensive claw and thicker hooves. Its head was black, elongated, and resembled that of a giant lizard, while its body tapered into a long tail. A protective spine, similar to that of a dinosaur, was situated along the back of this creature. A dozen hardened mounds with spikes protruded from each mound, with additional spikes along the tail. The jaws snapped closed with such force that the group took a step back.

The fourth and last creature was sinewy, lanky, and tall, except for its legs, which were short and stalky. It reminded Jet of a life-sized grotesque butterfly with an alligator's head. Its wings were gigantic, aslant, and ridged. They were segmented with an appendage-like structure with claws dividing the two segments. The wings could fold and unfurl at a moment's notice. The head had a long snout, a short neck, and numerous teeth. Despite its slender frame, there were spikes on its back. It stood a good sixteen feet tall. Its tail quickly wrapped around itself, flicked out, and resettled. From here, it looked like a dagger was at the tip of the tail. Jet imagined that this creature's skin was rough and thick and would be hard to kill.

Charcoit spoke. "The first elemental sentinel is Mammoth, and the next is Dierling. The first Runic demon is Kenapi, and the second is Flauge. These will be close to impossible to kill alone and even with most of your friends. The goal is to damage the beasts so they cannot continue to attack. If you accomplish this with regard to all four creatures, you will be granted access to the inner sanctum. If half of your troop dies, you will be given a moment to regroup. At that moment, the survivors will be given the choice to depart. If you do, the Mikado dies, but you will live. The Four Chevaliers will be released soon. You have five minutes to prepare."

The spell controlling the students of Chadwick's broke, and they peered around, then at each other. Jet hollered and screamed, but he wasn't sure what, if anything, he said was getting through.

Iris peered up at him briefly, and Jet knew she would fulfill his command. She slunk back to the groups as chatter intensified, and plans were created. He had the option to watch or turn his back on his friends to save his own heartbreak. It wasn't a hard decision. He needed to find unwavering courage.

Five minutes later, a bell sounded, and a shimmering protective curtain fell from the four creatures. The two groups separated, and Latisha, Jayco, Grantham, and eight other students faced the two Elemental sentinels. Autumn, Mckenzey, Seyanna, Eric, and six students confronted the two Runic demons. A countdown ensued: three, two, one, and the four creatures came alive.

A cacophony of screeches and yells reached Jet, and he forced himself to sit and watch the battle. Not participating might turn out to be the hardest thing he had ever done.

Mammoth, the walking tree, thrust both arms forward, firing a dozen thin crystal shards. Nolan rushed forward, and a wall of fire formed in front of the attack.

"Impressive," said Jet. Most of the ice crystals melted. Three small ones passed through the wall of fire and were knocked aside by others.

When Mammoth fired the ice crystals, the Elemental sentinel Dierling and the Runic demon Flauge rose into the air, circling both groups but staying far from each other. Dierling was a fire cloud; its wings of sand and dirt morphed as they beat down. From above, Dierling unleashed despair and sadness like a weapon against those on the ground. Three people fell to their knees.

Tominiko opened his hands ten inches apart, palms facing each other, and moved them back and forth. Within, sixteen spheres of mud formed. Then he hurled them, with speed and accuracy, at the moving creature. Jet was sure nothing would happen, but the mud glowed yellow and combined with the wings of sand, and the beast jolted, lost height, and was forced to bank away from the group.

Almost immediately, Flauge's ability became apparent. It tucked its wings, vanished, and reappeared ten feet from where it was. Then, dove at the group, keeping its body slim and nearly impossible to hit. On the second or third pass by, corrosive liquid gushed from its mouth. Drake used Water magic, freezing a portion of a gust of water and redirecting the poison to a spot near the wall. The instant the liquid touched the rock wall, it caused a half-foot-deep gash down to the floor. The liquid missed the golden lion by a few feet.

Kenapi galloped toward the center of the group, lowering its head, ready to collide with anyone in its path. Seyanna was slow to react, and the horse creature aligned its entire body. It wanted to knock her into the next century. Kenapi closed the distance in just a few seconds. It became clear that even with her speed, Seyanna couldn't escape Kenapi on her own. But using defensive tactics, she crouched and flung herself out of the way. Hiding behind her had been Leo and Wyatt and a large boulder. The Runic horse didn't have time to change directions and was lifted off the ground for a few inches with the collision, and the four hooves could not catch its balance. It careened into the ground on its right side, sliding for several feet.

Pandemonium broke out as the other three creatures attacked at once. Elemental spells were unleashed repeatedly. Most missed their targets or did nothing, but some did damage.

Mckenzey must've used her spell of Abzu as she manipulated ice to keep Kenapi from getting back to its feet. Seyanna aimed her golden bow and launched an arrow at Flauge. It impaled the left wing, but just seconds later, the arrow spun back and stuck in the ground to her left. Meanwhile, Wyatt charged Kenapi before it could stand and began punching one of the back legs. Then he took out his eight-inch sword with two shark teeth and slashed down. The cut opened. Kenapi kicked out, and the back hoof hit Wyatt's chest, cutting him near his left shoulder. The boy skidded for two feet.

Jet's heart rate accelerated, realizing there was nothing he could do. He always knew the risks that people might get hurt, but it was hard to swallow knowing he couldn't help. Focusing on Charcoit, he tried communicating with his mind. The white wolf either couldn't hear him or was ignoring him.

Focusing on the fighting, he watched as Phillip mishandled the spear with feathers. It spun to the closer side of the room, just below his encasement. Mammoth's long arm hit him directly, breaking his leg. Rushing forward, Jayco swung his fist, hitting the back of Mammoth, and the tree creature absorbed the hit with ease, spun, and shot a large ice crystal at Jayco. His Fire spell, Chango, melted the crystals. Jayco bent low and launched another punch, connecting with the left arm of the tree creature, and its entire hand and forearm shattered as if hit by a freight train. Mammoth spun uncontrollably due to the force. Jayco doubled over, gripping his hand in pain.

Ruby darted between other students, and Jet could tell she was using advanced defensive tactics. She was fun to watch. She never stayed in one position for more than half a second. She sent a spell at Mammoth, who was still reeling from Jayco's punch. Nothing visible happened, yet the tree creature tried protecting its head from the spell. Jet wondered if it could be Spirit magic, possibly confusion or pain. For the first time, one of the beasts looked vulnerable. Four or five students noticed the same thing and attacked.

Nolan gripped his thick sword and swung while Latisha expertly used her axe. They connected with the bark on both of Mammoth's legs. Nolan was capable and Latisha excelled. She was accurate, strong, and effective. Tessa and Conner connected with the right arm, but instantly, Mammoth swung a backhand, trying to catch Latisha off guard. She was ready. The girl rolled forward, the blow missing her by inches. When she stood, she swung her ax down, and it thumped against the chest, knocking out the ice chest piece. Ian leaped into the air, swinging his golden mace, and connected with the two obsidian meteorites. Mammoth was the first to fall, and the entire group cheered when it landed. The flame acting as its head dimmed entirely without the meteor eyes, and it moved no more.

Flauge dove dumping its poison onto both groups. Drake was ready with two frozen channels, like siphons, diverting away the toxin before they did any real damage. The creature circled again, screeching its displeasure. It alighted toward one group, landing a few feet away. The beast was still formidable, tall, predatory, and vicious. Jet could see the two claws on both winged appendages. Flauge lunged at Grace, cutting a deep gash into her left arm. Blood splattered the floor, and where it landed, it sizzled as if water was on a grill. The ground split apart, and two beetles, the size of a small car, crawled through the opening. Once they were in the grotto, the gap closed. Wyatt reacted quickly, pulling Grace from the creature's reach and preventing more blood from touching the ground.

The beetles began encircling the group. They had thick red shells on their backs that might open to reveal wings. Their undersides were black, with six legs and two large pinchers each, like scorpions. The head was fortified. Several spells sent at the beetle bounced off the outer shells. They kept their distance.

Nearby, Autumn bellowed something, and several Elementals understood what she said. Seyanna shot another arrow at Flauge, and this one caught it at the joint of the left wing. The beast stumbled back a few steps, attempting to flap its wings to get airborne, but couldn't. Mckenzey threw a knife and caught the beast somewhere low, but the most damage came from the golden bear, which had snuck behind and sprang onto its flank, missing the back spikes. The bear bit down on the right joint of the wing and tore a large chunk of the flesh away. The lion surged from the opposite side and did the same thing. Within seconds, the creature had been pulled onto its back. Both golden creatures sunk their jaws into the alligator's neck. Blood flowed from its many wounds, and the second creature was dead.

Dierling, Kenapi, and the two ginormous beetles attacked Jayco, Grantham, Remi, Eric, Ariana, and Phillip as if Flauge's demise meant nothing to them. The two groups had intermingled. One of the beetles knocked Ruby off her legs, and she hit the ground hard. The collision was more intense than Jet could have thought possible.

Even from here, Jet could tell Ruby was having trouble standing, and when she did, she stumbled and fell back to her knees. Kenapi did not hesitate. The creature bolted to the right of Ruby, almost passing her. The creature's movement was unexpected, but its hips twisted powerfully and flicked its enormous tail, connecting with Ruby's shoulder and neck. She was hammered with such force that she sailed across the room, bouncing twice, then sliding for another ten feet. When her body came to a rest, it was bent unnaturally.

CHAPTER 12

"No!" screamed Jet, and he pounded the invisible barrier so hard that his hand became bloody and his shoulder ached something fierce. But he didn't care. When the surge of energy was spent, he bent over and vomited, guilt rising in his body.

Both groups dashed to Ruby to check on her pulse, but it was clear that she was injured beyond repair. The golden lion and bear put themselves between the four remaining beasts. Hudson, Leo, and Wyatt crouched down next to Ruby's body. They dropped their weapons and began to weep.

Jayco shouted orders to the others, but everyone was flustered and unsettled. Grantham gripped Ariana, who was staggering on her own, directly in the path of Dierling.

"Why?" Jet slammed both hands on the barrier, wanting more than anything to find a way to escape. He feared that things were only going to get worse. Anger began to burn away guilt. This wasn't his fault. Something or someone was preventing him from helping his friends.

The remaining Elementals, except for the three near Ruby, huddled together. Autumn and Latisha stood at the front, Jayco and Grantham watching their sides. Behind these four, the other Elementals took their places, resolve and rage clearly visible. Grantham held his half-moon golden weapon. It was long, and he could extend it as he had done before. He showed Latisha what he wanted to do.

Iris and the other two golden animals broke apart and stalked Kenapi, pushing it away from the other three. The four-legged horse creature seemed to welcome the fight, flickering its tail back and forth.

Tessa broke away from the group and sprinted at Dierling. Jet swore the flying creature smiled at the tiny girl running at it. It shot Spirit spells at the girl, and she hopped back and forth as if she could see them. The concussive force shook the room as the missed spell hit the ground. Dierling's confidence wavered, and it beat its dust storm wings and rose into the air. Using what Jet thought was Varoun, Tessa caught the creature between flaps but only used the spell on the sand while the dirt and other particles remained airborne.

Every grain of sand plummeted to the floor as if called down by an electromagnetic force and stuck to the ground. Dierling tried pulling back up the sand to compensate, causing the dirt and other particles to separate from the creature. There was a tearing sound, and what lay behind was a skeleton of metal that moved and bent like no other creature Jet had ever seen. Dierling's body was made of metal bones, and it was grotesque and unnatural. Tominiko attacked from the adjacent side of Tessa. Propelling himself into the air as if he were riding an unseen wave, Tominiko gripped his golden paddle with two hands. The boy swung and crushed the center apex of the metal bones with such force that the entire skeleton shattered, and every particle of sand, dirt, or otherwise exploded away from Tominiko as if he were the center of a storm.

That leaves three, thought Jet. *Please pray no one else gets killed.* He watched as one of Seyanna's arrows flew back to her outstretched hand. It had been embedded in Dierling's arm.

The two beetles worked in tandem, blocking each attack and moving to help the other. Grantham or Jayco would position themselves on one side, only to have the second beetle flank him. Whatever they did, they couldn't separate the two creatures.

Kenapi was the final sentinel demon. It tore through the cavern as if playing tag, keeping as far away from the main group as possible. Sporadically, it would try to knock over an Elemental and trample them. Conner, injured, moved slowly and was a clear target. Four students, Phillip, Ariana, Autumn, and Grace, put Conner in the middle of them.

Seyanna unleashed an arrow. It collided with Kenapi's skin just above its front leg, near the shoulder, but bounced off. It couldn't have been a better shot, but nothing.

The next several attacks caused no damage to either side. Kenapi was too fast to be caught, and it appeared the creature had unlimited stamina. The two beetles weren't slowing down either. Jayco received cuts across both legs. Grantham's left forearm was bleeding.

Remi shouted, "The beetles are getting bigger."

Jet heard the pronouncement and focused on the two beetles. Their legs were thicker than they were when this started, with enlarged pinchers. They were becoming more dangerous.

A coordinated attack by the beetles and Kenapi was directed at Autumn's group. A shield blocked a pincher strike, and they were pushed back. The second beetle managed to surprise Ariana and sliced the back of her leg. She stumbled but didn't fall. The second beetle had been ready to plunge in to finish the kill.

Grantham announced, "Anyone have something that can disrupt the two beetles from communicating?"

A swirl of wind tornadoes erupted around both beetles. They staggered, and Jet couldn't tell if it was their balance or from a second attack. He scanned the group but saw no one. The golden animals kept their distance, trying to find the right moment to strike.

Jayco maneuvered, slamming his enhanced hand down on the beetle's hard shell. The shell indented slightly, but Jayco received most of the damage. He fell back, grasping his hand and screaming.

Mckenzey rushed to Ariana, trying to heal the wound. The two beetles regrouped and scurried forward. Kenapi also used the moment to strike from the opposite side.

Nolan shot another wall of fire, but Kenapi dove directly through the spell, undamaged. The beast landed, lowered its head, and ran full out. Grace, Tessa, Drake, and Ian stepped in front of the beast as it tried to find a clear way to get to Conner. Jet didn't understand the fixation Kenapi had on Conner.

Grace pulled out her golden sword as Drake swung his back and forth. Ian used a Water spell—Oblekii—and clouds stormed into the cavern. Kenapi stood a little taller and somehow ran faster. The horse creature lowered its head, intending to ram anyone in its way. Conner cowered. He couldn't retreat and dropped both his mace and shield to the ground.

"Move," Jet screamed, but no one could hear him.

A glancing blow hit Grace first, knocking her aside. Tessa sidestepped in the same instant that she swung her mace at one of the front legs. It connected, and the mace broke in half. Drake and Ian stumbled and were lucky they didn't get trampled. Conner scampered backward.

Time slowed, and everyone became aware of what was about to happen. Kenapi lunged at Conner. The moment the beast's four feet left the ground, Conner stood, gaining complete control of the situation, his assurance blossoming. Lifting one hand, he closed his eyes. Something in the room changed as if the ceiling of the cavern vanished. Bright moonlight shone in and fell onto Kenapi.

Kenapi did not stop moving, but the instant the moonlight touched the beast, it became like a shadow phantom, incorporeal and without a real body. It passed directly through Conner without inflicting any damage. Then, with a jerk of his hand, Conner removed the moonlight, and Kenapi became tangible once again. The creature crashed headlong into the side of the cavern with such force that the enormous beast's neck broke in one quick strike. Kenapi stood immobile for a full second, then fell sideways.

As the moonlight vanished, the barrier keeping Jet in the wall disappeared. The two beetles sank into the floor as if they had never been there.

Jet leaped from his hole, and he used a series of spells to reach the ground quickly. Upon touching the ground, he sprinted to the others. Some were shouting, others crying, and all hugged each other fiercely.

Charcoit's voice boomed throughout the cavern, "The four beasts have been defeated. You have won the battle of Diamond Falls. You may now enter the treasure chamber and collect your prizes."

A doorway the size of an entire house opened where the four beasts had been stored for their arrival. The dark hallway was unlit and foreboding. But no one moved. They all wheeled to stare at Ruby's fallen body.

"I got her," said Jet, and he hurried to the body. Iris reached him an instant before he bent low to look at her. The golden panther steadied him. Others arrived behind him. Ruby was pale, and her eyes were closed. The golden bear stopped on the opposite side, lowering his body to the ground. Jet understood the meaning. He lifted her up, placing her gently onto the bear's back.

"We've seen far too much of this already," said Mckenzey. "This is just too much. Ruby seemed so nice."

"She was," said Hudson, who stepped forward, produced some rope, and neatly bound her to the golden bear. "But she also loved the friendships she found with the Elementals. Me, Ruby, Leo, and Wyatt weren't friends before we chose to join. But we became instant friends afterward. The last few months were the happiest in her life. She told me so."

Grantham said, "She died helping us. That has to mean something."

"It does," said Jet, his voice low. "This may have started with a few of us, but without all of you and each Elemental, we would have no chance to win the war. Ruby ensured that you succeeded today. We can never forget her or anyone else who died because of magic, the Rivalry, the Azurites, or any other part of this. We'll bring her back to campus and add her and the others to the memorial."

Jayco said, "We will also remember Lucas, Quinn, and Victoria."

"That was messed up," said Nolan. "We needed Jet here to enter, but he couldn't help us."

Seyanna said, "Look at the scratch marks on his head and the hair he pulled out."

"Look at his hands," added Tominiko.

Jet admitted, "That was an entirely different level of anxiety. I'm sure I was on the verge of a heart attack."

"How did we do?" asked Jayco.

"You guys worked together with talent, skills, and brilliant minds. It was incredible to watch."

"That's what we experienced watching you fight Lucretius back in Silverton," said Grantham.

Jet nodded.

Eric pointed to the open hallway. "Let's go see what we earned and get the hell out of here."

Ariana and Autumn helped support Phillip, helping him walk. His leg was banged up.

As they strode to the wall, a tingle ran down Jet's spine, and he knew that he couldn't yet enter the treasure room. He stopped walking and said, "You guys go on without me. I'll catch up as soon as I can."

"You better not mean what I think you mean," said Eric. "You can't keep ditching us."

Jet lifted both hands passively. "I'm not."

"Then what is it?" asked Seyanna.

Jet pointed to the creature in the wall. "I'm being summoned for a quick conversation. I'll catch up when I can." He didn't wait for a response and jogged toward the far wall. Iris followed directly behind him.

The white wolf loomed large. Charcoit's eyes followed him as he advanced.

The beast spoke to him just as it had done in the Averseen. "That could have gone much worse, but the Elementals handled themselves well."

"Why was I not allowed to help?" Jet seethed. "I could have protected that girl."

"This can be the most difficult part of being the commander of an army. Ordering someone to a location where they risk perishing is far more challenging than fighting yourself. It takes character and empathy; you are never the same once it happens. That girl, or someone like her, has died before when fighting with you, but it is easier to justify because you were in the trenches together. Having someone die because you sent them there refines the soul or destroys it."

"Is that why this happened? Did she die to teach me a lesson?"

"No," Charcoit said emotionlessly. "And yes. It is a learning opportunity you can take away from this moment."

"What else?"

"The Elementals are proficient, talented, and able to work in connection with each other. It was impressive."

"It would have been more impressive if we had beat Shane here."

"Maybe. But he never went to Congo and never experienced what you have. It may hurt him in the end."

"If you say so," Jet mumbled. "We had the first four pieces, and now he has one. How are we ever supposed to get that from him?"

"Your goal should be to make sure he doesn't get the sixth piece; then, you can negotiate for the other one."

Jet nodded and saw the wisdom in this statement. "I'm sure I'll be seeing you in the Averseen soon enough. How can you be here and in my book?"

Charcoit said, "The Averseen is not in your book. Granted, it takes you to the fae whereabouts with ease. There's no other way to access the Averseen. I'm both there and here."

"Fascinating," Jet said, and he turned to leave, but Charcoit's next question froze him.

"Do you know who your biggest threat is at the moment?"

Jet said, "Let's see. The Coven, the Chupovanas, or the Khalicaans. It might be the Azurites, the Quills, and who could forget the Rufu squad."

"I see you conveniently left out one."

"Kevin would have been high on the list, but he's off the board."

"That leaves…"

"Faunal."

"Yes. The moment the sixth disaster happens, his bonds will be unleashed from the Rivalry, and he will take every moment to destroy you and prepare for the return of his master. He has been playing chess and stacking the cards against you."

"Can he be killed?"

"Not as long as he is under the protection of the Rivalry, but this gives you protection from him."

"He's already attacked me with his mind."

"Somehow, that method of attack was not censored."

Jet pulled out a necklace with a golden chain and a golden pendant of an open book. He said, "The Axenkind gave me this necklace to safeguard against attacks from Trimentis."

"Good," said Charcoit. "I was not sure if you were aware of this hideous form of magic. I'm nearly certain the Skeleton taught Faunal and the Grey Panther this form of mind assault. They both excelled beyond anyone before them. I believe the Skeleton has the knowledge but lacks the ability."

"What advice can you give?"

"Find and destroy the six deceitful tributes found in the Skeleton's cave and given to the tribes who helped during the war at Darcoff Pass. If Faunal or others reclaim these, the results could be catastrophic. This must be done before the sixth disaster unfolds."

"I'll do my best," said Jet.

He was about to walk off when Charcoit added, "Magic, as you know it, is constrained. It was not always as limited as it currently is. Your friends did an admirable job with what they know, but the future might be brighter when one Elemental might become two."

"What's that supposed to mean?"

"Time will tell." Charcoit's voice, but a whisper, added, "Other dangerous players on the board that you are yet unaware lurk in the darkness. Much needs to be accomplished before Arisol is released. There are ways to counteract magic. What you saw in Congo was just a taste. Not all enemies will be from the magical."

Before walking away, Jet said, "You're a fountain of good news." As he crossed the now deserted cavern, he contemplated all of Charcoit's words and loathed some of his unspoken implications. It wasn't enough to get ready for Arisol to return, but now, he needed to find and destroy these items. He hoped he had already taken a few steps in the right direction.

The hallway to the treasure room was no longer dark or dreary. On the other side was an elaborate and richly decorated room with walls with unique markings and enormous tapestries depicting wars and events from long ago. His eyes were drawn to a detailed account of the twins standing in front of an immense mountain range—Darcoff Pass. They wore the same cloaks they had worn when they attacked and killed Queen Aurora.

A colorful tapestry depicted a falling asteroid hitting the beach and sliding across the sand. Carved into the wall directly across from it was the gigantic sand creature from his vision. The title written overhead was: The Golem.

Along the back wall was a painting of the same pass and thousands of soldiers marching toward the opening as a horde of creatures and three enormous mountain trolls awaited them. To his right, the tapestry showed Arisol being forced back into his earthly prison and the precise moment when he unleashed a Runic spell, starting the Rivalry.

"Over here," shouted Seyanna, seeing him.

She and the others stood over a slab of granite in the center of the room, gazing down at the floor. Jayco, Grantham, and Ariana were tending to the gashes in their legs, bandaging them. As he came closer, he noticed chambers in the stone filled with weapons.

Before he said anything, Seyanna flung herself into his arms. He caught her, and she kissed him. Not once or twice, but a half dozen times. It felt good to be close to her, her warm breath, skin, and heartbeat. Everyone else in the room fell away for one of the best minutes of his life.

A cheer echoed around the room, bringing him back to reality.

When they broke apart, she said, "I should've done that sooner."

Her smile was unapologetic and shy at the same time. Her cheeks reddened slightly, but Jet reached out his hand, grabbed hers, and pulled her close. Her beautiful smile broadened.

"After that riveting moment," said Jayco, annoyed. "Take a look at what we have here."

Mckenzey stood on the opposite from the granite slab, refusing to look at him. Her cheeks were redder than Seyanna's, and she was ranting.

Grantham said, "Nine holes are cut into stone. Like storage bins."

Jayco pointed to a dais in the room. "I bet the fifth piece was there."

Jet glanced at each of the nine holes. "Tell me what we've found."

"The first three here...hold three different types of swords with nearly twenty swords in each hole. Around sixty swords."

Tominiko pulled out a sword from the first bin. "Looks nice."

The sword's blade was thick and central and would require two hands to wield it. The blade was three feet in length, thick, and sharp on both sides.

Next, Eric pulled out a sword from the center spot. It had a skinnier handle and a blade half the size of the first one. The blade went straight up from the handle, was gold in color, and the last third of the blade curved in the opposite direction. In total, the length of the blade was eighteen inches.

The third section held longer swords with handles that would require two hands. The golden blade was sharp only on one side and easily twenty-two inches long.

"There are another sixty weapons in the middle three groups," said Jayco. "The are different types of spears." The first twenty were shorter and could easily be thrown like a javelin. The length of this weapon was just beyond three feet. The handle was made of wood, but the end was pointed in golden metal.

The spears in the middle and right sections were about the same length, approaching six feet. The main difference was the spear blade itself. The spear in the middle section had a curved blade a few inches before the end and a wider tip. The third group had eight-inch spears as fine as a pen. These could cut entirely through a body for pinpoint accuracy.

The last row had a variety of weapons: thirty blades with intricate carvings and unique handles. The blade was nearly three inches wide, sixteen inches long, and sharp on only one side. It slimmed down towards the tip. The handle had a protective metal piece and a comfortable grip. The second weapon was a mace two feet in length. The end of the mace held a golden ball with a dozen three-inch spikes in all different directions.

The last two sections had dozens of bows, arrows, and fifty three-sided golden throwing stars. The bows were small, compact, and required strength. The arrows were skinnier but longer than Seyanna's. The golden stars were hand-sized, with three sharp edges, and the center circle was missing. There was a small area to grip this weapon between sharp blades. It was light yet sturdy.

"Over here," shouted Eric. "We have crates of shields."

Latisha was already looking through the items.

Jet, Seyanna, and others circled around and found three crates of shields. Again, there were three different types: a smaller circular one, the size of a basketball; a larger circular one, the size of a large tire; and a three-sided shield with one flat side and the other two breaking off and meeting together almost like an elongated triangle.

"How will we carry all these items?" asked Tominiko.

"Give everything to Jayco and the golden animals," mused Eric. "Let's start packing things up."

Jet hurried over to Conner, who was getting attention from Ariana, Autumn, Grace, and Tessa. "How did you know that moonlight would affect Kenapi?"

Conner said confidently, "I got to thinking. My weapon was a golden mace and a shield, which wasn't that different than anyone else. Something clicked in my head, and I knew I could call forth moonlight. I felt more than anything that Kenapi's weakness was moonlight. It called to me, if you can believe it. Glad it worked."

"Brilliant," said Jet, and he smiled. "That was the best thing I've ever seen."

Autumn winked at him kindly, as if saying he had said the right thing. She turned back to Conner and began wrapping a gash on his leg.

Retracing his steps, an idea popped into his mind. He rummaged in his hidden compartment and pulled out a multicolored stone. "Everyone. Come watch this before we get going."

He dropped the stone into the sand, and it hit once, then twice, then swelled ten times in size. A minute later, the outer crust of the stone, or egg, cracked, and out walked a salamander lizard.

"What's that?" asked Seyanna.

"It's called a Watcher Syntac. We used a few of them back in Congo. Depending on the type of spell used, these creatures can do different things."

Mckenzey asked, "What's the plan for this one? Protect this area?"

"No. We need its eyes to watch and tell us if anyone comes here after us. This place will have a greater importance after the Rivalry is finished."

"Did that creature in the wall tell you that?" asked Grantham.

"Yes," said Jet. "But so do these tapestries." He turned to the lizard, which had climbed the stone walls, swiveled, and stared at him, expectantly. He spoke "Doreskimo," and concentrated. Warmth spread across his chest. He added, "Incom Spruce Knob." The Syntac reacted to the spell by climbing to the ceiling, running across a part of it, then dropping to the floor. It rotated mid-air, landed cleanly on the ground, and took off into the large cavern, leaving them behind.

"This will give us a way to visualize this area even when we're back at Chadwick's," explained Jet. "These Syntacs will help us stay connected with the locations of the Rivalry. We left behind some Fighters in Congo along with a Watcher."

"Anyone see a way out of here?" asked Phillip. "I've totally had enough excitement for one day."

It took time to load all the weapons and shields. As they did, three students searched for an exit. Using the golden animals, they tied several weapons to each. Jet placed nearly half of the weapons into his hidden compartment. For the first time since he had received the ring, it was full.

Phillip said, "I think backtracking into the main room is pointless. The exit has to be around here somewhere." He hopped around on one foot, examining one corner after another

"This might be something," said Remi. She paused near a tapestry that was the least impressive in the room. Pictured was an enormous mountain at the far end of a desert valley. It was well done and vibrant, but the tapestry had no higher meaning. However, as he came closer, a dry wind brushed across his face, and there was a faint ocean smell.

"Check out the floor," she said.

Jet took another deep breath and looked down. Scratches in the floor, close to half a circle, were barely visible. He searched for more changes in the wall and noticed three small bricks hung farther out than the others. He touched all three, and the wall began to slide backward.

What happened next was hard to describe. The floor remained the same, or so Jet thought, but the ceiling vanished. Water flowed like a waterfall but only in the missing section of the wall.

"What now?" demanded Jayco, glancing between Jet and Grantham.

Grantham said, "We could try walking into the water."

Steam rose and water fell. Jet stepped hesitantly into the water and was jerked upward as if he were on a rollercoaster to the sun. The water cascaded against him, but he felt no pressure. The entire ride lasted a minute or so. When he broke the surface of the water, he was in the deepest part of the pond. Iris came up right behind him.

He swam for less than half a minute when his feet collided with the rocks below. He stood, only partly submerged. Iris pushed past him, made it to shore, and shook her entire body, drying her fur.

Seyanna was next, and she quickly made her way to him, smiling. "That was a blast."

"It was."

Together, they walked toward the shore, holding hands. Jet combed the nighttime skyline to see if anyone else might be around. But they were alone.

Over the next few minutes, everyone exited the water, smiling. It was described as "an incredible, once-in-a-lifetime ride".

Jayco exited the water. "That's everyone."

The first part of the hike back to the vans was the hardest. Carrying the injured and the weapons up the steep path required most of their energy. Jet hadn't fought, but his days of heightened activity and anxiety-ridden introspections had reduced him to a zombie.

As the parking lot came into view, Seyanna asked, "How was your fear of heights as you watched us?"

"It was outdone by my fear of you guys dying."

"Oh, crap," shouted Mckenzey. She was at the front of the group.

"What's wrong?" asked Nolan.

"Are we sure we're at the right parking lot? Could we have gotten lost?"

"Let me see," said Grantham, and he hurried forward. "Nope, this is the right one."

"That's bad," said Mckenzey. "Really bad."

"Why?" asked Jet. "What's wrong?"

"Our SUVs are gone."

CHAPTER 13

I'm going to kill Rysen and Charlie if they had anything to do with the disappearance of our friends. Jet's dark imagination threatened to take control. Anger simmered just below the surface, and he sprinted around the asphalt parking lot. It was empty. Glancing at his watch, he saw it was nearing 10 p.m.

"They're fine," declared Ariana, with relief in her voice. "They're parked at a lower spot and suggest that we don't walk down the road."

Grantham said, "Goodness gracious. I thought my heart was going to race out of my chest."

"Why didn't they say something sooner?" asked Jet, his jaw clenched.

"They were busy," said Ariana. "Professor Rysen, Charlie, and that woman are still nearby. Raul suggests we take a different, less dangerous route."

"How would they know about it?" asked Jayco.

"Phoebe found it when she was hiding from the trio."

"Seriously," said Eric. "This is not good."

Ariana stared directly at Jet. "Raul suggests that Jet doesn't look down." She added, "Rysen and company wanted to ambush us when we exited the lake but were forced to leave. Now, they're searching for our vehicles. Emmett and Zuri found a new spot, but it's only a matter of time before that becomes compromised. Phoebe had to climb down to them. It's not easy, but better than getting caught."

"We could take them," said Jayco.

"Not with Ruby's body and all the weapons. Faunal is with them. Climbing down is going to be hard enough."

"Maybe for you," said Grantham.

Jet rolled his eyes. "You're as sticky as Spiderman, so I don't want to hear it. But what about those injured?"

"We'll manage," said Eric.

"This way," announced Ariana, leading them back toward the forest but taking a path to their right instead.

Lathisha caught up to Grantham, kissed him, and soon they were hand in hand, following Ariana.

They weaved between trees for ten minutes, but suddenly, the space opened, and Jet's eyes doubled in size. Next to him, the cliff was a sheer drop.

"How's your fear of heights now?" Seyanna asked, and he could hear the smile in her eyes.

"Bad."

They followed the cliff's edge until it dropped severely into the valley through a narrow path. To get there, he would need to cross two ledges, the tiniest of trails, and a passage that went almost straight down. It was reasonable to think you wouldn't fall if you kept your balance. If.

"I can't," said Jet, shaking his head and stepping back a few steps.

Seyanna gripped his arm. "I'll help. And if you fall, you have magic."

"I'm not sure I really have enough energy to stop a grain of sand."

"You'll be fine," she assured him, and her fierce expression convinced him. Squeezing his hand, she led him forward.

Jayco, Grantham, Latisha, Mckenzey, Ariana, and most others had already dropped a hundred feet in elevation. Even the golden lion and bear weren't having an ounce of trouble. Soon enough, it was Jet's turn to begin down to the trail. The first hurdle was a six-foot fall, and if he missed by more than a few inches, he wouldn't stop until he smacked the bottom.

Iris leaped first, landing perfectly, then stared back at him. Seeing her soft golden glow, he experienced a tiny increase in his courage. After pretending to jump six times in a row, almost finding enough courage, he surprised himself when he sailed through the air on the seventh attempt. His arms flailed, and a whimper might have escaped his lips. He landed far from perfectly, and his upper torso continued its momentum forward. Iris's jaw clamped onto the back of his pants, preventing him from falling.

Seyanna scrambled down and gripped him.

"Thanks," mumbled Jet.

"Did you see that one tapestry?" asked Seyanna. "The one with darkness and the red triangle? Did it look like it was trapped or locked up?"

Jet wasn't sure he could answer and walk at the same time. He appreciated her attempt to distract him. After several steps, he stopped and said, "I'm not completely sure what it was. I saw darkness and manacles."

"Yea. That's what I saw. Was it a weapon?"

"It's quite possible." Taking a deep breath, he began moving again.

"Maybe a sword or something, without a handle? I have earrings of the same color. You know I love red."

Jet abruptly stopped walking, and Seyanna nearly stumbled into him. "You're right. That's remarkable."

"Is it important?"

"I think so." He continued walking. Now that she had said it, he could picture the black background and the manacles holding the blade in place. The blade was majestic, red, and beautiful. The tapestry had been small, but he should have spent more time looking at each of them.

After a moment, he said, "That color is called jasper. I'm pretty sure that was a blade made of jasper." He added, "I think it's one of the Insidious Six."

"The what?"

He explained the six items found in the Skeleton's cave. This time, talking calmed him enough that he began moving at a snail's pace.

She said, "Who would have guessed. I remember seeing that gaudy green necklace in that initial crate. Do you think Nana knew what she was sending you?"

"I doubt it. I had no idea what it was. Also, that black looped item. When we get back, we will have to see if it works."

"Any idea where the rest of them are?"

"I think the Azurites have one and used it to kill my parents and helped Charlie escape the bus. The horn was at Dillon Lake, and Kevin used the sword. I picked it up after killing him. We'll have to see if it really is. The rest, I'm not so sure."

"And the tapestry depicted the blade without a handle?"

"I wouldn't have thought so until you mentioned it. If it is...I have no idea where it could be."

The next portion, the last, was the trickiest. It dropped quickly, but parts of the trail had washed away. In two separate spots, you had to jump across a ravine. Staring back up from where they came, it was impossible to see the upper ridge. On the second leap, he missed the landing, tripped, and fell hard onto his right knee. Blood ran down his leg, but he didn't care. At least he didn't make his shoulders worse. A sense of relief ran through him when he stepped onto the lower level. His energy level plunged.

Seyanna was next to him a moment later, her arm under his.

Ariana said, "If we head toward the road, we'll find them behind some trees."

Phillip said, "I can't even tell where the road is."

"This way."

Sometime later, there was movement on their left, and Jet tensed. From behind a tree stepped Phoebe.

"We turn here," she pointed to a hidden pathway.

The group followed. Phoebe and Ariana began whispering. Jet wasn't the only one who was struggling. Phillip couldn't put any weight on either leg. Jet had no idea how he had made it down what they had just gone through. Jayco and Tominiko helped. They picked up the pace, and soon, Jet was breathing hard.

They hit an incline, and Phoebe announced, "We're almost there."

Once at the top, they leveled out for a minute, then slightly declined and rounded a bend to their left. The trees were thick but not as dense as back up on the ridge.

"I see the road," shouted Eric. "But no cars."

Ariana said, "I guess they're a bit farther down."

Phoebe added, "We'll stay parallel to the road, but we won't get closer than this. Charlie drove up and down about fifteen minutes ago."

Wyatt sprinted over. "Hide behind some trees. My ability gives different heat signatures to humans, animals, creatures, and the magical.

There are humans and dogs beyond the tree line. In a minute, they'll be at that overlook we were at. We're being followed."

"Hurry," said Jayco.

Jet pointed to several patches on the ground and spoke "Artemis," intending to create muddy places on the ground. Nothing happened. He didn't have enough energy to protect his friends.

But the others did.

A small patch of rain began to fall, and fog descended into the valley.

Seyanna dragged him behind a tree. But before he reached it, he saw Professor Rysen, Destiney Descartes, and five others step out onto the ledge. Three large dogs pulled at leashes. Jet eased to the ground and hoped he hadn't been seen.

Two minutes later, he was hauled to his feet, and they moved quickly through the forest. Dog barks and shouts erupted behind them. They were coming. Their group reached the two SUVs and two additional cars, ready to pull out. The vehicles were concealed from the view of anyone driving by. They piled in the gear and Ruby's body. Iris and the other animals transformed into pyramids.

Jet, Seyanna, Ariana, Phillip, Phoebe, Remi, Leo, Hudson, and Nolan got into the vehicle driven by Raul. All the prisoners, including Sarika, were put in the largest van with Jayco, Mckenzey, Eric, Latisha, Tominiko, and Drake. The rest of the students were divided into the two cars, with Grantham driving one and Autumn the other.

They took Route 112, heading north. They traveled along the back side of Spruce Knob, staying closer to Seneca Rocks. They switched roads and continued to Petersburg, then to the 81, keeping north to Harrisburg, which would eventually lead them to New York and Dillon Lake.

Raul asked, "What happened to Phillip?"

Ariana said, "Your boyfriend fought brilliantly." She described the battle with the four beasts and how Kenapi had attacked Phillip. She added, "He blocked several strikes and even saved Mckenzey. In doing so, he was knocked sideways and broke his leg."

"Will they be able to fix him in New York?"

"I bet they will," said Jet, unsure if this was true.

Phillip was barely conscious, his leg positioned on Ariana's lap. They found some ice in a cooler and some pain medications in the pocket of the first aid kit. His pants were cut away, and they found a splint and some other supplies. After getting some treatment, Phillip let out a sigh of relief, and his face seemed to relax. Raul never did, gripping the wheel and glancing back in the mirror.

Jet asked, "Do you know why Rysen, Charlie, and Descartes were forced to leave the lake?"

Raul answered, "Phoebe said that an invisible force pushed them away from the area. After an hour, they probably figured that we got to the area by driving, and they started going from vehicle to vehicle."

"What happened to Faunal?"

"I think he was injured. He cleared out in a hurry," said Phoebe. "His fur was burned."

"I can't say that I'm not cheering inside," said Jet.

Phoebe continued, "After they were pushed away, a van arrived with more Azurites. They joined the search."

Seyanna asked, "Is Faunal helping Shane or the Azurites?"

"I'm guessing both," said Jet. "I don't see any other option. Faunal must not have gotten what he wanted from Shane, or he's double-crossing one or both groups."

"Interesting," said Ariana. "It's hard to keep track with so many players involved."

"You're telling me!" hissed Nolan.

"Charlie got here fast," noted Jet. "It had to be Faunal watching the group, probably Shane."

"You're probably right," agreed Seyanna.

"How many people are involved with the Azurites?" asked Remi. "What's their purpose?"

Jet said, "Disruption of magic at any cost. They want the Rivalry to fail. That's probably a common belief they share with Faunal."

"From what I'm seeing," said Nolan. "Faunal is in leagues with Arisol, right? That means anything he does will have a long-term goal to help that creature trapped in prison. He can never be trusted."

Jet muttered, "I wish Shane could see that."

They continued talking. Questioning continued about Elemental magic, Runic magic, and the lost three magical books. Jet clarified as much as he could and hinted that things would change soon. About two hours into the drive, Seyanna took over driving. An hour and a half later, the four-vehicle caravan stopped, filled up on gas, and found something to eat at a 24-hour diner in Harrisburg.

Once they ordered, Jet called over Jayco, Grantham, Mckenzey, Latisha, and Seyanna.

"What's up?" asked Grantham.

"We need to contact the pilots and have us meet at the Warwick Airport," explained Jet. "Half of us will head back to Chadwick's, and the rest will go on to Dillon Lake."

Mckenzey, her voice distant, asked, "Why can't we all go to Dillon Lake?"

"We have serious injuries and prisoners. Phillip will need surgery."

"Where are we going to hold prisoners at Chadwick's?" asked Latisha.

Jet thought this was a good question. He really hadn't thought about this before.

Seyanna lifted her hand slightly, almost tepidly. "I can answer this."

Jet stared at her. "You can?"

She nodded. "After Shane and Jayco tried taking over the school, Principal Smuin began renovating the same building, but below ground."

"No way!" exclaimed Grantham.

Seyanna glanced sideways at Jet, then continued, "I only found out because I'm in charge of the school's defenses at night." She lifted her hand to stop his next question. "I promised Principal Smuin that I would tell nobody. Workers come in at night to work below ground. The other boarding schools recommended them as they have done work at each."

"What kind of work?" asked Latisha.

"I don't know all the details, but holding cells, escape tunnels, and more. I overheard Principal Smuin say there's a growing concern that magic could be manipulated and that the schools want options."

"That's insane," said Latisha. "Cells in a school."

Jayco said, "Rozene let slip that Dillon Lake has its own building. They used to have six holding cells below the sports building, but some flooding changed everything. They've had considerable renovations."

"Seriously," said Grantham.

Seyanna said, "It's my understanding that all the schools have them already built. Chadwick's is the last one. Principal Fletcher was on the fence, and when she died and Shane tried his little coup, it wasn't a far leap by Smuin."

Jet said, "Are ours finished?"

"Close. An interrogation room, and maybe a dozen cells." She added quickly, "I haven't seen them."

Jet wasn't sure how he was supposed to feel. "Then we take our prisoners back to Chadwick's. Tell the pilots where to meet us."

Grantham asked, "Who do you need to return to Chadwick's?"

Jet said, "You, Latisha, Mckenzey, and Eric, to go with Raul, Phillip, Ariana, and some of the others to Chadwick's. One priority is to get our prisoners back there. We must also be mindful that Shane might find this a perfect moment to strike to get the other pieces of the Phoenix."

"You want Eric and me to go back as well?" asked Mckenzey, but she wouldn't meet his eyes.

Eric said, "It's a good idea. We can take back the weapons and Ruby's body."

"Right," said Jet.

"Fine," said Mckenzey and she marched to the other SUV. Eric glanced between Jet and Mckenzey, but he said nothing.

"Good plan," said Jayco, whose eyes glinted slightly red. His voice was aggressive when he said, "But listen. Rozene is at Dillon Lake. You know this. So, there's no chance that I'm not going with you."

Jet forced a smile, still watching Mckenzey walk away. Pulling his attention to Jayco, he said, "I didn't. I knew you wouldn't leave without her."

Jayco's burst of anger slowly deflated.

Ariana announced, "Food is ready."

Grantham said, "See you at the airport."

Ariana took over driving duties, and Nolan helped guide her. They ate food as they drove, and then Jet, Seyanna, Remi, and Wyatt collapsed in the far back seat. Seyanna rested her head on his shoulder and they slept for the next two hours. Around thirty minutes outside of New York, Jet awoke. Ariana and Nolan chatted quietly. Seyanna snored, and the others were still asleep, except Phoebe. She stared out the window, and the airport came into view. At some point, she turned and smiled.

Jet whispered, "Did you get any sleep?"

"Not much. I think my ability allows me to forgo sleep for a few days. I'll crash hard when we're back on campus."

"That's a useful talent," he remarked.

"Sometimes." She turned and stared out the window.

Soon, they drove through the checkpoint and up to hanger six. It took half an hour to load Ruby, the weapons, and all those traveling back to Chadwick's. Mckenzey said nothing to him.

Seyanna whispered, "Is Mckenzey alright?"

"I think so," he said casually. "Probably tired." He watched as Raul and Arina helped Phillip onto the plane. Next went the prisoners and other Elementals. Grantham waved at them as the door closed.

Unfamiliar people hurried forward from the back of the hanger, got into the two cars and the largest van, and drove away. Jayco, Seyanna, Phoebe, Nolan, and Tominiko found seats in the remaining vehicle. Jayco insisted on driving.

Sometime later, they turned onto the road leading to Dillon Lake. The streets were quiet, and they hadn't seen anyone since they had exited the freeway. Only he and Jayco had been here before. They drove past the welcoming sign and a forest of enormous trees that were both wider and taller than some of those in the redwood forest.

"This is BloodMoon Pines," said Jet as everyone stared out their windows. He explained how, fifty years ago, a fire threatened the school.

Back then, there were only a few small trees. On the day of a blood moon, one of the last Fuerego Dragons landed and breathed the forest into existence. The fire was extinguished. Since that time, the school has been protected.

"So the trees are part of campus?" asked Tominiko.

"Not quite. There should be a gate up here."

As they drove through the forest, he noticed that the guard shack and keypad were no more. It was replaced by a gigantic building, a large metal wall, and a fence heading north and south. A large metal gate forced them to stop. The outer walls were eight feet tall, and the metal fence went another four or five feet above it. Flood lights were well-positioned in both directions. Two people sat inside the building. As they drove to the window, Jet saw monitors with camera angles showing the outer walls and some of the inner streets.

Jayco rolled down his window.

An intercom chirped, and a voice said, "Are you visiting a student, a prospective student, or a family member?"

"Uh," said Jayco.

Jet said, "Tell him we're here to see Principal Berry."

Jayco relayed the information.

"He's in a meeting until noon. I can get your—"

Jet interrupted from the back seat. "We're students from Chadwick's, and we need to see him urgently."

"Chadwick's?" the voice stammered. "You'll need to wait a moment."

In less than thirty seconds, the enormous metal gates opened inward. Driving forward, Jet thought they had been admitted into the school, but just as the doors closed behind him, he was dismayed to see another set of gates blocking their passage into the school itself.

The intercom voice returned, "Principal Berry is on his way, and he'll decide whether or not to let you in."

Phoebe said, "I'm starting to second guess my choice of coming here. I could be asleep on a plane home."

"Same," said Nolan. "But this is sort of exciting."

Fifteen minutes later, a golf cart summited the small hill where the entrance stood. From here, it was down into the campus itself. As the cart approached, it was apparent that Principal Berry had transformed nearly as much as the school itself. In less than a month, he had lost considerable weight. He was tall with bronze skin and a dazzling smile, but now he looked sickly. His face was guarded, even when Jet stepped out of the van and waved.

"Jet Black. Is that really you?"

"Yes, sir."

"I wasn't told if you would be coming back. Was it you who sent the other students here?"

"What have you been told?"

"That Kevin betrayed us, as did Charlie Eckenkeep. Some of our students were killed, and our school is at tremendous risk."

"Risk?" asked Jet.

"Do we trust Predilectors, or don't we? If Kevin was part of why Dart and Elliot were killed, then I'm not sure the school should remain open."

"Why don't you let us inside? We can help protect the school."

"How?"

"We can figure out who you can trust and how best to protect your students."

"What about those flying vultures? Will they come back?"

Jet said, "Charlie used glasses to control them. We broke the glasses. I don't think anyone controls those creatures, but I can't see them ever returning to Dillon Lake."

These words seemed to focus Principal Berry. Using a cellphone, he briefly spoke to someone, and then the gate opened.

"Follow me."

Jayco followed Principal Berry back toward campus. "He's changed a bit," said Jayco. "He seems jittery."

"Wouldn't you?" said Seyanna. "From what Jet told me, they put a lot of trust in Kevin. Them and the Brotherhood. Everything they thought was happening wasn't."

Jayco nodded.

They were led back down Middlesex Lane, but this time, they were taken to a building across the road from the main block of buildings where they had stayed before. The cart drove into a parking lot in the back, and Jayco followed. The van parked next to the cart, and everyone got out.

Principal Berry waited for them. He said, "I hope you're hungry. This is one of our cafeterias."

"You bet," said Jayco. "How's the food?"

Principal Berry smiled, but his words were direct: "The clock has started. You have one hour to convince me that I can trust you, or one of three things will happen: I lock you up, we close the school, or we figure out how to protect the kids here. I hope you have some great ideas. Rozene is acting student president, and we've already lost a hundred students and six teachers. Things have got to change."

CHAPTER 14

Eating breakfast was an odd occurrence. The entire group watched Seyanna as she approached each dish, ensuring that none of the tonic had been used on them. Principal Berry pretended not to know what was happening, deep in conversation with Phoebe. Mckenzey, who had been given the necklace in the first place, had entrusted it to Seyanna for the duration they were here.

The food satisfied some of his needs, but the picture of Dillon Lake's instability in the aftermath of Kevin's death and Charlie's treachery had been dramatically painted. The Brotherhood had taken a step back from campus, leaving only two teachers behind, as if trying to preserve the relationship with the school or allow it to implode if necessary. Principal Berry's outlook on reopening next year was dismal. He excused himself just before they finished but promised to meet up with them soon enough.

The instant he was out of earshot, Nolan said, "So there are multiple tonics. How many?"

"Eight," said Jet.

"And we could be exposed to any one of them?"

"Doubtful," said Jet. "Maybe only one or two."

Seyanna added, "Weren't you given one, and that's why you forgot about magic for a while?"

"Yes," said Jet. "The Olividar tonic. But I doubt we need to worry about that one. We only know specifics about four of them. Besides the Olividar, there is the Hira, which heals. There is the Alkuda that gives strength and the Zhendang that requires truth. The prisoners might be given these if the rumors are correct."

"We know nothing about the other four?" asked Tominiko.

"Barely. Best guess is there are ones that poison, induce sleep, remove doubt and fear, and, if I'm not mistaken, one that adds speed."

Phoebe said, "Sounds like they are like talents."

"I guess," said Jet. "I would hate to see a talent that allowed you to poison someone to death."

Jayco urged, "We need to find Rozene, Keesha, and the others."

"We will," said Jet. He noticed that the veins in Jayco's neck were taut and he sat on his hands.

Before Jayco could retort, a voice said, "I can help you with that."

A familiar face approached their tables—Marlon Flynn. "I would have given it a thousand-to-one odds that you would show your face back here so soon." His voice remained effeminate but harsh and unkind. His appearance had drastically changed. His hair was messy; like he'd slept in the same clothes the last week and hadn't shaved in a while.

"Sorry to hear about Dart and Elliott," said Jet.

Marlon swallowed hard. "They were my...my friends. I just don't know how you can sit here with smiles on your face, acting as if nothing happened after what you did?"

Seyanna and Jayco glanced at Jet.

"When we heard about Dart and Elliot getting killed, we were already back at our school in California," explained Jet. "We had nothing to do with that."

"That's not true," retorted Marlon. "You were here. You made the Azurites, the Brotherhood, Kevin, and Charlie Eckenkeep angry. We were punished because you wanted to make a show of it all."

Jayco said," That's not true—"

"It's what Rozene believes. She told me herself. She followed you to Congo and wanted retribution. She says she barely escaped the battle between you and Kevin. She saw you kill him." Marlon pointed at Jet, his hand shook with anger.

Seyanna spoke. "Do you know who I am?"

Marlon's head snapped in her direction. "Should I?"

"I'm Charlie's daughter, Rainbow. I go by a different name now. My father and Kevin kidnapped me. Jet and the others helped me escape. Kevin and Charlie were working *with* the Azurites."

Marlon's face contorted. "I wasn't talking to you in the first place, girl." He spat the words out. "The daughter of a traitor. I would have never let you onto campus if it were up to me. You'd better watch your back."

Marlon's kindness, which they had experienced when they were here previously, was gone, replaced by someone angry and vengeful.

Jet said, "That's quite enough." He stood, and energy surged through his body. Lightning danced on his fingertips, and a tiny bolt crossed from his right eye into his left. The tiny distraction prevented him from launching an attack. After taking a deep breath, he said, "We would like to see the other Elementals."

"I bet you would. But there's someone else who needs to meet with you first. His decision will determine the next steps for you and this school. You might end up being prisoners yourself."

"Who?" asked Jayco.

"Follow me." Marlon turned, expecting them to follow.

Jet and Jayco shared a glance.

Tominiko said, "I could knock him out with a single punch."

"I think that option will remain on the table for the foreseeable future," said Jayco.

Marlon was partway down Middlesex Lane, crossed the street, and continued walking in the direction of the front gate. The section of buildings to his right was enormous and more like an outdoor mall with shops and student housing, unlike anything at Chadwick's. The candy shop looked closed, and so did a few other buildings.

They hurried to catch up. When Marlon reached the end of the block, he turned right. This was the direction to the sports stadium, but that was a lot farther north. This road still had shops and buildings on their right, but across the street, there were three buildings they hadn't seen before. The first was a multipurpose open seating area. Jet imagined they could do outdoor theatre, band, or dances.

The second building was a small Gothic building with two stories, its outer façade green and brown. Its three different roof sections reminded Jet of upside-down cones with a broader base; each was a different size. Once again, Marlon crossed the street, and they followed.

The third building could be mistaken for a home. A wooden fence surrounded a tenth of an acre, and several large windows were visible on the front side, with curtains hung in each window. But several scientific experiments were happening in the front yard and within the house. Nine students sat huddled together, watching a teacher cut open plants. There were three different-sized microscopes, along with slides and solutions, on a table.

On the side of the house, a cluster of students watched as an animal was being dissected. Other equipment, including pliers, forceps, cutting tools, and metal bowls, was close at hand.

"What's she doing?" asked Tominiko.

"Checking the heart size and other organs of six different coyotes in the area," said a tall boy who stepped from the shadows. "And they're looking at the roots and stalks of six different flowers." The boy wore a black beanie, tight white jeans, and a button-up red Hawaiian shirt. The combination was not typical but somehow worked well for him.

"Why?" blurted Seyanna.

"Three of the coyotes have never had contact with magic. The other three were caught near Cranbrook Summit in traps and are believed to be under the control of Runic magic. There were eight coyotes in total, their eyes blue, traveling together, and they didn't react as a normal coyote would when gunfire erupted near them. Only these three were caught. Professor Marble asked the animals to be brought here for examination."

"Have they found anything?" asked Jayco.

"The coyotes both magical and nonmagical look and weigh the same. However, when you cut them open, the coyotes touched by magic have stronger muscles, larger hearts, and bigger lungs."

"Meaning what?" Seyanna asked, and her interest overtook her, so she stepped toward the coyotes.

"That magic might make us physically different from what we were before."

Seyanna nodded. "Are you going to study this in humans? What about someone who has died?"

"We aren't going to cut open any humans if that's what you're asking." The boy gazed appreciatively at Seyanna.

Before coming to Chadwick's, Seyanna and her family lived in Alaska and Svalbard Island, where they performed research. She had a knack and an interest in all things scientific. Coming to grips with magic had been tricky.

Phoebe said, "If only we brought back some of the students killed in Congo."

The boy shook his head as if he hadn't heard correctly. He managed to say, "We might test some Runics and Elementals before and after they're gifted with magic to see if we can identify changes. Maybe you guys could help us with that."

"I'm sure," said Seyanna. "What's your name?"

"Uri Gideon, and I'm the professor's TA. I'm a senior. Kevin dismissed my potential but chose me to monitor the grounds of Dillon Lake. I helped coordinate the new fence, the guard building, and the cameras. Our school is the most secure of the five."

"Are you a Predilector?" asked Seyanna, smiling at him.

He smiled right back.

Marlon stood at the building's doorway, observing the conversation.

"Yes," said Uri. "My ability is to feel the difference between the magical and the non-magical. For example, I can tell that this girl,"—he pointed to Phoebe—"has magic in her eyes. From that, I can deduce she can see magic in a way others can't."

"You can tell that?" asked Phoebe.

Uri pointed to Nolan. "He can hear things that others without his talent can't. The funny thing is that I can see the talent, but it's like it is contained in a box, unopened."

"I'm going to have special ears," said Nolan. "I can roll with that."

"We need to be going," said Marlon, dismissively. "These Elementals have a meeting with the Cicerone."

"Don't let me hold you up," said Uri. "The Cicerone is our most important guest. Enjoy the next few minutes. But find me when you're finished. I would love to chat some more."

"Why do you say that?" asked Jayco.

"You'll see." A broad smile crossed Uri's face, and Jet thought he saw him wink at Seyanna, who glanced away quickly.

Marlon led them through the front door. The inside was unexpected. Not a house but much more like a church. The windows were stained glass, and most of the building was open from floor to roof, except for a few small alcoves above the main door and on the right side of the building. Students could reach these recessed rooms by a tiny staircase to their right. Farther back was a statue of a wolf trying to walk on a stone slab, and it appeared to be morphing into something that could stand on its hind two legs. The statue was not alive or magical, but it depicted artwork. For Jet, it was a chilling reminder of Faunal.

Marlon pointed to the statue. "Touch the tooth in the far back, lower jaw, on the left side."

"Say what?" asked Nolan.

"You heard me. Follow the corridor until you reach a closed door. Knock on it twice."

"We aren't going underground, are we?" asked Tominiko. "That would be bad."

"You don't have a choice if you want to meet with the Cicerone. And if you don't meet with the Cicerone, you can't be cleared to see the other Elementals."

"Are you serious?" asked Jet.

"House rules."

"What house?" asked Nolan, confused.

"I've had enough underground adventures," muttered Tominiko. "I'll stay here and make sure nothing comes down after you."

"We would appreciate that," said Jet. "What is a Cicerone?" Nobody answered.

Jayco peered inside the wolf's mouth and found six teeth. Reaching in, he hit the one on the left side, the bottom jaw. The entire statue rolled forward until the wolf was standing. Jet's eyes focused on the beast.

Seyanna said, "There's a passage behind here, and the stairs spiral down. Do we go?"

Jet didn't answer as he tore his eyes away from the statue. Working his way to the back of the statue, he found Nolan and Jayco already descending some concrete steps that spiraled downward. He followed. A dozen steps later, they reached the bottom. The corridor heading away from them was illuminated by candlelight in several nooks. Fifty feet away was a closed door.

Jayco marched forward, and pounded on it twice.

From the inside, the door was unlocked and opened. A person stood in the doorway, and Jet recognized them. "Wh—"

The girl's face contorted as if warning him, and he stopped speaking.

"Can we come inside?" asked Jayco.

"Come," said a familiar-sounding voice from farther inside the room.

Jet demanded, "What's the meaning of having assassins in here? Is this a trap?"

At his words, his friends became instantly wary. The girl backed away, leaving the doorway empty.

"Come in," hissed the man. "You will not be harmed in any manner while you remain at Dillon Lake. I give you my promise."

Strolling forward cautiously, Jet asked, "What exactly is a Cicerone, Mr. Middlesex?"

He found the man seated behind a large wooden desk. The desk was full of scrolls, odd trinkets, lists, and books. Just behind him stood the three Myntra. They wore specialized robes with hoods and long hems. One was dark red robes, the other black, and the last dark green.

Karl said, "A professor who educates on the archaeological, the historic, and the artistic." Pointing to the three women in the room, he added, "There's no need to worry. These are my granddaughters, and they'll follow my directions."

"That does not give me any comfort," said Jet. But he secretly knew each of them. They worked together and fought together in Canada. He wondered why Karl Middlesex was not aware of this information. He had no clue why the Myntra were acting this way.

The man laughed. After a moment, he said, "I guess we don't know each other well enough for you to understand that I had this room built after I came here the first time. Only my friends are allowed down here."

"Why would you invite us then?" asked Jayco, who had come to stand next to Jet. "We barely know you."

The man added, "Or those whom I wish to be friends. This is a safe place, unlike what is happening outside the walls of this school. Please have a seat."

"We appreciate your hospitality," Jet said, who sat. Soon, Jayco, Seyanna, Phoebe, and Nolan were seated behind him. "What do we call you?"

"Cicerone Middlesex or Professor." His eyebrows rose, and he glanced around. "I thought there was another?"

"He's waiting upstairs."

"I see," said the man calmly.

The room was remarkable. It was well decorated with candles, tapestries, a magnificent oak desk, and seven chairs. Small statues depicted Quills, Dragons, and oddly grotesque creatures he'd never seen before. There were five creatures he had only seen in the Averseen. There were also replica weapons, like those of the Elementals and Runics.

"I see you have entered the Decontide Trials," said Cicerone Middlesex with a wry smile.

"How can you know of these creatures?" asked Jet.

"I have been doing things with, and for, and occasionally against, the Brotherhood for many years. I am a thorn in their sides and can be a valuable ally to you and your friends." He unfurled a scroll depicting Charcoit. The scroll proclaimed that he was a guardian of the Averseen.

Jet forced his eyes from the scroll and onto Karl Middlesex. Jet was awestruck at how similar he appeared to the man in Jet's vision from inside the Italian restaurant.

Karl Middlesex must've picked up on his expression. "You have seen me before, other than when I gave my speech here a month ago or so. How?"

"Through my tome, I witnessed when you gave the talisman to your five family members just before the Azurites came after you and your family."

"Astonishing," said the older man, and he looked genuinely impressed. "One of two things must've happened to see a vision like this. An Oracle was present, or one of their miniatures, like a toy or a small figurine. They can be positioned in any location by a Worthy. Some Predilectors can feel the presence of such a figurine. They can be broken, tamed, or imprisoned, and the Oracle's powers will weaken. Tell me exactly what happened."

"First," replied Jet. "What is a Worthy?"

"Someone chosen by the Oracle to carry the figurine. Another person cannot pick them up, but they can attempt to tame or destroy the miniature."

Jet thought back to the vision inside the Italian restaurant. "Well…," he said. "My vision started a few blocks from the restaurant. Your grandchildren, Lester and Ricky, were talking outside, almost arguing. Then I saw Christos Filo from Greece and the American representative of the Brotherhood." Jet spoke the words Karl Middlesex had used to introduce the Brotherhood's mouthpiece.

He continued, "You disapproved of your son Dexter and didn't care much when Rebecca went missing. You thought she joined the Azurites. Your granddaughter, Josephine, was working with Christos and came to warn you about the Müller family coming to steal the talismans." Once finished, he watched Karl Middlesex. Maybe a year ago, he would have missed the slight grimace on his face. The man was troubled by what Jet had said. The Myntra kept far better control of their faces, but even they flinched at the name Josephine.

Karl Middlesex peered at Jet's friends and said, "Magic is an impressive and annoying reminder of the past. I had no idea that

Rebecca was trying to locate a missing artifact and was kidnapped and later killed because of it."

Jet asked, "What type of artifact?"

"It doesn't matter. I can't be certain they found it or know how to use it."

Jet repeated, "What kind of artifact?"

The eyes of the old man fixated on Jet. "I don't know exactly. I was told it was a weapon that could fire a red flame with unimaginable power. It was the head of an animal, like a lion. I've never seen such an artifact."

"Why did you not believe your own son about his wife?" The question slipped out of Jet's mouth before he had time to process its full meaning.

"The Müller family sent three spies into our family over several years. One was a close friend of my youngest daughter. We believed she was genuine, which nearly broke my daughter's heart. If it were not for her husband, Dicky, and her children, I believe it would have. The second was a nurse who helped my wife during her cancer. The nurse was in our home for three years, and I caught her trying to find a secret passage. She confessed to being sent by the Müller family. The last one affected and nearly destroyed my oldest son, Kenneth, and might have had a part to play in his eventual heart attack. That story can be saved for another day. The Müller family has tried to destroy my family for decades, so yes, I was certain Rebecca had a part to play."

"Why did you want to see us?" asked Jet.

"Three reasons."

"We're listening," said Jayco, who had found his voice, no doubt spurred on by the thought of seeing Rozene.

"We need to talk about the sixteenth tribe that Darsil Müller spoke about when you were here last. Do you recall his proposal?"

"We do," replied Jet. "He would have control over one of the boarding schools for the information to help find the lost tribe."

"The Brotherhood has considered giving him Dillon Lake."

Jayco said, "That would be a terrible idea."

"Yes. But the rumors you heard are true. The children of the Darcurser tribe who are between the ages of sixteen and eighteen cannot be killed." Karl Middlesex held up a scroll depicting a rock outcropping adjacent to the ocean. An agreement of some form was being made at the center of the rock slab. "They're perfect for assassinations or full-out combat. They will become one of the more important pawns in the Great War. Their location is known to Darsil Müller."

Seyanna asked, "What would you have us do?"

"My granddaughters attempted to learn more about what Darsil Müller knows, but he keeps that information close to the chest. It's alleged that the Rufu Squad and several Azurites found the information along with a dozen high-powered weapons."

Jet shared a quick glance with Jayco and Seyanna. "We've seen some of the weapons in person. They are indeed formidable."

Jayco asked, "Why would Darsil Müller trade something so valuable?"

"That is the million-dollar question," said Karl Middlesex.

Jet said, "Imagine you have something incredibly valuable but no way of getting to it. Why not trade it for something equally valuable that you can access or control?"

"A boarding school," said Seyanna.

"That's an excellent idea," said the old man. "There may come a time that you'll need to decide if the cost is worth the find."

Jet tilted his head.

"That brings us to the second issue. My sources say that you're looking for the three missing books..."

Jet glanced almost imperceptibly at the Myntra sisters.

Karl Middlesex continued, "If this is true, and you were to choose Dillon Lake as the location where one of the magical groups is taught, I think Principal Berry and the Brotherhood would be willing to keep this school open. We would have a lot to work toward."

Jayco asked, "What about Predilector abilities?"

"A dying breed. Kevin was the only one who could grant the abilities with the Rohart dice. Something about him and the stones he used. The dice won't roll despite many different attempts.

Phoebe asked, "What do you mean it won't roll?"

"You toss it, and it refuses to land on a side. It stops on a corner, not allowing the gift to be given."

"Interesting," said Nolan. "What is the Rohart dice?"

Jet answered, "Predilector ability is given through the Rohart dice. I don't completely understand, but the dice rolls and lands on a particular magical group or talent. A portion of that talent is given to the person, but the specifics are learned over time."

"As accurately as I've been told," agreed Cicerone Middlesex. "But it's useless."

After a short pause, Jet said, "I cannot guarantee anything. I'm surprised that you know about the missing books."

"Why?" asked Cicerone Middlesex, almost defensively. "I've spent my life trying to build the boarding schools and protect the talismans. I am not unfamiliar with the magical types in the slightest. I know what to expect. I strongly believe you can't win the war without the other books. I'm just asking for you to consider Dillon Lake."

"You always did think this school was the best."

"It could have been if..." his voice trailed off.

"I give you no promises other than we will speak again on this subject in the future. I can foresee the Rohart dice as part of any negotiations."

"Gladly," the man said, with delight in his eyes. Karl shifted in his seat and said, "The statue over this corridor and this room is a Ravencat, and one of them, Faunal, was the guard of the Runics for a time. These beasts were remarkable at deception, war, and affecting groups of people with Trimentis. We can track the use of that magic when the statue is placed in a neutral position. We know that Faunal went to Canada recently, and I believe it was you he followed. You went there to find magical books. Am I wrong?"

"Yes," Jet said quickly. "I went to Canada to find out more about Nimliaki. The Azurites stole a brooch; we were fortunate to help them get it back. Rumors reached us that the true controls of the Nimliaki were in Canada. I'm assuming you know who they are?"

"From legends. Nothing more. An Oracle granted Runic magic the control over the Nimliaki." Karl rested his hand on his chin as if thinking. "Why would Elementals help the Runics? Shane Fallon's dislike for you is well-known." He turned his head to look at Jet directly. "I don't know if I trust your explanation. I will find a way to verify your response."

Nolan asked, "Why would Jet lie?"

"For several reasons. I'm aware that Jet saw Faunal in Canada and again in West Virginia just yesterday. There's a connection."

"I've told you about Canada," Jet said. "West Virginia is where we went looking for the next piece of the Rivalry."

"How do you know where to go?" This time, Cicerone Middlesex appeared greedy and intrigued. "Can I see it?"

"Not before we see our friends."

A frown fell over Cicerone Middlesex, and he shook his head as if clearing his thoughts. "The third request is that you allow the Myntra to go to Chadwick's with you. I know you believe them to be working for the Brotherhood, and they are, but they also have a greater mission. I will not indulge you now with the details as I'm not sure I can yet trust you, but it is vital that they are close to Elemental magic to become whole, and they are mortal enemies with Faunal. They recently uncovered information about the death of someone close to them, and they have a deep hatred for that wolf creature. They can be allies."

"I don't know," said Jet, pretending to consider the request. "Our campus is tangled with Axenkind, the Coven, and other protectors. This is an unnecessary complication. We have enough people to manage. I'm going to have to decline."

The three Myntra's faces became confused and uncertain. Karl Middlesex could not see their facial expressions, but it did not matter. They were his granddaughters, who might feel inclined to tell him information Jet did not want to be shared.

"I see," said Karl Middlesex hastily. "I guess it was pointless to bring you down here in the first place. I should have known that teenagers with power never see the bigger picture. Maybe if you spend a few weeks finishing your classes here, we can knock some sense into you. You are forbidden to leave campus."

"Wait just a minute," said Seyanna. "We've seen multiple friends die. I was kidnapped by a leading member of the Brotherhood, my father. We've discovered several missing artifacts and brought stability to the confusion magic brought when it returned. What have you done? Tell your children to start magical schools and suggest we give magic to the Azurites. You don't own us."

"Little girl," said Karl Middlesex. "You can only pretend to know what will happen when Arisol returns. It is unfathomable that you'll be prepared for it on your own. I try to suggest a manner to help you, and you scoff. Without the three missing magical books and the sixteenth tribe on your side, you will lose."

Jet interrupted, "If we accept help from Darsil Müller, then we won't be in control of one of the magical groups...the Azurites will. They killed my parents. They are unconscionable."

"Never you mind."

Jet asked, "What will it take for us to leave Dillon Lake tomorrow with our friends?"

"A promise to exchange information for the sixteenth tribe, give a magical book to Dillon Lake, and allow my granddaughters safe passage to Chadwick's."

"I can't promise all those things without talking with the rest of my leadership."

"It is a one-time offer."

Jayco stood. "You can't keep us here forever."

"You would be surprised what we can do," retorted Cicerone Middlesex harshly, and his true character became written across his face. He was angry but driven, but there was a measure of cruelty. He cared about the world so long as it went how he wanted. He knew something they didn't.

"Fine," said Jet. "We'll give the magical book as soon as we can. You'll contact Darsil Müller about an exchange, and the Myntra can travel with us to Chadwick's. We demand to see our friends, and we'll leave campus tomorrow."

"That's not possible," said Karl Middlesex. "I can't arrange a meeting before tomorrow."

"You can arrange for him to come to Chadwick's," said Jet. "You will be a welcomed guest as well. We've been away from school for a few weeks. We have classes; more importantly, we have the dead to bury and the next disaster to prepare for. Darsil hinted that he had information on the location of the missing magical books. We can discuss that when we talk. You provided the terms of our agreement, now, take us to our friends."

CHAPTER 15

Karl Middlesex stood and marched past them to the door. Gleam opened it obediently, and the man disappeared out into the hall. Jet and the others followed, ascending the stairs and into the main room of the Gothic building.

Tominiko was waiting for them, smiling, clearly relieved, when they reappeared. His pale face motioned toward Marlon standing in the corner. "He had a few visitors. The entire school knows we are here."

"Probably," agreed Jet. "Anything else?"

"They cut into more coyotes while you were below."

"Cool," said Seyanna.

Marlon pushed himself out of the doorway when he saw Karl, and together, they led the group outside. Their pace increased as they crossed the street, heading toward the Gerard Theater, known on campus as The Jungle. Jet and Jayco visited this bizarre building the last time they were here. The exterior was decorated with three enormous animals acting as art pieces: an armadillo, a turtle, and a puffer fish. The Myntra sisters spread apart, one in front, another behind, and the last off to one side.

"There's got to be a joke in there somewhere," said Phoebe as she pointed to the three animals.

"That can't be a real building," said Seyanna.

"It's a theater," said Jayco. "It's a popular building on campus and not so funky on the inside."

They continued past The Jungle and three smaller buildings to a single-story building resembling a detention center. As they walked, Nolan filled Tominiko in about the discussion downstairs.

"Your friends are in here," said Karl Middlesex. "I will allow you access for the next hour."

Jet hissed, "Are you kidding?"

"Rozene, Hebrew, Mikey, and Trinity brought in a group of prisoners. I know some were from Chadwicks, but some came from this school. We're familiar with Darium. Rozene described Kevin's behavior and his treachery. After Dart died, we had no idea that Rozene sent Mikey, Hebrew, and Trinity to find out what was happening at the other schools. I was surprised to learn that Charlie Eckenkeep was involved. I spoke with him often while he was here. It seemed that he had gone to great lengths to help the Brotherhood. He was the one who poisoned Kevin's mind, and it has come to our attention that more were tricked along the way. We had no choice but to put everyone in confinement until we received answers. Your friends have not been as forthcoming as we would have hoped."

"Are you intending to put us in confinement?" asked Seyanna.

"It had crossed our minds, and Rozene pushed for it, but in the end, Principal Berry thought it would be better to become partners with you since Kevin is gone."

Principal Berry materialized at the front door as if he'd been waiting for them. "We've moved the students from Chadwick's to a conference room. You can see and talk with them there. Rozene will be here in an hour. She has some questions for you."

The group walked up the five steps to the upper landing as Principal Berry held open the door. Karl Middlesex, the Myntra, and Marlon were last to enter. If they tried to detain them, Jet would demolish the building. His energy storage was nowhere near what would be required, but he would try.

The first section of the building had an enclosed glass room with chairs and computers for a security team. There was a metal detector, a single line to enter, and a glass wall dividing the rest of the space. One guard stood monitoring, and another was near the metal detector.

"That's bulletproof glass," said Principal Berry. "The contractor who put that up did so efficiently. We recommended them to your principal."

The officers wore the same uniform as those at the front entrance.

"How did this happen so quickly?" asked Jet. "I'm not sure I remember this building."

Principal Berry led them to a hallway near the back of the room. "They were just finishing up the cells below ground when you visited. The main building took just a few weeks." They turned down a second corridor.

Jet said, "Chadwick's never even had a gate until recently."

"The approach of war to our doorsteps has accelerated things." Principal Berry smiled. "I first thought you or one of your friends allowed the porcupine beasts onto our campus. That turned into an ordeal."

"It wasn't," said Jet. "We were already gone."

Principal Berry did not seem to hear this answer, replying, "It took time to find the video footage of Charlie sneaking them through a large van. There were six in total."

Jet wasn't sure what to say.

"My father fooled a lot of people," said Seyanna. "He tricked me for years, but I found a way to break free."

Seyanna's words, more than anything, affected Principal Berry. They stopped near a closed door, and he stared at Jet. "Rozene told me that by the time she reached you, she was shocked to find Kevin working with Charlie. He controlled those flying vultures, and you were engaged in combat with Kevin. It is my understanding that Predilectors, Elementals, and Runics helped him in Congo. You and your friends fought those porcupine creatures. You should know that if something like that happens again, we will close Dillon Lake permanently."

Jet said, "Rozene helped us. We wouldn't be here today if it weren't for her and the others. We will do whatever we need to ensure your doors stay open, safely."

"I appreciate you saying that. But words mean only so much."

Jet added, "All five boarding schools will need to come together and soon. I think that you will appreciate our commitment to Dillon Lake. We must all leave tomorrow to get ready and find the other missing magical books. We've been told of someone who has clues on where they might be."

"Our school is better protected," admitted Principal Berry. "Rozene has been active since she came back, changing outdated ideas on how our school should be protected. Marlon, Uri Gideon, and Rozene have closed loopholes in our defensive barriers. The three of them have been incredible."

"You have the right people for the job. By the way...the porcupine creatures are called Quills."

"Would you be willing to use some Elemental magic to evaluate our defenses?"

"Once we get through seeing our friends," said Jet.

Principal Berry opened the door, smiled, and looked more upbeat. He, Marlon, and Karl remained outside as Jet and the others entered. Several sets of eyes stared back at them, initially unsure, and then a cheer erupted when the door closed. Their friends were disheveled and in the same clothes that he'd last seen them but in good spirits.

"We knew you guys had made it when they dragged us out of our enclosed rooms," said Asher.

Jade demanded, "What took you so long?"

Jayco answered, "Things didn't go smoothly at Spruce Knob. Have you guys showered?"

"They were going to get around to that tomorrow," retorted Asher.

Keesha said, "They gave us some food and a bed to sleep on."

"Wish I had that right now," said Nolan.

Jet pointed to those who came with him. "For those who don't know, this is Nolan and Tominiko. They stepped up at Spruce Knob. Hopefully, you remember Jayco, Seyanna, and Phoebe."

Keesha stepped forward, hugging Seyanna and whispering something into her ear that Jet couldn't hear. The two of them were roommates back at school, and Keesha was clearly relieved to see her again. Maria rushed forward, hugging Jayco, Jet, then Seyanna.

Jet introduced those who had come to Dillon Lake, "Okay. Most of you know Keesha and Maria." He pointed to the two girls. "This is Asher and Jade." The couple raised their hands. "We also have the trio of friends Natalia, Allison, and Alivia. How's Melvin feeling? I don't see him here."

"He had surgery on his leg," said Keesha. "He went straight to the hospital upon landing. But I heard he came back to campus last night. We haven't seen him once."

Jayco whispered, "What about Rozene?"

"Haven't seen her, bro," said Asher. "She's not what you would call reliable right now."

Before Jayco could say anything else, Jet asked, "What happened to the Predilector prisoners you came back with?"

Alivia said, "They got better treatment than we did. Even Rozene was buddy-buddy with them."

"Good to know," said Jet. Next to him, Jayco's face turned a shade redder. Jet put a hand on his arm and whispered, "We'll see her soon enough. Don't freak out."

"Easy for you to say."

Ignoring this, Jet asked, "Where are the Predilector prisoners?"

"In the basement," said Allison. "I think on a different floor than we are."

"Darium?" asked Jet.

Natalia added, "Also went to surgery. I don't think he's come back yet."

There was a knock on the door, and the room went quiet.

"Come in," said Jayco.

The door opened, and Principal Berry, Rozene, and three other students entered, along with Marlon, Uri Gideon, Karl Middlesex, and another teacher Jet recognized. Mikey stood next to Rozene for an instant and then disappeared. Jet wondered if anyone else had seen him. He hoped that it meant Mikey was still on his side.

Principal Berry said, "Things always transition at high schools, and Dillon Lake is no exception. However, some things we've gone through in the last month could be classified as whiplash. As the principal, I'm hopeful to forge an alliance with Chadwick's and Dillon Lake." He pointed to Rozene and said, "Rozene Bluesky is our new student body president. The other students are Jericho McIntyre, Feather Zachnow, and Desmond Sacha. Jericho can see whisps of spirits, Feather can hear Chupovanas and other creatures speak to each other, and Desmond can detect magic. These are their Predilector abilities. Unfortunately, Charlie sent Feather to Cranbrook the last time you were here. That decision now makes far more sense."

Jericho was tall and lean, with olive skin, a shaved head, and bushy brown eyebrows. Feather was petite, less than five feet tall, with high cheekbones, light hair, fair skin, and dark brown eyes. Desmond was tall and looked like his descendants, with olive skin and brown hair, maybe from Spain or Greece. He was striking and kept glancing at Marlon, who patently ignored the looks.

Rozene spoke. "Welcome back to Dillon Lake, Elementals. I must apologize to you for my belief that you were somehow involved in the disappearance of my friend Marapi and the deaths of Dart and Elliot. I've kept in contact with Shane Fallon, who remained here when you ditched us the last time you were here." Her voice was anything but kind and was far more accusatory.

"Rozene," Principal Berry said quickly, but his facial features did not match his harsh tone.

She continued, "We believe that Kevin helped you leave school. It's useless to deny it now that he's gone, as we can't prove it. He was missing the night you left, and his whereabouts cannot be confirmed."

Jet said, "But—"

Rozene interrupted, "We're here to start over. Everything is in the past. We have a new student government, and the Brotherhood has far less oversight. We need protection like at Chadwick's and the other schools. I've been informed that an agreement has been made, and we appreciate it." She stopped speaking and took a complete step back, never making eye contact with anyone.

Principal Berry said, "Our students still wish to continue to learn and advance with their Predilector abilities. We cannot continue to recruit into the group. Rozene will become the Lideur, and the Dire Fraternity will continue here on campus. We'll maintain control of the Rohart dice and hope a new opportunity will prevent itself. We ask that some Elementals be sent here as students and help keep our school safe. Once the other books are discovered, the other schools will be expected to send students here, or one of the books will be taught here. You have agreed upon this?"

Jet glanced at Karl Middlesex and wondered if the older man had told the principal his plan to give a magic book to Darsil Müller. "We have."

Jayco asked, "Would you be willing to send some Predilectors to our school as improved cooperation?"

"That can be arranged," said Feather. Her voice was mellow and clear. "We must find a way to test our students and yours for duplicity with the Azurites. The Brotherhood has required a solution before they will return."

"Do you have any ideas?" asked Jayco.

"We're working on it," added Desmond. "We're hoping Darium can provide the answers."

Jet asked, "Can we talk with him?"

Rozene smiled. "He's in a secure location."

"I have some ideas about how to protect the school," said Jet. "I can share some of my information after we meet."

"That would be welcomed," replied Uri Gideon. "We might ask that you change the boundaries of the Claustra."

"We haven't agreed to that yet," said Principal Berry.

"My apologies. If Jet and his friends are to leave tomorrow, then we have much to do."

Desmond replied, "We can't let them have free rein of our school again. Who knows what might disappear."

"What disappeared last time?" asked Jayco.

"Nothing that relates to you, Chadwick's, or the Rivalry," said Principal Berry. "I agree. The students from Chadwicks will have limited access. Jet will be granted to some areas, but only if myself, Karl Middlesex, or Professor Marcos here can escort him, along with one of you three."

Professor Marcos was their guide previously when security had tightened following the death of a visiting student. He had enthusiastically explained some of the school's history, and Jet imagined that any further tours around campus would be equally entertaining.

"I think we're done," said Rozene.

"Can the students from Chadwick's leave this guardhouse?" asked Phoebe.

Rozene glanced at Principal Berry, who nodded.

Jet added, "We'll also want to see Melvin."

"Maybe later this afternoon," said the principal.

Rozene left, not giving Jayco or the others a second glance. Jericho and Desmond followed. Principal Berry escorted them all back to the penthouse suite. There were enough beds to accommodate them all. They spent the next few hours resting. Jet took a nap and was awoken at 4:00 p.m. by Seyanna. Principal Berry, Uri, Marlon, and Rozene awaited him at the door.

He was given access to two areas near the water, then around the inner portion of the outer fence. He vigorously searched for obvious risks that might be there. He asked about a few houses in the distance and learned they were uninhabited and scheduled to be demolished. Trees surrounded more than two sides of the school, with the last being water. Jet spoke infrequently, and Rozene didn't once talk to him directly. Six locations were highlighted as risk points for attacks. Three walls needed to be built higher, and two trees had to be cut down, preventing an effortless scaling of the wall. The most concerning spot was the northeast area, not far from the water. The wall and metal fence, with the razor wire, had been dismantled into a heap of debris.

Jet took up a defensive position as if this had just happened. He searched for any potential hostiles.

Uri said, almost laughing, "Chill out. We've known about this position." He pointed to trail cameras in trees and those fastened to poles in the ground. "These are motion sensors. The contractors will be back early next week to fix the wall."

Principal Berry asked, "When did this happen, and why wasn't I notified?"

Rozene said, "We don't know exactly. Uri brought this to Marlon's and my attention two days ago. We didn't want to worry you."

Jet stepped closer. "I think this happened weeks ago. There's dead grass under some of the fallen pieces of the wall."

"Exactly," said Uri.

Principal Berry said, "We need more sweeps in this area."

"Will do," said Rozene.

From there, they headed back to King Ken Palace.

Along the way, Principal Berry said, "I'm glad to have walked the perimeter. I'm comfortable with where the Claustra has been placed. The school has those areas of concern, but they've been identified and can be fixed. This is a clear improvement."

Nearing the end of the tour, Jet asked, "Are there any other places where staff or others can discreetly enter or depart the campus?"

Uri answered, "We can't divulge everything, but every conceivable entrance and exit has been accounted for."

"Chadwick's doesn't even have a fence. I think you are well protected. None of us is immune to what *might* happen, but you have done well."

"Glad you approve," replied Uri, bowing his head slightly.

He was escorted back to his room. It had taken two hours, and he doubted that they would be allowed to leave for the night. He was starving and ready to head home tomorrow. Marlon and Professor Marcos were waiting for him, Principal Berry, Uri, and Rozene.

Principal Berry asked, "Are we ready?"

Marlon nodded.

"What's going on?" asked Jet.

Open the door and tell your friend to get ready.

The door swung open; evidently, Jayco had heard them approach. He stood there expectantly. "What's happening?"

Professor Marcos said, "We've set up an outside dinner for you guys and a few students from Dillon Lake. No dancing, and we won't be able to take you out onto the lake for some fun, but once this is all over, feel free to come back and get a taste of all that Dillon Lake has to offer."

It did not take long for everyone to get dressed.

"No need to bring any weapons," said Principal Berry.

Jayco flashed a genuine smile, adding, "Whenever I'm told that, it feels as if I should do the exact opposite."

Marlon insisted, "We're just bringing you down to eat. No danger at all. Remember, your fearless leader inspected the entire area and pronounced us safe. The pavilion is a few minutes' walk. Let's go."

Once outside, they crossed the street, heading in the opposite direction from King Ken Palace. They went down a charming path toward the shore, weaving in and around trees illuminated by stylish outdoor lighting. The path opened onto a breathtaking pavilion with spacious outdoor seating, sand volleyball pits, and an incredible view of the bay.

"You didn't let me see this gem," said Jet.

Marlon said, "It's called a grand finale."

"Touché,"

Professor Marcos pointed out where the water rose after the natural disaster in D.C., but the entire school was protected. "The Claustra deserve all the credit," said the Professor. "Rain fell, and some areas of campus flooded, but the damage was insignificant."

He pointed out over the water. "Thirteen of the one hundred tallest buildings in the world toppled over in New York City alone. D.C. and Philadelphia weren't much better."

"Where are we?" asked Maria.

Marcos answered. "This is Westerval Pavilion. One of the most picturesque views for fifty miles."

The aroma of baked bread, seafood, and something with honey assailed their senses. They turned and watched as a dozen kitchen staff emerged from a tunnel system with food carts.

Keesha asked, "Why does that bread smell so good?"

"It's one of our finest foods at Dillon Lake," said Principal Berry. "Our kitchen staff is unmatched. Much of the food is made in our state-of-the-art central canteen. We have secure tunnels allowing for quick distribution. We have five main dining halls. Two always have the basics of sandwiches, salads, pizza, hamburgers, and similar. Two have food that is specific to that month. This month is Italian favorites. Similar things are given in the first two weeks, then it shifts. It makes it enjoyable. One of our most popular classes is culinary cooking. It's full every semester."

"What's the fifth cafeteria for?" asked Jayco.

"A restaurant. There are five options that any guest can choose from. It allows our students to work and eat well. The reservations are usually made a day or two in advance."

"Wow," said Natalia. "I wish we could have enjoyed this campus a little more than we did."

"What about that tall building?" asked Jade, pointing to a tall steeple to the northeast.

Marlon answered. "That's Fillmore Tower. It helped, decades ago, when arriving by boat was more useful. It was the third building ever built. The lantern at the top still works, and when it rains or becomes foggy, the light helps the students in the area to see better. I personally believe it should be torn down."

Professor Marcos said, "After dinner, we'll have a volleyball tournament with some of the students at Dillon Lake. They'll be dining with you as well. Please introduce yourself and learn something about a student here. Have a wonderful night."

Principal Berry announced, "Tonight is a celebration for the new world. We value new friends and new adventures, as well as the collaboration of all the Boarding schools. Times are changing." Pointing to three pots on his right, he added, "This is a crayfish boil. There are corn and potatoes. On the far left is the spiciest food, and it gets spicier from there. Water and lemonade are already on the tables, and other sodas are in the coolers. The food should be set up in five minutes. Eat, relax, and enjoy a little volleyball competition. All teams will have students from both schools. We'll stay here until nine or ten, so we have plenty of time."

They hurried to grab spots and then lined themselves up for the food. Jayco leaned over and whispered, "I don't see Rozene."

Jet answered, "I'm sure we'll see her soon enough. Relax."

Jayco said, "I don't like how distant she was earlier."

"It'll be fine," added Jet, but he wasn't sure what to think. He hadn't seen Mikey since earlier.

Seyanna and Jet found seats next to Jayco, Marlon, Uri, and Feather. The conversation was effortless. All dislike or stuffiness had evaporated. They laughed and joked and learned more about each other. Uri was on the track team, and Marlon performed in theatre. Feather enjoyed debate class and poetry.

Seyanna slipped her hand into Jet's and squeezed twice. He wanted to enjoy the night and forget about what would happen soon. Several students from Dillon Lake stopped by and introduced themselves. It was impossible to learn each of their names.

"Game on," shouted someone from Dillon Lake.

Those who wanted to play came forward and was divided into teams. Jet was on a team with Natalia, Jade, and three locals. Tominiko, Seyanna, Jayco, Alivia, Keesha, and Asher were divided onto the other three teams, while the rest watched. He thought his skills were middle-of-the-road, but he was the weakest link among the others. Natalia was incredible, as was a boy from here. Jet was in awe as the ball moved around efficiently, set up for each other, and violently knocked over the net. They dominated point after point and won the first game quickly. High fives were given as they moved to the next court.

Three tall players from Dillon Lake and Asher, Tominiko, and Keesha waited for them, brimming with confidence.

Asher announced, "Be prepared to lose badly."

Jade countered, "Don't hold your breath."

The first game was contested for the first three serves. A fifteen-hit volley went Team Asher's way, and the score was 2-1, with them leading. That was the last point they scored for the next ten. The outcome wasn't complete domination, but close. Jade mocked her boyfriend, but it was all in good fun.

Jayco, Alivia, Seyanna, and three students from Dillon Lake stood across the net from Jet in the championship, the final game.

Alivia whispered, "I know how good Natalia is. She's probably the best in our school."

"Seriously," said Jayco.

"She got an invite to try out for Nationals."

Jayco nodded appreciatively. "We have Cassandra, and she has a scholarship to a D1 college, so I think we got this. I know how Jet plays."

"Jet pointed to Megan, Frank, and Aaron and said, "These guys are pretty good."

"Did you beat Asher's team?" asked Jade.

"We wouldn't be here if we didn't," replied Cassandra. She was tall, athletic, and confident.

The game began, and both sides traded points until the score was 9-10. There were incredible blocks, serves, and passes on both sides. Cassandra's team caught up and passed Jet's, but Natalia served three straight aces. On the next play, Seyanna blocked Jet, and Natalia dove for it. She wasn't fast enough, and the other team got the point. That closed the gap, but like the second game, that was the last point they got. Aaron dominated serve, and Natalia spiked that final point to win them the game.

The instant the game ended, Cassandra sprinted onto their side and shoved Aaron. Soon, they were rolling around, a mixture of fun and something more romantic brewing between them.

"Finally," said Marlon, who had watched the last portion of the game. "I don't know how long I've been talking with both of you." A flicker of his old self reemerged.

Aaron shouted, "Oh, wise one!" Moments later, he and Cassandra kissed and cheers rang out

Bang!

The loud sound echoed around the pavilion. Jet ducked and moved instinctively to discover what had made the noise. Seyanna was close to him, while Jayco, a dozen feet away, pulled out a golden sword. Other Elementals reacted in similar ways.

"Chill out," yelled Marlon. "Everything is fine! There are walkways below ground and steam will build up every once in a while. Watch."

One of the cooks sprinted to a small panel near where they had entered with the food and opened a small vent. A puff of steam rose into the air for several seconds. Fragrances of food mixed with laundry permeated the area.

"Not everything is an attack," added Uri. "You guys really need to chill out."

"Trying," replied Jayco as he hid the sword back with his stuff, Cicerone Middlesex glaring at him the entire time.

Seyanna hurried up next to Jet, their shoulders touching. "I blocked you twice." Her eyes were ablaze. "And I had you going the wrong way more than I can count."

"I carried the team," replied Jet.

"Nearly into the ground," said Nolan, who appeared behind them.

"Why didn't you play?" asked Seyanna.

"I had a friend come to chat with me."

"A friend?" asked Jet, curious.

"Mikey," whispered Nolan, leaning in. "He wanted a word with you, but it would've been too obvious if you hadn't played."

"What did he say?" whispered Seyanna.

Nolan glanced around. Jayco sauntered over, close enough to hear. "Mikey wants Jayco to know that Rozene is the same as before. Things aren't as they seem at Dillon Lake. There are still a few Azurites in leadership. That should change by tonight. Rozene hopes that she'll be free to speak openly tomorrow. She's optimistic that Principal Berry and Karl Middlesex will listen."

"Is he still around?" asked Jet.

"Nah. He left before the match finished. I guess Cassandra can tell when someone invisible is around."

"Thanks," said Jet. "We might be heading back soon, but there's something I want to do." Reaching down, he clasped Seyanna's hand and pulled her toward the water.

"Don't have too much fun," chortled Nolan. "You might make the rest of us jealous."

As they came closer to the water, he became mesmerized by the small waves splashing on the shore. The sun had set half an hour ago, and the glimmer of bright lights from New York shone across the water. It was exceptional. A feeling to pull her close surged within him, and he hoped she was feeling something similar. He let go of her hand and slipped his arm around her waist, bringing her lips. She flowed with the movement, a small smile playing on her lips.

His first kiss touched the side of her neck, and she shivered, leaning into him, her head tilting slightly. He kissed her in the same spot three more times, and she tried to remain still. Something was building within her, and suddenly, she kissed him back with hunger and need. Her hands went into his hair, pulling softly. Her eyes were wide open, staring into his. Then they closed. So did his. He held her tightly and never wanted to let go. The bliss was unmistakable, and he wasn't sure he'd felt anything so joyous. The sights and sounds around them evaporated. He wasn't sure if he was still standing on the sand or floating to the skies.

Then...every ounce of happiness vanished, as if air had been pulled suddenly from the room, replaced by cold water. Compulsion gripped him, and he knew precisely the source. His eyes flashed open. Seyanna still kissed him, and he wished he could feel her. He tried to force his eyes closed and block everything else but her, but it was impossible.

He broke away and muttered, "Seyanna."

Her eyes flew open as if something was wrong. "What is it?"

"My tome," he managed to wheeze.

"What about it? Is it missing?"

He shook his head, unable to formulate the words.

She stepped back. After another few seconds, her expression changed. She whispered, "You have to open it."

He nodded. She helped him into a seated position. He muttered, "Bookcase," and removed *The Sorcerer's Guide*. It opened without any effort.

From a distance away, and only inside his head, someone yelled, "The Cursed Land!"

CHAPTER 16

The daytime warmth rapidly dispersed as the sun sunk below the horizon and most creatures returned to their homes, but... this coldness invited darker ones to enjoy their newfound freedoms. Frost gripped the land adjacent to an enormous outdoor colosseum as a storm of change threatened to send the realm into a calamity.

Standing in a large alcove in the highest position of the colosseum, Jet acknowledged the lamps, large candles, and three central fireplaces kept the frost at bay. Across from him, on the opposite side on the first row, was a large stage, partially built into a rock wall, shielding it from rainfall. In front of the stage were nearly a hundred seats, sloping slightly upward to give everyone a perfect view. Another thirty seats were placed on the second floor, but they remained empty.

Ancient magic permeated the air as if the memories of those who had passed on clung to the walls of this exalted edifice. Reaching out, Jet touched the cold, green marble of the walls and appreciated the brown and white minerals comprising the floors. Six black columns lined the outer perimeters and two more bracketed the stage. Dark purple curtains were positioned next to the columns. On the stage sat three unclaimed chairs.

Doors clattered open, and three dozen people entered from below, divided, and found seats grouped together. Three groups emerged, each with thirteen disciples. On his left were men and women dressed nearly the same in battered white cotton shirts and brown cotton pants. They sat in two rows, huddling together. They had matching flat ears, crooked chins, and sandy hair.

The middle section contained thirteen men of various ages with different strengths and sizes. They wore thick pants and white tunics, and their hands were dirty and calloused. On his right were thirteen women dressed extravagantly in elegant black pants and shirts made of fine linens with thick red embroidery along the seams. Each wore a matching golden crown.

The groups whispered among themselves, pointing to the walls and floors, startled at the warmth within the colosseum. Stepping onto the stage was a tall woman of immense beauty and strength, built like a bodybuilder, wearing an elegant strapless silver dress. She appeared to be strong, agile, and cunning. Her skin and hair were as dark as Latisha's, except for a grouping of hair next to her left ear that had turned bright white. She displayed a braid, and the white streak continued the length of the thread.

An older woman emerged with pale skin and gray, frizzy, unkempt hair, except for two thin lines of black hair near both ears. She was fragile, with swollen joints and a hunched back, and required a walking stick. The elegant woman helped the old lady to one of the three seats on the stage. The younger woman took up the second seat.

Jet felt a peculiar sensation as if a cool breeze was stinging him, creeping up from behind, only to pass beyond him to the others. Those in the colosseum shivered in its presence. A heartbeat later, an intense magical power careened against his face and chest. Jet sucked in but could not breathe. Blue fog drew near from the outer edges. It came within a few feet of the threshold of the colosseum's outer pillars.

Back on stage, a man stepped into view—a man he recognized. He was handsome, tall, and regal. It must've been a few years since he'd last seen him. The Grey Panther looked healed from the goring he'd sustained from a Chupovana. Queen Aurora and her stones had healed him, and now she had disappeared. The man who would become Arisol, the demon prince, stood forth confidently. The expanse became silent.

"Thank you for coming," his voice boomed. "I am the Grey Panther, the leader of the Council, and I welcome you to the Savannah of Fensca. We are on the border of Illustina and await the arrival of Queen Safamora, Prince Proteus, and Prince Salmmon, who should be here shortly. We need to find out where Queen Aurora has vanished to."

The man turned to the other two guests on stage. "But for now, I would like to introduce and welcome my Lieutenant, the Silver Fox, second in command within the Council. Sitting next to her is the revered Myntra Dormacloud."

Cheers erupted upon the pronunciation of the second name as if the three groups had been permitted to come out of a trance. Jet found this odd as he assumed the first two held more fame and distinction. The elegant Silver Fox bowed, and then she mimed with her hands, presenting Myntra Dormacloud again to another round of thunderous clapping.

"We also would like to welcome you," said the Grey Panther, gazing out over the crowd. "We have thirteen nobles from the Hearthstone plains with Incrementum magic. Thirteen members of the Balak family possessing Shaman magic, and lastly, thirteen priestesses from the Resitituals. You are our valued guests, and you have the privilege to do something that will bless Goth Airtha for eternity."

One individual, possibly an advisor from each clan, respectfully bent their head.

From behind a curtain appeared a celestial messenger, who glided forward without taking a step and passed a note to the Grey Panther. He read it swiftly. A flash of anger crossed his face for less than an instant, but Jet wasn't sure who'd seen it, as everyone else was distracted by the beautiful and scantily dressed winged succubus. The mademoiselle kissed the Grey Panther on the cheek and swooped over the crowd, unleashing a small commotion.

The Grey Panther smiled insincerely and said, "Queen Safamora and Prince Proteus have been detained momentarily. Prince Salmmon has been located." Swishing his cloak, he changed directions to his movement, his face becoming serious. "There are mounting concerns among Goth Airtha that the limitations of magic are on the rise, and there might be a connection with the disappearance of Queen Aurora." He waited as a murmur rolled through the crowd. "You've heard them, and so have I. I am here to tell you...that they are true."

"I knew it," cried a voice from the Hearthstone plains.

"We're doomed," added the youngest of the Balak family.

"But we have a plan." The Grey Pather, again, swished his cloak, reversed directions, and a broad smile crossed his face. "We might have the answer." He pointed at the Silver Fox. "Our Lady Sion envisioned us coming together and inviting you to listen to her verdicts and present a plan to alter the course of this catastrophe."

The Silver Fox let go of the hand of Myntra Dormacloud and stood, sauntering to the center. Her demeanor and countenance were far kinder than the Grey Panther. Jet wondered if it was his own knowledge of what was to come or if he was the only one to see it. In less than a second, Jet read the emotions of the two Kings, and a look of disdain sprang momentarily onto the Silver Fox's face. Everyone else had missed it, and the Grey Panther retreated half a step.

Her voice was majestic and enchanting, "It may come as no surprise to you, my friends, that the strength of magic is waning and no longer what it used to be. The Council has heard your fears, your agony, and your worries. We were victorious at Darcoff Pass and rejuvenated with hope not long ago. I know many of you wished to greet and thank the twins, but the Elementals and Runics could not attend today as they are searching for the Skeleton's lair. I anticipate they will be present at our next assembly in Deshret."

She strode back and forth across the stage, and Jet was mesmerized by her authority, candor, wisdom, eloquence, and beauty. "Not long after the fighting at Darcoff pass, one of the last Rhoenixes vanished into thin air. If you are unfamiliar with Rhoenixes, they are brave and loyal creatures who have served alongside the 10 Kings for many years. They have brought prosperity and strength to those nearest them or those called upon to be heroes of our day. When Sarcoff disappeared, none of his power was transferred as it should have. To my knowledge, there were only three Rhoenixes still remaining. I became fearful that something was afoot. I departed and began searching for the last two Rhoenixes."

She continued, "To me, this signaled an end of the magical and galvanized a new era of resourcefulness, self-worth, and self-reliance. We must work together to triumph in this new era. All is not lost; I believe magic can return stronger than ever if we play our parts. Finding

Sarcoff will help hasten the return of magic, as will a monumental sacrifice and unending humility. Therefore, this day, we ask you to give back a portion of what you were given."

The Grey Panther placed a hand on the Silver Fox's shoulder. He tried hard to look pleased at her words, but there was an underlying hostility. When he spoke, however, his voice was kind and respectful. "Thank you to my loyal Lieutenant. What she has discovered may help save all of us."

The Silver Fox continued, "I searched for the last two Rhoenixes, but what I found may be more significant. Inside a long-forgotten tomb, I unearthed a prophecy from one of our last Oracles, hinting that there would be a foreigner scheming to acquire all five types of magic. But to do so, magic must be lost initially and completely. When all five magical types had vanished, they would return at the right time to be claimed by the Heir of the Myth. I searched for and tracked down the ancient Oracle, and was shown a path to prevent magic from being lost. He has consented to explain what is required."

The Silver Fox and the Grey Panther shifted, allowing a figure behind them to be revealed. The man, with a crooked back, downtrodden with age and infirmities, shambled ahead. He was over eight feet tall, wearing a cherry-black cloak with a hood and long sleeves that covered his arms and legs. Each in the crowd could feel the Oracle's supernatural power. Like a wave, the surge of blue fog flowed from under the Oracle's cloak.

The man pulled a thick yellow scroll from his pocket. Blood dripped from its corners as he opened the crusted page. The oracle spoke, but he wasn't reading. His voice was deep and guttural, "The legend of 'The Shadowed Lovers' is as old as time itself. It depicts devotion, bred of trust, fidelity, and resolve, by two prohibited to adore each other.

The legend happens. It demands the birth of a child, and magic must consummate its origin. That is why magic has become misplaced like the memories of the insane."

At these words, a horrible feeling touched Jet's soul.

The Oracle read from the scroll:

"Ista Migipa fresh for the Sinagala.

Lomika Saza taking of these wills Frizillia.

Qoncuso Vumen into our desired servitude Norisha."

Yellow vapor extended from the scroll in three separate directions, directly at the crowd. The instant before the high priestesses were overtaken, all thirteen women vanished, leaving their clothes and crowns behind. The central section, the Balak family, could not react in time and became instantly cursed. They dissolved from physical beings into spirits, no longer full of flesh. They became grotesque beings. The youngest resembled Kardsten the Assassin.

The Hearthstone nobles could do nothing to escape the vapor. Shielding their faces from the vicious attack, they began to offer prayers to the skies.

Myntra Dormacloud reacted, crying out, "Dare Vim Vitalem."

The thirteen nobles, in response, quickly replied, "Vitalem."

Jet understood her intent. Myntra Dormacloud gave her lifeforce to protect the nobles. The Grey Panther removed a silver sword, closing the distance to the Myntra. A single slice cut her head from her shoulders. The transfer worked, and her lifeforce protected the Hearthstone clan, but they lost their bodies, becoming spirits. They drifted from the colosseum.

The Silver Fox stared in horror at the body of Myntra Dormacloud and the approaching blue mist and yellow vapor. Somehow, she created a barrier —possibly from a ring she wore—keeping the blue mist and the yellow vapor at bay as she retreated. An instant before vanishing, her head faced Jet, seeing him, and her silver eyes bore into him knowingly.

The Grey Panther and the Oracle turned to face the Silver Fox, but she was gone. The Grey Panther lifted his hands and signaled to the Oracle to stop the flow of blue fog. The yellow vapor dispersed as well. An emblem formed on the handle of the silver sword, then onto the Oracle's cloak, and lastly, it burned into the ground before the two destroyers.

From where he stood, the emblem was like a wheel, with five spokes and weird images between each rod. Curvy lines, something like a female symbol, a circle on a mound, a beaker of sorts with two lines near the apex, and two mounds. He had never seen anything like it before.

The Grey Panther shouted, "Welcome Balakcursen!" His pronouncement burned the same emblem into their skins, or rather their souls, and they received the symbol with groans of pleasure. "Let me introduce you to the Shade Zorican. To become the highest-level shade to have ever walked this earth, you must kill an Oracle, which transpired today because I allowed it. Now, under my direction, he has brought you into our fraternity. Obey your master and serve me."

CHAPTER 17

"Jet," screamed Seyanna. "Come back to me. What happened?" The voice tailed off for a moment, then it returned. "Help him. I don't know what's going on."

"Is he sick?" asked a second voice.

Seyanna spoke again, "He was reading from the tome, and then a faint yellow hue came out of it. He tumbled back onto the ground and started convulsing. The book is closed, but I can't pry it from his hand or wake him."

Something pulled at his face, tore at his shirt, and reached under his arms.

Jayco's voice bellowed, "Even with my strength, I can't move him an inch."

The force holding Jet in place abruptly ended, and he was launched into the air, his tome gripped in his right hand. He sailed over the pavilion and onto the opposite side of the peninsula. He would have gone into the water, but spoke "Enlil," stopping mid-air. Releasing the spell a touch here and there, he lowered himself to the ground.

Seyanna arrived first, as her speed was unmatched. She leaned in as if wanting a hug and then had a second thought. It was a half-second before everyone else arrived.

Jet whispered, "I'm fine. Explain later."

"What was that?" cried Marlon. "Doing tricks?"

"Trying something stupid," replied Jet, and he tried looking embarrassed. "It failed."

"Looked cool," said Aaron.

Several other students arrived, along with Principal Berry and Professor Marcos.

Jayco, beaming, demanded, "How in the world did you do that?"

"I've been practicing some of my magical strengths. That one is not one I'll try again."

Cassandra asked, "Was that Elemental magic you were using?"

"Yes," said Jet.

"Show us more?" cried a girl who hadn't played volleyball.

"Indeed," added Bobby.

Jet created a fireball, turned it into a frozen ball, then made the entire thing evaporate. He next triggered temporary memory loss and fear for several seconds. There was a cheer of excitement. "Questions?" He and the other Elementals answered as many questions as they could. Jayco and even Seyanna showed their strengths. Marlon and nearly everyone else were intrigued; his anger was long forgotten.

Principal Berry announced, "That's a wrap. You have about ten minutes left. Those from Dillon Lake, see you tomorrow, and don't be late for your classes. I'll take Jet and Jayco to see Melvin. The rest of you can go back to your rooms with Professor Marcos."

The cleanup was well underway, and Jet helped wipe down some tables and move some chairs. He had no chance to talk to Seyanna. Several students stopped by to say goodbye, and soon, Jet and his friends were walking back to their dorm.

Principal Berry and Professor Marcos were dozens of paces in front of them. Cicerone Middlesex was behind, watching them closely.

Jayco asked, "What in the hell happened back there?"

"Something weird," admitted Jet. "What did it look like?"

Seyanna wrapped her arm under his. "You were looking at that book like you always do, but then a yellow smoke somehow escaped from the pages. You were so rigid, I thought you were going to have a seizure."

Jayco added, "I came over and couldn't pry your hands apart or pick you up."

"The next second, you were flying through the air."

Jet shook his head. "Yellow, huh." And he explained what he had seen in the vision. He described the Shade Zorican and what happened to the Balak family as best as he could.

"The priestesses escaped, and the Hearthstone plains were only partially affected," recounted Nolan.

"That's what I thought."

"Was the yellow vapor an attack on you?" asked Asher.

"I would have never guessed...but, yes."

They reached the far end of the street. Principal Berry waited for them.

"I'll take you guys this way."

Seyanna let go of his arm, but reluctantly.

"See you soon," said Jayco.

Natalia added, "Tell Melvin we said hi."

"Will do."

Glancing back, Cicerone Middlesex had disappeared. Jet and Jayco were led to a building they hadn't looked closely at before. It was just north of the Lexington block but hidden by several large trees. There was a twelve-foot wrought iron fence encircling the building and some grass. Jet could see a magical wall, probably unseen by others, much like he had seen in Congo, surrounding the entire building. He wondered who might have put this barrier into place.

Principal Berry hit a few keys into a machine, and the gate opened. The magical wall vanished until they were inside, then it re-engaged. Inside the building was a small foyer, like a waiting room, and two nurses sat behind a desk chatting. The girl was showing the boy something from a patient's chart.

Principal Berry said, "Melvin was in bad shape when he arrived and required surgery the same day. Both bones in his lower leg were broken. The surgery went well, and he's recovering. Doctor Wong cleared him to travel back to Chadwick's with you tomorrow. They fixed the bone with a plate, but healing will still take time. He can walk short distances, but he should be careful."

"Wow," said Jayco. "He's already walking."

"Slowly."

They approached the desk. "This is Nurse Sheila and Nurse Vance. It looks like it's a change of shift."

Nurse Sheila said, "I was just reviewing some of the incidents we saw today. A couple of allergic reactions, and someone nearly cut off their finger."

"Wow," said Jet. "Are you always this busy?"

"Yes," replied Sheila. "Of course, there are days worse than others. Today was pretty typical."

Jayco asked, "How's Melvin?"

Vance said, "Not bad. He'll be glad to have some visitors. He's been a little lonely."

"Is there an upstairs and main level?"

Sheila replied, "Yep. You can be selected for an upper-level room if you are here for more than a week. Surprisingly, most of our students, like Melvin, choose to stay on this level."

"This way," said Vance, leading them down the hallway to the right. They passed spacious rooms on the left and right, each more colorful than the last. They had a television, sink, and a large bed and couch.

When they reached room 111, Principal Berry opened the door, revealing Melvin in bed, playing chess with another student. A broad smile crossed his face when he saw them. "Hey, Jayco. Hey, Jet. Glad you could finally make it. This is Ben. He's in the room down the hall. A snake bit him and has been here for a few days."

"Hello," said Jet.

"Hey," replied Ben.

Principal Berry said, "I'll give you fifteen minutes. I'll be back at the nurse's station." Ben shadowed the principal from the room.

"Fine," said Jayco.

Once the door was closed, Jet asked, "You good, bro?"

"Fine. I just want out of here." Melvin's head jerked at a curtain shielding the only window in the room.

"What's up?" asked Jayco.

Melvin placed his finger to his mouth. Instead, he asked, "How's everyone? How was Spruce Knob? Am I really going home tomorrow?"

The curtain shifted slightly, and Rozene's head came into view. Jayco started to move toward her, but she lifted a hand to stop him.

Jet said, "Spruce Knob was intense. Shane beat us to the piece of the Phoenix, but we did well. We learned a lot and got some weapons for the war."

"Any sign of the Azurites?" Melvin's voice and expression were weird.

Jet suddenly became concerned.

Melvin's hand moved as if pushing Jet to answer. He said, "We haven't seen them at all. Maybe we scared them into hiding."

Relief crossed Melvin's face.

Jayco asked, "How has the food been here?"

"You know," —Melvin leaned back, clearly more relaxed—"nothing is as good as our school's food."

Jayco took a single step toward Rozene. "How was the surgery?"

Rozene inched forward and inclined her head purposefully.

Melvin hissed softly, "Put up a spell so they can't hear us."

Jet had used such a spell before. He spoke "Enlil," and focused his mind.

"Did it work?" asked Jayco.

Rozene typed something onto her phone. After the response, she whispered, "Keep talking casually."

Jet said, "Seyanna is feeling better. She is recovering from her ordeal."

"Good. I was worried she would be exhausted," said Melvin.

"She crashed on the plane."

Jayco added, "We did something cool just before we came to see you. We had some Italian food and played volleyball. We almost won the championship."

Melvin asked, "Who did?"

Jayco pointed at Jet.

Jet said quickly, "It wasn't because of me. That I won was more luck at being on the right team."

Rozene glanced at her phone, then glanced up. "We're good. They can't hear us, and they've walked away from the door."

"Who?" asked Jet.

"The principal, Karl Middlesex, and those three Myntra."

"We didn't see them in the hall."

"They've been here for a while, waiting. They almost walked into me in the bathroom. Good thing Mikey warned me."

Jet asked, "Is he out there now?"

Rozene nodded.

Jayco rushed forward, kissing Rozene. She kissed him back. Jet had never seen him so relieved and happy. He whispered, "What's going on?"

She gripped his arm and burrowed into his chest. She was an incredible actress. Until this moment, he had never believed she was on their side. But how she acted with Jayco was undeniable. She leaned in and kissed him several times. "We're good. It's been a little tense. They don't trust you guys. They hate Charlie and the Azurites. They haven't made a decision on Shane yet?"

"That much is clear," said Jet.

"But considering the deaths of students, the loss of the Brotherhood, and the duplicity of Kevin and Charlie, they're doing well enough. They're strong and will get through this."

"Does that mean you are staying?" asked Jayco.

Rozene flashed a dazzling smile. "Why? Do you miss me?"

Jayco grinned. "That's indisputable. I can't be without you."

"It won't be for very long. I'm class president, but once things have been settled, I can travel more, including this summer. We won't have regular classes, but most students will be here during the break."

"We'll have classes," said Jayco.

"What do we need to know?" asked Jet.

"The Brotherhood was stung by Charlie Eckenkeep. They'll keep a low profile for a few weeks. There are five Predilectors at each of the other boarding schools. They'll remain there, for now, undercover."

"What about closing the school? Is that an option?"

"No. That's just the face they're showing you. They are confident about their strengths. When you regarded the school's protections, the trees on the border were a test. You passed and pointed out other factors."

"They used me?"

"Tested you."

"Good to know," said Jayco.

She reached into her bag and pulled out the Fogle Horn. "Is this what you needed?"

"Why?" asked Jayco.

"Poisons," said Jet quickly. "There's a rumor that Charlie and Kevin made off with some of the school's poisons. This horn will come in handy if the Azurites try to learn or alter the poisons for future attacks. I foresee us asking students from all schools to come to Chadwick's. We have some things planned."

"Is that a good idea?" asked Rozene.

"We've discovered the missing books for the other magic groups," said Jet, and he was surprised at himself. He was willing to tell the truth about the books but not about the real purpose of the Fogle Horn. He would tell Jayco the truth about everything when the time was right.

"I didn't know," said Rozene. "Where are they?"

"In a safe place. Keep that information a secret until we contact you in the next few weeks."

"That'll change everything for me," she said.

Jayco turned Rozene to face him. "What do you mean?"

"I love my Predilector ability, but I want to experience magic. I've dreamt about it. I just want a chance, and knowing that all the books have been found gives me a clearer picture. I'll need to make some hard choices in the next few days. If I get chosen for a magic type, I may never return to Dillon Lake again. I still love this school and will need to choose someone to take over for me if I don't come back."

"Who?" asked Jayco.

"I would choose Bobby or Cassandra, but they are both graduating. I'll come up with someone."

"What about Marlon?" asked Jet.

"Maybe," she said. "He gets a little disagreeable if he's angry at you."

Jayco said, "Don't we know it."

There was a knock at the door. Rozene handed the horn to Jet, who took it and expertly hid it in his hidden compartment. Stepping toward the door, he passed through the sound barrier without dropping the spell. "We're almost finished."

"Good," said Principal Berry. "Five more minutes. Is everything good?"

"Yes," said Jet. "Just filling Melvin in and planning for tomorrow."

"We'll be outside."

"Okay." He caught onto the "*we*" part of the comment. Turning back to Jayco and Rozene, there was a sense of surrealness as he watched them kiss. Melvin looked confident and hopeful, even though he didn't know much about the boy.

Jet went to the hospital bed and asked, "Where are you from?"

"Sacramento."

"I'm from Silverton."

Melvin smiled. "I know."

"Siblings?"

"A younger brother and sister. My brother starts at Chadwick's next year, and my sister in two years."

They chatted for the next few minutes, giving Jayco and Rozene a few more minutes together. Rozene stayed behind as Jet and Jayco left the room.

Principal Berry and Karl Middlesex walked them back to their building. There was no sign of the Myntra or Mikey.

At their door, Cicerone Middlesex nodded at Principal Berry, who stepped away, giving them some space. He turned to Jet and said, "Earlier. You and I tested each other. We made promises that may not be necessary. This entire trip has been a big test. I know you know the Myntra. I sent them to Canada with you. They're connected with you beyond what I know. They keep your secrets. You protected them and came out of Canada with a secret. I have my guesses on what it could be, but I don't need to know the details. I still need you to allow them to come to Chadwick's with you. They have their own destiny."

"What do you want?" asked Jayco.

"I would never trust Darsil Muller. I don't want him to have a book, but Principal Berry fears what will happen to Dillon Lake. He made me make you make promises. But we will endure."

"You speak contradictions," said Jet.

"As do I suspect, so do you. But we both have our reasons."

"Fine," said Jet.

"Will you protect and help the Myntra?"

Jet answered, "As best as we can."

Cicerone Middlesex nodded, appearing relieved. "That's all I ask. Goodnight and Godspeed." He hurried to Principal Berry, and the two disappeared into the night.

"That was weird," said Jayco.

"Unsettling," agreed Jet. "I feel manipulated."

CHAPTER 18

Jet and Jayco climbed the stairs, chatting a bit about Karl Middlesex's inconsistent behavior and if they could really trust the Myntra. He shouldn't have been surprised to see Seyanna waiting for them when they got inside. She wasn't the only one. They were each seated, waiting patiently for an update on Melvin.

Jet announced, "He looks good. Surgery on his leg went well, and he can walk short distances."

"Why wouldn't they tell us anything?" demanded Natalia.

Alivia added, "It would have helped if we could have seen he was doing fine."

As they explained everything that happened, he waited for Jayco to say something about Rozene, but he said nothing. Instead, Jayco peered into corners or turned his head quickly as if trying to catch something that didn't want to get caught. Jet understood immediately.

Standing, he said, "It's time to get some rest. I'm exhausted. We'll see Melvin in the morning."

"When are we leaving?" asked Keesha, and the group dispersed.

"Pretty early," replied Jet. "At least that is what I think."

As the lights went out, Jet went to use the restroom and took a shower. Returning to his bed, he changed and put on some fresh clothes. He was about to get into bed when he noticed a figure in a chair in the corner. It was Seyanna, asleep. He tried waking her, but he couldn't. Picking her up, he placed her in his bed and crawled in next to her. Kissing was the furthest thing from his mind. He was exhausted and fell asleep within less than a minute.

When he woke the following morning, Seyanna was gone. Voices murmured, just out of reach of understanding. He packed, and fifteen minutes later, he sat down to a plate of a toasted bagel, fruit, and grapefruit juice. He devoured his food.

"You snored a little last night," said Seyanna, sitting next to him. "I'm not sure why you moved me into the bed rather than just rousing me."

"Really?" he demanded. "A freaking hurricane wasn't stirring you. I tried."

"Sure. You just wanted some alone time."

"I wish I had the energy. I was drained. How'd you sleep?"

She smiled. "Better than I have in a long time."

Jet's eyebrows rose. "Even with my snoring?"

"Even," she said, leaning in and kissing his cheek. "I heard we're taking a limousine to the airport."

"What? No way."

"A fancy Jeep limo. It arrived twenty minutes ago. I guess we're leaving in style."

"Or a perfect target."

"Three of them pulled up to the curb," said Seyanna. "Two fakes."

Jet's mouth dropped open, and bagel pieces tumbled out. "Three?" He shook his head. "Seems like the water might be a better option. That's how we left last time."

"Oh." She snorted. "There are three boats. And three helicopters."

"No way. That's a bit ridiculous."

Jayco strolled to the table. "Time to go. Leave the food and the bedding. It's time to roll." His voice sounded miserable as he added, "Kids from Dillon Lake, including Rozene, will be in the other vehicles. Even some teachers. Nothing bad better happen."

"Why go through with all the unnecessary risk?" questioned Keesha, as she hurried to the table to grab some food.

"They don't want any additional students getting injured," said Jet. He pushed away his plate and drank some juice.

"Putting Rozene at risk seems to say the opposite," huffed Jayco.

Taking his mostly empty suitcase, Jet and Jayco moved to the front door. Seyanna, Keesha, and Natalia were a step behind. The rest of the students followed them out and down the stairs. When Jet reached the bottom, he opened the door. In the briefest second, he saw Principal Berry crossing the street and felt an overwhelming sensation of someone watching the building's front. He slammed it shut.

"What's wrong?" asked Seyanna.

A second voice spoke from slightly behind them. "Sorry. I did that." Jet spun, pulling out a golden sword. A girl around his height and hair color stepped out from the shadows. Behind her was a narrow corridor that Jet guessed led to the back side of the building, possibly for trash or storage. The girl was stout, and her look was piercing. "Stand down. I'm not here to harm you."

"Who are you?" asked Jayco, who glared at her.

"I'm Dawn Doyle. I was being considered for acting president."

"What's going on down there?" demanded Asher from several steps up.

"Getting some last-minute directions," shouted Jet. He turned his attention to Dawn. "You caused that feeling that someone was watching."

"I was ordered to make sure you didn't go out the front door. Last night, we found some Quills in the streets and in the fields outside of school. They have an entrance that we don't know about. Marlon and others have been searching but haven't found the entry point. We didn't catch any of them, but we know they're there. "

"Is there a change in plans?" asked Jayco.

"Do we go back upstairs?" wondered Maria.

"The school's council hopes you haven't been spotted on campus. We've spread the word that the limos, other cars, helicopters, and boats are for our seniors and a special retreat to New York. We do have something spectacular every year, so it isn't a stretch. The hundred or so kids leaving today will go together. Only seniors and student council members can go, but we'll bring others. I'm here to make sure you don't ruin the plan. The Quills are here for a reason. We hope to find out what that is. During which, you'll make your escape."

"You don't want our help?"

"That proposal was voted against by the council, in case you have something to do with why they're here."

"Are you freaking serious?" shouted Jayco.

Dawn lifted her hands. "I didn't get a vote. But you can see their logic. Quills here when you were here before, and they're back again."

Jayco was about to argue when Jet asked, "What do you want us to do?"

"You'll love it," said the girl, and she pointed somewhere below their feet.

Seyanna said, "I'm not escaping school through the sewer."

Dawn said, "Nope. It's required to enter, but it won't help you escape. You'll use it for a few hundred feet as we reach one of the main buildings. The real fun will be smooshed in the back of a trash truck."

"Stop," said Seyanna. "Some of the kids are going to be in limousines and helicopters, and you're suggesting we frolic through the sewer and get in the back of a trash vehicle."

"A garbage truck," said Dawn. "We leave in two minutes."

Seyanna rolled her eyes, and Jayco hurried to Keesha and Maria. Soon, everyone was told the plan. A few minutes later, the group hustled down, dragging their luggage.

"This way," said Dawn. Instead of going out the front door or the back corridor, she turned and hit a latch on the wall adjacent to the door. A full-length mirror with decorations on both sides swung outward, revealing a dark, hidden passage.

The door swung inward. Dawn pointed for Jet to go first. "There's a boy named Glue...and yes...that's his name. He can stick to anything and walk anywhere. He'll lead you, and I'll be at the back."

Keesha asked, "What can you do?"

Dawn unleashed her ability, and several people ducked down in fear.

Stepping through, Jet was ready for anything. Faded sunlight shone through the top crack of the corridor. They were near the front edge of the building but were in a space between corridors with wooden beams and the backside of drywall, but this was not a finished room. They traveled ten feet and were forced to turn left. Dust particles floated around them, and a layer of dirt clung to both walls and the floor. After rounding the corner, a young boy with brown hair stood upside down on the ceiling as if he were a bat. The kid laughed and strolled down the side wall without any limitation.

Jet rolled his eyes. "Glue, I assume."

"You've got a great memory. This passageway goes between rooms, under staircases, and sometimes between buildings. Most of what you'll see is known only by a select few."

"We'll take your word for it," said Jet. "Carry on."

The expression on the boy's face fell as if he was disappointed. "I thought you would be better travelers. This is cool stuff."

Jayco hissed something, and warmth suffused the boy and the area. Within seconds, the boy was sweating. Glue asked, "What are you doing?"

Jayco growled, "Showing you real magic."

"Cool," Glue replied once the heat had dissipated. He moved quickly and was out of sight in seconds. They hurried to catch up. The passage was seldom straight or long. They went up or down, often in the basement or on the second floor. When they had gone a decent distance, Glue suddenly raised his hand, and the group stopped.

"What is it?" asked Seyanna.

"We're not alone in here."

"What's that supposed to mean?" asked Asher, a step behind Jayco.

"Good question," said Glue.

There was movement in the ceiling, and a panel opened. The group, including Glue, stepped back. The murkiness above them made it impossible to get a clear view. Someone tried using a flashlight, but the space was empty. Then suddenly, Mikey appeared, waving for them to climb.

"Climb what?" asked Jet.

Mikey mimed hitting himself on the head. A moment later, a ladder was dropped, fitting perfectly against the wall. Glue looked annoyed and walked up the wall to give Mikey a piece of his mind. Jet was the first to ascend. The crawl space above wasn't huge, and getting their suitcases up the incline was frustrating. They had to crawl for a dozen feet. Jayco pulled up the gold bands on his arms and tossed the suitcases to Glue, who caught them ridiculously easily.

At the end of the crawl space, Glue opened another entry point, and they found themselves climbing out of a picture onto a staircase of the laundry building. Jet thought it was ironic that they also had a passage in their laundry building.

The group settled in the main room with enormous machines and earsplitting sounds. Glue took Jayco and Jet to a damp staircase going under the building. When they reached the bottom, they found a storage room. Instead of going into the room, as Jet expected, he did something near the opposite wall, and a concrete panel swung outward. When it was pulled away, it revealed an opening. Poking his head into the area, Jet found a concrete slide leading to somewhere unknown. It smelled horrible, and there was running water, and he knew it was the sewer.

Glue whispered, "I haven't been down here since the storm hit. Who knows what we're going to find." There was a gleam in his voice.

"That's reassuring," said Jayco. "Why couldn't this have been easier?"

When they returned to the others, Jet explained where they were going. "It's gross down there. Don't wear your most expensive shoes, but something is better than nothing."

"How's Melvin leaving campus?" asked Nolan. "We'd better not be leaving him behind."

"Oh, yeah," said Glue. He winked at Jet. "I was supposed to give you this note."

Pulling a note from his pocket, he tried handing it to Jet, but Jayco snatched it and asked, "Does it suck to have your hands sticky, like when you're trying to get close to your special someone?"

"My Predilector ability only affects my feet, so I'm cool. Have you ever kissed someone upside down?"

"We've seen that movie," said Jade. "Cool but impractical."

"It's better than cool," said Glue.

"It's from Principal Berry." Jayco read the note aloud, "'Things are going as planned. Don't worry. We moved Melvin early this morning, and he'll leave with you. He's fine. This plan will work.'"

Glue snatched the note and said, "Forge forward."

Jet watched as Jayco forced down his frustration. For an awful second, Jet held his breath, worried that Jayco would punch the boy. It passed.

They climbed down the stairs, and it creaked loudly. A measure of focus and intensity spread onto Glue's face, and he stepped to the open hole in the wall. After several steps, he said, "Be on guard. This is the weakest part of the plan. I doubt anything is in here other than what should be."

Jet pulled out Gravity and returned the golden sword to his hidden compartment. Elementals began pulling out weapons. Jayco pulled on his biker cloak, and Seyanna her white, smudge-less cloak.

After several seconds, Jet entered the tunnel. He only slid down a few feet at a time. After twenty feet, he found Glue standing next to a metal gate that had been welded shut.

"No lock...no key," said Glue.

Jet spoke "Kali," and small firebolts hit the wielded portion. After a minute and several newcomers, the gate swung outward.

Peering out, Jet found they were in a four-foot, large circular metal conduit bisecting the central underground sewage system. They hunched as they exited the tunnel and stepped onto a small concrete platform. Water flowed in the center of the large sewage tunnel. Trash and debris lined both sides, and the water flowed in the center. The tunnel was eight feet tall and ten feet wide. They had two choices: left or right.

"Which way?" asked Jet.

Glue pointed to their left. "That goes to the outside, but through a locked building that has been given the highest security, including the medical unit and the detention center." He pointed to the right. "The working plan is to go down a few hundred yards to a place where we can leave the sewer before it reaches the water."

"The water?" asked Tominiko as he hopped down beside them.

"Most of this is rainwater. The sewage is taken to a different place."

"Right," added Nolan.

Glue continued, "There's a building past a small park and a parking lot. There will be trash containers on the far side. We will sneak through a door on the side of the building facing the park. If we get separated, we'll meet there. Down here, avoid anything that moves or smells."

"Haha," said Jayco, who splashed into the tunnel next to Nolan. He was the last one down, having helped everyone else. Mikey and Dawn remained with them.

Jet peered into the water. It was mostly clear and moved deceptively fast, but the amount of debris in the tunnel was unexpected. The water was less than two feet deep, and they would need to cross to the other side, as that was the only path. He spotted broken trees, trash, several tires, couches, and dozens of other items strewn around the area. He doubted this space had been cleaned in a decade. It wasn't bright by any means in the tunnel, but he could only see clearly for ten or fifteen feet. There were sporadic small lights on the ceiling in the direct center, but only half of them worked.

Jayco came up next to him. "Thoughts?"

"You, me, Nolan, and Tominiko help everyone across. Position yourself at the front or the back as we move forward. Be ready for anything."

Jayco smiled, pulled off his shirt, tossed his suitcase aside, and dove into the water. Jayco was like a fish, and his ability to see and breathe underwater was exceptional, but diving into potentially sewage water was insane. He loved it and swam hard up several feet, then floated down.

When he got out on the opposite side, Seyanna yelled, "No one is going to kiss you for weeks."

Jayco shrugged as Maria tossed over his shirt and luggage. Quickly, all the luggage was thrown over. Glue hung upside down and walked over to Jayco's side.

"Tominiko and Asher, head over to help Jayco."

The two boys splashed into the water. It was waist-high and tricky to navigate, but they made it across.

Asher said, "Come on over, Jade. It's not as cold or gross as you would think."

"Nasty," hissed Phoebe, who wore a specialized backpack holding the golden chalice. Its contents, black powder, created an area of darkness.

Jade crossed, followed by Natalia, Allison, and Alivia. Nolan and Jet helped push them beyond the first half, and Jayco and Tominiko caught them.

"Someone is going to buy me some new clothes," said Maria. She and Keesha crossed next.

Jet said, "Mikey and Dawn. You guys don't have to follow us. I bet we can make it on our own."

Dawn said, "I think we'll come anyway." She crossed quickly.

Mikey struggled and couldn't cross on his own. Jet and Seyanna leapt into the water to provide stability. Mikey surged forward and was nearly swept away. Seyanna reached out and caught him, and Jet latched onto her. Tominiko and Asher pulled all three of them to safety.

Once across, Jayco spoke "Chango," and warmed everyone up. It took ten minutes to dry off. When they set off, they formed a line. Jayco wanted to be at the front, which meant Jet was last in line. Seyanna stayed with him. The amount of trash was staggering and it only worsened. At times, the water was pushed to one side or another. They either got their feet wet or climbed over some items. A new conduit, often only a foot in diameter, bisected the sewer every thirty feet.

"How do you know they aren't dumping human waste back into the ocean?" asked Alivia.

"Not happening," said Glue. "That waste goes into the city. The city and the school had massive problems after the disaster in D.C. Building new infrastructure, especially a new sewage treatment plant, was a top priority. This is from water when it rains, overflows, and floods. Gates will block items like these from getting in here. It looks like we have a broken substructure upline somewhere."

"This has been going on for a while," said Jayco.

"Looks like it," agreed Glue.

A smashed couch blocked the way forward. Jet considered pushing it into the water, but instead, he used magic to lift it and move it behind them, placing it softly out of their way.

"Oh, my," said Phoebe, and she pointed to two bodies lying under where the couch had been. The stench that hit them was powerful. "Are those what I think they are?"

Jet answered, covering his nose. "Quills. What would they be doing here?"

Seyanna covered her mouth, and someone vomited behind them.

"It wasn't like they were killed in the last few days. This seems to be a week or more."

Asher asked, "Why do they smell like burned toast and sulfur?"

Before he could answer, a shadow emerged from within the next conduit on the opposite side of the water. The frame was either stocky or bent over. No one else seemed to notice. Jet wasn't sure if he should react.

"Maybe it's from the manner he was killed," he said. He stepped up to the bodies and over them. There were burned marks on their backs and faces.

From the corner of his eye, Jet watched Mikey disappear. Maybe he wasn't the only one who saw the figure. A board moved slowly into the water, but Jet doubted Mikey could get across on his own. "Don't do it, Mikey."

The others glanced around. Mikey materialized close to the water.

Jet pointed Gravity and said, "Show yourself. You can't win against us."

"I know exactly who you are," said a voice, and the figure moved. "You're the reason I'm down here."

"Me?"

"Elliot!" shouted Glue. "Is that you?"

Dawn added, "No freaking way."

"Why?" said Elliot Sanders, a boy Jet had believed was dead.

"What are you doing down here?" asked Glue.

"Nowhere else to go. There's no way I was going to be caught by Jet Black or the Elementals."

Jayco said, "Hey, Elliot. It's me, Jayco. Do you remember me?"

"Sure. What of it?"

Jayco glanced around. "Why are you blaming Jet for being down here? What gives?"

The boy swung his legs and sat on the metal edge. In one hand, he held a knife, and in the other, a Quill sword. He was dirty, exhausted, and had lost ten pounds. He glared at them with contempt. A steady stream of water cascaded around him and he didn't care.

Jet noticed someone else farther back in the shadows, keeping just out of view.

Elliott continued, "Those porcupine creatures arrived the same day that Jet and his friends left. A student died. I can't unsee that flying vulture. Nothing has been the same, and the school is barely keeping things together. Then we were attacked again, and more students died. Jet launched those porcupines to attack us. Kevin knew it. Dart and a few others were in denial, and they're dead."

Jayco said, "They were sent, but not by us."

"Like I'm just going to believe you," said Elliott.

Seyanna spoke. "Mikey can tell you that we fought Quills in Congo. They are no friends of ours. Kevin was the one who discovered a way to work with them."

"Who the hell are you?" Elliott demanded. "These are lies."

"I am Charlie Echenkeep's daughter. He and Kevin kidnapped me. Rozene, Mikey, Trinity, and Hebrew helped Jet and Jayco rescue me. Kevin fought Jet and died. Kevin is the real traitor."

Elliott turned to Mikey. "Is that true?"

Mikey nodded, his head emphatic.

"No lies."

Mikey began shaking his head.

"Mikey?" a timid voice asked. "Is that you?"

Mikey's eyes widened.

Elliott pointed over his shoulder. "Yuki and I have been hiding down here for a few days."

Mikey began splashing in the water, and Jayco had to help the boy cross to the other side. A tiny person stepped next to Elliot.

Elliott continued, his face glancing from person to person. "Yuki and I recently became friends. She was born in Japan, but her mom and dad died. She had a bad injury. She came to school but never fit in."

Mikey rushed forward, and Yuki slipped down onto the ground. They hugged and nuzzled each other. Jet was surprised at their reaction. He felt bad that he didn't know more about Mikey.

Glue said, "I didn't know they knew each other. Yuki is in my economics class. She is brilliant."

Mikey smiled, but Yuki answered. "We've had to be sneaky. Two dunces together, the insults would be never-ending."

Yuki was slightly taller than Mikey and about the same size. She had a short left arm and fingers. She walked with a slight limp. Burn marks covered a portion of her face. She smiled, appearing enamored with Mikey, who returned the look.

"A girlfriend?" asked Keesha, playfully.

A broad and mischievous smile formed on Mikey's lips.

Elliott asked Yuki, "Can we trust them?"

She nodded and hugged Mikey again.

Jet asked, feeling uncomfortable, "Yuki. I hope you don't think this is rude, but how did you get those burn marks on your arms and part of your face?"

Yuki stared at the ground. "In Japan, there was an apartment fire, and my parents died. I barely made it out alive. I was sent to America with my aunt. She sent me to Dillon Lake."

"That's terrible," said Maria. She moved closer. "I lost my brother. I'm from Argentina."

Yuki looked impressed and sad at the same time.

"Elliot. What happened?" asked Glue. "Why are you down here?"

"First," said Elliot as he jumped down from the conduit. "Tell me what happened in Congo?"

Seyanna asked, "Have you ever heard of the Azurites?"

Both Elliott and Yuki shook their heads. Even Glue and Dawn inched closer to hear what was said.

Jet explained, "The Azurites are a group like the Brotherhood, and some of their founding members were from the Brotherhood. They want to change how magic is given and taught and are willing to kill for it. They're against the current boarding schools. Kevin and Charlie are members. The Azurites can be composed of non-magical beings, Elementals, Predilectors, Runics, and others. They are secretive. They kidnapped Seyanna and tried interfering with the Rivalry, intending to cause it to fail."

"Are the Brotherhood and the Azurites working against each other?" asked Elliot.

Jayco said, "To the best of our knowledge."

Yuki appeared lost. Mikey wrote something on a piece of paper and showed it to her. She smiled and nodded at him.

"Do you know a boy named Samson?" asked Jet.

"Sure," said Elliot. "He was close with Kevin."

"He was a jerk to me," said Yuki.

Jet said, "He was in Congo, too. He threw you and Dart under the bus."

Elliott eased himself onto the ground. "Why am I not surprised?"

"We fought those flying vultures, Quills, Kevin, and other Azurites." Jayco reached out his hand to help Elliot cross. "Some of our friends died. We captured a few, and they were brought here. A few of our friends were injured and came here to recover. Now, we are getting out of here. There are Quills on campus."

"This entire school is in a mess," said Yuki.

Keesha said, "We're trying to make it better."

"It's your turn," said Dawn to Elliot.

"I'd just seen Dart killed. Quills had invaded the school; they came up through the sewers. I thought it would be easier to escape. I came down here and never left. Four days later, I found Yuki down here. We've been here for a week. We had to kill those two Quills."

"Burned them?" asked Asher.

"And stabbed them," replied Elliot. "There are also small flying creatures, like imps or fairies. They fly back and forth. There has been a flurry of activity."

Glue said, "On the orders of Principal Berry, I'm taking these guys to the Depot. They need to leave campus, then we can get you back to the surface."

Elliot scoffed. "Not on your life. Yuki and I are leaving school. We will come with you or find our own way out."

"Come with us," said Gleam.

"Dillon Lake is no longer safe," said Elliot. "There have been breaches. The Depot is the last place that I would go."

"Why?" asked Keesha.

"In the last hour, Yuki and I were almost caught. There are new hunters on campus. We watched six Quills and two flying imps escort a feline creature with three horns down this tunnel. A girl rode on its back."

"A Chupovana?" cried Jet. "They can sense magic. Are you sure?"

"They took the tunnel leading to the Depot. This is the first time we've been back to this section since we killed the porcupines. There is no other way out of the school. It has to be this line. We heard you guys and hid."

Dawn said, "We were told the Claustra would prevent those creatures from entering."

Yuki spoke. "It's not true."

Jayco asked Jet, "What do we do?"

"We can't leave Melvin," insisted Allison.

"I know," said Jet. "Why don't Jayco, me, Tominiko, Seyanna, and Keesha go forward to check things out? The rest stay here and wait for our signal."

"We can't fight a Chupovana on campus," retorted Jayco.

Jet said, "We might not have a choice." His head bobbed a few times. "But I've got a plan."

"I really hate the sound of your voice right now," said Seyanna.

CHAPTER 19

Jet, Seyanna, Jayco, Tominiko, Keesha, Allison, and Glue hustled down the sewer, turned left, and splashed through water, climbing over debris.

Glue asked, "What happens if we manage to lure the Chupovana away?"

"The priority is getting it away from the school. If it found a way in, there's got to be a space big enough for us to escape. It's here for our magic. Seal the entrance once it leaves."

"Kill the remaining Quills," added Jayco.

"Did they break in, or did someone let them in?" asked Keesha.

Seyanna said, "We are missing something."

She was right, but Jet had no idea what it was.

Ahead, the tunnel sloped down, the water flowing faster.

"Seventy feet ahead is the end of the sewer," announced Glue. "A large metal grate stops the trash from continuing, but the water keeps moving.

From here, Jet sees trees, pieces of metal, insulation, a broken door, and more piled together.

Glue added, "We'll need to cross up ahead. We're looking for a metal door."

"Well...that's a problem," said Jayco.

Jet followed his gaze and saw the large hole in the side wall with sunlight pouring through.

Glue Blanched. "That was a metal, locked door."

"It's not locked any longer," said Keesha.

Jet widened his stance and crossed the faster moving water. Once on the opposite side, he climbed four concrete steps. Glue burst outside, followed by Jayco and Keesha. They stopped suddenly, a millisecond after as a small explosion rocked the morning.

"What happened?" demanded Allison.

"Half the Depot is on fire," cried Glue.

"Am I supposed to know what that is?" she demanded.

"It's where the trash is compacted and shipped out of the school." Suddenly, Glue's voice changed. "Get back! Get back! Back! Back!" Jayco and Keesha were driven back into the tunnel.

"What's wrong?" asked Tominiko. "What did you see?"

"He saw me," hissed Glue. "He's telling the others. What is happening here?"

Jet gripped Glue's shoulders. "What did you see?"

"Uri Gideon is helping the Quills. He spotted me and alerted the Chupovana."

Jet yanked Glue, shouting, "We've got to go."

Jayco ran to some debris, pulled up his golden bracelets, and threw item after item, blocking the hole in the wall. Jet tore up the incline, dragging Glue. Speed was the only way they were going to survive.

Seyanna reached the upper portion first. Jet bellowed, "Keep going. Tell the others and don't look back."

A moment of apprehension crossed her face, then she sprinted ahead. Jet considered firing some magic, but what would it take to stop a Chupovana at this point? Damaging the school was the wrong move.

"They're coming," cried Jayco, several steps behind.

His cry was muted by the detonation of detritus being hurled back into the tunnel. They were coming. Bellows erupted from behind them as if those pursuing them were frustrated.

From behind, Jayco shouted, "I guess they encountered those jagged sticks."

"How did you manage that?" asked Jet.

"Broke them in half and pinned them against other debris."

"Quick thinking," shouted Jet.

Up ahead, he could see the others hustling forward. They were slower, still carrying luggage. Two minutes later, Jet had caught up with Maria and Seyanna. Suitcases were handed out, and the group moved more quickly.

Seyanna said, "Asher and Dawn are farther ahead. Get up there, and Jayco and I can help the stragglers."

"Fine." Jet tore off.

The sewer drain went straight for a hundred yards, then abruptly turned left. They climbed, turned, and mounted piles of debris three or four times. Rats, cats, and other animals scurried in the darkness. Sometimes, they were seen, but mostly, they remained in the shadows.

"They're catching us," bellowed Jayco, still at the back of the group. "Find an exit or we'll have to turn and fight!"

Ahead, the largest pile of debris blocked their path, except on the left side. Asher and Dawn looked unsure about where to go. When Jet arrived at the base, Glue was climbing over the left side of the pile to get a vantage on the tunnel.

"What do you see?" asked Jet.

Glue said, "Beyond this, the passages split into three."

"That gives us a chance to find a way out."

"Look," said Phoebe, pointing upward to a small section near the ceiling. He'd been wrong. Things had been purposely positioned or shifted down the pile. It was like a staircase to the top. A large piece of plywood covered a hole in the ceiling.

"Up there!" cried Jet. "Go!"

Asher sprang up. After a few seconds, he reached the top and pushed at the plywood. It was stuck for the first few attempts. "Almost got it," grunted Asher. The wood broke free and revealed a giant hole. "There's an abandoned house up here. It looks empty."

"Get going. Don't stop."

Glue effortlessly slid back over, and within seconds, he disappeared into the house. His face reemerged a short time later. "No one is here. Come on up."

Asher and Glue helped pull everyone into the house. Jet, Seyanna, and Dawn stayed below while Jayco moved to the end of the sewer.

When all but a few were left, Jayco sprinted in their direction, shouting, "They're coming."

Dawn said, "I can seal this."

"Hide behind this mound," said Jet, pointing to where Glue had gone. "Once they follow us through, seal it closed."

Jayco launched debris down the tunnel.

"Let's go," said Jet, and he and Seyanna climbed. He let Seyanna go through first. As Jayco ascended the pile, Jet sent firebolts, hitting several pieces of waste. Soon, the tunnel was ablaze. Jayco scurried up. Reaching an arm down, Jayco pulled Jet into the abandoned house. Jet hoped he hadn't just killed Dawn or suffocated her with smoke.

Asher gripped Jet's arm while covering his own mouth. "All the doors and windows are boarded up."

"That's why we saw so much furniture below," coughed Seyanna.

Maria muttered, "Plenty of broken glass on the floor."

"We've got animal bones," said someone. "And blankets with porcupine quill pieces."

The wood creaked above them. Jet thought there might be a second floor or that it was coming from the attic. Yuki cowered down, trying to cover her eyes. Mikey reached over and put an arm around her.

Natalia mouthed, "What do we do?"

Jet pulled out a golden pyramid and spoke softly, "Pyramis of Aurum," and Iris transformed before him. The instant she appeared, she was on alert, sniffing the air, somehow understanding the situation exactly as it was.

Someone shouted, "We gotta go."

Jet rushed for what he hoped was the front door, with Iris a step behind. Glue placed the plywood over the hole. Elliot went to a boarded window and repeatedly slammed his elbow into it. On the fourth hit, the wood shattered. Jade guided Mikey and Yuki toward Elliot.

A step before reaching the door, Jet spoke "Urania," and a wind explosion knocked the door off its hinges, sending it halfway across the yard.

"Get out!" bellowed Jayco. "You've got two options."

Stepping outside, Jet released the other two golden pyramids and took several deep breaths. Iris touched them, and they transformed. Mikey and Yuki were the first out the window. They coughed and stumbled toward the street. Others poured out of the window or the door, hacking up their lungs.

This house was one of six in a small cul-de-sac, with one road in and out of the area. Pounding erupted on the garage door, and it ominously slid up two feet. Five Quills burst from the gap a dozen feet away and sprinted directly at them. Two had bows, one an ax, and two held swords. The golden lion and bear reacted first, knocking four of them over. One recovered quickly, jumping to its feet, as the other three screamed in agony. Asher and Tominiko dispatched the remaining two without hesitation.

"Where do we go?" demanded Keesha.

Pounding from within the house told Je they only had seconds to spare. "Pull out your weapons and follow me." The only real path was directly up the street. To Jayco, he asked, "Did everyone make it out of the house?"

"Everyone is accounted for."

"What about me?" demanded Glue. "What weapon do I use?"

Jet said, "We'll find you one."

The house faced northwest, and they trotted down the street. Seyanna fell into step next to him. It was slow-moving at first. The plywood snapped back inside the house, and they began sprinting.

As they passed the second house on the left, Jayco shouted and pointed across the street. "Over there. Look."

Jet smiled.

They crossed the street and entered the front yard of one of the houses. Sprinting past a group of four trees, they continued along the side of the house with the golden animals leading the way. Turning toward the backyard, Jet glanced back. The feline Chupovana exited the abandoned house, caught their scent, and tore off after them. Jet's heart leaped into his mouth. He bellowed, "Don't stop!"

The back fence was partially broken, and they crossed into the terrace of the adjacent house. Directly ahead of them, across the street, was a large park.

"That open space will make it easier for them to see us," said Yuki.

Jet said, "It doesn't matter. That Chupovana can track our scent wherever we go. We need to find a place that gives us the advantage."

"We're going to fight that thing, right?" said Asher. "I'm stoked."

"Probably," said Jet. "Let's see if we can find a position where our backs aren't exposed." Mikey and Yuki slowed as they crossed the street. Keesha, Maria, and Tominiko stayed nearby to help.

He heard Elliott mumble, "I hope Dawn is safe."

Jet opened his mouth to say something, then closed it. What did he really know? Behind them, the Chupovana turned the corner.

Alivia shouted, "On the left are some trees and a blocked area with a wooden fence. Is that a good place?"

"Let's hope," said Phoebe.

"Run!" screamed Jet.

Iris and the golden animals peeled away, putting themselves between the group and the attacking predators. When they reached the field, they turned left, ran behind some trees, and continued to the back fence. On their right was a playground and, further along, an outdoor basketball court. People played on both but stopped instantly upon seeing Jet and the others. Sensing that something was happening, they retreated.

"There are people in those houses," said Allison.

Jet said, "Let's make this count."

Branches snapped back near the three trees, and Jet and the others turned to face that direction. The three golden animals were striding backwards. In front of them, less than twenty feet away, was Taraqeu, the feline Chupovana.

Jet spoke. "Most of you have fought with us before. We're powerful, but so is the Chupovana. Taraqeu is fast and lethal. We need Mikey and Yuki to be the lookouts and tell us if they're attacking from the side?"

Yuki said, her voice wavering, "I...I think."

"Tell us more about the Chupovana," said Elliot as he accepted an Axenkind ax from Jayco.

Shadows stopped at the tree, and it was clear that there were more than just Quills and the Chupovana following them.

"Her three horns are thick and curve back toward her tail. She's fast, agile, and lethal. A Khalicaan, a clanswoman, rides on her back and directs her. Taraqeu has a tail that can shoot porcupine quills. She has a large chest and a long torso. She can climb as well as Glue. She doesn't like Water magic, but Wind can't damage her. I think Fire, Ice, and Confusion won't affect her either."

"My wall of fire will do nothing?" asked Nolan.

"Look," said Allison.

Taraqeu pushed past the grouping of trees and five feet into the clearing. Her head was lowered, but her keen eyes took in the entire area. An electrical current swirled between her three horns. She was riderless, but the branches of the tree, several feet in the air, parted, and the Khalicaan emerged. She was tall with green robes, dark brown skin, and chocolate brown hair. She would be majestic if it weren't for the red splotches encircling her eyes.

Tominiko nervously brandished his carved golden paddle as Nolan swung his thick sword with shark's teeth back and forth. Elliott tested the ax, trying to get a feel for it. He moved his feet and had more control than Jet would ever have, but he was far from an expert.

"Remind me how we kill the Chupovana or the Khalicaan?" asked Jayco.

"With an enchanted blade," answered Jet flatly.

"Do we have one of those?" asked Elliott.

Jet mumbled, "Gravitas," so that only he could hear. The blue blade he pulled from the bottom of his staff was majestic and bewitching. "We do."

Tree branches shifted, and ten humans, each holding a white crystal, marched into view. Surrounding them were a dozen Quills. Uri Gideon and two other Predilectors came to rest next to Taraqeu, and they finished comprising this attack squad.

Yuki screamed and retreated a few steps.

Elliott bellowed, "I always knew you were backstabbing Uri."

The boy shouted back, "You cockroach. Lived for a few days only to get killed by a Chupovana. Killing you and the Elementals will be as sweet as honey."

"Why are you helping the Chupovanas?" demanded Glue.

"It's an enemy of my enemy thing. If we kill all the Elementals, Faunal has promised we won't be attacked."

"You can't trust him," shouted Jet.

Taraqeu growled.

Uri bellowed, "Well, I'm not fighting a war alongside the son of traitors."

"Traitors?" questioned Jet.

"Jet Black, I know that Elemental magic was not intended for you. Your parents stole it when Kevin's family had been chosen. Then you killed Kevin, like the troll you are. Revenge is imminent."

Jet explained, "The book opens for who *it* chooses."

"Liar!"

"What are the humans doing here?" whispered Asher. "What are those crystals?"

"Trying to buy some time to find out." Jet added, "Khalicaans can perform mind control on humans. Those crystals are a problem, right behind that feline."

Elliot demanded, "Who killed Dart? Was it you?"

"Stop stalling," bellowed Uri.

"What's the plan?" asked Keesha.

The Khalicaan brayed something, and the ten humans trekked forward in unison, spreading out so that they were the same distance from each other.

Jet announced, "Use defensive movements only. Don't attack humans...for now. The goal is to kill the Khalicaan."

Elliot said, "And Uri."

"That's up to you," breathed Jet.

The Khalicaan beckoned, "We just want to talk."

"What do you want to discuss?" asked Jet. "We're not surrendering."

The girl laughed, "That I know."

Jet examined their options. It might be flight or flee. "What do you want?"

"The Fogle Horn," said the Khalicaan.

Jet's head snapped back.

"Plain and simple. Give it to us, and you can depart. Freely."

"No," said Uri. "That wasn't our—"

"Quiet," hissed the Khalicaan.

Glue yelled, "How many people did you kill back at the school?"

The Khalicaan answered her voice husky, "Such things do not matter. What is important is that we don't kill you and your friends here and now. You have two minutes to think it over."

When Uri reached for a limb to climb, he stopped suddenly, as if he couldn't move...or breathe. The Khalicaan stared at him for nearly a minute. No one could tear their eyes away from the scene. When she released him, he toppled to the ground. Then she whispered something they couldn't hear.

"Why do they want the horn?" asked Jayco. "Should we give it to them?"

"No," said Jet. "We can't."

At that precise moment, a cacophony of sounds erupted to the right of the humans. The ground shook, the grass lifted and domed until it tore open. Six creatures pushed through. Jet had seen the other three types of Drekavac Demons before, but not these ones.

With their narrow heads, elongated bodies, and six short legs, they looked hideous. When their mouths opened, retractable pinchers appeared. Expanding to their full height, in tandem, four of their legs remained on the ground and two became useable arms. A high-pitched cackling sound passed between the six creatures, and they fanned out.

The Khalicaan announced, "You only need to worry if you don't give us the horn. No one will get hurt if you obey."

"Yeah, right," said Natalia.

"What now?" asked Maria.

Jet said, "If you're injured or not strong enough to fight, move to the back." He glanced at Seyanna.

She smiled weakly back. "I don't have a ton of energy, but I'm not sitting this one out."

"Same," added Natalia. "I've got a few working limbs."

Jet said hastily, "If things go sideways, you two protect Mikey and Yuki. The rest of us will fight. Killing the Khalicaan is the main priority."

Jayco stepped up to Jet. "Are you seriously thinking of fighting? We can't win. Just give them the horn."

"If they get it, one day, we will regret it. It's powerful."

Jayco stepped back, a look of doubt etched on his face.

"What do you want us to do?" asked Asher.

"We need five to focus on those digging creatures. They're called Scorepos. Five will focus on humans. The last few will watch the Predilectors and help where needed."

"When?" asked Jayco.

Jet said, "We have fifteen seconds left before two minutes have elapsed. When it's time, I'll unleash a series of Water spells. Depending on what they do, we'll know how to proceed. I keep up a barrier and keep everyone preoccupied. If they do nothing, we will need to retreat."

"I think we can take them," said Asher.

Maria and Phoebe moved close as if preparing to team up.

From the back, Yuki cried, "We can't fight that thing. We're all going to die."

The Khalicaan called out again, "There's no place to go. The Scorepos could have attacked you from underground if we wanted to hurt you. We just want the horn. Don't make us kill each of you."

CHAPTER 20

Pointing to the sky, Jet spoke "Oblekii," once, then twice. The number of clouds that appeared was less than he would have wanted. But he didn't stop. He next spoke "Ogen," and a torrent of rain fell from the skies. He howled, "Keesha and Alivia, use your Water magic."

They joined him with their spells. The air pressure changed, and the temperature dropped instantly.

Jayco bellowed, "We are just attacking them."

"We are," shrieked Jet.

"We have no clue about those crystals."

"We are about to find out."

Several people roared.

"We have our answer," cried the Khalicaan, who nimbly dropped from the tree onto the back of Taraqeu. The feline stalked forward purposefully as Khalicaan spoke to the humans. The crystals began to glow, and then electricity sprang and connected all ten crystals together. The ten humans became a blur, traveling at impossible speeds for ten feet, then reappearing. They took another three steps, and the process repeated. The electricity moved with them the entire time. The

Quills moved to guard the humans. The Scorepos pulled out their own weapons, brown-blade long swords.

"Kill them all!" wailed the Khalicaan.

"Oh, crap," cried Jayco.

Every Elemental unleashed their magic, even Seyanna and Natalia. Fire, Wind, and Earth magic had little effect on the group ahead. The Khalicaan's primary focus was on keeping the humans safe. Jet became convinced those white crystals could kill them, and that she was banking on his fear of harming the humans.

Jet spoke "Kali," and a firebolt struck a human who was less than twenty feet away. The woman crumpled, and the crystal toppled to the ground. The intensity of the other nine humans diminished marginally, but visibly. He unleashed another firebolt at a young boy. A Quill hurdled into its path and shouldered the attack in its arm.

"Disrupt and kill the humans," hollered Jet. A surge of nausea nearly caused him to collapse onto one knee. He could not believe what he had just said.

No sooner had the words left his mouth than the Scorepos and Quills changed tactics. Three Scorepos burrowed into the ground, and the other three rushed forward. Six Quills unleashed arrows in their direction.

Jayco, Tominiko, Elliott, Allison, and Alivia broke off to defend against the Scorepos. Jet heard Jayco yell, "Watch for attacks from below the surface."

Jet's back stiffened. His next spell created a barrier, preventing flying arrows and anything below the surface from coming too close. Using the chalice and black powder, Phoebe made it impossible for anyone to get a clear shot at them. Latisha, had used the same chalice, back when she had power over it.

Seyanna shot golden arrows at four Quills, separating them from the others. Iris, the lion, and the bear rushed the humans. The bear shredded a Quill, and Iris tracked down a Scorepo, only to retreat as the creature swung its brown sword. This gave the lion a moment to attack. It vaulted onto the beast's back, and Elliot swung his ax.

Jayco uprooted two trees and swung them like clubs. He connected a glancing blow at a Scorepo as it dove underground.

Jet spoke "Abzu," and a hundred ice crystals descended into the battlefield. For some reason, this spell wasn't limited like his other water spells, and there were ice crystals as large as a baseball bat. He crushed another two humans, three Quills, and a Predilector who moved forward to attack. Taraqeu dove aside to avoid being struck.

Seyanna screamed, "That's three humans down."

"Ouch," cried Glue.

An arrow had caught him in the back of the shoulder. A Quill had positioned itself behind a tree adjacent to the path. His second arrow sailed directly at Yuki. The girl screamed hysterically.

Mikey pulled out a tiny, slender sword and expertly knocked the arrow out of the air. He lost his balance and toppled to the ground.

Nolan and Keesha stepped back to protect Yuki.

Maria used her golden orbs and guided them at the Quill. At the last instant, the creature dropped from view. The orbs smashed into the tree's trunk, splintering it in half.

"The humans," cried Seyanna.

All eyes turned to the humans. The crystals pulsated, and a thick electrical lightning slashed forward and connected, center mass, with Jade's chest. She was knocked backward several feet.

Before anyone could react, small yellow containers sailed through the air. They hit the earth, and a deep white smoke swirled upward.

"Smoke bombs," bellowed Nolan.

Three grenade-like devices came to rest near two Scorepos, and they backed away. The humans were forced to stop as more devices landed. Still, they sent an electrical jolt at Seyanna, but the instant it hit the smoke, it dissipated.

"The smoke is forming a barrier," announced Jayco.

"Iris," yelled Jet. "Back!" The three golden creatures withdrew.

Four dove into the soil, but one collapsed and died before it could reach the safety of the dirt. The Khalicaan screeched in frustration. The humans were immobilized. Quills shot arrows, but these too stopped mid-air as if stuck to floating honey. Taraqeu weaved back and forth, unable to advance.

In the distance, two engines revved, and two black SUVs sped down the road, coming to a stop on the far side of the playground and the basketball court.

Gleam stepped out of one and Faris the other. They had canisters in both hands. Em was partially hidden on the playground with swords.

"Follow me," cried Jet. He saw a clear lane to the SUVs.

Five steps later, a Scorepo surfaced and swung his blade. Jet reacted, dodging its attacks and using his enchanted blade to slice one leg as he rolled on by. Before he could strike again, Keesha shot the creature with two golden arrows, ripping through the shoulder and the neck. The creature swayed and dropped.

The group sprinted past, with Asher slowing and helping Jade to her feet. She didn't appear injured but muttered, "I don't feel my magic." Keesha helped Glue as blood from his injury soaked his shirt.

Two humans managed to block their path, each holding a white crystal. Suddenly, they face each other, smashing their crystals together. A bolt of electromagnetic force came at Jet and those behind him. The single wave was visible, white, and grew in intensity.

Em screamed, "No!"

A speckle of fear threatened to overcome Jet, but he planted both his feet, spoke "Gongpae," and directed his air shield as a triangle, with the tip in front of him. The barrier widened to cover the group. He wasn't sure he could match the power racing at them, but he needed to redirect it.

The wave hit the tip, dividing into two paths, just as a rock diverts water in a river. The wave and its intensity washed past them on both sides, crashing into the fences and houses behind them.

The two humans, now empty-handed, froze for an instant, drained of color, and toppled to the ground, unbreathing.

"Go," screamed Jet. He watched as Gleam and Faris released other canisters so the barrier would block anyone from following them or returning to the school.

Using his Predilector affinity, Uri soared into the air as if carried by a tornado. He navigated over the yellow barrier, keeping himself ten feet off the ground. He removed a bizarre-looking gun Jet had never seen from his pocket and aimed it directly at Seyanna.

"I'll kill her first," said Uri. "I know how important she is to you. Lay down your weapons and surrender."

The growl that escaped Iris was more than a warning. The golden panther took two steps forward, sprang onto the back of the golden bear, and sailed upward so quickly that Uri barely had time to adjust himself to the left. Iris cruised past harmlessly without even landing a scratch.

Seyanna expertly notched an arrow, aimed, and fired. Uri could not avoid it. The arrow stuck deep into his abdomen, followed by a cry of pain. As he drifted down, he settled on the opposite side of the barrier, crumbling into a ball. Elliot crashed into the yellow barrier, trying to get at the injured boy.

"Run," cried Gleam. "What are you waiting for?"

No one needed to be told twice. The Khalicaan unleashed a cry of frustration as Jet and his friends reached the two SUVs. The group separated as the three golden animals transformed into pyramids and were stored in Jet's hiding place. He got into the car with Gleam and Em.

As the doors closed, he asked, "What was that stuff?"

"Songs of Mist."

The answer was given as if the entire explanation had been done in those three words.

The SUVs shot down the street.

"Dillon Lake is at risk," said Jet. "We have to help them."

"They're protected," replied Gleam.

"Are you sure?" asked Seyanna, who sat next to Jet, along with Keesha, Mikey, and Yuki. They were stuffed together. Maria, Jade, Asher, Natalia, Allison, and Alivia were also in the SUV. The rest followed in the second vehicle.

"Dillon Lake was never at as much risk as Principal Berry alluded. They didn't know if Uri or Marlon was helping the outsiders or where the last entrance was."

Jade said, "That means you used us as bait."

Her words sent a cold realization down Jet's spine.

Em, driving, said, "It wasn't our choice."

"You could have warned us," hissed back Jet.

"When?" asked Gleam. "We were being watched closely. Everyone was."

Em said, "The Chupovana was a surprise. They were ready to seal the opening; they just needed to find it. That's why you were needed. No one is getting back into the school."

"Good to know," said Jet.

Asher asked, "How are you, Jade?"

"Different," she answered.

Maria asked, "What was with those white crystals?"

Gleam answered, "They're a creation from the Skeleton called Harbor Crystals. There were forty in total, and if that lightning hits you, it will deplete the strength of a magic wielder for forty hours. If the crystal itself touches you or if two are combined and the wave hits you, all your energy vanishes...forever."

"What?" cried Jade. "I was hit by a wave."

"No," said Em. "You were lucky. No magic for a few days, but it will come back."

"Are you sure?" Tears fell onto her lap.

"Yes."

"Can anything block it?"

"Not really," said Gleam. "Truthfully, I never would have guessed your spell would have worked. I cannot tell you how happy I am that it did."

Natalia said, "For the future. It would be more helpful if we knew these things in advance. Without Jet, we would be kibble right now."

"Fancy shooting," said Keesha. "Seyanna saved the day."

Jet reached for her hand and squeezed. "Darn right."

"I'm about tired of being threatened," Seyanna said. "I don't always have to be everyone's favorite target."

They took the next corner at almost full speed.

"Where are you taking us?" asked Alivia.

Em answered, "On a plane and back to Chadwick's as quickly as possible. You'll be protected there."

"What about Melvin?" asked Natalia.

"Taraqeu came after him first. No one saw it coming. Once it received the boy's magic, it became fortified. We held it at bay, kind of, before it turned and ran off. It wasn't until we followed and discovered the truth about the battle outside that it became clear they were here for you."

Asher blurted, "That green rider wanted the Fogle Horn."

Em said, "That can't be real."

"Why?" asked Jade.

"The Fogle Horn, along with the other crafty palisades, has been missing for centuries."

Jet said, "No. Chief Charlie Eckenkeep found it and delivered it to the school." He didn't want to say anything more. "The Azurites are working with the Chupovanas to drain as many students of their magic as they can. We were lucky."

"Yes," agreed Keesha. "And Melvin paid the cost."

The SUV drove north for a few blocks, then onto a different road. Ten minutes later, they crossed over the Hudson River.

"Where's the airport?" asked Jet.

"A few hours away. That'll give us enough time to drive there, and you can have your plane meet us there."

Sleep came quickly for everyone but Jet. Guilt seethed deep about losing Melvin and for retreating from Dillon Lake before he was absolutely sure it was secure, and for ordering the deaths of humans.

Gleam spoke quietly from the front seat. "The school is safe. The Chupovanas, the remaining Quills, and the crystals are gone. The humans, all dead, were left behind. Once you are forced to touch the Harbor Crystals, you are already slaughtered. Principal Berry sends his thanks for all you did *and* his condolences for Melvin's death. Without you guys, they would still be in danger."

Her words calmed him, barely, and he dozed off for the next forty-five minutes. When he woke, he sent texts to Mckenzey, Grantham, and Latisha about the last few days. Each responded individually.

Rumors were already swirling that something awful had happened at Dillon Lake. An alarm had sounded at Chadwick's, and several leaders of the Elementals and Runics were summoned to a meeting. The other four boarding schools were being searched, right now, especially for any underground tunnels, drains, and sewers. No one wanted anything like this to ever happen again.

PART 2:

THE COALESCENCE

CHAPTER 21

Upon arriving at Stewart International Airport, they were taken through a side gate and out to a hangar. The plane had landed but was still being refueled. Some gathered around and talked, while others cried about Melvin's death. Exhaustion, guilt, regret, and anger were a powerful mix, but not a constructive one.

Jet approached Glue, Dawn, Mikey, Yuki, and Elliott. The five were huddled together, chatting. "You're more than welcome to return to Dillon Lake. I've been told it is safe. I'm sure you could catch an Uber back."

"Nope." Elliot shook his head. "We've agreed that we're going to Chadwicks. We owe you guys big time and want a better picture of magic."

"All of you?"

Mikey grinned and nodded emphatically. The kid was courageous and fun to be around.

"Time to go," announced one of the pilots. "We've been cleared to leave in the next fifteen minutes. Where's your luggage?"

"Stolen," said Jayco. "It has been a rough trip."

Jet hadn't realized exactly when the suitcases had been thrown out. When he boarded, he was happily surprised to see the black canoe still in the middle. The back of the plane filled up fast, but Seyanna grabbed Jet's hand and pulled him into one of the first few rows. They talked casually for almost the entire flight until Seyanna fell asleep, and his thoughts overwhelmed him.

Ten minutes from landing, an intrusive thought forced itself into Jet's mind. *What if an ambush is waiting for us?* After everything that had happened to them, it would be the spoiled garnish on top of the worst meal of his life.

When he was about to voice his thoughts, there was a tap on his shoulder. "Are you and Seyanna officially together?"

Jet couldn't tell if Jayco's voice contained anger, jealousy, or both. "Nothing official. Just a long trip, and glad to be back."

"Have you talked to her?"

"A bit, but things have been hectic." He watched the rhythmic rise and fall of Seyanna's chest. "We haven't had that perfect moment to discuss our relationship between her kidnapping and the Chupovana."

Jayco said, his voice softening, "I hope it works for you too."

"So do I," Jet said to himself.

When the plane touched down, his fears of an ambush resurfaced like an old injury. He held his breath until they were driven to their usual aviation shed. Relief flooded through him upon seeing Grantham, Mckenzey, Latisha, Eric, and some teachers step out to greet them.

"Our welcoming committee," suggested Asher as the bus slowed to a stop. "I hope they brought some food. I'm starving."

He wasn't the only one to feel the excitement as hugs and embraces were freely given. Seyanna watched him, beaming radiantly.

"Is that for your excitement and being back or how I handled Jayco's question?" Jet asked.

"Both." There was a playful twinkle in her eye. "He's not entirely on board, but his answer could've been worse."

"I can see that."

The canoe was the last item removed from the plane and immediately tied to the bus.

Seyanna was pulled into several different conversations as Latisha, Grantham, Principal Smuin, other students, and teachers wanted to hear how she was doing. She cheerfully answered dozens of questions.

Someone bumped their hip into his, and he tore his eyes away and found Mckenzey examining him. Her face was slightly sunken as if she hadn't eaten or slept in a few days. Her brown hair partially blocked her golden-brown eyes. Leaning in, she hugged him, remaining attached to him for as long as she could. She whispered, "Was going back to Dillon Lake all you thought it would be? I missed you."

He delayed answering as his heart fluttered on its own, but it wasn't like that had never happened before. He broke the embrace and said, "Missed you as well. Dillon Lake was a mess. I'll be glad if I never have to go back."

"A Chupovana, huh? Every time I am not around, you make a mess of things."

"Tell me about it. They had some Azurites still in the school. One was working with Faunal."

"What?" Mckenzey appeared as if she wanted to lean into him.

"He said that he'd made a deal with Faunal. Help kill us, and he wouldn't die himself."

"What a deal." After a moment, she added, "But honestly, if I didn't have magic and that deal was presented, I might take it."

Jet's head tilted, and he considered Mckenzey. She had been distant and irritated with him just a few days ago. "Are you okay? You seem different."

"Just going through some things. Nothing you need to worry about." She straightened, and the sweetest smile crossed her face like someone had turned on a light switch. "Eric, over here."

They walked toward the bus. The various students and teachers converged. Jet introduced the new arrivals, "We have four students from Dillon Lake. This is Glue, Elliott, Yuki, and Mikey. We are also playing host to the Myntra sisters. They have some suggestions on how to keep Chadwick's safe, especially for what's coming up."

Principal Smuin, standing next to Professor Namish and Professor Dickerson, exclaimed, "My counterpart won't be thrilled, but he barely survived the attack from a Chupovana. Let's quickly get on the bus back to campus, where we'll want a full accounting of what happened."

Nolan asked, "Did you hear about Melvin?"

"Unfortunately," replied Professor Namish. "We've contacted his parents. They'll fly to New York to get his body. We've also heard from the Brotherhood, and they'll be returning to Dillon Lake and sending additional representatives to all boarding schools."

Jayco asked, "Was anything found at the other schools?"

"Not as far as I've heard," she said. "The search of Chadwick's ended an hour ago. Another reason I'm focused on returning to school."

"Time to get onto the bus," announced Professor Dickerson.

Seyanna tried sitting next to Jet, but Professor Namish forced her to sit with Nolan while Jet sat with Keesha. It was a clear and purposeful maneuver. He tried not to show his disappointment as he chatted with Keesha as the bus left the airport.

Partway back to school, Principal Smuin stood and peered at the new arrivals. He asked, "Did one of you say you were Elliott? I've heard that name before."

Elliott sighed. "I'm one of the students they thought was killed when the school was attacked a few weeks ago. I didn't know who to trust, so I lived in the school sewers. Jet found me, and I didn't want to go back to school. If you could wait to announce that I survived. I want to try to explain things to my parents first."

"What a predicament," said Principal Smuin.

Jet learned new things about Keesha during the bus ride. He was surprised to learn that her older brother refused to attend Chadwick's and that her younger sister intends to go to Valley Sun in Florida next year.

"What does he think of you being able to do magic?"

"Jealous," she said, then laughed. "He says that I get all the cool things in life." She added, "Cool, dangerous, and likely to kill me."

"Kill all of us," muttered Jet.

The northern gate of Chadwick's boarding school came into view, and Jet was startled by how much it had changed. It had tripled in size, and someone sat in a booth, pushing a button to allow visitors to enter or leave. The campus had an East Coast feel with large trees, several cobblestone walkways, and magnificent buildings. However, compared to the sophistication of Dillon Lake, it could be viewed as inferior. But not in Jet's eyes. He let out a sigh of relief that they were home.

As they stopped at the front gate, Grantham asked, "Where's Darium?"

"In a secret location," answered Jayco. "We didn't see him at all."

"We saw him once," said Maria. "Darium was taken to another room for...how do you say...*interrogatorio*." Her accent accentuated the last word in Spanish.

Phoebe answered, "Interrogation."

"Exactly."

Allison added, "I heard he was there for one night and then taken to a secret Brotherhood hideout."

"Really," said Professor Namish, her voice skeptical.

Gleam spoke. "That is precisely what happened. I questioned him for an hour. He refused to speak. The Brotherhood has six primary compounds. Chances are he was taken to one of them for enlightenment. I wouldn't recommend visiting if you have a choice. They're intense."

The bus parked near the CeU parking lot, and the sun was just starting to set.

Principal Smuin stood and announced, "Those who went to Dillon Lake and the Myntra should follow Professor Namish, and we'll get you settled. We ordered some food, and the rest of you should head to the second floor of the CeU building. Tables and chairs have been set up. We'll spend an hour debriefing the last few weeks. Two additional teachers, three Runics, and two non-magical students will be part of the discussion. They should be made aware of what you've experienced, and having student deaths is unacceptable."

"Wait," said Jayco. "That wasn't all our fault."

He continued, "The next few weeks are equally important. Many of you are far behind. We have some ways to make up the work. The Predilectors and Myntra might need to be called in to corroborate what is said."

Tominiko groaned, "Do you know what we've been through?"

"No, I don't," Principal Smuin noted. "That is the precise reason we need to hear firsthand what happened."

The CeU building was one of the largest on campus, featuring three gyms on different floors. The basement was recently transformed into a medical clinic equipped with X-ray capabilities, exam rooms, oxygen therapy, and other medical treatments. The top of the building held two restaurants. Porter's was more of an outdoor café, offering hamburgers, fries, ice cream, and more, while The View was a typical restaurant with a great view of Santa Barbara Bay. Their specialty was Sunday Brunch, but they had excellent sit-down dining every day of the week.

College Avenue divided the campus into east and west sides. The northern gate went back to Santa Barbara, and the southern gate connected to the 101 Scenic Highway. The dorm buildings, bookstore, three cafeterias, and most classrooms were on the west side. The CeU building, administration buildings, staff apartments, most sports fields, and several parking lots were on the east side.

They mounted the stairs to the second level and found half the gym set up. Sandwiches, chips, soda, and cookies were being unloaded onto a table. Famished, Jet took two of each and sat at a table with Grantham, Latisha, and Seyanna. He ate slowly, in silence. Mckenzey, Eric, Keesha, and Maria sat at the next table, and the rest found their own tables.

As he finished his first sandwich, the inner door opened, and Jessiva, Clyde, and Trina Madden walked in. Jet was mildly surprised to see who Shane Fallon sent to listen and that he hadn't come to gloat. Jet was not a fan of any of them.

Upon learning he had magical abilities, he confided in Mckenzey first. Shane, wanting to find out who in the group had abilities, tried to bully Jet into talking. Jessiva, Clyde, and other Runics had cornered him and Mckenzey. It deteriorated into a skirmish, and he'd been punched a few times. Mckenzey jumped in to help, kicked Jessiva, and the girl had never forgiven either of them.

Trina Madden was another story. She was attacked early in the school year. Everyone had believed it was just the worst sunburn in history. When she recovered, it was discovered that Shane had attacked her with this powder. Instead of hating him, she joined him, becoming infatuated. She had gone to school in Silverton, like Jet, and lived in the same town that had been destroyed. For the life of him, Jet couldn't understand why she had sided with Shane.

Grantham whispered, "When Shane learned that Julian had double-crossed him, he went ballistic. He was in the inner circle and one of the bearers of the Nimliaki. Can you guess who he nominated to take his place?"

Jet groaned. "Don't tell me it was Trina."

"It was."

Principal Smuin moved to the front, pulling out two chairs. "I would like Jet Black and Jayco Carter to come to the front. It will be best to hear from them directly."

Jet took a sip from his soda and decided to take the entire can with him. He was going to wink at Seyanna, but found that she and Mckenzey were staring at each other.

Once they were front and center, Principal Smuin said loudly, "Let's invite our teachers to join us."

Through the same door the Runics entered, Jet watched as Professors Marcella, Rufian, Cheio, Sidewinder, and Gimshe walked in.

"Guess 'two teachers' was an understatement," said Jayco.

"A better group to evaluate your choices," Principal Smuin replied.

Jet's mouth fell open upon seeing Marcella. She smirked on seeing his reaction. As a witch with the Coven, she had been cursed to remain in the water. Somehow, she had made a pact with Shane, allowing her to come onto land but could only go a few hundred feet from the shore. Marcella had tried bewitching Jet, Jayco, and Grantham.

Principal Smuin stood off to one side, joining Professor Dickerson and the new additions. Rufian, Sidewinder, and Gimshe were Axenkind from Svalbard Island, and they didn't appear happy to be here. At present, they appeared like any other human, but in their true form, they had colorful skin and hair. They specialized in defensive tactics and sword fighting, and most of the students loved them. The Axenkind and the Coven could be most easily described as enemies.

Professor Namish spoke. "We request that Jet describe what took place at Dillon Lake. What happened to Melvin Sacco?"

Jet hesitated for a second. He hadn't even known the boy's last name. When he spoke, he did so slowly. He described the moment they arrived at campus, meeting with Principal Berry, then Karl Middlesex, and eventually seeing the detained students. He gave no background information on the ancient man.

Jet recounted dinner and how he and Jayco were taken to meet with Melvin. Then Jet explained their attempts to leave campus, how the original plan was altered, getting into the sewers, escaping, and fighting the Chupovana.

Marcella asked, "Whose plan was it to take the sewers?"

Seyanna answered, "Principal Berry and Cicerone Middlesex devised the plan—"

"I wasn't asking you," barked Professor Marcella.

Jet said, "We woke up to a shell game with helicopters, boats, and a limousine. But when we descended the stairs, the plan had changed."

Professor Cheio asked, "How did Melvin die?"

"We don't know exactly," said Jet. "The Chupovanas, Quills, and some Predilectors attacked the building. It exploded."

Professor Cheio asked, "Whose choice was it to leave Melvin alone?"

"Alone?" asked Jet. "We were guests and had no say in any of that. We were to meet him at the Depot."

"Interesting," said Professor Dickerson. "That's not what we heard."

Jayco retorted. "That's exactly what the plan was. We were not permitted to walk around campus on our own."

"How did a Chupovana get onto campus?" asked Rufian. "Why did you have to fight it?"

"We lured it away from school so that they could seal it closed. There was a Predilector working with the Khalicaan. Uri Gideon." He explained about Taraqeu, the ten spellbound humans, the Quills, and the Scorepos.

Principal Smuin listened intently, then said, "You left Dillon Lake to fend for themselves. The Chupovana will certainly attack again."

Jet said nothing.

Professor Marcella asked, "Don't you think you were strong enough to defeat this Chupovana inside the school? It seems that you were mistaken in your strategy."

Jet was about to defend his actions when Principal Smuin raised his hand to silence him. Jessiva, Clyde, and Trina chortled as if he had failed miserably to explain something.

"There were twenty-five students killed at Dillon Lake, along with two professors," said Principal Smuin. "Principal Berry broke his leg. It was a downright disaster."

A musical voice spoke, but her words were harsh. Gleam, standing in the doorway with Professor Namish, said, "These questions are nonsense. Strength is often defeated by wisdom, and it should rarely be used to force an obstacle to move, especially one as crafty. Taraqeu and the Khalicaan planned this for months. They found an abandoned home and dug until they found a weakness in the school's security. Beyond that, they set a trap for the Mikado and his friends. If they had fought on campus, hundreds would have perished."

Principal Smuin asked, "Who are you again?"

Gleam bristled at the question, her black robes parted to reveal her chest plate and weapons. "We are the Myntra and work closely with the Brotherhood. But we are heirs to the Hayawan Kin, and we are allies of the Mikado."

The color drained from Principal Smuin, and it was clear he was familiar with them. He muttered, "We apologize. We had heard from a contact at Dillon Lake that things had gone afoul."

"Who is your contact?" asked Faris.

"I would rather not say."

Elliot, Glue, Mikey, and Yuki also entered. Elliot said, "The entire thing was a trap. They killed Dart, drawing Jet to return. I was tricked."

"What kind of trap?" asked Professor Namish.

"Once we exited the school and went through the abandoned house, the Chupovana found us quickly. It was after something." Elliott glanced over at Jet.

"Yes," said Professor Marcella.

Jet spoke. "We know that Chupovanas can sense magic. It brought ten bewitched humans with white stones. The Myntra explained that if the stones touch the magical, we're drained of our magic. Completely."

Jade said, "I was hit by the stone. It will hopefully wear off."

"What was the Khalicaan searching for?" demanded Marcella.

"A lost artifact," replied Jet. "We did not have it, so they attacked, intending on—."

Trina interrupted, "You're telling us you couldn't stop a few entranced humans. What kind of leader are you?"

Jayco replied, "They moved so fast. Combined with all the defenses around them. Without the help of the Myntra, a few of us would have lost our magic today."

Trina hooted, "Guess Jet isn't as all-powerful as he thinks he is."

Marcella put her hand to her mouth, hiding a smile.

Professor Sidewinder said, "The Harbor Crystals should not be overlooked. They can only be touched by humans. Often, they are used in secret, as a punishment, or as a torture device. I had hoped they had been lost long ago. Humans who touch them are immune to magical injuries themselves. Even a golden blade wouldn't harm them. If they had touched Iris, she would have lost her life. Only once, during the Ataga War, have I heard of ten stones being used at once. This was indeed a trap to destroy Elemental magic."

Jet said, "It almost worked."

Mckenzey asked, "What was the Ataga War?"

"Genuinely, that war is the most mysterious of all the wars in the time of the 10 Kings," explained Rufian. "As far as I understand, a Shade was born, and some believed it was working with the Silver Fox. Many people were massacred. The Grey Panther demanded that the Silver Fox be removed from the Council. She, in turn, blamed the Grey Panther, and the first inklings of deception and disunity began to emerge in the Council. The Shade created the Balakcursen tribe, and the war was severe. There was also a disconnect between the involvement of the Skeleton and his minions. The Grey Panther was nearly defeated, but the Shade came to his defense. The truth became known to many, and evil, lurking on the horizon, was unleashed. The Grey Panther became the leader of the Shade, Faunal, the Skeleton, and the Demon Kirche. Jet has slain Kirche, but other adversaries are preparing for the release of Arisol. This inquiry has revealed that evil is cunning."

"That was dramatic," said Marcella, but the room had fallen silent.

Jet felt paralyzed by the depth of what he heard, and the connections *The Sorcerer's Guide* had given him. He had watched the Shade create the Balakcursen tribe and knew it had killed an oracle.

Marcella continued, "Professor Darnshaw is correct about most things." She spoke using Rufian's professorial name.

Jet glanced over at Jayco, and the boy was staring at Marcella as if he wanted to reach over and strangle her. His expression of blood thirst unsettled Jet's nerves. Reaching out, he touched Jayco's arm, and the boy snapped out of his trance.

"Thanks," Jayco whispered. "She bothers me."

Marcella continued, "The Shade is an outright mystery. Some believe he is a figment of the Council's imagination, used to protect against the true person responsible."

Rufian replied, "We know you are on Arisol's side, witch. Stop mudding the waters."

"Enough," said Principal Smuin. "We need to return to the issues at hand. Death has become prevalent at every turn. Melvin at Dillon Lake, Ruby at Spruce Knob, and Lucas, Quinn, and Victoria in Congo. I heard there were others as well, like Julian. These deaths are unacceptable."

A lump formed in Jet's throat. He had witnessed many of these deaths, and they were his responsibility.

Trina emphasized, "Don't forget Kevin McCormick, who once walked these streets, wasn't killed by a mythical beast but by Jet Black in combat."

"What happened to you? You're from Silverton." Seyanna glared at Trina. "Kevin was working with the rebel Charlie Eckenkeep, and they kidnapped me. Jet, Jayco, and others saved me. Kevin became perverted."

Jayco said, "There were Runics who witnessed it."

Principal Smuin said, "I've spoken with each of them. There are still some unanswered questions."

"Like what?" Grantham asked, standing and joining Jet and Jayco. Soon, Mckenzey, Eric, Keesha, and every other Elemental stood next to them. The Myntra and those from Dillon Lake did as well.

Principal Smuin continued, though his voice was less accusatory. "Why was Julian there? Why were the other members of Shane's group and students from Dillon Lake helping you? How did Ruby die?"

Em spoke, her voice bitter. "The Azurites are deceitful. They sent students to infiltrate Dillon Lake, Chadwick's, and the other boarding schools. Julian was one of them, as was Darium Fitz. We will break him. I believe you hired his father, one of the leaders of the syndicate."

"I didn't," he blustered.

"See how accusations can be misleading," said Em. She continued, "Charlie tricked even the highest within the Brotherhood. We have been sent to help track him down and protect the school during the next phase."

"Really?" asked Jet.

"What phase?" asked Professor Namish.

Em said, "The Azurites want to stop the Rivalry and prevent magic from advancing. Julian, Darium, and anyone else who has died are casualties of war. They are not unimportant, but they can't help us now. The Brotherhood demands that Chadwick's continue the course. The worst has yet to take place. We have a lot to do."

Principal Smuin nodded and considered what he wanted to ask. "Why was Julian there?"

Jayco told how they had found Julian and Marapi, and about the battle outside Kal Beni.

The principal asked, "Are you saying they used Julian's hand to remove the black items? Is that even possible?"

"It is," said Jet.

Seyanna added, "It's why my father kidnapped me. To force me to move the golden items."

Principal Smuin stepped forward and leaned on the side of a table. He muttered, "Convenient for Shane to avoid mentioning that to me."

"He didn't," said Jessiva. "He didn't know the extent of things."

Principal Smuin cut her off quickly. "Things are worse than I was led to believe. Death is never something that should just be buried. I hope we can have a quiet next few weeks to end the school year. I trust you have no additional adventures planned."

"Well...not exactly," Jet said loudly.

Professor Namish demanded, "Where are you thinking of running off to?"

"Nowhere. Chadwick's is about to become the party of the century. We will be inviting dozens of people from each boarding school and each tribe. If we're lucky, all the boarding schools will have magic by the end of next week. Party commences this weekend."

"What?" cried Marcella.

Jet said casually, "Didn't you know? We've found the other three books. We plan to invite students from Dillon Lake, San Mateo, Cranbrook Summit, and Valley Sun to come to Chadwick's and see if magic chooses them. The plans are in place, and the invitations have been sent. It's about time we turn our full attention to defeating Arisol."

CHAPTER 22

As the meeting ended, Jet wanted nothing more than to disappear, escape to their hideout, and soak for an hour. The Axenkind clay soak, the Vetex, would help his magical energy and his physical pains. He needed some serious recovery, with the muscles in his legs, his ribs, and both shoulders screaming out in pain each time he moved.

Principal Smuin left after saying, "Take the rest of the morning off. But you need to be in your classes this afternoon. You have the week to catch up on things. Each of you has homework assignments, some projects, and one debate topic to prepare. Those assignments will be dropped off tonight. To finish the year, you'll need to do more than just accomplish each assignment. Miss one and you'll regret it."

The door closed, and Jet thanked the others for joining him, defending him.

Rufian bowed his head, and the three Axenkind professors left the building. He hoped to talk with them tomorrow in their Defensive Movements class. The Myntra were assigned to stay in an apartment assigned for parents or visitors. Professor Namish had assigned rooms to the Predilectors, and Eric and Raul were designated mentors for all new students.

Jayco suggested, "We'll have some eyes on us for the next few hours. Get some rest. Let's head down to our secret hideout just before dinner."

"Fine," said Jet.

Grantham said, "I'll tell the others."

Jet lied, feeling several eyes on him, "I think my tome is about to open. I need to get back to my room. See you." This abrupt departure was nothing new. He had suddenly felt an overwhelming need to make sure the other Phoenix pieces were where they should be. He had the fourth one in his secret compartment, but Shane now had one. That would need to be rectified soon.

From across the room, Jet heard Professor Dickerson ask, "Seyanna Motick, can you stay behind with Grantham, and five others, so we can arrange a schedule to protect the school? Things have been a disaster since you left. The mirrors haven't been entirely reliable."

"No problem," said Seyanna, walking opposite to Jet, but eyeing him closely.

Jet slipped out a door on the inner section of the building, ran down a level, and ducked out a side door. He turned south, avoided the staff apartments, crossed a field, and kept to the back side of the football field. Five minutes later, he crossed College Avenue, near the southern gate, and found the path leading down to the beach. It was once hidden, but was now well-known.

The path had become more prominent and easier to descend, with many trees and boulders removed. He remained concealed off the path and within the remaining trees. The instant he stepped onto the sand, he turned left and into a small crevice between the rock wall leading to an entrance door, accessible only to those who had been given a necklace with a shark's tooth.

He placed the tip of the tooth in his mouth and positioned it near a small hole, like a panel beside the entrance. The solid outer rock vanished, revealing a doorway and a hallway. Stepping in, as always, he wondered what he would do if he were not allowed to enter. After a few quick steps, the solid rock wall reappeared.

Swiping sweat from his forehead, he felt relieved that it wasn't the beginning of the school year, when the temperatures had been significantly hotter. He would have been drenched in sweat. A heat wave had crippled the entire lower forty-eight states. It had been associated with the fifth disaster, the one linked to Spruce Knob. The four previous disasters had occurred about eleven months apart, and Jet and his friends had located the missing Phoenix pieces at each site. The first was in Silverton, Oregon, and the second in Catamarca, Argentina. The third had been Starbuck Island, the fourth in Congo, and the fifth at Spruce Knob. That left one remaining in the next few months, and after that, Arisol would be released. He was far from ready and wasn't sure he would ever be.

The hideout was empty, and he sighed with relief. Beyond the hallway, the space opened into a large area with a television, table, fire pit, refrigerator, couches, and the old hallway, which was the previous entrance. The entire hideout was built into the rock wall and was nearly impossible to penetrate. To his immediate left was another hallway breaking off from this central space—which held a room containing the Vetex. A spiral staircase led up to the second floor, where the weapons were stored. Those they had retrieved from Spruce Knob would join the other unclaimed golden weapons stored there. They had swords, maces, shields, and everything else they could gather.

Bunk beds were positioned on the first floor near the end of the Vetex hallway. All four soaking chambers were empty, and instead of picking the first, he went to the last one. He quickly undressed, pulled out some swim shorts, and descended into the mud-like sludge. It was a wonderful and disconcerting feeling, as if he were being pampered by the most capable group of massage therapists in existence, yet it felt foreign, as if it were created for someone else. Every muscle knot, injury, dislocation, and bruise began improving forthwith.

He'd entered the Vetex for the first time with Seyanna on Svalbard Island, in a place called the Cherished Soaks, with the monarch of the Axenkind. She lived in the substance and spoke to them telepathically, but only if they touched the same material simultaneously. Sinain was wise and insightful. He'd thought about her admonitions many times. She had taught him about the history of Ella and Tigerus and had advised on how to defeat Chaos inside the Heart of Demaro.

But his mind now centered on her other words—He had asked:

"How can I help the other magical groups?"

"You need to find them and form a truce. Give the gifts of their animals, and this will bring forth great pleasure and joy."

"I hear that the other forms of magic were lost."

"There's a difference between lost and hidden. But it's true, the other magic groups have far less magical ability. First, because of the Rivalry, and second, their books are concealed."

"Any idea where?" he'd asked.

"Some. But not anything concrete."

He shook his head and completely submerged himself, staying under for as long as he could. His need for oxygen diminished, and he remerged ten minutes later, a new personal record. He pushed the

Vetex out of his eyes and sat back. He had discovered the other magical books. Sinain had given him the pyramids for the other three groups. She had understood the importance of having all five of the magic types found, healthy, and growing. Jet needed to make this happen—and soon. A truce must be formed.

He remained in the Vetex for seventy-five minutes, and when he withdrew, he had renewed energy, relief, and determination. The sludge dripped off his body, fell onto the floor, and edged back into the pool of its own accord.

He sent out a group text, saying, "*Guys. I'm at the hideout. I need ten minutes. Let's meet before class. I have some things to explain.*"

"I knew I would find you here."

His head shot up, and he found Mckenzey standing next to the doorway, wearing a cherry-red swimsuit. He couldn't help but smile. She sauntered in his direction, her hips swaying, and her eyes never left him.

"Will you join me?"

He mumbled, "Any excuse for more recovery."

Mckenzey sat on the edge of the third chamber and dipped both feet in. She then leaned over and felt the temperature with her hand. Winking playfully, she slipped into the substance as Jet returned to the fourth one.

"I've never seen our friends so divided yet so unified," said Mckenzey mischievously. "Many feel isolated, unable to learn magic, while others have nearly been killed."

Jet wondered if a hint of playfulness masked that annoyance in her tone. He guessed she was irked by Seyanna and for not being asked to go to Dillon Lake. "You're probably right," he said. "I haven't been the best leader. So many people have died. I wish I had made different choices."

Mckenzey leaned forward; her eyes met his. "I didn't expect you to say that."

"Shane beat us to the fifth piece. Seyanna was kidnapped, and several people died. I get an update from *The Sorcerer's Guide* at the worst time, and I can't remember who I've said what to. I came here to think about how to improve things. Any suggestions?"

She didn't answer this question but asked, "Why did you send some of us to Chadwick's and didn't allow us to come to Dillon Lake? We could have helped with Taraqeu."

"Or more people could have been killed."

"That's not what Jayco thinks," said Mckenzey quickly.

A few pieces of understanding fell into place. He asked, "What else did Jayco say?"

"That you're purposely keeping things you learn in your book from us."

"He's not wrong." Jet had decided to tell the truth. "But he's not completely right either. There are things that I've been explicitly told not to divulge. Some of it concerns magical spells, advanced information, and other concepts."

Mckenzey's mouth dropped open. After another few seconds, she adds, "You could choose to tell us anyway."

Jet thought about this answer, and it was the same one he'd considered. "What if I did and the book stopped opening?"

"Would it?"

"I'm not sure," he said truthfully. "But I worry it could happen." Another moment later, he said, "People have died, and they'll continue to do so...because of *my* choices. That's a hard pill to swallow. I wonder if Jayco has ever considered that?"

"He has a group of supporters that push him to say things behind your back." This time, her voice was less bothered. "He disagreed with staying and fighting the Chupovana. Professor Namish overheard him talking and asked to have a private conversation. That's when I left."

"What other students was he talking with?"

She hesitated. "The three Runics – Jessiva, Clyde, and Trina, along with Maverick with Water magic, Piper with Spirit magic, Gabriella with Earth magic, and Navaeh with Fire magic. There were another five or so. You ran off quickly, and the Runics demanded answers. I only saw them because they asked Eric to join the meeting about border security."

Jet's feeling of renewed energy dipped slightly. "Sorry you have been put in this position."

"I want to help."

"I know, and I appreciate it. But I bet it also feels weird talking about Jayco in this manner."

"He's changed."

Jet's eyebrows rose. "He wishes he had been chosen to be the Mikado. He had a few chances in leadership and failed."

"He still blames you."

Jet wanted to exit the Vetex, find Jayco, and shake him until the boy could see clearly. Being the Mikado was nothing but impossible, exhausting, and demoralizing. "Whatever Jayco tells people, I don't choose when *The Sorcerer's Guide* opens and what it reveals to me or who I can share it with."

Mckenzey said, "I know that. I remember when it was just you and me who knew about magic. Remember when we thought everyone else would reject us?"

Jet laughed. "I do."

"We were a team back then."

"We still are."

"A team, yes, but it's not just you and me any longer." A flash of her annoyance returned.

"What's really going on?" he asked.

Mckenzey ground her teeth. "You're such a frustrating boy."

"About what?" he protested.

"Seyanna!" Mckenzey shrilled emphatically. "Why would you tell Jayco before the rest of us that you and Seyanna are together?"

"I didn't…" blurted Jet, then he stopped immediately. A minute later, he asked, "What exactly did Jayco say?"

"He went on and on gushing about him and Rozene. Then he added that you and Seyanna were trying to outdo their love affair. He caught you getting cozy and admitted that you guys have been a couple since before she was kidnapped."

"Wow," said Jet. "None of that is true."

"To make matters worse. When Jayco told us, Marcella walked by at that exact time, saying how cute you and Seyanna looked together. Jayco had added, 'See!'"

Grantham tried to say nonchalantly—that it wasn't a big deal. But Jayco insisted he'd heard that you and Seyanna slept together. His final jab was that 'Melvin would never have died if he had been in charge.'"

Jet's anger began to boil, but he forced himself to remain calm. More pieces had fallen into place. "You know that Marcella is excellent at identifying our weaknesses and exploiting them. She's trying to divide the group. She's got something planned."

"That's what Grantham said, but several people walked off with Jayco."

Well, Seyanna and I weren't kissing on the airplane. Jayco knows this; he was sitting right behind us. I don't know what's going through his head. Seyanna fell asleep in a chair, and I moved her to the bed."

"Have you kissed Seyanna?"

Okay. Now we're getting to the crux of the conversation. He had the option of avoiding the question, deflecting, or answering. "Yes. We have."

Mckenzey's mouth opened then closed. She remained silent for a few more seconds. "Does that mean that you're together?"

"We are not," said Jet honestly. "Jayco asked that question on the plane. And I told him the same thing I'm going to tell you. Seyanna and I have had no chance to talk. It could have been a one-time thing or not."

"What do you want?"

Jet said, "I'm worried that a relationship will fail, and I'm equally worried about not trying."

"You should try," she said, but her voice was distant and hurt. "What's the worst that can happen?"

An unintended chortle escaped his mouth. He considered switching to Eric but thought that would be a poor tactic. "We'll see," he said, barely above a whisper. They sat in silence for several minutes. When his emotions were better under control, he asked, "What's happened on campus since you got back?"

"We were put under house arrest. Principal Smuin had reports and wanted confirmation on certain events that had occurred. Shane beat us back to Chadwick's by two days. I heard he was rubbing our noses in it for the first several hours until Jocelyn came back with the news that Julian had double-crossed them."

"What did he think Julian was doing?"

"I heard from a Runic in my math class that Shane was enraged with how Congo turned out. Shane had a similar plan to yours and divided his forces. He thought Julian had a way to get to Congo without any problems. He sent Trina and several other students with him. They got ambushed. Rumor has it that Julian summoned a Predilector from Dillon Lake whose talent is to cause whomever she touches to doze off. She came to Congo and brushed up against the entire group, entrapping them, allowing Julian to make a clean getaway. The girl stayed with the group for the next few days."

"That's a bold risk."

"The plan was for Julian to go missing and blame you."

"And why not," hissed Jet. "What about Sarika?"

"She has been placed in lockdown. No one will tell us if that's on campus or not. There are others as well. I heard she was visited by Rufian and revealed a few things."

"Is Raul feeling better?"

"I think. I haven't seen him much either. No one from the Elementals or Runics has been allowed to get together in large groups. Principal Smuin keeps saying it was just until you got back safely, but I think there might be something worrisome going on with the school's borders. What happened in Dillon Lake won't make anyone less paranoid."

Jet said, "It was crazy to see the entrance to the sewer. I bet they had been working on finding a way in for a few weeks."

"How would they know that you would come back?"

"Not sure exactly. That changed, though, with the arrival of some of the Elementals with Darium. I never considered a Chupovana attacking Dillon Lake. We need to do something to ensure all the boarding schools are safe."

"Like what?"

Before he answered, he heard Jayco call from the entrance. "Hello. Anyone here?"

Jet's anger boiled, and he was ready to lash out at Jayco. "In here."

Jayco and Grantham entered first, and a roguish smile crossed Jayco's face. An instant later, Seyanna, Latisha, Keesha, Eric, and Maria followed behind.

Jet asked casually, "Anybody else need a good soak?"

"We're good," said Grantham. "Maybe later. Are you ready for us?"

"Sure."

"We'll wait," said Jayco forcefully. "Until you guys are finished. It'll give Eric, Grantham, and me a chance to do an inventory of the items and add the new ones we retrieved from Congo and Spruce Knob to our stash."

"Wait," Jet said. "Don't do anything. We need to talk first."

"More news," hissed Eric. "Why am I not surprised?"

Latisha, ignoring the tension, came and sat next to the pool where Mckenzey sat. She removed her shoes and dangled her legs in. Jet motioned for Seyanna to come, but she shook her head slightly, and she leaned against the wall.

"Hey, Latisha," said Jet. "How are things?"

She looked worn down, confused, and unsteady. Her makeup had been placed with an unsteady hand. Her clothes were wrinkled, and her eyes flicked back and forth. She said quickly, "Pretty good. How about you?"

Jet said, "Better now. A few more days of the Vetex and I'll be as good as new."

A silence fell over the room. Keesha, Maria, Raul, Autumn, and Ariana stayed back, as if not part of the conversation. Jet knew that

Latisha wanted to say something, but he couldn't imagine what it was. She stared at the pool of clay as it slowly bubbled repeatedly. Jet shifted, sitting up and looking directly at her.

The words began to pour out all at once, "I've been invited. I need to leave the Elementals. Professor Gimshe asked me. She says that I have an aptitude she hasn't seen in humans before. It's like I can see a moment in the battle happen before it does."

Raising both hands, Jet said, "Can you please slow down?"

A tinge of a smile played at the corner of her mouth. "Sorry. I hate the idea of disappointing you."

"What are you talking about, Latisha? Not possible."

"Professor Gimshe approached me a few days ago. I haven't slept since. I didn't even tell Grantham." She looked for him, then mouthed...I'm sorry. She continued, "The Axenkind are preparing for war. They're manufacturing and distributing weapons to various parts of the world. They've asked that I become part of their mission. I will get personal training with specific weapons and will become one of their commanders. If I choose this, I might need to leave the Elementals and maybe Chadwick's."

"Not happening," said Grantham. "Jet, you tell her."

"Please," whimpered Latisha. She started to silently cry.

Jet lifted both hands. Grantham's face became neutral, and he stepped back. After a moment, Jet asked, "Why can't you do both? We need you, and you're the best in school with the Axenkind weapons. I can't imagine Rufian and the others would ask that you leave the Rivalry. I'll talk to him."

Latisha said softly, "I *want* to become a commander with the Axenkind."

"No doubt."

"They did tell me that at the end of the school year, they want me to travel with Gimshe and Sidewinder to Svalbard Island and meet the infamous blacksmith who creates most of their weapons."

"I bet you'll have a blast, Latisha," Jet said honestly. I encourage you to do both. We can't lose you. Every Elemental, and especially every Echoes, is vital to our success. We'll make it work."

She stood and said, "When you get dried off, I'm going to give you a hug." She hurried from the room.

"Gladly."

He and Mckenzey exited their pools and began drying off. No one else had left the area, and when Jet glanced over at Seyanna, her eyes were wide as she took in Mckenzey's swimsuit. Eric appeared to be on the verge of exploding. Autumn covered her mouth, preventing herself from laughing.

Mckenzey whispered, unaware that anyone was staring, "That was nice of you. From what I've heard, I'm not sure the Axenkind will let her do both."

"Are you two about done?" demanded Jayco. "Why did you send that text if you were just having some quiet time with Mckenzey?"

"She arrived after I sent the text. Relax."

Eric growled, "Are we putting these golden items away, or are we going to have some Elementals see if these weapons choose them?"

"I need to talk with you first, then we can decide what happens next."

"This is annoying," said Jayco. "If you have something to say...then say it. Why are you being so unhelpful?"

"Do you want to know what *The Sorcerer's Guide* told me or not?" asked Jet coldly. "If you don't want to be here, then leave."

"That's enough," said Grantham.

Jet didn't stop. "He complains when he's not informed and complains when I'm trying to share some information."

"It's been a long day," said Grantham. "That's it."

"Let's table the discussion until later," said Jet, and he walked toward his clothes.

"I want to hear," said Latisha. "If you called us here, it has to be important."

"I agree," said Mckenzey.

"You would," whispered Eric, but Jet heard.

"I need to get an item before we talk," said Jet. "It was sent by Nana ages ago. Give me a second."

As he hurried away, he heard Jayco mutter, "He couldn't have had it ready for us when we arrived."

"Knock it off," said Seyanna.

Maces hung on the left wall of the weapon room, and there were spears, bows and arrows, and more. Armor, some shields, and other items were placed on the right side of the room. Along the back wall were several unique weapons and swords awaiting the right person to choose them. Anyone could use some of the golden weapons, while others could only be used by a single person.

"Where's that crate?" murmured Jet. Moving to the left corner, he moved a few items and found the crate Nana had sent him at the beginning of the year. Throwing it open, he pulled out the necklace.

Rushing back, he found Grantham and Jayco whispering.

"Did you find what you were looking for?" asked Latisha uncomfortably.

"I did." He pulled out a green gaudy necklace.

Rolling his eyes, Jayco scoffed, "What the hell are you talking about? This is stupid and a complete waste of my time. I could be calling Rozene right now."

Jet lost control. He spoke "Vesta," concentrating on Jayco and no one else. He knew he had the option of pain or fear. He chose fear. The color of Jayco's face paled, and his eyes widened.

"What are you doing?" Jayco demanded, stepping back once, then twice.

Jet advanced. "Getting your attention."

CHAPTER 23

Arms wrapped tightly around Jet, and he was lifted into the air. He was spitting mad and wanted to attack Jayco relentlessly. He cried, "Let go of me."

"Not until you end your spell," grunted a voice in his ear.

Grantham spun Jet, and the instant he could no longer see Jayco, his anger faded. He let the spell end. He was set down but knew instantly that it wasn't over. Eric, Mckenzey, Seyanna, and the others had stepped into Jayco's path, and he was trying to fight his way over to Jet.

Grantham rushed toward Jayco and said, "It's over."

"Then I'm leaving."

Jet's anger simmered, "No, you're not. Give me five minutes to explain what needs to happen next, then you can go on your way."

"What is it you want to say?"

Jet tossed the greenish-gold necklace to Grantham and asked, "What do you feel when you hold this?"

Grantham caught the item, holding it in both hands, then his face contorted. Jet knew he had felt it.

"Pass it along before answering."

The necklace was circulated from person to person. Keesha held it for a second before giving it to Autumn. Raul said, "Don't make me touch it. I trust you."

Jet inclined his head. Lastly, Jayco held it.

"What do you feel, Jayco?" asked Jet.

"Malice. This item wants Evil to win." The air in Jayco's annoyance vanished.

From his hidden compartment, he pulled out Kevin's silver sword with a broken tip. "Do you feel anything different within this?"

The sword went around. A look of surprise fell onto each of their faces. Lastly, he removed the Fogle Horn and did the same.

"Uncanny," said Seyanna. "What are these things?"

Jayco asked, "The Khalicaan wanted us to give her this horn."

"Yes. Because she knows the true nature of these three items. When Rozene won it, we were told it protects against poisons. I don't think that's the whole truth. I sent part of the group to Dillon Lake, knowing we would return and try to retrieve this item."

"Are they connected?" asked Latisha.

Pulling out *The Sorcerer's Guide*, he read from the tome. First, he recounted the Fisador Pact, which had caused magic to be taken from the world, and how some of the magic was siphoned to an object called the Kindred Loop.

"Do we know what the six items were?" interrupted Maria.

He read, "The six items were given out to the Machitis tribe, the Geistes, the Khalicaans, the Coven, the Wandering Nomads, and the Narvanians. They became known as the Insidious Six. The Insidious Six included, an eighteen-inch curved horn, a beautiful and antique green necklace, a book of recipes with a spine of crushed blue amethyst, a silver-bladed sword, a bull's head relic with curved horns and an open mouth carved of red stone, and a jasper crystal dagger without a handle."

"You surmise these three items are part of the Insidious Six?" asked Eric. "That seems to be a stretch."

Jet held up the loop and twirled it in his fingers. "Four items." Picking up the greenish necklace, he said, "The loop and this necklace were sent to me by Nana. My parents or my great-grandfather must've had them. I remember playing with this loop when I was younger."

Jayco said, "Is there a way we can test them?"

Jet read, "These wicked weapons can only be destroyed by the Kindred Loop and the keyword—Uovu Vernietik."

"Intense," said Latisha. "Only one problem. That green necklace is far from striking."

The group chuckled.

As Grantham reached for Latisha's hand, he said, "Eyes of the beholder, babe. I'm sure someone out there thinks it's glamorous."

She countered, "They would be idiots with terrible taste."

"Let's put the items on the ground and circle around them," advised Jet.

The sword, necklace, and horn were placed side by side. The significance of the moment washed over him. He stood up a little straighter, holding the loop firmly. He knew that gripping the amulet would not work. It was designed as a cursive, elegant, lower-case L. He slipped a finger in the top area of the talisman and spun it on his finger. Once, twice, and when it passed over five times, he knew it was time to say the words: "Uovu Vernietik."

A silver flash brightened the room, and the loop transformed into a black mamba coiled around his hand. The snake's deadly eyes matched the silver light from a moment ago, and it spotted the green necklace. It unwound and elongated, pulling its body closer to the piece of jewelry. Jet watched in fascination as it swayed back and forth.

The necklace reacted as if it had been awoken from hibernation. It took less than a second to acclimate, shuddering as if cold, then changing into a hideous creature—a combination of lizard and dinosaur. It was as big as a medium-sized dog but longer, with four legs, a tail, and a lengthened head and massive jaw. The grotesque lizard had green scales, fangs like daggers, and liquid frothing from its mouth, with irregular horns on its back and claws sharp enough to cut through diamonds. The creature lowered as if it were about to spring at Grantham.

The black mamba lunged, and its mouth opened. Black and silver fangs appeared for a millisecond before the creature latched onto the grotesque lizard's neck, never letting go. The end of the snake's tail remained attached to Jet, but barely.

A black smolder of decay spread, consuming the lizard until it was nothing more than black ash. The creature's remnants remained connected for a long time, keeping the same outline, until the ash fell into a pile on the floor.

"Did everyone just see that?" asked Grantham. "That thing was going to attack me."

"Hard to freaking miss," gasped Eric.

Ariana added, "That was somehow wrong and right."

Glancing back at his hand, the mamba returned to its loop form. Jet handed the amulet to Jayco and said, "Hold it steady. Don't let go."

Jayco's fingers shook as he took the amulet. "Are you sure?"

"Give it a whirl."

Jayco spun the amulet; his egotism had entirely evaporated. This time, it rotated seven times, and he spoke "Uovu Vernietik," and the black mamba reappeared. Instantly, the silver sword altered into a silver coyote with fangs, claws, and a long tail. The left ear was missing, as was a patch of hair on its head. It wasted no time, vaulting at Jayco, but the black mamba was ready. Its fangs dug into the coyote's chest, halting its attack and putting it back on the ground. As before, the creature decayed quickly, becoming nothing more than a pile of black ash.

"That was the coolest thing," admitted Jayco. "Who wants a turn?"

Latisha said, "It has to be me." Jayco handed her the loop. Turning to the Fogle Horn, Jet watched a protective transparent barrier spread out over the horn. Latisha spun the loop four times and spoke "Uovu Vernietik," and the snake appeared. It was silent and deadly, but this time, it did not strike; a few moments later, it transformed back into the amulet.

"What happened?" asked Seyanna.

Jet said, "I think the horn has a defense mechanism."

"I sensed it was protected, but I couldn't see anything," said Latisha. "I'll be ready when the time comes." She handed the amulet back to Jet.

"It's clear these three relics are the devilish artifacts from the story," said Grantham. "We still have to find the other three."

"No," said Seyanna. "We have two to find and one to steal."

"What are you talking about?" asked Mckenzey.

"When Charlie was liberated from us, I saw the Azurites using a bull's head with curved horns. It shoots an intense fireball. The Azurites have one of the Insidious Six."

"Two if you count the silver sword," said Autumn.

"That's right," added Grantham.

Jayco said, "We have two items left. How are we going to get the Azurites close to us?"

Jet said, "Announce that we're bringing the other schools to Chadwick's to give them magic."

"That will put all of us in danger," said Eric.

"Not that we already aren't," answered Maria.

"I say we do it," said Keesha. "And I might have a plan."

"What kind of plan?" asked Grantham.

"Remember how I was friends with Chin Nguyen, and now he's at Valley Sun? I could try talking with him and see where it goes. I could let it slip that we have information about the missing books. If there are Azurites at each of the schools, they'll eventually hear the information. We could set up a meeting outside of the school, say at the building where you first met with the Brotherhood."

"That's still on school property, right?" asked Jayco.

"Yes," said Seyanna. "It isn't within the boundaries of the Claustra. I don't think we've patrolled near there in weeks."

"Needs work," said Jet. "But a great start."

Coming forward, Jayco held out one hand and said, "Sorry about earlier."

Jet shook it. "Sorry about shooting a spell at you."

"That was a bit much...but I guess I deserved it. I'll try to chill out. I see you had a plan the entire time."

"Not always." To the others, he said, "Thanks for having my back. I lost it for a second there."

"That's an understatement," replied Grantham.

"Do we actually have the books?" asked Keesha. "The other magical books."

"We do," said Jet. "And the sooner the other schools can get them, the better off we will be."

"You really want to invite the other schools to Chadwick's after all that happened at Dillon Lake?" asked Ariana.

"It's the only way," said Mckenzey.

Jet added, "The sooner the better. I need Grantham or Jayco to tell Principal Smuin, and it needs to be next weekend. Hopefully, we can trick some Azurites."

"Will the other schools come here, and we'll just give them the books?" Seyanna asked.

"No. I think it's going to be more complicated than that." Jet added, "But once that's done, we won't be staying that long."

"What else do we need to do?" asked Eric, more curious than before.

"Remember when Raul, Mckenzey, and I met with Rufian and Marcella to get some information? Before we left for Canada?"

"How could we forget?" joked Jayco.

"I wasn't here. What happened?" Seyanna asked.

Jet explained, "Our research and information from the Myntra and *The Sorcerer's Guide* pointed to a location called the Lagoon of the Arches."

Seyanna shook her head. "Which is what?"

"The location of the missing books," said Jet. "Marcella had a clue, and we needed to get it from her."

Mckenzey's face drained of color.

Jet continued, "I promised Marcella to help find a way to release the Coven's children."

"Where?" asked Latisha.

"Egypt."

"Wow," said Seyanna.

"I know. I'll be leaving for Egypt sometime after we give the three magical books to the other schools." Jet raised a hand to forestall the questions. "I know nothing of the exact plan or who will want to come with me. I just wanted it on your radar."

Jayco said emphatically, "You can't *trust* Marcella."

"True...but trust isn't the issue. I committed to keeping my side of the bargain for the information she provided. We would never have survived that lagoon without her."

"Anything else?" asked Latisha.

"During our trip to Canada, we agreed to help fix the throat or something of one of the Myntra."

Mckenzey said, "They said that it had to be me."

"Exactly," said Jet. "I was hoping I could still count on you."

"Always."

Keesha asked, "When do you plan to leave for Egypt? How many people are you taking?"

"Not sure on both accounts. I'll let you all know."

Jayco stood quickly. "I think this meeting is adjourned."

"Not so fast," said Jet. "One last thing."

"Seriously?" asked Mckenzey. "I'm not sure we can take much more."

"The Rivalry focuses on the release of Arisol and the impending war that will follow." We control four pieces of the Phoenix, and Shane has one. However, I've come to learn that Faunal plays a significant role in Arisol's army, as does the Skeleton and the Demon Kirche.

Seyanna said, "You destroyed the Demon Kirche."

Jet nodded. "I've seen something recently that tells me there's another player."

"What do you mean, seen?" asked Mckenzey.

"From the tome."

"Like what?" asked Grantham.

"Thirteen magical Shaman, Incrementum, and Resitituals members met with the Grey Panther, the Silver Fox, and Myntra Dormacloud. At first, it seemed like they were all working together, but the situation deteriorated quickly. An important Oracle had been invited, but it seemed that a secretly invited guest had killed the Oracle. The guest was a Shade named Zorican. The Silver Fox escaped while Myntra Dormacloud gave of her lifeforce and protected some of the magical members. The Shade excels at creating a blue fog."

Mckenzey said, "Like the type we see at the disasters…and in my dreams," she mumbled.

"Seems to be," said Jet. "My guess is that he has been brought into the Rivalry and will be waiting for us at the opening of the sixth disaster."

Jayco said, "Honestly. This was fun once, but now it's an impossible task. You could have waited to share some of this information with us.

His temper rose, but he dropped back into his chair, keeping a lid on the comment itching to be spoken.

Grantham stood and said, "Let's call. This afternoon, we need to catch up with our classes. Let's do our own things tonight rather than get together. See you tomorrow."

CHAPTER 24

Unlocking the door, Jet stepped into his dorm fantasizing about having the next twelve hours to rest and relax. If that comprised a nap, a movie, and snuggling with Seyanna, he was all for it. He had absolutely no regrets about skipping his afternoon classes. He felt better after his soak, but he needed mindless relaxation.

Should I be the one to call her? he asked himself, then answered quickly: *Nope.*

Flipping on the light, he wailed at the disaster before him. His bed was unmade, spoiled food sat on the counters, and a rotten milk smell came from the sink or the fridge. The stench worsened the instant the fridge door opened. He had six boxes of cafeteria leftovers, decaying fruits and vegetables, and three cups of smoothies with moldy frothy tops.

He tried remembering when he'd last been here. It was hard to recall. Probably before he'd gone to Canada with Mckenzey and Raul. He thought Mikey had been staying with him at the time, and he wondered if the boy had rampaged through his stuff before setting off to save him and the others in Congo. His anger dissipated instantly as he thought of what Mikey and Rozene had done to save them.

His phone chimed, and he smiled as Seyanna's name brightened the screen. Her text read, "Mom and Dad just got into town. Spending the evening with them. See you tomorrow."

Jet picked up a pillow and screamed into it. He just wanted things to go smoothly for once. He quickly typed out a reply. "Have fun. Tell them I said hi. I'm exhausted. Heading to bed."

He set down his phone and fell back onto his couch. There was a knock on his door. He called out, "No one's home."

"Bro. Come on, let me in."

Jet smiled as he heard Raul's voice. Upon opening the door, he found Raul, Phillip, Autumn, and Ariana standing there. "Good to see you guys. Come on in."

Stepping back, the group hurried in. Phillip used crutches, and his foot was in a large black walking boot.

"What died in here?" asked Raul.

"My sanity," huffed Jet. "I just got here. Let me take this trash out."

"We're opening the windows," Autumn said, her smile faltering only slightly.

"Do you have a candle?" asked Ariana as she plugged her nose.

"Under the sink," yelled Jet, and he ran down the hallway to the trash chute. Upon returning, it smelled both better and worse. He knew he had acclimated to the smell. The candle helped.

Ariana had found Febreze under the sink and was aggressively spraying the couch.

Jet explained, "I didn't make the mess. I just got back."

"Sure," said Autumn playfully.

Phillip stared at Jet, tilting his head slightly. "Is this status quo for you or is something else going on?"

Raul said, "He was pretty clean when we were roomies."

Autumn added, "Must be overwhelmed."

Jet rolled his eyes. The way she said it, it sounded like a mental health condition for the insane.

"Lost his will to survive," added Ariana.

"I'm standing right here," implored Jet. "Tell me what's been going on."

"When's the last time you ate anything?" said Raul, opening the fridge. The foul odor worsened. "Get me another trash bag. It's all got to go."

Jet considered the question. He'd been given sandwiches a few hours ago, but it felt like ages ago. The soak must've consumed all his energy.

Autumn said, "I'll clean the sink."

"Dishes," said Raul.

"His room, but I'm not touching any underwear," added Ariana.

Phillip said, "That means I'm calling for some pizza.

"No, really..." said Jet, but no one paid him an ounce of attention. As he watched his friends, a smile spread across his face. He crossed out of the kitchen, past the half-wall dividing the space, and sank into the couch, closing his eyes.

A moment later, there was a nudge on his shoulder. Opening his eyes, he found Ariana smiling at him kindly. "Go take a shower."

"But...," he protested.

"You need it, and it'll make you feel better."

He sniffed at his clothes and bowed his head.

Nearly half an hour later, he stepped out of his bathroom, and his entire dorm looked cleaner than it had since he moved in. The warm water and a change of clothes were a minor miracle.

"Dinner is served," announced Phillip.

The pizza's aroma was intoxicating. Jet said, "You guys are the best." He took two slices of pizza and asked, "What have you guys been up to?"

Phillip said quickly, "I had surgery at Cottage Hospital, and Raul came and visited me once."

"We've been on lockdown," replied Raul.

Phillip gave him a quick wink. "I know you had a bad experience, but it went well enough for me."

"It was fine," said Jet. "When I had surgery on my collarbone, I didn't have any problems."

Raul cleared his throat. "Here at school, things have been superb."

Ariana added, "Grantham worried that Shane would try to approach the Elementals or the hideout while you were gone. There probably wasn't going to be an outright attack, so we watched for anything suspicious."

"That was so boring," said Autumn. "They had no parties or activities, and both restaurants were closed." She finished by adding, "Lame."

"What did you guys learn?"

"What?" Raul asked, feigning offense. "You think we disobey every order to remain in our dorms and only attend our classes?" He reached for his own pizza and soda.

"We fear the wrath of Principal Smuin," said Ariana.

"What really happened?" demanded Jet.

"We stayed clear of Shane. I am mostly better. There has been a lot of traffic near the machine shop. That's where the cells where Jayco and Grantham were held."

"What type of traffic?"

"Workers."

Jet thought back to the changes that had happened in Dillon Lake. "Okay."

"Beckham is a whole different ballgame," replied Autumn.

"Huh," replied Jet. "Why Beckham?"

Raul said, "He was malicious, especially to those of us whom Runic magic didn't choose. He watched us and enjoyed needling us to the point of pain."

"And?" asked Jet.

Ariana replied, "We wanted to uncover something about him or his group to use against him in the future..."

"No harm, no foul," said Raul, regretful.

Autumn announced, "We think Beckham and Trina Madden are an item. They hang out a lot. They have also become paramounts. Do you remember what those are?"

"Leaders of secret groups on campus," said Jet.

Exactly," said Autumn. "The paramounts are the leaders of the five different types of Runic Magic."

"Motion, Life, Darkness, Matter, and Mixture," said Jet.

"Wow," said Raul. "I'm surprised you remember all of them."

"My tome discusses them, and I didn't want to look stupid.

"Makes sense," said Arianna. She asked, "Do you understand Runic magic?"

Jet said, "They design signs in the air that correspond with each category of magic. There are five Elemental groups and five Runic groups. Each category has a certain number of spells."

"Exactly," said Autumn. "Shane knows them all."

"Do you know who the other paramounts are?"

"There is also Jessiva, Julian, and Clyde. Clearly, Julian was a liar and was killed; he'll be replaced."

Raul nodded, "It'll probably be Jocelyn or Derek. Other lesser-known Runics, such as Skylar, Jax, Freya, Oslo, or Siena, might be picked. They are some of the more talented Runics."

"I don't think I know any of the last group you mentioned," said Jet.

Ariana said, "You've seen them around, I'm sure. We'll help you get the names down."

Raul continued, "Matter is about moving something, blocking something. I would say it closely resembles Earth magic. Trina is the leader of Matter."

"Interesting," said Jet.

"Beckham is the leader of Mixture," explained Raul. "It vaguely mirrors water. You can have water, vapor, ice, and others. Mixture is combining two thoughts together, like physically combining anger and a dragon. The dragon will do your bidding, but neither you nor I will see the dragon."

"That is a bit more confusing," admitted Jet.

Autumn said, "Runic magic is secretive, but what isn't when it comes to Shane. Suffice it to say, the full effect of this type of magic occurs when two forces are combined."

"Jessiva is over the Darkness category," explained Autumn. "Which is more like Spirit magic. There isn't an actual ability to cause darkness. However, this magic can deceive others, distort how you feel, create false images, and more."

"She's the perfect person for that," replied Jet. He sat back and accepted a third piece of pizza, a combo slice.

Phillip said, "Runic Life is akin to Air magic. They can pretend someone is dead and can cause small animate objects to move on their own. They can use spirits for communication, and they can exacerbate certain insecurities. Runic Life is all about manipulation. None of them can ever be trusted. I've seen Jocelyn be mean and nasty when the time calls for it. If she's chosen, she'll be perfect."

"She hates me," whispered Jet.

"Why?" asked Autumn.

"I killed or caused the death of her two closest friends."

"Oh," said Phillip.

"Clyde is the leader for Motion," continued Raul quickly. "It is similar to Fire, a strong, in-your-face type of magic that incorporates movement. They can create a gravitational pull between objects, alter speed, change mass, make something lighter, cause an object in motion to lose its momentum, and even conceal something in plain sight."

Frowning, Jet said, "I never knew you guys knew this much about Runic magic."

Raul placed his fork onto his empty plate. "We spent more time with them than we would have liked."

"The stories are horrible," said Phillip, wrapping an arm around Raul. "It's a beautiful thing that you freed them. I'm eternally grateful."

"You're my friends. Even if you hadn't joined the Elementals, I could never have stood by and done nothing."

"We appreciate that," said Ariana, smiling at him. Although they had dated, this look was more profound than a crush, more like an eternal friendship.

Jet asked, "Did you learn anything else by following Beckham?"

"We watched him from a distance, thinking he might be dating a few girls or sneaking off campus," said Raul. "He interacted with other Runic leadership…a lot. We think they're working on something."

Jet cringed. "Let's hope they aren't thinking of overthrowing the school again."

"Don't think so," said Autumn. "Raul and Phillip are convinced they're going to leave Chadwick's. I fear they know something we don't and are planning to act on it."

"Not this again," said Raul.

"What again?" asked Jet.

Ariana answered, "The boys aren't on the same page, but Autumn watched Motion meet with Darkness, and then Matter encountered Motion later that day. Autumn thought she saw messages being sent with weapons and other symbols. The next day, Matter met with Darkness, and those same weapons were passed on. They're building a camaraderie that we don't have in the Elementals. Autumn and I think they're hiding weapons around the school, and eventually, they're going to try to take the Phoenix pieces."

"Or they could be preparing in case the school is attacked," retorted Phillip.

"Maybe," admitted Autumn. "But unlikely."

"What do you think?" asked Raul.

Jet considered what he would think if he saw two groups passing weapons. It took a painfully long few seconds to picture the encounter in his mind. Something else was trying to grab his attention. He muttered, "On the one hand, physically seeing weapons passed from one group to another is interesting."

"See?" replied Ariana confidently.

"But the Runics must have a hideout where exchanges could happen secretly. Why do it in public?"

"A good thought," added Raul.

"I know Shane wants all five pieces," said Jet, pondering. "We have four and they have one."

"What?" asked Phillip. "I know for a fact that Shane thinks he has two, and we have three."

"One of his is a fake," confided Jet. "It's a replica."

"He's going to be pissed when he realizes it," said Raul. "I hope I can be there to see it."

"Getting back to the thought at hand," said Ariana. "We should be getting ready for an attack."

"Always," agreed Jet. "My gut is telling me that this is a distraction from what is really going on. We need to bring other Elementals into the conversation and establish a more effective surveillance group. But you're right, we need to get to know one another better."

He paused. For the last five minutes, a memory or a thought had been nagging at him, running amok in his mind, and when the pieces finally fell into place, he took a deep breath. Charcoit's words rang in his head.

Raul's voice spoke from a distance. "Is everything okay?"

Jet said, "We should be prepared for an attack from the Runics, and we should build solidarity among the Elementals, but I think Shane is preparing for something related to magic more than anything else."

"What do you mean?" asked Phillip.

"Each of you is limited to one magical Element and one spell within that Element. What if that changes, and you can learn more spells or another Element?"

Raul said, "That would be crazy cool."

Jet said, "I bet Shane knows something we don't. But I've heard the words—the future might be brighter when one Elemental might become two. I didn't understand it before now, but I bet the Runics plan to train to learn two spells at some point. So should we."

CHAPTER 25

Jet left his dorm, heading for his first class, feeling more optimistic and well-rested than he had in days. Today, his classes consisted of English, math, defensive tactics, and swordplay. The soaking and spending time with friends had worked miracles. At some point, Raul and his friends left, but Jet was sure he'd already fallen asleep. He crawled into bed close to midnight. A text had awoken him in the morning. Rolling over, he read it was from Raul, directing him to his door. Three sacks of groceries lay outside with bagels, cream cheese, milk, orange juice, iced coffee, bread, lunch meat, and other snacks. He had the bestest of friends.

Entering Professor Cheio's class, he hoped this was a good token for the day. She smiled pleasantly and waved for him to come to the front of the room. He hurried down, and she handed him a stack of papers. "You have two weeks to finish these and prepare for the final."

"Wow," said Jet. "This is like fifteen assignments."

"We must be fair to all of our students. I did the same for Shane when he and his friends returned." Professor Cheio pointed to the back of the classroom where Shane, Clyde, and Jessiva sat, smirking at him.

Turning back, he said, "Shouldn't be a problem. I look forward to it and if I have any questions, can I contact you?"

"No," she shook her head. "Except for the fifteen minutes before class begins. Otherwise, you'll need to speak with my TA, Trina Madden."

Jet had to strain himself from rolling his eyes. "Thanks for the information." He turned to find his seat.

Before he'd taken two steps, Professor Cheio added, "No points will be accepted for late work, Mr. Black."

Not long ago, Professor Cheio was one of his supporters. She had been kind and excused some of his other missed assignments. That time had come and gone. He worked on some of the assignments during class, first sorting them by book title and questions. Whenever he glanced down, Professor Cheio asked him about a book he hadn't read or didn't know he needed to. It was tedious but effective. She didn't call on him once over the last fifteen minutes of class because he stared at her the entire time.

His next class, math, with Professor Dockord, was met with equal hostility. If possible, he received more homework than every other student. Half was to be done by the end of this week and the other half on the day of the final. The best part of the class was the three Elementals sitting with him. Felix, Aaron, and Sadie. They agreed to help him with his homework. It was not lost on Jet that Professor Dockord glared at the four of them as he left the classroom.

After eating alone in his dorm, Jet caught up with Latisha, Mckenzey, and Autumn as they passed the CeU building toward the three stadiums crucial for Defensive Movements. Mckenzey greeted him coldly, and Latisha and Autumn said very little, but he was unconcerned as everyone looked as if they were in their own little world. He guessed their first day back hadn't gone as planned either.

"We're here," said Jet, trying to infuse a measure of positivity. "Where do you guys want to go?"

Near smiles broke out, and his friends escaped their inner thoughts.

"Already?" asked Mckenzey. "I don't remember crossing through the trees."

"I was out of it," agreed Latisha.

Autumn pointed to the stadiums. "Look how many people are here."

The four of them faced the arenas built into the ground by the Axenkind. The central one was the largest, yet the other two were smaller but equal. Students lined the main stadium and others were on a nearby hill, packed to see what would happen in the next class.

Jet worried he would be asked to fight someone or show off his Capocea movements. The defensive movements were being taught to the Elementals, Runics, and non-magical. He was the only one he knew who had a grasp on Capocea. His eyes found Rufian, who stood next to Marcella.

"This is horse crap," groaned Jet as they made their way to the stadium.

Mckenzey said, "Is that a new grandstand?"

"Principal Smuin and Professors Namish and Dickerson are also here," added Autumn.

A large, covered wooden seating area with standing room and seating was positioned on the far side of the main stadium, big enough for twenty people. Pushing through the crowd, Jet and his friends found a spot directly across from the pavilion.

Rufian spoke. "The last two weeks, we have been working with Marcella on the defensive illusion spell. This works for those of you without magic. You can't practice it while asleep, but use the words 'Ilusao dupla' during a self-trance. This tactic lets you blend in like a chameleon in most circumstances. It is not a magical spell but more of an incantation to the non-magical. I am grateful to Marcella for sharing this incredible insight. The Coven has been working on this for many years, and we can see why. We've seen some of the capabilities some of you possess."

Rufian continued, "Today is slightly different. Marcella is willing to bring some advanced training, which is why we asked additional students to come here today. But first, I would like to reintroduce Deputy Chief Vicario, a guest of the Brotherhood, who has been appointed to oversee magical instruction at all boarding schools. Because this is new information, he desired to be here. We have the same three students from Dillon Lake, Molly, Figueroa, and Tenney."

Jet recognized the three students and wondered how long they had been here. Molly was tall, with fake eyelashes, blond hair, and a perfect complexion. Figueroa was short, without hair, with tan skin and brown eyes. Tenney was taller than Figueroa but much shorter than Molly. They were each dressed in combat clothes today.

"Today is about preventing mind control," Rufian Continued. "Some mythical creatures may attempt to attack using their minds. The attack comes from the misuse of Trimentis, and it can be deadly. The attack will not be by someone who is a Runic or Elemental, as they don't have this ability, but it could be done by the Foresworn, a group of Wandering Nomads who felt betrayed by the 10 Kings. They formed a secret group and discovered a way to alter Trimentis. The Ravencats became their disciples in this area of study, and more recently, we learned this process is how the Chupovanas can track those with magic in greater precision than before. Defending this is key."

Principal Smuin stepped forward to stand next to Rufian. "The Brotherhood is willing to pardon Marcella significantly, and an agreement has been made with the Axenkind for this information. Other schools will come here to learn this lecture, as Marcella still cannot be far from the water."

Marcella bowed her head at Principal Smuin, keeping her facial features flat and neutral.

Rufian continued, "No magic will be used during this lesson. A complete understanding of what is required must come first." Smiling at Marcella, Rufian said, "The classroom is now yours."

Marcella's sweet, bewitching voice filled the air, "Mind magic is an ancient agreement with the lost water fae of the Southern Winds. It was used to communicate telepathically with other magical tribes, non-magical, and the magical. The Foresworn of the Wandering Nomads perverted the magic and turned it into Trimentis in attempts to control your thoughts and actions. As a Coven Witch, I have the ability to influence you and bewitch you for knowledge, information, and some control over you. This is referred to as Glamor, which is pointedly different than Trimentis."

Marcella paced back and forth, and each student present, including Jet, watched her closely. She had attempted to use Glamor on him, Jayco, and Grantham. Her ability was undeniable, but for some reason, it hadn't entirely worked on him.

"I've seen the deepest secrets removed forcefully from a prisoner using Trimentis. There are ways to block some thoughts, but they become obstructed to the person who owns them as well, permanently."

The hairs on the back of his neck stood on end.

"To protect yourself from Trimentis you must do several things. First, you must create a Golem from clay, rock, or stick. If you can use magic, your Golem should be made from rock. If you don't have magic, it must be a stick. A clay Golem is for tribesmen."

Marcella pulled out a purse from around her waist. From within, she removed a thick brown clay statue, only a few inches tall. Even from here, Jet could see the stocky legs, thick arms, and a broad head. "This is my Golem, and this is very similar to what the others in the Coven have created." Quickly, she stored the item back in her purse.

"The word to control the Golem is 'Tambiko'. It is pointless to say now, as you have no connection with your Golem. But one day, this will allow you to store some memories into it. When you are attacked, you say this word, and the Trimentis spell attacks your Golem instead of you. Once the connection is made, your Golem will be at risk. Keep it safe." The witch glanced at Rufian for less than an instant. Jet thought a wisp of malice crossed her face.

"Those with magic," Marcella continued as if nothing had happened, "can use your specific magical ability to further block the attack by adding your magic into the Golem. This is vital. Place specks of Fire, Darkness, Spirit, or Motion to create a greater connection. Those without magic don't have this opportunity, and you must work to strengthen your Golem in other ways. To increase the wisdom of your Golem, you will need to add Sacrifice. The more you do for someone else, the more Sacrifices you will get. Without a Golem, your Sacrifices vanish into the world, but with a Golem, you can find strength and purity. Your Sacrifice will alter the Golem to become more like you. The final thing you will need is something to connect you with your

Golem beyond its form. Look for something that suits you. It may be musical, metal, wooden, or cloth. It will be effective if it resonates with you; if not, you might have a problem. Overall, this process might seem easy, but it isn't. It could take weeks, so start as quickly as possible."

Rufian began clapping, and the rest of the class and the professors joined quickly.

"Is there an age limit?" asked Principal Smuin

"Sort of," replied Marcella cooly. "The older you get, the less likely your Golem will mesh with you, but any age can design and create one."

Jayco and Grantham appeared suddenly at their sides.

Lathisha kissed Grantham and asked, "Where have you been?"

"In the back. We couldn't get over here."

Jet glanced around for Seyanna, but he couldn't spot her. But his eyes were drawn back to Marcella, who stood relaxed and casual, but she was trying far too hard. Something wasn't sitting right with him. He knew she didn't like the Axenkind or the school and was only here because of the imprisonment charm placed on her. They were a good distance from the water, the farthest he'd ever seen her, so maybe that was it.

Marcella continued, "We have several different types of wood and rocks to choose from. These particular varieties are most useful for creating a Golem. There are large and thin pieces of wood. There is a kit that will allow you to cut, tie, and use cloth at joints. There are directions to follow. For those with magic, you will need to match with a partner, and you will be given a twelve-piece chisel kit and instructions on how to form a stone Golem."

"We have the wood on the left side of the stadium and the rocks on the right. When we dismiss you, go to your respective areas and choose wisely," said Rufian.

Marcella said quickly, "The wood or stone will call to you. But you must be listening."

They were allowed to divide. More than half of the group went toward the rock. It went surprisingly fast. Jayco and Grantham talked excitedly about things happening around campus, who was seeing who, and other details about students. Jet listened...but didn't. When it was his turn, his choices were soapstone, alabaster, granite, sandstone, limestone, and marble. Some were easier to work with than others. He was drawn to a white marble instantly, but Jayco chose it. In the end, he noticed a black rock at the bottom of the granite pile. When he reached down, picked it up, he felt a connection. It was dark black, almost like coal.

Rufian said, "That is soapstone, from the Tabaka Hills in Kenya. That is an interesting choice."

"Does that mean good or bad?"

"It mostly depends on how your Golem turns out."

Jet's eyebrows rose, and he wanted to say more, but Principal Smuin swooped in and picked an alabaster stone.

"Take this," said Rufian and he handed over a chisel kit. "This is going to take you some time."

As he and his friends returned to where they were before, they chatted excitedly. Jet joined in every few minutes. He searched for Shane and other Runics. He wanted to see whether they would participate in creating a Golem.

Once all the students were back in their places, Rufian turned to the students in attendance and announced, "For our meeting on Thursday, I expect you to have begun this project. Bring your work to class, and we will inspect it. Please email one of the teachers if you have trouble with the directions. If you have done nothing, you will get a failing grade for the day."

Marcella was led from the small platform; nearing the last step, she again glanced in his direction. She knew something he didn't.

Grantham said, "I don't trust her."

"Is it this Golem thing, or something else?" asked Latisha thoughtfully. "We need a better understanding of the true nature of the Golem."

"What do you mean?" asked Mckenzey.

"Can it be used to control us?"

The thought was frightening. His hand touched his necklace, given to him by Rufian, to prevent him from being attacked by Trimentis. He wasn't sure why he'd been given a necklace if a Golem was the better option. "I'll get to the bottom of this."

Rufian continued, "Those not in this class regularly are dismissed. We will turn the rest of the time over to Professors Sidewinder and Gimshe. They will be addressing you shortly."

"I wish we could stay around," said Jayco. "This next part is exciting."

Doris, an Elemental with Earth magic, asked, "Do you know what is happening?"

Jayco nodded. "We've been working with the ax and the longsword. The rumor is that the Axenkind have brought in a new weapon to work with. The entire school is buzzing."

Latisha waved, and Grantham and Jayco left. Those left behind began guessing what the next weapon would be. Jet thought it would be a different type of sword, and Latisha hoped it might be a club or a mace. The arenas slowly thinned out, but several students stayed behind and were quickly kicked out by the Axenkind. Deputy Chief Vicario, Molly, Figueroa, and Tenney remained at the stand talking.

Jet asked Latisha, "Have you heard anything about becoming part of the Axenkind's mission?"

"A little. It involves weapons, strategy, and getting others involved. They've asked several non-magical."

"Can still be an Echo?"

A broad smile formed on her face. "Yes. I can do both."

There was a commotion, and Professor Gimshe and Professor Sidewinder called for silence from the class. Gimshe was lean, quick, and agile, while Sidewinder was tall and skinny with broad shoulders.

"Let's gather around," said Professor Gimshe in her musical voice.

Shane Fallon and his entourage strolled to the front of the class. He looked as excited and confident as Jet had seen him.

Mckenzey whispered, "That boy knows what's happening next."

"What kind of weapon are we going to be using?" asked Trina Madden, then she winked at Shane.

Professor Sidewinder said, "You have been using the Arma and the Zenith or the ax and the longsword. You've done well. Autumn is marvelous with the longsword, while Latisha excels with the ax. They should be commended for their talents."

Just over half the class clapped, comprising Elementals and some non-magical. Not a single Runic turned in their direction.

"Our blacksmiths have been working tirelessly on some new weapons. We call them Fireflies."

Behind them, a good forty feet away, an enormous overlay was pulled back, and six large chests materialized.

Professor Gimshe sprang out of the arena and came to stop before them. "There should be enough for everyone."

"Typically, you are most effective with Fireflies when you use two, but for today, you will practice with one," added Professor Sidewinder, a partial grin on his face as he watched Gimshe.

Rufian divided the class into two halves. "Those to my right," —he waved his arm—"go to the first set of weapons while the others should use the second chest."

Jet took a step forward, but Rufian shook his head slightly. He didn't want to look like the only one who didn't follow directions, so he followed his friends.

"Take one," said Mckenzey.

"Rufian warned me not to."

"Why?" asked Latisha.

"Not sure."

As he walked back with the others, Tenney, one of the Predilectors, materialized at his side and thrust something into his hand. He caught it, surprised to see he was being given a weapon.

When they were back in their spots, Professor Gimshe spoke. "This is a curved sickle blade. The edge on the inner edge is sharp enough to kill the person next to you, just as the longword and ax are. The handle is shorter and allows a single hand to grip it."

Jet felt his weapon and knew it was entirely made of wood.

From the far side of the stadium, one of the students began swinging his weapon back and forth. Professor Gimshe hadn't yet seen the student, but Shane had. The boy drew something in the air. It took only a second, but his hands moved in a blur. Suddenly, two rocks flew out of the forest, and one went on each side of the boy's head. Noiselessly, they smashed together, hitting the boy with force, and he dropped to the ground unconscious.

"If I see anyone acting recklessly, you will cause the entire group to do pushups," finished Professor Gimshe.

Shane was watching and listening to the professors as if he hadn't just attacked another student.

Professor Sidewinder held up his own Firefly. It was a different metal and slightly larger than theirs. He moved his sickle from one hand to the next. He swung, cut, threw it from one hand to the next, danced, and attacked. The movements were aggressive and defensive simultaneously. His body was compact and precise. He looked like he was using the outer edge to block and the inner edge to cut, slice, or attack.

Professor Gimshe brought out a longsword and an ax and slowly attacked Professor Sidewinder. They watched as the sickle could easily block something as big as the ax and as long as the longsword. The professor stopped and faced the class. "I hope you can see the importance of this weapon. It is first and foremost for defense but is quite effective in close-quarter combat attacks."

Rufian stepped forward. "The weapon you have touched has imprinted on you. Much like some of the weapons from the Rivalry, only you can touch this going forward. Principal Smuin, myself, Gimshe, and Sidewinder know the override spell if you should decide to take it from the classroom. For now, the weapons are for practice. If something should happen and you need it, it will become available."

Jet glanced down at his wooden weapon. He wondered why he wasn't allowed to have one of the sickles.

"If you achieve a certain level of ability, you may be given a second sickle, which is the preferred manner of using them. Cut and block is the motto for this weapon because you can do both at once."

The class was separated and placed into the arenas to practice. Everyone formed a line on the side closest to the CeU building and faced the canyon behind the stadiums. Gimshe, Sidewinder, and Rufian taught them the moves of the first level of the sickle fledgling. It was only blocking, with no attempts to slash. Two non-magical students and one Runic were as light as feathers, and they excelled. They shifted into a blur for several steps as they blocked and advanced, much like the humans holding the white crystals had moved. He didn't think the three students realized they were moving so quickly.

Latisha was irritated. Her ability with the sickle was poor. Jet wasn't much better, and he wasn't surprised. Shane was decent, but no one compared to Manteo, the boy with Runic magic. After thirty minutes, he'd separated himself even further. Even second place was several steps behind, a non-magical named Daniela. She had once tried to get Runic magic, but it hadn't chosen her. Marcus, the third best, was also non-magical but hadn't attempted choosing magic yet. Mckenzey was probably the fourth best.

She whispered, "They look as shocked as the rest of us."

Rufian announced, "A unique byproduct of this weapon. If you have two of them in your possession, holding them, when you fall asleep, you will only need half the time to sleep as before. It is remarkable and useful, especially on the battlefield. The ring at the top of your handle will change color to match your eye color. That stays in place until you pass to the other side; even if you lose the sickle, no one else can use it."

They spent the next hour swinging, moving, and learning from the instructors. Jet used his wooden sickle, which resembled the others, ensuring no one knew that he didn't have a real one. He grumbled more than once, and Latisha glared at him repeatedly.

Near the end of class, he thought his movements and balance had improved. In the final five minutes, Manteo, Daniela, and Marcus were given a second sickle, and their speed increased, if possible.

"Sickle weapons in the hands of those who have been given a Lifeforce can be temperamental. We will want to see how it works for you, but not with so many people around."

Jet hadn't heard Rufian get that close. Without turning around, he asked, "What about the Golem? Should I make one?"

"Why not?"

"Because you gave me a necklace, preventing an attack."

"Yes," said Rufian. "But a Golem is more like a piece of you that can be attacked. If someone were to attack you now, they would know that you have something preventing them. They might want to find a way to remove it. A Golem is a piece of you, so the attacker might think they're attacking you. Having a Golem is becoming more essential. Truthfully, yours will need to be far superior to the average person. I can help with that."

CHAPTER 26

The procession of cars for those arriving began promptly at 3 p.m. on Friday and continued for more than two hours. Those first in line were delegates from other states, communities, and tribes. Chadwick's students sat in awe as the collective amount of the magical, tribesmen, and magnificent beasts had not been assembled in such a way for thousands of years.

The vehicles transporting students and professors from Dillon Lake, Cranbrook, San Mateo, and Valley Sun were some of the last to arrive. Palpable excitement ran through the crowd like electricity. The exterior of the CeU building was adorned with welcoming signs, celebratory wreaths, announcements, and other enhancements.

Security was the tightest it had ever been. Measures were added in the form of scrolls, paintings, statues, and relics from the Brotherhood that arrived on Wednesday. These items could do far more than what Jet could imagine. He'd seen illusions, Glamor, energy fields, alarm bells, spectral soldiers, and a moat encircling the outer boundary.

Seyanna and her team created a guard watch to monitor the area. The Cyndral mirrors, created by Marcella, were in use. Braverly, Jet's protector, observed from a distance.

"Are you sure your plan is going to work?" asked Grantham as they waited for the last two buses to be allowed through the northern security checkpoint. "No one took the bait on Sunday. We waited in those shrubs for two hours and came away empty-handed."

Jayco added, "I still have a painful rash that won't go away."

Jet eyed Shane and his welcoming committee on the far side of the parking lot. "We couldn't wait any longer. Everyone has spies at all the schools. They'll be close by. Hopefully, Braverly can spot them before they attack."

But inside, Jet felt the level of panic growing. This day was going to be worthless if they didn't lure the Azurites into the open. He still had no idea what tonight would bring.

Mckenzey asked, "Do you want to try and talk to the students away from their principal's prying ears?"

"Probably." He watched as Jocelyn was called forward and spoke briefly with Shane. She glanced in their direction and scurried over.

She might be friendly or unfriendly, depending on how she feels when talking with him. It was the luck of the draw. This time, she scoffed, "Shane wants insight into your plan here, Black."

"You know that we have the three missing books—"

"And the four pyramids for each magic type," she finished. "What's the game plan?"

"We want to monitor their training and have them help us in the coming war."

Jocelyn frowned. "Then why do that now?"

"School is a week from ending. Summer vacation is nearly upon us. It was the only time."

She seemed mollified by his response, yet she stared at him closely. As if determining she was satisfied, she turned and walked away.

Latisha asked, "Is that the actual plan?"

"Partially," said Jet. "It sounds like a good option. Just thought of it."

"You're winging this," bellowed Eric. "This seems significant."

Jet winked. "Everything we do is important."

The two buses stopped in the parking lot, near where Principal Smuin and Professors Dickerson, Darnshaw, Marcella, Namish, and Cheio were huddled together, talking. They attempted to be a welcoming crew to the visitors. Then each school would be joined by the Runics, paraded through the onlookers, and brought to the Elementals. Afterward, they would be shown their dorms. The party would end in three days, with each school returning home. Despite all his blustering, he wasn't entirely sure the schools would be leaving with the new books. His tome had been stubbornly quiet about what was to happen.

Dillon Lake was the first to exit the bus. Despite his height, Jayco stood on his toes to see if Rozene was among them. She hadn't contacted Jayco all week.

"Good girl," Jayco said affectionately when Rozene stepped from the bus. She was followed by Principal Berry, Karl Middlesex, two professors, and Marlon. Three additional students, whom Jet didn't recognize, shadowed Marlon.

Mckenzey gasped. "That's Professor Felicia, who helped Eric and me escape."

"Why would she come?" wondered Eric.

"That's strange," Jet agreed. "I'll ask Rufian to keep an eye on her."

Diego Axel from San Mateo led the students from his school. Jet had barely spoken with Diego, but the kid was tall, with dark hair and a dark complexion. He appeared older than when Jet had last seen him. That probably had more to do with the death of Oaklyn, a friend, while they had been visiting Dillon Lake. Diego chatted with Joey Reich, Chase King, and Brayden Coleman as they took in the school's atmosphere. A tall, blond-haired girl pushed through four adults, likely teachers, and stopped beside Diego. She muttered something, and they all laughed.

The six people who stepped out next were unexpected. The Brotherhood had sent several emissaries. Li Wei, the commander of the Brotherhood, led the group with his long white hair and white beard. Chiefs Lara Brancoff, Ethan Davenport, and Junjie Su followed him. The last two were Geb and Nana.

Jet inhaled deeply, and a rush of relief flooded through him upon seeing his grandmother. He'd only received letters from her. She smiled and waved her hand twice. Geb never glanced in his direction.

"Is that Nana?" asked Mckenzey. "What's she doing here?"

"No clue," said Jet honestly. "I haven't spoken with her in a few months."

"Weird," agreed Grantham. "Are they holding her hostage?"

Latisha answered, "Does it look like she is an unwilling participant?"

"No," said Grantham. "But why wouldn't she have warned you?"

"That's a great question," said Jet.

The first bus, having dropped off all its passengers, departed. The three groups of people were ushered to the sidewalk in front of the CeU building, where they waited for instructions from Principal Smuin.

The doors on the second bus opened. Evelyn Ulm, Chin Nguyen, and three other students whom Jet didn't recognize stepped from the bus. These students were from Valley Sun, but only two had been at Dillon Lake.

Jayco said, "The last three are new to the leadership at Valley Sun. I wonder what happened?"

Next, an exceptionally tall woman appeared. Jet guessed she was the principal. She immediately gave orders that were followed.

The students from Cranbrook were the last to descend. Jet identified Nylah Veeda, Austin Buckley, Ellie Giron, Vani Warde, and Wade Sandusky, the same five who had gone to New York. He'd spoken with them only briefly, so he was surprised he remembered their names.

All five groups surrounded Principal Smuin, and instructions were given. Then they moved toward Shane. Jet was curious about how he would greet the Runics. He was crafty, with a kind smile and magnetic commands. The Brotherhood went first. They smiled politely and spoke softly, and even Nana seemed genuinely happy to see the Runics. Everyone shook hands with all the Runics present. The Cranbrook students barely said anything, and those from Valley Sun were even more distant. Dillon Lake expressed sincerity, but they strode past the Runics as quickly as possible. Those from San Mateo were ecstatic to see Shane and his friends lingered back to talk.

"Here they come," said Seyanna, inching closer to Jet. "This should be interesting."

"Hello, Mikado," said Lei Wei in nearly perfect English. "Thank you for inviting us to this glorious moment. Seeing all five books in the same location at the same time has been a distant dream by many of our members."

"It does feel a little surreal," replied Jet warmly. Nana remained at the back of the group. She must've known that Jet wanted to ask something as she furtively shook her head. "Thank you for coming. I feel that we might be out of our depths with what happens next with magic, and it will be helpful to have the Brotherhood's voice of reason."

"I hope you mean that," replied Li Wei.

"I do."

"We should chat later and formulate a plan going forward."

"I look forward to it."

No one else in the Brotherhood's group said anything as they navigated through. Nana winked. Rufian greeted the Brotherhood and escorted them to the teachers' apartments.

"If you want our help in the magical war, we're going to need a seat at the proverbial table," said an extremely short girl with brown hair, white skin, and long fingernails that looked far more like weapons than aesthetics. The number of tattoos she had could not be counted. Strolling emphatically towards Jet, she added, "Shane's proposal is quite convincing. You'll need to do better."

"Hello, Nylah." A warm smile crossed Jet's face. "That's an interesting attempt at negotiating. I hope you remember that Cranbrook is on the table for control by the Azurites. They want to make a deal and have the leverage. Your school might not be chosen to receive a book, even if I allow it in the next few days. Moreover, magic might not choose you, and just because you're the student president today doesn't guarantee you'll be the leader tomorrow."

Nylah stopped walking as her mouth dropped open.

Jet added, "I'll be repeating this to each school. The Elementals control the other three magical books and the pyramids. No book will be released without discussion with the Brotherhood, some other tribesmen, and all the boarding schools. This isn't a game or a popularity contest. Having magic is a responsibility and one that you'll have to qualify to receive."

"Are you sure this is how you want to proceed?" asked Nylah.

"Wrong question," replied Jet. "You should have asked, 'How will we work together going forward?'" He nodded to Mckenzey, who pulled out illustrations of the Chupovanas they had fought or had seen. "Here's Kee-faux, Taraqeu, Dalkiate, Urslacisus, and Zediathon. There are others. We fought each of them and killed Zediathon. Chupovanas will come after those with magic, and it'll be your responsibility to stop them. You'll surely have some defensive spells if magic chooses you. Elementals will be willing to protect you, but do you honestly believe that Shane will send talented Runics to help you in your time of need?"

"Um—" Nylah hesitated.

"We'll talk again soon."

The Valley Sun students were next, and he watched Chin's eyes find Keesha, who stood a little behind him. The boy's face paled when she glared back at him, and his eyes shifted to stare at the ground. Chin was once a student at Chadwick's and liked Keesha. He had become friends with Shane near Christmas, their freshman year. He had been recruited for one of Shane's secret groups. One day, he vanished from Chadwick's and ended up at Valley Sun. His leaving was the driving force behind Keesha joining the Elementals. Jet knew she wanted answers.

"So, what are we doing here?" asked Evelyn Ulm. She was as tall as Jayco, with black hair and golden-brown skin. She stared at Jet unflinching.

"One time, you asked if war is coming. It's already here. We're trying to decide if allowing the other magical books to be released will hurt or help the war. The next few days should answer those questions."

Evelyn's eyes narrowed. "Who decided that you're the gatekeeper?"

Jet said, "I possess both the pyramids and the books for the three missing magical groups. That speaks volumes."

"What do you want from us?"

"Want?" asked Jet. "It's not that straightforward. Things will become clearer soon."

"Okay," whispered Evelyn, her voice calm. "We're with you. Just tell us what we can do."

"We will," replied Jet, equally calm.

Rozene strode forward, acting as if she didn't like them. The only thing she or anyone from Dillon Lake said was, "Don't waste our time."

The last group was San Mateo, and surprisingly, they were equally thrilled to see Jet and the other Elementals as they had been to see Shane and the Runics.

"It's a privilege to be invited to Chadwick's," said Diego Axel. "I hope you remember Chase, Brayden, and Joey. When we lost Oaklyn, it was hard to fathom a replacement, but Mary Albright has been a real inspiration for our school during the dark times. I'm not sure what we would have done this last month or so."

"Glad you could make it," said Jet. "We hope this will be an enlightening few days."

"I'm sure," said Diego. "Your campus is incredible. I love how close it is to the beach. I don't know if you'll ever get some of us to leave. I seriously love surfing. Do you think we'll have time to get out?"

Jet glanced at Jayco and smiled. "Maybe. I guess that depends on how things go here."

Grantham asked, "How are you guys?"

Chase replied, "Fine. Shane made some promises he can't uphold, throwing a few of us off."

Jet asked Diego, "What are your thoughts about Shane's promises?"

"Here for the ride," said Diego, but he winked at Jet.

Mary said, "We have concerns. All the schools do. Magic is unsettling."

"Ain't that the truth," said Grantham. "And I think it's about to get weirder."

The rest of the students from San Mateo waved and smiled, then walked past without another word.

The Elementals moved in close and Jayco asked, "What's the plan?"

"Use the strategies in place to identify any secret meetings that happen tonight," said Jet. "We don't want this to get out of control. If the Azurites are here, we need to be ready."

"Have we let the wolf into the sheep's pasture?" asked Latisha.

Jet answered, "They were already here."

"This is going to be a crazy weekend," added Mckenzey.

CHAPTER 27

That night, the entire school and their guests traveled to Devil's Landing for an evening of rock climbing, food, and mingling. Jayco, Grantham, and a few of Shane's friends showed off their excellent skills, but no one compared to Grantham. His ability allowed him to scale up the entire rock wall without a rope, but Grantham held himself back so as not to show off too much. Jet kept both of his feet firmly on the ground.

Seyanna and the Brotherhood arranged for guards to be stationed on the western side of the school just for this occasion. Tensions evaporated as fellow students and professors intermingled, and new friendships blossomed. The Myntra openly welcomed everyone, introducing themselves, showing off their weapons, and sharing insights into fighting and combat. Like the Axenkind, they had years of military strategy and knowledge of the enemy.

Yuki, Mikey, Dawn, Glue, and Elliott stayed close to each other at first, but they opened up to Rozene, Marlon, the other Runics, and Karl Middlesex. Jet thought Glue might be able to rival Grantham on the climb, but he looked unsteady and swayed back and forth after the first forty feet. Rozene stayed away from Jayco, Jet, and the others, but she appeared calm and relaxed. She even smiled and laughed as she scarfed down some food.

When the night officially concluded, Jet considered the entire event a success. Shane had left fifteen minutes ago with most of the Runics. Jayco, Latisha, and other Elementals had followed them to see if they met up with anyone. Jet walked back to the CeU building with Seyanna, Mikey, Grantham, and several other students. A comfortable heat settled around them, and a slight breeze brought the smell of salt and the ocean to them. They overheard several groups of students as they talked, laughed, and debated on what would happen tomorrow.

The principals from each school, several professors, and other adults separated themselves from the students, acting as watchers. He wondered if they realized how much pure talent and power stood here this night?

Seyanna explained, "The Brotherhood brought twenty extra adults to patrol the outer border. They think someone or something is planning to attack tomorrow. I heard Chief Lara Brancoff imploring Principal Smuin to cancel the meetings. They're convinced an attack will come once the books are revealed."

"Twenty?" Jet's eyebrows rose. "Do they have information that we don't?"

"If so...they didn't say anything to me."

Grantham asked, "Are there any students?"

"A few," said Seyanna.

"Iris, the lion, and the bear are patrolling. Braverly is guarding the water."

"Do we want the Azurites to attack?" asked Glue.

"Only if we can surprise them. I don't want anyone else in danger."

"That's a thin line," said Keesha. "If you don't give the other books, you might make everyone lose trust in us."

"It's a chance we have to take."

"What's the plan for tomorrow?" asked Grantham.

"I was just informed that Principal Smuin wants the Echoes and Runic leadership to meet with the Brotherhood," said Jet. "They want to pass along information and to come to an agreement. They say there was a breakthrough with Darium and Dania. Something to help protect the schools."

"Really," she said. A buzz sound in her walkie-talkie. Her response was succinct and in code, "Green. Fifty-seven. Send three." After lowering the device, she asked Jet, "Anything else currently scheduled?"

"Yes. Tomorrow afternoon, but Shane has been put in charge, and he'll inform us of our part in the morning."

Seyanna smiled at everyone else. "I think that's all for tonight. I want some alone time with Jet. Would that be alright?" Before anyone answered, she gripped his arm and pulled him toward some trees.

"Have fun, you two," shouted Keesha.

"Way to take charge, Seyanna," said Grantham. "Jet. Give me the details when you can."

"Will do."

When they came to a stop, well hidden, he turned and smiled at Seyanna. She wasn't smiling back. Instead, she glared at him.

"What did I do?"

Seyanna said, "Jayco is publicly suggesting that each school swear fidelity to the Echoes in order for you to give them the missing books.

He wants Rufian to perform the Axenkind magic like he did when binding Marcella so she couldn't attack us."

"That is a horrible idea."

"You think. Trust is beneficial but forcing it on the other schools will undermine any trust we're trying to create."

Jet asked, "Did you think I was aware of his demand?"

Her face relaxed slightly. "I wasn't sure."

"How did you find out?"

"Everyone knows."

Jet groaned. "What am I supposed to do?"

"Give me your phone."

"Huh."

"I'll text Autumn something. She has numbers from half the delegates so far. She can spread the truth quickly."

"Of course she does," laughed Jet.

Seyanna spent a minute typing on his phone. She showed him, and he nodded. She hit the send button and handed his phone back. "It was a good thing we addressed this now."

"Thanks to you. I would have been clueless."

She faced him, both eyebrows as high as he'd ever seen."

"More clueless," he clarified.

She leaned in and kissed him several times. A warmth grew in his chest. Their kissing, although delightful, ended far too soon.

"I got to get back," she whispered, her breathing rapid.

"Me too," he managed to stutter.

A few minutes later, they stepped back onto the path, toward the CeU building. They walked in silence, holding hands. Seyanna held his hand tight, as if worried he was about to get lost. She finally said, "I know you know this, but be careful of Shane."

"Always."

"He's going to try to divert everyone's attention from you to himself."

"It's a game of chess. He's always playing."

They fell back into silence and soon reached the asphalt of the parking lot at the CeU building. A few moments later, they stood, ready to cross College Avenue.

"What are you thinking?" she asked.

Jet said, "All night I've been thinking about the Elemental and Runic Prisoners we have on campus. Jayco reminded me of them. I'm not sure who has talked with them. There's Sarika and the others. I've got to see what they know."

"Will Principal Smuin even let you see them?'"

"Can he really stop me?" He smiled, attempting to joke with her, but it was clear that her thoughts were preoccupied. There was another buzz from the radio.

Jet's head pounded, and he knew he had to decide about tomorrow. Should he give the missing books to the other schools? He had so many other thoughts competing with him. They were unprepared for the next disaster. He had to find the Coven's lost children. They must find and destroy the remaining Insidious Six. Getting the fifth piece of the Phoenix from Shane and retrieving the bodies of Alces and Kaya were just as crucial. He was pretty sure he wasn't getting any sleep tonight.

Seyanna's words pulled him out of his musings, "I've been asked to write out a schedule for everyone who will be working to protect the school over the next three days. I am going be up late tonight. Text me if you need something."

He said hastily, "That sounds boring."

"So…I'll see you in the morning?"

"Yes."

She leaned in and kissed him quickly. A second later, she was gone.

A voice spoke from the shadows before he took two steps toward his dorm. "That seemed like a brush off, if you ask me."

Jet turned, a spell of protection ready on his lips.

Shane Fallon stepped out from behind the side of the building. His handsome looks, smug face, and self-confidence accentuated his domineering personality. He was likable until you got to know him. He would cross any and all lines to ensure he won.

"What's the plan here?" Shane asked.

Jet immediately worried about what Shane had overheard. How long had he been listening to them? "I think I've been clear on why we've asked the other schools to come to Chadwick's."

"Sounds like you want to control the other schools."

"Not control," answered Jet. "Just assurances that you won't manipulate them."

"Manipulation is the definition the weak give out to explain their lack of control and leadership of a situation. I don't manipulate, but I've been asked to guide others and help them gain control of the situation."

"Call it whatever you want, but you've made promises you can't deliver. You don't have the books or the pyramids."

"I helped you get them," retorted Shane cooly. "But you would never give me credit for my accomplishments. You're blinded to the Elementals' path, but the Runic's way is just as difficult. Remember that."

Shane took five steps, then spun and said, "I've been asked to help Seyanna with whatever she needs to guard the perimeter. I might call her and see what that entails." He left, following the path Seyanna had gone.

Jet hurried to his dorm, fuming, then showered, his mind thinking of Shane and Seyanna the entire time. Despite everything he needed to accomplish, their images sprinted freely in his head. Jet let loose a small scream, bent down, and started doing pushups. The first thirty were smooth and rhythmic. The next thirty were harder. When he stood, he had to take rapid breaths. Five minutes later, he did thirty more. He nearly collapsed when he stood. Ten minutes later, after having paced the room repeatedly, he pushed out forty more, and the last ten were grueling. These final ones did the trick, and his mind loosened, and he was freed from his racing thoughts.

Unsurprisingly, a different feeling overcame him. Compulsion. Reaching over, he pulled out *The Sorcerer's Guide*, but he was drawn to a page he had already read:

There is a clear picture of the involvement of the Chupovanas, who pleasure in the destruction of all magic. Aurora's daughters attempted to uncover the exact plan and learned of an obscure tribe that may have formed an alliance with these foul creatures. The Chupovanas have ravaged the magical communities and caused the loss of the Lexicon's governing power.

Jet paused to think about what he understood to be "the Lexicon's governing power". In truth, he knew very little. He was directed to another page in the book. This time, he knew he needed to read the entire page and recognized Wier's handwriting.

In the beginning, Magic was unstable, unusable, and dangerous. The Five Goddesses of the Four Realms of Earth began to formulate a plan to find a way to control magic. They formed the Lexicon, an agreement and an advocate, and by cutting down the oldest tree in the land, they created five books of creation, later called the Five Books of Terra Maleficis.

Lady Gaea, Atmos Geni, Ella Dastria, Aqua Felis, and Bio Vita reigned over the Four Realms. Atmos Geni discovered Elemental magic and called on it to come to the Earth. It took centuries for magic to be wrangled and disciplined, and when it was finished, five tomes of divine workmanship were produced. I showed you the thirteen priests who used Atmos Geni's instructions to finalize Spirit, and the Cloaks of Armandour were shaped.

Mikado, you wear one of the Cloaks of Armandour, as do your friends.

These five tomes allowed for writings, words, songs, and spells to be understood by the chosen. In essence, the tomes were indestructible, but the words and meanings could be lost or forgotten. All five books were named, and a leader was chosen. When Atmos Geni left to entice the final pieces of Elemental magic, he never returned. Lady Gaea, Aqua Felis, and Bio Vita became the gatekeepers of the Phoenix and other hidden relics.

Created in Goth Airtha, the five types of magic, their tome's name, and the position of their leader as well as the chosen are as follows:

Elemental magic—*The Sorcerer's Guide*—the Mikado and Occultists
Runic magic—*The Mage's Letters*—the Czaric and Mages
Shaman magic—*The Book of Shadows*—the Flamanis and Spirituum

Incrementum magic—*The Recipes of Life*—the Aedificum and Dabant

Resitituals magic—*The Adaptation Guide*—the Ficher and Mutatio

As he read, there was a pang of guilt because he hadn't protected his cloak well enough to keep it and use it today. He missed his cloak and the security it provided him. These words meant something more profound than the first time he had read them. Sure, they gave the name of each book and the chosen leaders and such, but the words—They formed the Lexicon, an agreement, and an advocate... and they were vital.

Jet immediately knew the next page would turn, only requiring a thought in his mind.

Wier's handwriting was visible.

THE LEXICON DEBACLE

The Five Goddesses of the Four Realms of Earth couldn't imagine losing magic, as it had been part of their lives for so long. For centuries, they strived to encourage, tame, and control magic. They designed for it to continue and evolve as it wove its vital connection among those who used it. Diamond Falls became the meeting place and the birth of the Lexicon through Sacrifice, Love, and Work. This agreement was far more than anyone truly understood. Attacking and killing other magical individuals weakened the harmony established by the Five Goddesses. The Fisador Pact was the final tenet in the dissolution of magic because those in authority believed they had no other choice. This allowed for hope that it could someday heal and blossom again.

Specific steps must be taken to allow magic to be reborn to its fullest. The Rivalry provides an avenue for Runic and Elemental magic to return. Leotyton gave his lifeforce to allow *The Sorcerer's Guide* to become powerful again. But for the other lost books, Sacrifice must once again be mandatory. To breathe life into the books, a lifeforce must be given to each of the three newly discovered tomes. This lifeforce must come from a tribesman rather than from the magical or nonmagical. This is but the first of three steps.

The second step involves Love. Three individuals present must terminate their feelings for someone else. They will use the magical words of "Leia Alofa" and their love energy will be removed, igniting a breath within the lifeforce provided.

The third step involves Work. Five individuals, one designated or attached to each magical group, will provide a human shell to accept the Sacrifice and Love provided. This shell will become an Oracle. They must be a Mayeian or non-magical. They will then depart the land, never to be allowed within the confines of any Chalua from that time forward. The five newly chosen Oracles will be required to meet once every other year with the five magical leaders and other assigned attendees, and the Wepet Sumuran will be revitalized. The previous Oracles, if still alive, will have their connections to their magical groups severed, but they will continue to act as who they are—an Oracle.

Once these steps have been accomplished, the newly discovered tomes will open, and magic can choose its newest leaders. All five magical leaders shall strive to work together to defeat Arisol and bring forth peace. The Rivalry prevents other magical types from finding and handling the pieces of the Phoenix and becoming directly involved in that process with golden and black weapons. Still, Incrementum, Resititual, and Shaman magic will be essential in winning the war. So much is still yet to be discovered. The deceit of Arisol is more widespread and devious than ever before known. Any slip of one type of magic or another will bring death to the entire world.

CHAPTER 28

A force of nature began stirring as Jet realized that reviving the Lexicon would be nearly impossible, and the information to do so had blossomed in the final moments. Why hadn't his tome given this information last week? He wanted to throw it out the window. Why couldn't it have given him this information before he invited everyone to Chadwick's? How in the world would he be able to accomplish all these recommendations?

Swoosh

The muffled sound came from the hall outside his door. He wondered if Seyanna had changed her mind. He hoped so. When he reached the door, he looked out the eyehole. The hallway was empty. Despite this, he opened the door, expecting something to have been dropped outside his door. Instead, he noticed the carpet held an imprint of someone's shoes.

"Mikey," Jet hissed. "Are you standing there?"

The boy appeared abruptly, a broad smile plastered on his face. He wrote something on his pad.

Leaning in, Jet read: *It usually takes others several times of opening and closing the door.*

"Ha ha," laughed Jet, but he was happy to see the boy. "Do you want to come in?"

Mikey shook his head once, pulled out a phone, and texted something.

"Do you want me to come with you?" asked Jet, slightly confused.

This time, his head moved back and forth, neither indicating a yes nor a no.

"Are you here to give me a message?"

Mikey's head continued in the same movement but faster.

The elevator chimed down the hallway and opened. Rozene Bluesky stepped out and strolled down to his open door. "Why don't you invite both of us in?"

Jet was shocked to see her. Stepping back, he held the door open. "Please take a seat. What brings you here?"

"Things are more perilous than you can imagine." Rozene wore white shorts and a navy blue tank top. The color of her shirt matched his. She seemed to notice this but said nothing.

"What do you mean?" asked Jet, and he closed the door and followed them.

"Mikey is the best Predilector that we have. Something about his inability to talk makes him all the more capable of becoming invisible. He says you noticed right away, and he's impressed. The last time he was on campus, he didn't feel the presence of another invisible Predilector. Today, there are three. I think one of them is working for the Azurites."

Jet said, "One would tend to believe they're students from Dillon Lake. Does he know who they are?"

Rozene smiled. "Normally, that would be true. But I remember when that girl from San Mateo died, Kevin said that he had visited each school. Oaklyn was his chaperone, and he knew her. His deceit is still completely unknown. I wouldn't be surprised if he placed Predilectors in all the schools."

"That's a sobering concept."

"Mikey was the first to think of it. The three Predilectors aren't any that he recognizes."

Jet said, "If he can feel them, can they feel him?"

"I don't think so," said Rozene. "But I can't be sure. Not until we catch one and ask them."

Jet crossed the room. "This makes things more difficult."

"That's just the beginning. Do you know why the Brotherhood wants to meet you and Shane tomorrow?"

"Something about something that Darium Fitz said."

"Yes," said Rozene. "I was involved, distantly, with his interrogation. He ended up giving information about two safehouses in New York and one in California. The Brotherhood raided the one near here; it was in Ventura. They caught some low-level people, but they also caught Dr. Destiny Descartes. They cornered her. She did not go quietly. In the end, she swallowed something that stopped her heart."

"No way," said Jet. "Is this some KGB crap? Swallowed something?"

Rozene continued, "Darium insists that there's a mole inside the Elementals, maybe even in the Echoes."

"What?" Jet said, temporarily rigid with disbelief. "That better not be true. I can't imagine it is."

"I was there. He had no reason to lie."

"Except to cause us to lose trust in each other."

She considered this, then added, "He was quite convincing. He told us about your hideout inside the rock mountain near the secluded beach. The traitor has been inside and provided details about the trap door in the water and the large open space inside."

"Who interrogated him?"

"Karl Middlesex and Polina Abramov, a deputy chief from Russia."

"Russia?" asked Jet.

"The Brotherhood spent two weeks performing a vetting process of the Chiefs and Deputy Chiefs since Charlie Eckenkeep's treachery. There have been some changes. You've seen Alejandro Vicario on campus. He's from Bolivia and the leading candidate to replace Eckenkeep. There's also Amanki Latu from Tonga, Mostafa Salah from Egypt, and Polina Abramov. Everyone except Vicario has been at Dillon Lake this last week. They all interrogated Darium."

"We were just at Dillon Lake, and no one said anything. They told us the Brotherhood had distanced themselves from the school."

"Partially true. But they knew they had a leak in their security, and you helped close that breach. I've been permitted to tell you the truth as an attempt to bridge the gap and meet on common ground. Some of the more intense interrogations happened after you left."

"Right. They lied to our faces."

Rozene shrugged, and Mikey smiled again, watching him intently.

Seeing that he wasn't going to get anywhere with arguing, he asked, "What are the responsibilities of Chiefs and Deputy Chiefs?

"I don't know everything. Chiefs sit on the governing board and make decisions. Deputy Chiefs control magical missions, searches, and identify problems within a geographical area. Currently, there's an opening in the American branch."

"Was that Charlie's position?"

"Yes," replied Rozene. She stared at him for a moment as if contemplating something.

"What is it?"

"Geb Morvich has been nominated to become a Deputy Chief, and the Brotherhood has agreed."

"Geb?" Jet questioned. "Is this the same Geb here with my grandmother?"

"Yes."

"Did he get nominated because of me? He has been around me and my family for years."

"I don't know the details. From everything I've heard, he'll be a good candidate. He'll replace whoever is chosen to be the replacement of Eckenkeep."

Jet had to forcefully move this new information from the front part of his mind. "Getting back to a traitor inside the Elementals. Do you have any idea who it could be?"

"The Brotherhood thinks it's most likely Eric."

Jet let out a long breath that he didn't even realize he was holding. He wanted to scream and shout. Instead, he said, "I hope you're wrong. That would tear us apart."

Rozene stood. "Just what I heard."

Mikey, who had said nearly nothing, stood, but Rozene's facial expressions softened.

"Is there something else?" asked Jet.

She whispered, "I'm worried about Jayco. He's acting a little off."

"What do you mean? That guy is hard to read."

"He has always been open with me."

"How much can you guys talk while he is here and you're in New York?"

"More than you would think. Faris, one of the Myntra, has been helping us. She has a special phone that allows her to communicate with me and others at Dillon Lake."

"Is she spying on us?"

"Not really. But she informs us of the players at Chadwick's and what's happening."

"That would be a yes."

"Anyways," she muttered. "Jayco has been spending less and less time with Grantham. He has been going out on walks around school, especially at night. He swims in the ocean whenever he can. He's distancing himself."

"Even from you?"

"No. He's very kind and genuine. He surprises me with gifts. But I'll catch him staring off at something, pondering. I'm worried."

"I'll talk with him," said Jet. "I'll see what he's thinking."

She smiled. "Thank you."

"I bet he's thinking about you. He's always talking about you."

"That's nice of you. I hope so."

Mikey and Rozene made their way to the door.

"What should we do about the other Predilectors?"

"Nothing for now. We need to identify them and see who they're working with. I've given Mikey that task. Tomorrow should be a really interesting day."

"What do you mean?"

"Between the Brotherhood's plans, the books, and the potential of finding a traitor. Tomorrow may drastically change all our worlds."

Remembering something she had said one of the first times they met, he said as he opened the door, "You've always wanted magic. What will you do now?"

"When Dillon Lake is stable, I'm coming back here and seeing if Elemental magic chooses me. I have a feeling I would be great at Water magic."

"Good for you," said Jet. "Opposite Fire magic. You could give Jayco a run for his money."

"That's the plan." She winked.

Mikey shook his hand reverently as if he had just met with royalty. Jet laughed as they disappeared. Closing the door, he began searching his refrigerator for something to eat.

There was a loud knock at his door. "Forget something?" he called back, opening the door. Standing on the threshold with takeout Chinese food in her hand was Nana. Despite everything, he smiled.

"Hello Joshua. Can I come in?"

"Please do. That smells delicious."

"I knew my grandson needed a full meal."

"You're not wrong."

She entered and began looking around, as if deciding whether to ground him based on how clean his dorm was. She said, "This is nice. Better than your last one. Grab some plates while I clear off the table."

Opening the cupboard, he asked, "Where have you been?"

"A lot of different places," said Nana, opening the lids to their food. "Mostly with Geb. He and his team have been wonderful. I've seen some peculiar things, and we've discovered a lot."

He stared at his grandmother in disbelief. She had never wanted anything to do with the magic world, going as far as shielding herself.

That was…until Jet got involved. That's when everything changed. "Are you working *for* the Brotherhood?"

"Since your mom and dad died, along with my brother, so much has changed. I was blind to the importance of magic, or at least, I convinced myself to be blind. But now, things are happening at an alarming speed. I fear you're walking a tightrope. One false step, and I'll lose you forever. The Brotherhood gives me purpose, and so I am working with them."

Rushing forward, he hugged Nana harder than he had ever done in his life. He refused to let go for a long time.

She began to cry softly, and she shivered.

He asked, "What's wrong?"

She answered, "The Brotherhood thinks someone will try to injure or kidnap me to get to you."

"What?" he demanded and pulled away. "Are you in danger?" He had worried about something similar just after he and his friends had found the first missing piece of the Phoenix in Silverton. He had called her, and that's when Geb stepped in and began helping her. "Is Geb aware of this?"

"Of course." She found a napkin and wiped away the tears. "They are protecting me. I'm safe. It's just so good to see you. My emotions ran away from me for a moment there."

Pulling out a chair, he helped her sit down. "Where have you been?" Looking closer. She appeared healthy but had aged over the last six months. Her wrinkles on the sides of her eyes and on her forehead had deepened. When she genuinely smiled, the light in her eyes was still there.

"After Silverton, I told you someone came to my home around midnight. In truth, it was three guys. They said they were from

Chadwick's and that you had left early and couldn't be found. I had just seen you, and you told me of your plans, so I knew they were up to no good."

"That wasn't very well thought out," agreed Jet.

"They must not have thought you had stopped by the house yet." She shook her head disapprovingly. "They went to their car, but only one got inside. Geb approached my back door. He said nothing, but through the glass he showed me an old picture with him, your mom, and dad. When I let him in, it only took a few minutes to explain. I grabbed some things, and we left."

"Did you go to Canada?"

She divided the two main dishes, along with the rice, onto two plates. They began eating, as they used to when he was in high school.

"We did," she confirmed. "I told you the truth about going to Calgary. The natural disaster that hit D.C., New York, and the rest of the East Coast didn't affect them. Planes weren't flying much, but we found a place in northern Calgary for a few weeks. You called and told me you would stay with Grantham's parents in Los Angeles. I think that was when you ended up going to Argentina. By then, we were in Winnipeg. The next thing I knew was that you were missing and presumed dead. Geb was angry that we hadn't been there to help you. The Brotherhood was making it difficult for him to get direct information, and you were making it difficult for the Brotherhood to track you."

"Are they watching us that closely?"

Her eyebrows rose as if in answer. "While you were missing, I spoke with Jayco and Grantham a few times and your principal. They provided some details about what happened in Argentina. Geb and I flew from Winnipeg on a private jet to Dallas, a smaller Brotherhood compound. They allowed us to enter, giving us access to information, and helped them with a few things. When you were found, that was pure relief, and we rushed to see you. I can't believe how sick you looked. Then we broke you out of the hospital."

Jet asked, "What was the Brotherhood having you do?"

"Checking up on a few people. Nothing really that exciting."

This time, Jet raised his eyebrows as if questioning her response.

She ignored this and continued, "You probably remember, but after getting you to your dorm, Geb and I learned that six other students were found dead in Argentina. Geb has a close contact who shared that information with us. This pushed Geb and me to travel to Silverton and then Argentina."

Jet asked, "Junjie Su?"

"Not bad," said Nana. "Then, Geb and I returned, and you were in a coma. Talk about taking years off my life. You've caused me more heartbreak than…" She stopped, having seen the look on his face.

He felt horrible. "I didn't mean to," he managed to say.

In a soft voice, she said, "I know. But it was still incredibly hard to watch you suffer. Then, one night, you were gone. At first, no one would tell us what happened. A phone call from the Brotherhood informed us that you were heading to Iceland with Miss. Motick. Honestly, I wasn't too pleased you left me in the dark."

Jet couldn't even form the words he wanted to tell her.

She continued, "I returned to Chadwick's with Geb and Junjie Su and talked about Silverton and Argentina with you."

"I remember," Jet managed to say.

"Geb and I believe that the students killed in Argentina and those who went to Silverton were part of the Azurites. Some of their injuries were from the local beasts, but a mythical creature killed some. The Brotherhood believes it was Faunal."

"What? How?"

Junjie Su and Geb surmise that the Rivalry gives access to only a portion of the resources at each site. The Azurites discovered this, as Darium mentioned. That's why the submarine was so close to Starbuck Island. They planned on returning once you left. Darium stole the brooch and forced his father to surface and attempt to help him."

"Wow," murmured Jet.

"In Silverton, we know they removed those alligator creatures. We firmly believe no school has them, but the Azurites do. We're guessing that ten people went to Argentina. Those who died had sword cuts across their chests, and a few had bite marks. We don't know what might have been uncovered."

"Faunal can't attack me, Shane, or anyone involved in the Rivalry. He seemed to be helping Shane at the beginning, especially in Silverton and Argentina." Staring at Nana, he wondered, "That must mean that Shane is working with the Azurites."

"Darium confirmed that Professor Rysen, your father's college roommate, tricked Shane. The Azurites are helping Arisol, and the Brotherhood is helping the schools. Those in Argentina could have found something that scared them, or someone changed their minds. Faunal killed them and took whatever was found. Shane is misguided in many of his steps, and the Brotherhood is worried about him as a leader. Trying to take over the school was another mounting concern."

"That kid is an idiot."

"But a powerful one."

"Did you end up going to Egypt after all?"

"Yes. Cairo. I saw some of the inner workings of the Brotherhood. I can't give you all the details."

"Why?"

"I made a promise," she said. Her voice made it perfectly clear she would not answer any more questions about Egypt. "We were there for a few weeks, and then we were instructed to go to Starbuck Island. When we arrived, another ship was there, along with a submarine."

"Professor Rysen!"

"We couldn't get any closer. The Brotherhood sent in drones at night. Part of the island was underwater. They sent divers below and brought out five or six crates of items to the surface. We couldn't visualize what it might be."

"Did you get inside?"

"They collapsed the entrance before leaving."

"I don't get them. What's their goals?" asked Jet. "What could they have found?"

"Darium said that he explained their plans to you. They think Arisol is the liberator of the world, not its destroyer. They're trying to find every available artifact, weapon, book, or creature that can stop you and Shane from fighting Arisol when he is eventually released. They will join his side.

"At first, they tried helping Shane win the Rivalry. Darium said that a mind magic attack on an Azurite leadership while visiting Silverton in the days after it was destroyed gave Faunal the information about Shane Fallon. That person knew about the plan to help Shane become the student who controlled one of the books. Faunal befriended him and then tried tricking him. Professor Rysen did the same thing. For all the despicable things Shane is, he botched their first plan. Even Faunal failed in the end. Some of his closest friends double-crossed him. When it became clear that Shane wouldn't help the Azurites, Charlie Eckenkeep created a plan to trick Kevin and turn him. Who would have guessed? That stung the Brotherhood more than they will ever admit. He was their prize. The Azurites will gloat about that until the end of time."

For several long seconds, he was full of compassion and empathy for what Shane had endured. The moment passed as Shane's divisive actions returned to his thoughts. His mind shifted to Darium and his attempt to disrupt the control over Nimliaki by stealing the brooch. Again, this is another attempt at chaos by the Azurites. "We met Darsil Müller, and he's a fanatic for the Azurites. This entire war between them is ridiculous."

"Most feuds are. It's been going on for years."

"How close have the attempts been on your life?" asked Jet flatly.

"Not close. The information has been found on a few different platforms. Geb and my guards have stopped any serious threats."

Jet paused, staring at Nana. She didn't flinch or react.

"I'm fine," she finally said.

Jet asked, "Anything else I should know?"

"Geb had been nominated for an important position in the leadership of the Brotherhood. He believes it is partly due to his relationship with you. The Brotherhood needs a win. I would ask that you work with Geb, even if only at face value. The Brotherhood needs to be seen as in control."

"What do I get from the deal?"

"Information and insight."

"I should be able to do that."

"Good to hear." Standing, she pulled him close, and they hugged for a long time. She set off to wrap the rest of the food and cleaned up their empty plates. He was tempted to help but knew he shouldn't. When she finished, she said, "This was good. I needed to see and talk with you. To hold you is comforting. So much has happened since the beginning of the year."

Jet wasn't sure what to say. "Classes end next week. I don't think we have a choice but to stay on campus. Going back to Portland is out of the question."

"I know."

"What about you?" asked Jet.

"They sent another team to Congo. After this weekend, Geb and I will be heading to Spruce Knob. You guys have been busy."

Jet nodded.

"How does tomorrow look for you?"

"Like walking into a burning house."

"It'll be fun from the sidelines. I'm excited to watch what happens."

"Thanks."

"Let Geb or me know if we can help you."

"I have something in mind for Geb. If he can help me out. I will work with the Brotherhood, and it won't be just for show."

"Interesting," said Nana. "And unexpected."

"I'll give him more details tomorrow."

"Goodnight," said Nana, and she let herself out of his dorm.

CHAPTER 29

The next morning, Jet ate breakfast in his dorm, deliberating on everything from the last twenty-four hours. Pulling out his phone, he sent a group text to the Echoes with new information. He wanted to bounce a few ideas off them. By the time he'd finished eating, no one had replied. He sent a text to Jayco privately, but there was no response.

He found it impossible to involve all his friends in every decision that he had to make, especially since *The Sorcerer's Guide* opened on its own accord. Was it unreasonable to hope they would trust him enough to make the right choices? Too often, he felt guilty that he was keeping something from them, and he usually was. It wasn't necessarily by desire or to be secretive, but it was just how things worked out.

In the pit of his stomach, he knew today would turn out to be a disaster. He wanted to trust his friends, but after hearing from Rozene and Nana last night, he wasn't sure he could...not completely. Darium had the layout of their secret hideout. Who was the traitor? Could it really be Eric? The conflict between the Azurites and the Brotherhood was no secret, but the depth to which the Azurites and Faunal had gone was insightful.

As important as these concepts were, they served as distractions from what needed to happen. To rekindle magic, he would require all his focus on figuring out how to incorporate Sacrifice, Love, and Work into a ceremony to bring back magic fully. He couldn't stop thinking about Love and what it would take. He wondered if he had the strength.

The first official meeting of the day was scheduled to take place at 9:00 a.m. in the English building with the Brotherhood and the Echoes. He assumed the Brotherhood wanted to express their beliefs on how magic should be given, if they had any idea of how that was to happen.

A text arrived from Jayco as he left his dorm: *Shane has not been invited to our first meeting. I just spoke with Li Wei. I've sent Keesha, Eric, Autumn, Raul, Phillip, and Ariana to make sure Shane doesn't schedule a secret meeting without our knowledge. I have invited the class presidents of the other boarding schools.*

There was a small sense of relief. At least Jayco had followed his recommendations...this time. He stepped from his dorm with plenty of time to spare. He wanted a few moments to discuss plans with his friends. Inside the English building, he went upstairs rather than down the hallway to the classroom he was familiar with.

When he reached the top floor, Mckenzey's voice echoed from a closed door down the hallway. "Jet has had a lot on his mind. He hasn't overlooked his promises to help the Brotherhood or keep them informed."

Principal Smuin retorted, "Jet does things his own way. Li Wie here is concerned. Jet has accomplished so much, and yet, look where we are. We're no closer to being ready for the upcoming war than we were a year ago. Shane's proposal is not ideal, but it has merits."

Jayco said, "She has a point."

"No, she doesn't," said Grantham. "Why doesn't Shane give up his two crystals? We're in a better position than he is."

Latisha asked, "Why does the Brotherhood think they have a say in this?"

"Because," said the voice of an older woman, Junjie Su, "the fate of the world rests with the decisions that are made today. Not just the pride of one group or one person."

Jet stopped at the outer door and considered his options. Barging in and arguing might turn out to be the most fun.

Seyanna said, "We received your proposal last night. We don't completely agree with you, and I'm certain that Jet is acting and doing his best. I don't believe he has been hiding something this big from us without a reason."

"You say that because you're involved with him," hissed Jayco. "You need to separate common sense from your feelings. The evidence is right here."

"Jayco," said Mckenzey. "That's rich coming from you. When Jet and I initially brought the idea of magic to you, Grantham caught on first. It wasn't that long ago that you sided with Shane, only for him to lock you, Grantham, and Latisha up. You've been jealous of Jet since day one."

"None of that matters now. If this picture gets out to the rest of the school, the integrity of the Elementals will be gravely injured," argued Jayco. "I don't want to work with Shane ever again, but Jet is a sinking ship."

"Whenever it comes to friendship with Jet, you have one foot halfway out the door," said Seyanna. "You haven't even talked to Jet about this picture. You should hear his explanation. Didn't you just defend him a second ago?"

"I was attempting to be polite. But the reality is that he's struggling under the burden of leadership."

Jet's hand touched the doorknob.

Li Wei's majestic voice spoke. "We've verified the picture. It is authentic and hasn't been altered or, how do you say, photoshopped. This is happening. The Brotherhood will ask Jet to step down. If he won't, we insist the Elementals transfer the remaining three pieces of the Phoenix to the Runics. We need to have a solid force to confront Arisol."

"Jet won't back down," insisted Mckenzey. "Not after everything he's been through."

Jayco asked, "Can you explain this photo? It looks recent."

Seyanna added, "I held things from you guys. They were huge. I had a reason, and I bet he does as well."

"Fine," said Junjie Su. "We will hear his explanation."

"Our minds were made up on this from the moment Shane approached us with this photo," said Li Wei. "I just wish we had had it sooner."

"What's that supposed to mean?" asked Grantham. "This better not be about Kevin McCormick."

"No," said Chief Lara Brancoff. "Kevin made fundamental misjudgments, and there are no excuses. Shane will receive the blessing of the Brotherhood going forward."

Lathisha asked, "What are the Elementals supposed to do?"

"Join Shane," said Geb Morvich. "If Shane's the final choice of the Brotherhood, Jet could remain the leader of the Elementals in a manner. All decision-making would need to go through Shane."

"We can't," said Grantham. "This is ridiculous."

Jet was overwhelmed and confused by what he was hearing. Jayco, Junjie Su, Li Wei, Principal Smuin, and Geb were against him. He always knew the Brotherhood didn't like him. They couldn't control him. Was that their intention? What was happening?

"Does his grandmother know?" asked Latisha.

Geb said solemnly, "I told her this morning. I showed her the pictures."

"Why would he lie to us?" asked Seyanna, sounding injured.

"Control and power," said Jayco. "Think about it. He only tells us what he wants us to know. Usually, it benefits him and keeps him in power."

"Do you hear what you're saying?" asked Mckenzey. "Jet has almost died several times. All of us have. And you think this is about power."

Mckenzey said, "I'll never trust Shane. We're not giving him the three pieces of the Phoenix. He can go suck it."

Grantham added, "I agree. I trust Jet."

Jayco said slowly. "We will see. But..."

Jet burst into the room, a gigantic smile on his face and fire dancing in his hands. He'd never had so much control over magic. "Hello, Principal Smuin, the Brotherhood, and the Echoes. I hope I'm not interrupting. You guys are so loud. Heavens. No wonder everyone knows our plans from the beginning."

His sudden appearance shot waves of panic through the room. Seyanna glanced at the floor while Jayco's mouth dropped open. Latisha and Grantham flinched as their hands found each other. Li Wei snarled, but Junjie Su winked at him astutely. A sly smile was on Geb's face as if he was trying to communicate with him.

Jayco blurted, "The meeting doesn't start until 9:00 a.m."

"Which is in twenty minutes, you idiot. You didn't think I would try to be early and talk with my *friends*? Regarding Arisol, I joined forces with and released him last week. He's rampaging around Russia and China. I'm not going to release the other books. I feel bad, but we're cronies now, so it's all good. As for Shane, he's still a pompous prick, so that's stayed the same."

"Glad you're here," said Li Wei hastily. "We would like to discuss a few things with you."

"What is Shane's proposal?" Jet walked forward self-assuredly. Something shifted in his vision, and he thought someone else had entered through a different door.

Seyanna spoke. "Shane will leave Chadwick's and go to Dillon Lake peacefully, if he has all five crystals, or he will begin a war and cripple the Elementals permanently. He'll use a picture of you. He has threatened to send it to every student and boarding school. The picture will question your ability to lead the Elementals. He has shown it to Jayco, Principal Smuin, and Li Wei. This is the first time we've seen it."

"Let me see the picture," said Jet.

"Why?" asked Jayco. "So, you can make up a story about it? The evidence is clear."

"Shut up, Jayco," said Jet. "Let me see the damn photo."

Geb held it out. It was a 4 x 6 photo. Jet glanced at it, and the entire room began to spin. His anger, frustration, and sadness were sucked from the moment, as if a black hole had swallowed everything around him. Gone were his friends and the Brotherhood. The fire in his hand vanished.

"Oh my," he wheezed.

The picture was of him, probably around fifteen, sitting with his mom and dad at a restaurant, eating dinner. Three others were in the picture, enjoying the evening. Across from his parents sat Dalf Rysen, Alex Wozniak, and Dr. Destiny Descartes.

Jet's mind flashed back to the bus in Germany. He watched from outside the bus as it rolled five times. It was partially submerged underwater, and bodies were sprawled on the ground. Suddenly, he was pulled inside, next to Geb, and his parents were dead. Three people strolled forward: Rysen, Descartes, and Wozniak. They had been the ones to kill his parents.

Stumbling to his knees, he vomited on the floor. Someone touched his shoulder, and someone else snatched the photo from him. The instant the photo left his grip, he improved slightly, but the picture was implanted in his mind. It made him feel gross.

He thought a door slammed somewhere behind him. It was probably just a figment of his imagination.

Rufian's voice spoke from far away. He had no idea why Rufian was there. "Get him into a chair. There's poison in the photo. He needs to relax."

"A poison," asked Jayco. "How?"

"Never you mind."

Jet heard some mumbling.

Rufian spoke again. "Jet told me about a time when kids were attacked and turned red. He said he used a powder to get rid of the skin changes."

Mckenzey said, "I remember. I took some of it as well."

"I need a cup full of that powder."

"I'll go," she said.

"Wait," said Rufian. "Be careful in how and where you go. This might be a trap for all of you."

"What are you talking about?" asked Jayco. "A picture can't poison someone."

Latisha said, "Grantham and I will go with you."

"Thanks," said Mckenzey.

"Jayco!" Someone asked, "Can I see the picture?"

"Rozene. What are you doing here?"

She answered, "Mikey followed Jet this morning. He heard that something was going on. He called me as soon as Jet arrived. I need to look at that photo."

"I guess," answered Jayco.

"Oh, boy," said Rozene. "This isn't a fake photo, but it isn't real either."

"That doesn't explain a thing," said Seyanna. "What's happening to Jet?"

Something pricked his arm, and he lost all control of his movements.

"I've caused him to sleep," said Rufian. "It'll prevent the spread of the poison."

* * *

Jet awoke in the English building and lay on a recliner chair. His head was fuzzy, and he didn't know how much time had elapsed. Rufian, the Myntra, some of the Brotherhood, his friends, Rozene, Mikey, and others sat and talked. Seyanna sat on the floor beside him, tear marks running down her face.

"Wow. That was enjoyable," his voice cracked. "Can we do that again?"

Seyanna jumped, and Rufian, Mckenzey, and Latisha rushed forward.

"How are you feeling?" asked Seyanna.

"Sick and tired of all this happening to me. Where's Rozene?"

"Here."

"Before I passed out, I heard you say something about the picture."

Rozene asked, "Can you remember the picture?"

Jet's vision was slightly blurry. He felt exhausted as if he'd run two marathons. He wasn't sure he could stand. "Unfortunately. It was me, my parents, and some Azurites. My parents are dead, and those three are some of the worst people in the world." Jet couldn't bring himself to say what they had done.

"Several things in the picture tell us that this was a manipulation. The first is your parents' eyes. They are offset. But after that, there's a mark on the neck of all six people in the picture. Did you see it?"

In his mind, Jet focused on the picture and the necks of all six people. "A line on top, a small circle, then a line below. I didn't notice that before."

Rozene said, "Those six are regular people sitting there, but a Predilector has superimposed pictures on top of the people. When this is done, the mark happens."

Jet's throat was on fire. "Were the Runics involved?"

"Well," said Rozene. "Yes and no. But I don't think Shane was complicit in what happened. At least not the photo part."

"What does that mean?"

"Take a look for yourself," replied Rufian.

The picture was held in front of him. All six people were still there, but only as shells over the real individuals he was looking at. He saw Darium Fitz, Julian Kelley, and Kevin McCormick. The next two he recognized were Lincoln and Zoey, who helped Darium on the ship leaving Starbuck Island. They were both caught. That last person was mind-blowing, and Jet was dumbfounded. It was Brenda, the girl who had worked in the mailroom at the beginning of the year. The girl who had been killed by his old roommates, Rick and Jackson, after they had become traitorous and joined Shane, only to be turned into Wraiths.

"This can't be possible," said Jet, and he shifted. But he stared into her green eyes and her awkward smile. "Latisha!" he cried out. "I thought you said you saw Brenda die. How can she be in this picture?"

"Brenda?" she asked softly and hesitantly. She came forward and took the picture, concentrating on it. "That's not Brenda. I didn't see this girl die. I've never seen her before."

Jayco said, "That girl in the picture is Rick's girlfriend. I found her crying once near our hidden beach. We became decent friends. She and I talked a few times."

Jet asked, "Did you ever let her see inside our hiding spot?"

"No," said Jayco defensively. "She was curious about what I was doing."

Grantham asked, "Did you let her see inside?"

Jayco finally admitted, "Only once. It was not a big deal."

Jet coaxed the chair to sit up straighter. "How could I have been so stupid? Everyone in this picture works for the Azurites. She wasn't

Rick's girlfriend. She was playing me the entire time. I gave her a magical ring before I knew what they were."

"That doesn't explain the poison," said Seyanna. "Or how this picture came to look like it did."

Rozene said, "A Predilector used their ability to alter what you were seeing. I have no idea about the poison."

"That was a specialty of the Coven. It was meant for Jet and no one else. It was a warning." Rufian's eyes connected with Jet, and he knew this was about his promise to Marcella.

"Did you have to sprinkle the black powder on me?"

Rufian said, "No. You had to drink it. A black shadowed cat clawed out of your mouth. None of us wants to see that again."

"A cat?"

Rufian whispered, "A warning from Marcella."

"I really hate her," replied Jet.

"Me too," replied Rufian.

Li Wei said, "So, we know this photo is a fake."

"We do," replied Rufian.

Glancing down, Jet found that his hand was intertwined with Seyanna, who had heard their conversation but said nothing. She squeezed his hand. Jet forced a smile on his face. He asked loudly, "Can we get this meeting going?"

"No," said Seyanna. "We can try again tomorrow."

"We don't have time. There's a lot to discuss."

Jet stood unsteadily, letting go of Seyanna's hand. She and Rufian helped him to the chairs surrounding the conference table. Quickly, the others found their seats. Taking a moment to gather his energy, he glanced around. Jayco sat between Latisha and Grantham. He wasn't sure he could ever trust Jayco again. He had crossed a line. Next to him was Seyanna, then Mckenzey. On the opposite side, Geb, Junjie Su, Li Wei, Lara Brancoff, and Ethan Davenport were next to Karl Middlesex. Geb and Junjie Su smiled as if they knew something the rest didn't. The Myntra stood behind the Brotherhood. Rozene sat near Jayco but next to Latisha. Next to her were Nylah Veeda, a boy he didn't know, Diego Axel, Evelyn Ulm, and two others he didn't know, along with the principals of each school. He assumed they arrived after his near-death experience.

Jet muttered, "We need to call Shane to attend this meeting."

"We can't," said Jayco. "We talked about this."

"Things have changed," said Jet, without glancing at Jayco.

Diego said, "He's in the building. I saw him."

"Leave it to me," said Grantham, and he left. Thirty seconds later, Shane, Jessiva, Jocelyn, and Beckham entered the room, but there were no seats, so they stood in the back.

When Jet finally spoke, his voice was hoarse and deeper than usual. "Valiant effort, Shane. The photo was a deepfake. You'll not be getting our Phoenix pieces. And tonight, we need to meet with all the schools and determine if we will bring back magic."

The boy beside Nylah asked, "Is this even a question?"

"Who are you?" demanded Grantham.

"Javier Malcom. I'm a student at Cranbrook. I fear that with the request made by Darsil Müller, our school is at the greatest risk. Having magic and protection would create stability."

Jet asked, "Are you willing to allow members of the Runics and the Elementals onto your campus to provide protection?"

"Protection from what? We'll have the Claustra."

"So did Dillon Lake," said Rozene. "The Chupovana found a way inside."

"I don't know," said Javier, and he glanced at Nylah. "We will have to discuss our options."

"Exactly," wheezed Jet. "There is much we must consider."

Evelyn replied, "I hope you aren't suggesting we came here for nothing. Chadwick's invited us here for our magical books."

"No," said Jet. "We invited you here to discuss the options. But, as long as we come to some sort of agreement, I don't see why it can't happen. But, trust me, the cost will be great."

Diego replied, "What sort of cost are we talking about?"

"We will get to that."

With his hands steepled in front of him, Li Wei said, "We would formally suggest that Shand Fallon lead this conversation."

"Shane?" asked Jet. He bent his head to stare at the leader of the Runics. "Do you have insight into how the Lexicon will be accomplished?"

"The what?"

Jet's eyes narrowed on Li Wei. "I hope that answers who will be directing the proceedings."

Li Wei mumbled something no one could understand.

"Additionally. We need some assurances from the Brotherhood."

"Us?" replied Ethan Davenport, who sat back comfortably. He could be an executive from a stock exchange company with his expensive suit and fresh haircut. "Why would you need something from us?"

"The Brotherhood has long been involved in the instruction of kids in hopes that they would one day be governed by the Brotherhood when magic came back to the earth," said Jet. "The first round of students was given a golden necklace with a small golden open book. I was part of the group, and so was Devon Dartmouth, also known as Dart. I'm pretty sure Shane was part of this group as well. The second group involved Evelyn, Stefan, Sakura, and Javier, two of which we have in this room today. Evelyn and Javier, if I'm not mistaken, have been working with Shane. Evelyn sent notes to Shane even through our defenses as some from her school were searching for Spruce Knob."

Evelyn shouted, "You don't know that."

"I saw the note you sent Shane. You were watching the school. You've been working with Shane because he promised to find your missing book. I assume the same is for Javier."

"Stop," said Li Wie. "You don't need to say all this to everyone."

Jet turned to face Li Wei, his intended target. "That's the problem, Commander. The Brotherhood and the Azurites are playing games behind our backs. You're using the Runics, the Elementals, Kevin, and the Predilectors to your own set of rules. It's time for you to come clean. There's something you aren't telling us about the upcoming magical war."

"No idea what you're talking about," mumbled Li Wei, but his face betrayed the lie.

Jet spoke slowly and calmly. "You've meddled so much that you've forgotten that we are putting *our* lives on the line. We need to know the truth. Why are you so involved in magic?"

Li Wei licked his lips, his hands still steepled. "It isn't that important."

Mckenzey asked, "Why have you been holding out on us?"

"We haven't," said Lara Brancoff. "We're just trying to ensure that we're as prepared as possible—"

Jet interrupted, "So, you haven't even told some of your closest advisors. It's time to come clean."

Li Wei didn't glance around at the other members of the Brotherhood. He stared directly at Jet, his eyes unfocused, as if he were seeing something that only he could see. His voice was low and mechanical. "Before the Azurites broke off from the Brotherhood, four of us were led to a discovery in Oman, near the Arabian Sea. This was years before I became Commander. I have always been able to feel magic and am a true Predilector. The students of Dillon Lake are created Predilectors. I was born this way, as were many of those in the Brotherhood.

"We were guests of the county and had a group of tour guides as we traveled in the Hajar Mountains. When we reached a location with an unseen black key overlapping a crevice, this was not a well-known area. Our guides couldn't see the magical spotlight, but they recognized the evil residing there. They fled for their lives. Myself, the previous commander, and two others that shall remain nameless went inside."

"Why won't you say their names?" asked Junjie Su.

"They have died. Their misdeeds will die with me." Li Wei continued, "The cavern descended into the depths. Following the magical signs, we eventually arrived at the tomb of one of the oracles of the 10 Kings. Arisol had been imprisoned, but we were about to learn about the Rivalry and the eventual release of the Demon Prince through a series of events. In this location, we found the Talismans and the Claustra. We uncovered scrolls explaining where to find other books and such. We uncovered the recipes for the tonics and a dozen more relics. The Azurites later stole an ancient weapon we located. It was used to attack the bus that killed your parents."

The story enthralled Jet. "Keep going."

"There was a price to pay to be given the Talismans, Claustra, and other items. The four of us had to promise not to reveal what we learned until it could not be helped. The other three never spoke of what we learned."

"What was the knowledge you learned?" asked Jayco.

Again, Li Wei only spoke to Jet. "We learned that if Arisol gets hold of the tablet known as the Phoenix, not only will he win the war, but every living human soul who has touched magic will die. Every student who has ever attended any of the boarding schools, their families, or anyone who has stepped onto the grounds of the school will die. Every Azurite, Brotherhood, or anyone who has helped will die."

"There's no way you would withhold this from us," cried Lara Brancoff.

Li Wei ignored her. "The Elementals and the Runics hold *our* lives in their hands."

"Unbelievable," said Geb. "All these years we've been lied to."

Again, Li Wei said nothing but stared at Jet, this time waiting for a response.

"It took a while for me to understand why you would work with Kevin and Shane and allow some of the things you've allowed," said Jet. "Shane has always been unpredictable. But you told him, didn't you?"

Li Wei swallowed. "After graduating from Dillon Lake, his father worked closely with the Brotherhood. I wouldn't say he was within the leadership. He uncovered a portion of the threat and confronted the Commander at the time. I was forced to placate him with partial truths. He guessed the rest, and I would bet he has told Shane."

"When did you visit Oman?"

"Nearly sixty years ago."

"You've spent this entire time—

"Preparing for magic to return," finished Li Wei. "And preventing the deaths of thousands or hundreds of thousands."

Junjie Su said, "You should have told *us*."

"We told you what was necessary," argued Li Wei.

"How did Shane get *The Mage's Letters*?" asked Jet.

"We had them initially and learned immensely from them. The oracle from Oman pointed us to where they could be found in Indonesia. They were discovered in an underwater cave at the bottom of Lake Toba. It's the largest volcanic lake in the world. However, the book was stolen many years later. We had been given the word to open them and were advised what to add, but we couldn't read the words that were already there. We added some letters and other items where we could. It was a surreal process. Slaves removed other artifacts from the cave."

"We were always told," said Junjie Su, "that the books came from the cave itself."

"That was a lie."

"Why?"

"To protect the truth." Li Wei continued, "Jstor Farish learned the truth and did not like how we were testing young children to see if they might be capable of opening the books, and he stole them. I still don't know how your parents found *The Sorcerer's Guide,* but we believe Jstor Farish hid or gave *The Mage's Letters* to someone in Germany. Your parents were on their way to get the second book. They were as talented as anyone." Li Wie's voice trailed off.

Jet added, "Shane said that he, Clara Yarrow, and Charlie Eckenkeep met someone in Germany and were given *The Mage's Letters*."

"Yes. A lady named Freya Hahn held the book and gave it to them. I never knew if she found it or was helping Jstor Farish."

Jet asked, "Did you know the book would open to Shane?"

"It was a high probability," said Li Wei. "During our testing of some of the children, we learned that Shane has the ability to ask a question and can tell if the person is lying. He must ask the question and hear the answer. That's why he was there. The book opened to him a few years later, when he turned sixteen."

Jayco said, his voice thick with derision, "Okay, Commander. Let's make sure we understand. The Rivalry is real, but more importantly, if Arisol touches the Phoenix, we're all dead. So...you change your allegiance to whoever gives you the best chance to control all six pieces. At times, it was the Elementals, then Kevin was brought in, but you lost control of him. Now, you want us to give all the pieces to Shane."

"Yes," Li Wei said bluntly. "In war, you play to your advantages. Having the Phoenix in the hands of one person decreases the chances it falls into the hands of the wrong person."

"No," said Jayco. "That's not true. You would divide the pieces and hide them. That's exactly what they did in ancient times. The Rivalry is bringing them back together. We should split them so that Arisol can never find them."

"No," said Jet and Li Wei in chorus.

Jet added, "We need the Phoenix to defeat Arisol. There are enough of Arisol's comrades that he will eventually find them."

"But if he gets the Phoenix, we all die," pleaded Jayco.

Jet nodded. "Nothing has changed for us. The stakes might seem bigger, but it's all the same."

"No, it's not," said Jayco. "It's far worse. I say we divide the pieces. Shane has one, and we have four."

Jet's body tensed. He hoped no one heard what Jayco had just let slip. "It doesn't matter. We need to control all of them."

"Wait," said Rozene. "It's common knowledge at the other boarding schools, largely because Shane won't shut up about it. He has two pieces, and you have three pieces."

Jayco said, "Shane cheated on the second task, and his piece is a knockoff, not the real thing."

Grantham asked, "Why did you have to tell everyone?"

"We need to work together and not apart. We need everyone's help. If everyone is going to die, we need everyone working together."

"I'll agree with that," said Jet. "And that's why tonight, we'll find a way to bring back the other three types of magic."

"And how are we going to do that?" asked Shane.

"*The Sorcerer's Guide* gave me the steps to do it last night. But it's going to be much harder than we ever imagined."

"What's that supposed to mean?" asked Evelyn.

Jet said. "It will require choices and sacrifices, and more than one person will walk away, forever changed. The party starts at 6:00 p.m. Invite everyone." Jet stood to leave the room. "I'm going to my dorm, and I don't want to be disturbed. We'll meet on the football field at the time selected. See you then."

CHAPTER 30

The fiery golden sun was nearing the end of its daily expedition as Jet set off for the football stadium, with far too much on his mind. He had ignored several phone calls and texts, but he didn't sleep. He had sent out a single text of instruction and one phone call. He had spent his time packing clothes, weapons, food, and other items in case things went badly. There was always a chance, and he needed to be ready. He worried that Seyanna was hurt by his partial retreat over the last few hours. Iris paced next to him. Other students gave him a wide berth, and no one approached.

He strolled past guards posted throughout campus and was unaware of the full extent of the security implemented by the Brotherhood, Principal Smuin, and the other schools. The two golden animals, Braverly, and the four black Runic animals guarded the campus perimeter, along with adults, mirrors, and other students. Still, he suspected there was more than even he was aware of. Entrapping the Azurites was no longer a priority, but keeping safe was.

A large crane, a construction trailer, and piles of supplies were situated east of the football field. The final repairs were nearly completed on a building where an explosion had happened weeks before. Every worker had been escorted from the property hours ago, and the area had been thoroughly searched for stragglers and assessed for risks for tonight's affair.

Students from each boarding school, their principals, and members of the fifteen tribes would be in attendance tonight. The largest number of those in attendance would be Elementals and Runics. But like back at Dillon Lake, there would be non-magical, important community members, and others invited by the Brotherhood. Meeting in the open posed risks, the largest of which was an open attack by the Azurites or a group of Chupovanas.

Jet smiled at the two guards at the southern entrance and was quickly waved through the instant they spotted Iris. He arrived on time. Most of the other Elementals would be seated. The Echoes had been tasked with getting a layout of those who had arrived and monitoring for anything unusual.

A vast four-sided platform was situated on the eastern side of the field, near where one team would stand on the sideline. Forty or fifty chairs were situated on the stage, and another two hundred chairs faced it. Some onlookers chose to sit in the stadium's seats. This would be perfect for sneak attacks, but harder to escape. Jet, three Elementals, Shane, and three Runics, twenty teachers, five principals, members of the Brotherhood, and three other guests would be seated on the stage, behind a single lectern and a small dais.

The Elementals on the stage with him would be Raul, Keesha, and Phoebe. He had deliberately chosen not to have any Echoes and invited them to spread out in groups of three or more to watch the proceedings. Seyanna had stopped texting after this information had been sent out. Jayco, Grantham, Latisha, and Rozen sat together. Mckenzey, Eric, Seyanna, and Maria were closer to the seating area. Others were spread out among the other guests.

Over two hundred individuals whispered as Jet crossed the open area to the stage. Many eyes turned in his direction. His mind was brought back to the phone call to Seyanna just before heading over.

"Why won't you tell anyone the plan for tonight?" asked Seyanna.

"The required choices must be given to all."

"What choices?"

"Certain individuals will be asked to make choices and sacrifices to allow the books to be given and the Lexicon recreated."

Seyanna replied, "You've managed to make everyone worried, mad, and hopeful, all at once."

"I didn't do all of that," he insisted. "Starting tonight, many cards will be on the table for all to see. I can't be blamed for keeping things hidden."

Seyanna's voice dropped, "You should know the potential consequences of this plan of yours. Jayco and several others almost left tonight."

"I'm not surprised."

She added, "He's a boy who believed himself to be the most important, who is coming to terms with reality."

"This isn't a contest," said Jet.

"Someone forgot to tell Jayco," she said.

"See you soon."

The conversation ended.

As he approached the platform, he saw the Myntra talking with Karl Middlesex. With his hands, Karl made it clear he wanted to ask him a question. Jet shook away the request. The Rufu squad was there, as were three official leaders of the Azurites, including Darsil Müller. Peace must've been brokered for a few hours, but that meant nothing. Fresh off a defeat in Congo, the Rufu squad glared at him.

Several members of the Wandering Nomads stood together, and another stood apart. His clothes were darker than the others. As the main turned to face Jet, the word "Foresworn" was embroidered near his left shoulder. Jet sucked in two quick breaths.

Rufian appeared next to him. Jet had stopped to stare at the tribesmen, "Those are the Arma Arches. I think that's Arma Petacid, Arma Davine, and Arma Atticus, though I can't be certain. I haven't met some of their newer leadership. So much has changed since I was free to roam."

"You know them?" asked Jet, enamored by their clothing.

Rufian said, "There are fewer than two thousand left. I know I should have better relations with them. Hopefully one day."

"They look like they live in the swamp."

"They have transformed since the days of Goth Aritha. They are evolving." They wore long, damp robes, with braided hair and thick-soled, waterproof shoes. It almost seemed like their skin sagged in areas. They weren't overweight; in fact, the opposite was true. They were lean and muscled. "That group created many of the elite weapons of the time. It is believed they created many weapons used in the Rivalry."

"What about them?" asked Jet, and he pointed to eight tribe members who were oversized on everything. They held gigantic spears, maces with spikes, or both. Their clothing was nearly as thick as Jet's winter coat, but only covered the essential areas. They had a protective chest plate, along with arm and leg bands. No matter the color of their skin, their hair was caramel brown.

"Those are the Machitis. They're comprised of ninety percent males, and the rest are females. The women run the tribe, like queens."

"How did you manage to get so many of the Coven on land?" Jet stared at more than thirty members of the Coven's leadership. Jet knew the names of two, Camora and Bigorea.

"A temporary border change and some added ocean water. They are being monitored constantly."

They were all seated in a raised section, with an ocean swimming pool below them. Marcella's seat was on the stage, near Rufian's.

Turning, Jet spotted Dorthwallow and a dozen Axenkind. "How did they get here so fast?"

A sly smile crossed Rufian's face. "They weren't that far away to begin with. We are concerned about your safety and the safety of the school. They are on high alert."

Jet's eyebrows rose, but he said nothing.

The next group resembled a group of avid learners—scholarly, with calm robes the same color as beach sand. All ten were vastly different in height, skin color, and build. They held scrolls, wore glasses, and engaged in deep discussion with one another. "Discerests?" he asked.

Rufian nodded. "That last group is the Narvanians. They are shorter than the Machitis, but not by much."

Jet noted that this group of nine travelers wore earth-colored cloaks with dirt stains. They drank water freely from beautifully carved cups. They brought gardening tools and planted plants in pots.

Rufian and Jet had reached the stairs, and they climbed the few steps. Raul, Keesha, and Phoebe were already seated, as were Shane,

Jocelyn, Jessiva, and Beckham. The five principals divided the Elementals and the Runics. He was relieved he didn't have to sit next to Shane or Marcella.

Rufian said, "Best of luck. This may be the best day in our history or one of the worst."

Jet gulped at these chilling words. "Thanks!" he managed to say.

Principal Smuin said, "Jet Black. Can you step over here for a second?"

He did. Shane was also called over.

Principal Smuin said, "This is the most scrutinized gathering in the history of men. Congratulations on being a part of it. Don't let it turn into the most dreadful moment in existence. Promise that neither of you will start a war tonight."

"Shouldn't happen, sir," said Shane shamelessly.

"Promise," added Jet sarcastically. He found his seat and checked his phone. Principal Smuin sat next to him. A text chimed from Seyanna. It read: *Meet me at the hideout when this is all over. We need to talk.*

Jet texted back. He thought about his words...then hit send: *Sorry. I can't. If things work out as I think they will, please know I am sorry. I never really knew how complex this would get. I never had a real chance with you in the end. No matter what happens, it will be my biggest regret.* He turned off his phone and concentrated on what would happen next.

Principal Smuin whispered, "Do you have any idea what will happen if today doesn't go well?"

"An inkling."

"Is this going to turn into a war?"

"Maybe. But even if I knew, I don't think I would tell you."

Principal Smuin shook his head. "What is your problem?"

"I've come to believe that you've known more than you led us to believe. I'm also certain you haven't kept your side of the agreement. You know what Shane did to this school, and you were so ready to give him back the power. Your decisions have given me pause." Jet turned toward Raul, turning his back on Principal Smuin. "How are you guys?" he asked the others.

"Nervous," said Keesha.

Raul nodded.

Phoebe asked, "Why did you choose us?"

"I trust you three. I need you to watch my back if anyone should try to attack me."

Raul asked, "Are you serious?"

"Completely."

A bell chimed loudly, and people began to take their seats. The moment of truth was upon them.

It took the audience no more than five minutes. Jet focused on the podium, five feet away, placed near the middle of the platform, with some open space behind it. Their seats overlooked the audience, and intense and anxious faces stared back at them. The importance of this moment was evident.

A tall woman stood and walked to the lectern. Jet thought she was a member of the Wandering Nomads, but she hadn't been with the others. Her cloak was darker than her fellows, but not as much as the Foresworn followers'. Her hair fell to her lower back, but it had tight curls. Jet had never seen anyone so magnetic, not even Marcella. She strolled from the opposite side of the stage, also seated in the first row, at the end. She glanced at him an instant before she turned, preparing to speak.

"Welcome, community of the magical. I am Ivy Wren and the grande dame of the Wandering Nomads. Some sixty years ago, we froze in time, and now we are alive again. We don't age, but we can die. We've been transported here to correct the mistakes of the past. I've spoken with other tribesmen, and your experiences are much the same. One day, we were in hibernation, and then we were awake. It took a while to understand that magic had vanished from the earth.

"There were whisperings of those with some powers, but we felt lost in this new world. Now we feel more comfortable, yet things changed again when, less than one year ago, magic returned. We were stunned to learn the Rivalry had begun again. Elemental and Runic magic were back on earth. We did not want to believe past errors could repeat themselves with these two young men. In some ways, they haven't, and in some ways, they have.

"More recently, we began to see signs of Chupovanas and other devilish creatures wandering the land. We have remained hidden, unsure if we should pick a side or remain apart from the battles. In the last several months, word came that the Demon Prince would be released again. Some said it was the Grey Panther, and some said it was the Silver Fox. The truth remains unclear.

"We have been asked to gather here to witness the rebirth of all five types of magic. We hope this is true, but we are hesitant that this is why we are truly here. Our eldest sage insists this is impossible, but I am willing to watch in wonder to see if it will come to pass. If Arisol, or whoever is set to attack us again, we must be prepared. This day will be forever celebrated if all five magics can be reborn. Let's see what the humans have to say. But beware. Don't be fooled into believing in illusions or trickery. Trust is hard to earn, yet easy to lose."

The response to Ivy Wren's words was mixed. Jet realized how unsure the other Tribesmen were, except the Axenkind and the Coven. Both had worked closely with Jet and Shane and knew the truth. Some humans clapped, as did several of the Runics.

Karl Middlesex stood from directly behind Jet and moved to the podium. When he spoke, his voice was steady and strong. "Not long after speaking with my children, near the time the boarding schools were started, I too was placed in hibernation to be reawakened. War is coming. I hope the five magical books will be enough, but I fear it might be too late to win with our backbiting and disdain for each other. Only unity will conquer our foe."

The older man turned, stepping away from the lectern. He gave a small nod of his head. Someone stood behind Ivy Wren. Jet's eyes focused, and he realized it was Darsil Müller. The man muttered, "He's gone soft in his old age."

When Darsil Müller reached the podium, he placed both hands on the lectern. His voice was cold and calculating. "Wickedness has brought forth indolence. It is clear from the Nomads and other tribesmen that your inactivity has revealed your desire to allow the Silver Fox and her underlings to take over the world without any resistance. She has been the most dangerous villain the world has ever known. A master manipulator and deceiver. The Brotherhood has poisoned the waters, and the Elementals and Runics will hand the most important weapon over to the enemy because they aren't worthy to hold it.

"Only the Azurites have maintained the correct course. We were formed because the truth became too obvious, not that the Grey Panther or the Silver Fox were involved, but that the Rivalry would be used to gift the Demon Prince the weapon to destroy the world.

You've known that the Azurites have been trying to teach magic as it was designed to be taught. I asked for a boarding school to instruct magic as it was intended. I was categorically denied this request, even when I was willing to give the most important tool to the Rivalry, the knowledge of the whereabouts of the sixteenth tribe.

A wave of rumblings spread through the crowd.

"The realm of the Darcurser tribe is closer than ever before," continued Darsil Müller. "The Silver Fox will call out to them if we don't. Without the Darcurser tribe, the Phoenix will fall into the hands of the Demon Prince, and all will be lost. Many of you will die the moment the Silver Fox touches that weapon. Why are you so prideful that you can't see the truth?"

Darsil Müller turned to face Jet and Shane. "You boys are puppets, and there's no way you can beat the Demon Prince. I don't blame your ineptitude, but stop being mind-controlled by those searching for power." He strode away, shaking his head.

The crowd became even more unsettled.

Shane smiled confidently. "Guess it's my turn. I think you're going to like this." The boy sauntered forward.

Shane began by saying, "I am the leader of the Runics and the first to open a magical book. *The Mage's Letters* unsealed when I turned sixteen last June. But I knew for over a year that I'd been chosen. I began to have dreams, and I started to see magic around me. I watched as I could sense magic in different things. I contacted my old mentor, Professor Rysen, and he agreed to come to Chadwick's to help guide me. He never suggested that I come to Dillon Lake to allow Runic magic to thrive there. He built a trust with me, and it was not until later that I learned he had fooled the Brotherhood and was a member of the Azurites.

"Even worse, I confided in him about the voice inside my head, urging me to do certain things. This might sound crazy," said Shane, quickly drawing a rune and producing three gaudy black rings and two darkened, chained necklaces. He kept them afloat using Runic magic. "My friends and I were led to some jewelry that gave us strength and reduced the amount of energy required to perform magic. At first, I thought my speed in learning Runic magic made me the natural leader of Chadwick's. I was surprised that Jet Black was chosen to lead the Elementals. The Rivalry pitted us against each other to find the first missing tablet piece. When Jet escaped with the first piece, the voice I'd heard earlier turned out to be Faunal. I had once believed he was an ally to Runic magic.

"I was wrong on both accounts with Professor Rysen and Faunal. In Argentina, Faunal flaunted a special entrance into the underground cavern. I supposed I had discovered the second Phoenix piece, but I recently learned I was given a fake because I had not followed the rules of the Rivalry. I've learned since that Rysen used me for the Azurites, and Faunal used me to help the Demon Prince. I was unprepared for some of the tasks required. You see, in Argentina, Faunal couldn't enter the prison alone, but needed someone from the Rivalry. I was that person. There are important items at each of the sites of the bestowal, and in the case of Argentina, it was both someone and something. I will strive to repair the obstacles I have created.

"I was deceived, and it took some time before the Runics got back on track, but this did not happen before I lashed out and tried to take over the school. My lessons have been ingrained in my mind. I have disappointed my family, friends, and the other students at Chadwick's.

"Along the way, I've worked with some wonderful students from the other boarding schools. I believed I could find the missing magical books. A month ago, at Dillon Lake, I realized I could not do it alone. Jet Black and the Elementals had the time and knowledge to discover the missing books. They agreed to work with me, and Runics found the next piece of the missing tablet. Today is a day to celebrate the Elementals and the missing magical books. This will forever be an important day.

"As part of the agreement, the Runics will be in the best position to unite the six missing artifacts and stand up against the Demon Prince. Only one bestowal remains before the demon is released. We need to be ready for that day, and the Runics plan to be. Once again, we will be the protectors of the people. To do this, I met with the Brotherhood, and they have agreed to allow open enrollment for all the boarding schools, starting the day after school ends.

"This means that the Runics will do what we should have done at the beginning. We will move to Dillon Lake and allow Runic magic to be taught openly. Chadwick's will teach Elemental magic here without the competition of a rival. This will not displace the Predilectors in the slightest. But you can choose to attend a school that teaches the magic you might want, even if you are from a different boarding school or have Predilector powers.

The five boarding schools will fulfill their intended designs, and magic will once again be complete on earth.

But for this to happen, we must turn our attention to Jet Black, Mikado of the Elementals, and trust he has the power to give back magic to the world."

CHAPTER 31

Shane smirked at Jet from the lectern, dripping with loathing, contempt, and jealousy. A thunderous explosion of clapping erupted from the crowd, including all the boarding schools, and even Dillon Lake. Shane had perfectly set the stage for his failure, and even if he managed to succeed, it was based on the agreement that Shane had made with him. He had maneuvered a win-win for the Runics. Jet's blood boiled with anger, and he nearly lost control. It was both triumphant and conceited. Shane believed he had pinned Jet into an impossible corner of making magic return.

Raul gripped Jet's arm firmly, grounding him.

Rotating back to the crowd, Shane held up *The Mage's Letters* and hollered. The crowd reacted in kind. As he sat, he whispered, "My spirit mentor, Huchon, believes it impossible to bring back magic. You don't know what is required. This is going to be an embarrassing, public failure."

Shane's pronouncement of his impending failure calmed Jet more than anything else could. Standing, he muttered, "The only thing embarrassing is your facial acne. That blemish on your forehead is the size of Rhode Island. But at least your pretend girlfriend still loves you."

"Good one," said Shane a bit too loudly. Several people glanced at their encounter.

Jet said into the microphone, "Thanks for that great introduction, Shane. The Elementals and the school will be happy to see you go. Good luck, Dillon Lake. Let's give another round of applause for Shane Fallon."

Shane just sat in his chair, and the clapping was far more subdued this time. The crowd had sensed a pending skirmish but had been sorely disappointed. He pondered the words he wrote last night. They sounded incredible then, but today, he wasn't so sure, especially in the face of Shane's attestations. Reaching inside his back pocket, he pulled out a talk he knew he wouldn't give, just to give himself a few more seconds. Those in the crowd began to quiet down, and there was silence when he focused on them. He saw, in his friends' eyes, how precarious things really were.

Jet yelled, "Iris!" A moment later, he yelled, "Braverly!"

From the stadium's entrance, Iris, the golden panther, tore onto the field. The gigantic protector with an enormous sword and protective armor materialized out of nowhere, landing near the stage. Iris sped past Braverly, up the stairs, and came to rest near him.

Many in the crowd stood, unsure if this was a joke or an attack. Jet cried, "Don't be alarmed. This is my protector." To Braverly, he asked, "Would you tell us a little about your first master?"

Braverly's face contorted, and a smile spread across it. In a booming voice, he began, "Many moons ago, I was the protector of Ella Dastria, one of the Five-Goddesses of Goth Airtha. She became mortal after falling in love with Tigerus. I became her protector. She was fair, clever, good-natured, and wanted more than anything to unite magic and orchestrate peace on the earth. She strived to enlighten the world's leaders with insight into magic and how we can exist with the other tribes of the land. She blessed all that came into contact with her."

Jet asked, "What happened to her?"

"She was deceived and left the world and went into exile."

A low murmur spread through the crowd, and several took their seats. A few people glanced over at Shane.

Jet continued, "Do you know what happened to her?"

Braverly's head jerked up in surprise. "You were dying. She gave her lifeforce to save you."

Jet nodded. "When I was younger, I was given a potion to cause me to forget magic. The Brotherhood created it. It didn't work completely, and I was also mind-attacked by Faunal on a rock cliff not far from where we stand. *The Sorcerer's Guide* chose me. But I was incomplete, and Ella Dastria's lifeforce made me whole."

Jet asked, "Who do you protect now?"

Braverly smiled again, "The Mikado of Elemental magic, Jet Black."

"Thank you," said Jet. "You can return to protecting this school."

Braverly vanished.

It took a few seconds for the muttering within the crowd to stop. Jet explained, "Iris here is the leader of the Sagitta tribe. Shane has four animals as well. The Elementals have uncovered the animals that will be given to each new magical group. And the Elementals have uncovered the missing three books. This should be enough reason to celebrate, but it isn't. Bringing back magic will be more burdensome than you can ever imagine. Shane Fallon would like you to believe he has all the answers but does not. He would never have been able to discover the whereabouts of the missing books, as only an Elemental could. His words of flattery are only words of ill will and contempt."

Lifting both arms, he shrugged and continued, "Today, I stand here with the guidance of unleashing the three missing magical types, but I will not be going forth with the process."

Shouts of displeasure rang out through the crowd.

Behind him, Shane demanded, a false derision in his voice, "This can't be. You promised. We will all fail without the other schools."

"You must," cried Li Wei. "We will not survive without more help."

"Instead," bellowed Jet, and he began pointing to the crowd over and over again. "It will be up to you today to determine if magic is truly reborn. I cannot bring back magic...only you can. You must act. You must sacrifice."

Jet softly spoke "Oblekii," and focused on creating a tiny cloud on the lectern. Then he spoke "Kali," and tiny firebolts rained down from inside the clouds. He pulled out *The Sorcerer's Guide* as if the entire thing were a magic trick. In his mind, he allowed both spells to fade. The desired results were obtained. The crowd stood on their feet, watching him, as entertained as they had ever been. Shane's words were long forgotten. A circle of flames erupted in a small space on the ground, in front of the stage, creating a half circle. Jet held his tome so that everyone could see. "Will the students from Dillon Lake, San Mateo, Cranbrook, and Valley Sun come forth. Students from Runics and Elementals must also participate. The choices required tonight include all five magical types. If one declines to continue, the process fails. We are to begin."

Five minutes later, nearly twenty students sat in front of the stage, just outside the half circle of flames. Those on the platform stood and moved to the left and right, giving Jet a wide berth. He opened his tome.

"For magic to return, those among you must perform three steps. Some of the steps will fall to students from each of the boarding schools, while other steps may require someone within this school or nearby. We know that each of you has other individuals close to campus. You may need to call on them to fulfill the requirements."

Shane shouted, "He is lying." But his words were hollow and unconvincing.

Jet continued, "Those who lived during Goth Airtha never imagined that magic could be lost or hidden. Noblemen from those tribes were mystified as to why it was happening. Evil gained a significant foothold in the world, and Queen Aurora, Queen Safamora, and Prince Proteus created the Fisador Pact, which slowly removed magic from the land. First, it was Shaman magic, then Incrementum, then Resititual. If magic had not been taken, the land would have been destroyed. Despite the betrayal of some of the Resitituals, all magical groups are essential. Therefore, a significant cost must be freely given to bring magic back. That is what is required today."

Jet turned a few pages of his tome to the most recently opened page. "Long ago, magic was controlled through the Lexicon, which created five books for the five types of magic. An agreement was made, and magic was wrangled. Therefore, we must make another agreement. This will require three steps."

The crowd leaned forward. Shane scowled, but all the other delegates were enthralled. Iris perched at his feet, protectively.

"The rebirth of the Lexicon will take Sacrifice, Love, and Work." He couldn't help but look at Seyanna as he said these three words. Her head jerked slightly, almost like a twitch, and he wondered if she had seen the intentions on his face. "The primary reason for the loss of magic was that those with magic were attacking each other. This weakened the bonds on the agreement, and Evil snuck past like a prowler entering a home at night through a door left ajar."

"Ensuring that magic returns is essential in the protection against the upcoming war. We need as many students as possible to learn magic and be ready to fight. Some of the magic types will help in different and unexpected ways. Not everyone can fight in the traditional sense, but there are other options. Once Arisol is defeated, we must find peace and connection. I strongly doubt this will be our only fight in the future. Balance and unity are required. By accepting magic being reborn tonight, you accept that you will do all in your power to work toward unity. If you are willing, the tasks are at hand."

Marcella demanded, "Who will lead the magical world? Will it be you?"

Jet smiled. "Like in the days of old, we will create the Kings. This will consist of leaders of the five types of magic, the leader of the Predilectors, the Brotherhood, the Azurites, and two from the non-magical. Others will make up this council, including tribesmen in good standing. If we quarrel, that risks a war; we will form a collaboration process. Additional wise individuals will be invited. If you're willing to embark on this future, the time has come to begin to give your assent by saying yes."

Hundreds of voices spoke the word in unison. Iris stood alert, staring at something in front of the podium. Jet said, "Show yourself."

Mikey appeared suddenly close to Jet, who was unfazed. Over the last few minutes, he had sensed the boy in the crowd working toward him. The boy pulled out a card from his hand and handed it over. You don't look surprised.

Jet answered, "I perceived you coming. First time that has happened."

The next card read: Interesting.

Jet asked, "Is someone coming?"

Mikey nodded. The next card had been written more quickly: Chupovanas, Ratas, Razors, Quills, and more.

Jet continued, "If we are united, they can't stop us. Feel free to leave before our enemies arrive. If you stay, you agree to the new council and what occurs next."

No one voiced any concerns, and no one left their seats. Iris prodded, and Mikey took a few steps back.

"To renew the Lexicon, it will take three steps. Again, I urge you to know that I cannot be the only one to move this forward. It might require you." After a long pause, he said, "The first step requires someone to give their lifeforce into the three hidden tomes. They must think fully about what they are doing and what this could mean. Your lifeforce is partly your will, your experiences, and your memories. You will not die, but you will never be the same."

A cacophony of murmurs erupted, then died immutably as a man stood. Jet's heart raced. The man wore sand-colored robes, carried scrolls, and was the shortest of his group. He was from the tribe Discerests. Falling into place behind him was a tall lady from the Machitis tribe with a deep-purple cloak stained with earth. An instant later, one of the Axenkind joined the queue heading toward the podium. Jet was relieved, it was someone he did not know well. Gasps spread through the crowd.

When the Discerests scholar reached the podium, he said, his voice like a professor, "I am willing Mikado, though I don't know the words."

"Neither do I," muttered the lady of the Machitis tribe, her voice sweet and grounded.

"I do," said Jet. He had first been given a lifeforce by Alces before the first fight on campus, against three Chupovanas. As the three guests stood shoulder to shoulder, Jet pulled out the three newly rediscovered tomes. A thrum of excitement ensued, but he was ready for any type of attack. He opened a space in the fire, and the three approached. Quickly, the fire resumed. When they were close enough, he whispered so they could only hear, "The three words to give your lifeforce are Dare Vim Vitalem. You must pull it from your mouth. I will answer and place the lifeforce inside the book."

The Axenkind asked, "Are you sure this won't kill us?"

He was impressed by their bravery. "You will still live. I don't think you can perform magic or have any old abilities. But you will find happiness."

The three of them nodded. They said the words and pulled their lifeforces from within. Each was a sphere, but they were far different from what Alces's had been. The Axenkind's was ocean blue, smaller than a fist but powerful. The Discerests was yellow and as big as a melon. The Machitis's was forest green and the size of a marble. The three lifeforces hung in the air.

Jet whispered, "Vitalem."

The yellow lifeforce merged with the Shaman book, the forest green one united with the Incrementum, then the blue combined with the Resititual book. The covers of each book glistened and came alive, as if energy had been zapped into them like a defibrillator restoring life. The three books rose into the air, for all to see, and a haze of fern green permeated the air.

Jet announced, "The first step is complete."

The crowd cheered, and the first three volunteers departed the circle.

He glanced at his friends. He wished to be seated next to Seyanna so he could squeeze her hand one last time. The next step may change him and those around him forever. "The next step requires a sacrifice of Love. We need three people willing to give away their feelings of love for someone else. It must be done uncoerced and will be permanent. You will never have the same feelings for that person again."

Jet's vision expanded, and he analyzed Seyanna's face. The moment she understood the meaning of his words, she tried pushing through the crowd in protest.

A voice behind them asked, "Are you saying you will take the love that we have from us?" The voice belonged to Darsil Müller.

Jet repeated the question into the microphone, then answered, "No. I'm not taking anything from anyone. The magic required will only receive the gift, much like a lifeforce. I cannot force the feeling from anyone."

A wave of humming spread through the crowd. Jet was unsure how long he should wait before he needed to calm the crowd.

Someone stepped off the stage to his right.

"No. Don't do this," cried Karl Middlesex.

One of the Myntra, Gleam, hurried forward. Jet was startled to see her. He couldn't imagine she would be willing to do this, but the look in her eye was laser focused. He remembered when he first met Gleam and Faris, something had been said about each of the Myntra. They were missing something or were injured. Could this be the case for Gleam?

Karl Middlesex pushed through others on the stage. Gleam turned, stared at Karl, and he came to a dead stop. "I've lived with this for too long. It is like it's burrowed inside my heart. If this will release me, I must."

"You don't know it will work."

"I must try." She moved to the edge of the fire, standing in the same spot as the Discerests who had just given their lifeforce. The circle of fire ended, and Gleam stepped forward.

Jet whispered, "The magical word you must say is 'Leia Alofa.'"

The instant the last syllable was spoken, an orange lightning bolt crashed, colliding with Gleam's chest. She did not scream with terror or release a single gasp of pain. Like a ghost, a translucent heart fluttered into the air. It was only visible for a few seconds. It dipped into the book for the Resitituals. The book visibly bounced twice, like a heartbeat.

Gleam peered up at him, a tear in her eye, and she smiled so kindly that Jet was taken aback. She muttered softly, "I am free." She returned to stand next to her two sisters, slightly less burdened by life.

The wait for the next volunteer was two minutes of uncomfortable silence. There were three separate moments when Jet was about to say the word himself. He refused to look at Seyanna, but she knew what he would do.

"Me," shouted Evelyn Ulm, standing from her group from Valley Sun. With dignity, she strolled forward. Her classmates glanced at each other as if confused.

Chin stood and followed her. Jet heard him ask, "Is it me? Did I do something wrong?" The boy suddenly appeared downtrodden.

Jet watched as Keesha stood, interested in the exchange like everyone else, but he knew she had some personal involvement. It was as if Chin had chosen Evelyn over Keesha. The complexities were intense.

Evelyn continued forward. Chin followed, whispering. Finally, Evelyn stopped, putting a hand on his chest and forcing him to stop. She said, "It's definitely not you. This has prevented my feelings for you from growing into what they should. Let me do this."

She left him standing dumbfounded. Her eyes connected with Jet, as if pleading for strength. Jet nodded, smiled, and allowed her to enter beyond the fire. She spoke to Jet quietly, "I've known Shane for a long time, since we were young. I always thought he loved me back. I now know better."

Jet spoke the same magical word to Evelyn. She repeated it. This time, a purple lightning bolt hit her chest, creating another heart, purple in color. This time, it combined with the Shaman tome. Relief flooded through Evelyn once it was done.

"My turn," bellowed Jayco. "This looks fun."

Rozene turned to stare at Jayco. The boy looked feverish and not in control. His face was red, and sweat poured down his face, as if from a hose. Jet didn't think he was doing this of his own accord. Jayco's face contorted with anger and frustration, and he pushed through the chairs, knocking over Grantham and Eric. It was as if he were possessed. Grantham stood almost immediately, grabbing onto an arm. Lathisha seized the other. Eric went for a leg. Nothing was stopping this boy.

Jet wondered if he should just say the word and end this display. He closed his eyes, feeling he didn't have a choice.

"Lei—"

"Don't you dare," cried a voice in his ear. Opening his eyes, he found Seyanna standing beside him, gripping his arm. Iris had stood, but even she had been too slow. "You don't need to sacrifice everything for the Rivalry. I can't lose you."

"But…"

"Jayco!" screamed Rozene, using her Predilector ability, focusing on Jayco. The intense sounds she made caused everyone near her, including Jayco, to tumble to the ground. She ended her ability. "Are you doing this of your own free will, or is something else going on?"

Jayco looked at her, shaking his head, "It's not me. I would never."

"It has to be me," cried a voice, and Jet studied the new volunteer.

Jocelyn Delgado leapt from the stage and came to stand just outside the fire circle. A chill ran down Jet's spine.

CHAPTER 32

Jet's mouth fell open in shock. It took several long seconds, then he slowly closed it. The girl stood defiantly as if waiting for him, or anyone else, to say something. Jocelyn detested him. She and two of her closest friends had bullied him. He had killed one of them, and a Chupovana had killed the second, moments after fighting with Jet. The one he had killed had been on the verge of killing Mckenzey.

Jocelyn spoke. "The anger I have in this world since Jake died has taken hold of me. You know this! Losing Vinny was a second blow. We grew up together in Huntington Beach. We were the closest of friends, maybe something more. I need this." The last words were pleading.

Jet understood and regretted the part he had played. "Is this really what you want?"

"It is."

He opened the flame, and she stepped inside. Seyanna moved back several feet so Jet could tell Jocelyn the word, privately.

Jocelyn repeated it. Green lightning flashed down. The heart that emerged immediately combined with the Incrementum tome. She didn't look as relieved as Gleam or Evelyn, but a brief smile crossed her face.

"Thank you," she whispered, spun, and strode back to some of her friends, avoiding the stage entirely.

The crowd was stunned. Some were crying, and yet others were angry. Jet saw Gleam, Em, and Faris hugging. Darsil Müller stood not far away, shooting him daggers, as Iris sat perched, ready to attack any threat.

Returning to the podium, Jet waited for the crowd to quiet, but also quieted his own soul. He had been so close. The three books still hovered in the air. He spoke slowly, "The third task isn't something that can be taken lightly. It won't require something you can give up today, but a charge to do something for the rest of your life. The volunteers won't age as normal men and women. You will become part of the story like only a few have. You will have a deep responsibility and cannot shirk from what is asked of you. Again, do not take this *work* lightly."

Shane asked firmly, "What kind of work are we talking about?"

"Each time a significant change in magic occurs, shepherds are compulsatory to bring forth peace, knowledge, and truth. These shepherds will not die on their own, but they can be killed. They will replace the previous shepherds and will have a direct connection with magic. Their work will be essential, unpredictable, and often lonely. Therefore, only a person, without magic, from each of the five boarding schools can choose to enter such service. One person from Dillon Lake must choose. It cannot be a teacher, a former student, or a tribesman. These volunteers will become Oracles attached to the magic they connect with."

Shane demanded, "Why can't two people from Chadwick's volunteer?"

Jet said cooly, "Because you've already agreed to change schools, and magic has taken you at your word."

The color drained from Shane's bronze-colored face as he realized what he had said was now a binding agreement.

"I do not know the full extent of the requirements when an Oracle is chosen. But the five Oracles must meet each other every other year, along with the five leaders of each magic type, and other assigned participants. They will gain knowledge, wisdom, and insight into our world. Beyond that, I have not been given any other instructions. Choose wisely. Five people must be chosen in twenty minutes, or we will have to wait one year to attempt this process again. Trust me when I say, it will be too late."

Stepping away from the lectern, Jet reached for the three books but could not remove or touch them. He came to stand near Seyanna. Iris padded up close.

Jayco, Grantham, Latisha, Rozene, Mckenzey, and Eric came onto the platform. Jayco was pale and unsteady. Grantham and Rozene helped him cross the stage. Raul, Keesha, and Phoebe hurried over as well.

"I am so sorry, bro," muttered Jayco. "That was crazy and stupid. I don't know what came over me. It's like I don't always have control of my thoughts or actions."

"We will figure it out," said Jet, surprised at the guilty look on his friend's face.

"I didn't want to go up there. Something was compelling me to do so."

"Rozene saved you," said Grantham. "That is one powerful girl you have there."

"I know," said Jayco, smiling kindly.

Mckenzey asked, "How did you know what to do tonight?"

"That's why I wanted to meet this morning. But Shane, Principal Smuin, and that picture threw everything off. *The Sorcerer's Guide* opened last night, and I learned what would be required to connect all five magical books. Many requirements were given, but I was also given some thoughts from previous pages. It helped me get to this point, and my thoughts started sticking together, and I knew how today was supposed to go."

Latisha asked, "You thought it would go like this?"

"Not precisely. This entire thing has gone in the opposite direction. Crazy though."

You can say that again," said Keesha. "What was Chin thinking?"

"I pretty much ask myself that about some of you daily," said Grantham. "Chin looked like a lost puppy. I felt bad for him."

"Not me," hissed Keesha. "He should have stayed at Chadwick's."

No one was brave enough to argue.

"Who will we pick to be our oracle?" asked Raul. "I know several people who would be great options."

"We can't choose for them," said Seyanna. "Didn't you hear what Jet said?"

"We could strongly encourage them," retorted Jayco.

Eric said, "Three people are headed in our direction. I know each of them was not chosen by Elemental magic."

Jet recognized the tall boy. His name was Samuel. The other two, a boy and a girl, he recognized.

"This is Sameul Thornton, JJ Hamblin, and Fatima Pike," Eric introduced.

Phoebe asked, "What can we do for you?"

Samuel replied, "We're gathered on the lawn over there with other supporters of Elementals. We might be willing to consider becoming an Oracle. We hoped for more information."

Jet said, "I can't. The information I provided is all I'm allowed to say. Think over each thing that I said carefully. This is a tremendous opportunity and a major responsibility."

Fatima asked, "What if we all want to do it?"

Jet considered this question. The answer came quickly to his mind. "Elemental magic will choose the one who is most worthy."

There was a pause in the conversation as the three non-magical students walked away. His mind raced at what he should say next. Suddenly, he was yanked to the end of the stage. He smelled her perfume and knew the warmth of her skin.

Seyanna growled at him. "You were on the verge of sacrificing yourself again."

Fidgeting with his shirt, he didn't want to answer, but she didn't look away. "It was the last thing I wanted to do, but what if no one had volunteered?"

"Then we would have found another way. I would have been left with my feelings for you, and you with nothing. Did you ever think of that?"

"Sort of," he mumbled.

"What were you thinking?"

Jet answered honestly. "I find it difficult sending people to fight for me. I have trouble asking someone to do something I'm unwilling to do. I don't want to disappoint you or anyone else."

"Were the feelings you were going to surrender for me?"

This time, he looked away. "Yes."

She nudged his head, so he stared at her. "Why not give up any feelings you had for Mckenzey?"

Frowning, he said, "You can't give up feelings for someone that you don't have."

Her face reddened. Lunging forward, she hugged him fiercely. Into his ear, she whispered, "Don't give up on us yet."

He squeezed her back.

They stood there for several seconds, lost to everything happening around them. Jet had to pull himself away from her intentionally. "It's time we finish what we've started."

They walked back to the others together, Iris in tow, and Mckenzey watching them the entire time. Jet went directly back up to the podium.

The crowd quieted as he approached, and he took a moment to stare around. Others had joined them, likely from outside the stadium. "The Elementals have three volunteers. They can approach. Please allow those wishing to be considered from the other schools, including Dillon Lake, to come forward."

A single person approached from Cranbrook, San Mateo, and Valley Sun and introduced themselves.

A stout girl said, "Ellie Giron from Cranbrook."

"Joey Reich from San Mateo," said a taller boy.

"Ryker Garvin from Valley Sun," muttered a boy who stared at the ground.

Seven people from Dillon Lake advanced, but it didn't seem to him that they had any choice. They glared at Shane, unmistakably upset.

He wasn't sure what to do next. He needed to buy some time. Before him stood thirteen students. No word or phrase had been given to him by his tome. Once they spread out, on the other side of the fire, a moment of insecurity passed through him. In the next instant, the answer became crystal clear. Pulling out *The Sorcerer's Guide,* he tossed it to join the others, hovering.

"We neeed *The Mage's Letters*".

Shane stomped forward, keeping his distance from Jet, and released his book into the air.

The spell came into his mind, and he spoke loudly, "Polney Lexicon." The top corners of each tome touched the edges of another book, forming a circle in the middle. The instant all the books came into contact, a deep voice spoke to the collective. Jet's head shot up. He heard Wier's voice within. Shane did the same, and Jet wondered if the mentor inside each book was speaking as one.

"The power of magic is innate. It was born to be used. But as with all around us, it has been and will be used for Evil. Only Wisdom, Sacrifice, Love, Kindness, and Work will prevent magic from being lost forever. This Lexicon agreement has been years in the making. A unified magical cooperation is the only way it will survive. The overseers of magic have always been the Oracles. They provide the insights and clarity required to settle disputes, initiate kingdoms, and preserve rituals. The 5 Goddesses were the first Oracles. More has come and gone since the beginning of time. We collectively bless the next Viconian Sages with a gift of vision."

An incandescent yellow mist burst from the center, created by the five books. Five intricate metal bracelets, in vibrant colors, materialized from the core as if removed from a hidden compartment. The bracelets hovered, separated from each other, and latched onto five of the students. Fatima Pike was chosen from Chadwick's. Ellie from Cranbrook, Joey from San Mateo, and Ryker from Valley Sun.

Jet learned that the boy chosen for Dillon Lake was Didier Macron, a French foreign exchange student. The instant the bracelet touched their arms, it felt as if a bond had formed. They grew taller, smarter, and more confident. Along with the bracelet, he noticed a metal thimble slide over the pointer finger with the thinnest of chains attaching the thimble to the bracelet. The five Oracles straightened, and a shroud of importance and wisdom fell over their faces. Each turned and bowed to Jet, their eyes met for an instant, and he could see the power they held.

Fatima spoke to him, but her voice carried so that all could hear. "No book can change the world unless its word precedes action."

Jet bowed back to the five Oracles.

"No kingdom is set in stone, no war is a foregone conclusion, except for those who refuse to lean, build, and fight...then all is lost," added Ryker

Jet agreed, "War is coming."

Didier answered, "War was already here."

"You just misunderstood when it started and where to look," finished Ellie.

Without another word, all five Oracles strolled from the platform, the football field, and into the twilight.

"Look!" bellowed Karl Middlesex once they departed.

A fluorescent purple light outlined all five tomes as if an invisible figure were tracing them. A deep-seated feeling assured Jet that the Lexicon had been reawakened. The bright light shone through the green haze, evaporating it completely. *The Sorcerer's Guide* shot into Jet's hand just as *The Mage's Letters* landed in Shane's.

The Shaman's *Book of Shadows* rose steadily, higher than the other two. The book opened near the middle, and six semitransparent apparitions stepped out and surrounded the students from Valley Sun. Evelyn, Chin, and the other students were brought forward and led past the open book. When Evelyn approached, the tome flipped pages to the front in a blur.

After reading the words, she replied, "I accept." The apparitions paled slightly, as if relieved, then bowed to her. Evelyn grasped the book as if it were a prized possession and moved to the side.

The Recipes of Life opened, and a dozen bees, butterflies, and other flying creatures escaped to surround the students from San Mateo, ushering them forward. The students formed a line to walk in front of the book, but there was no need, as Diego Axel was chosen immediately as the leader of the Incrementum. He read the first page and said, "I accept." As he turned to leave, he dipped his head toward Jet in appreciation.

The Adaptation Guide opened, and an eerie tune began playing, which seemed slightly off and distant. Apparently, those from Cranbrook did not agree. The enchantment brought forth excitement, and they scurried forward, gaining strength and insight, and stepped into line. Nothing happened for the first three students, but on the fourth, Nylah Veeda, the eerie sound stopped as she passed by, and the book turned to the first page. She became fascinated by the words on the first page. She spoke. "I accept."

The purple vanished instantly. All eyes turned back to Jet. He thought the ceremony was over, but now the ever-familiar compulsion caused him to reach for his tome. Absentmindedly, he opened his book to a page near the back and began speaking.

The opening of the newest tomes will release the truth on the land. This includes forgotten theories, symbols, influences, evils, and misfortunes, but will also allow the gathering of lost spirits, the healed, and the exalted. Unbalance will become more expected and far-reaching.

Controlling and fixing these calamities will become the tasks required for the newest magical classifications, and their tomes will point them toward these mishaps. They will be required to strive to regain balance in the world. The Rivalry will continue with only the Elementals and Runics, but the war will be fought by all.

A Henosian Unity is required to finalize the Lexicon's rebirth. Each magical leader must repeat the binding agreement—Uni Monard Dyad. The bond is strengthened through Sacrifice and weakened through Pride. Go forth and regain control.

In unison, five voices, including Jet, said, "Uni Monard Dyad."

Glancing up and returning to his senses, he blinked twice. Everyone stared at him, and he wondered if he had a momentary lapse in thought. The audience held peculiar expressions, as if waiting for something. He said quickly, "Thank you for joining us for this monumental moment. We await the sixth disaster, for the continuation of the Rivalry, and then Arisol's release. Join us as we prepare to fight him. Much will change from now until then. Peace be unto you."

Commotion erupted, and the spectators, previously forbidden to speak, were now granted full freedom.

The half-circle fire still burned, and fifty students stepped closer.

"What just happened?" asked Jet.

Evelyn said, "You just spoke to us in an exalted tone."

"Really? What did I say?"

Diego replied, "Unbalance will become more expected and far-reaching. We were given a word to repeat, and we did."

Jayco said, "I didn't hear the word. The last thing he said was that—the war will be fought by all."

"Exactly," agreed a boy from Dillon Lake.

"There was more," said Nylah, glancing at Shane. "Perhaps it was only for the five of us to hear and say."

"So, no one else heard what we said?"

Jessiva said, "Only Jet spoke."

"Interesting."

There was a slight nudge from *The Sorcerer's Guide*, and the half-circled fire extinguished instantly.

"That was exceptional beyond our wildest dreams," a voice boomed behind them. Li Wei towered over all five leaders. Other members of the Brotherhood surrounded him. "To watch magic work in such a graceful and commanding manner will be a highlight in my service. Thank you for adding a member of the Brotherhood to the council. We will submit a name by the end of the week. We are pleased that you have not forgotten all that we have done. We expect to meet with each of you in the coming weeks."

"Sir," said Jet. "We have a fair number of things to do—"

"No worries," the Commander interrupted. "We will come to you."

Shane gripped his arm as the Brotherhood left, pulling him a few steps away from the others. "You're an idiot and a dirtbag. You knew you had the recipe to bring back magic, and you let me make a fool of myself in declaring we would go to Dillon Lake."

"I had no idea what you would say."

"Still," hissed Shane. "Before, it was a bluff, but now, I have a deep-seated desire to move to New York. This is not what I wanted." He stormed off.

Dozens of Elementals pushed forward, joined by the other boarding schools. Jet returned to where Evelyn, Diego, and Nylah were huddled together. He shook each of their hands and congratulated them. The reality of what had just happened was written on their faces.

Grantham said, "Bro. That was the coolest thing. How did you do all that?"

Jet, holding tightly to *The Sorcerer's Guide*, lifted it slightly. "I wouldn't have known, without this."

Jayco added, "I don't think I could have handled all that. You did well, Black."

"Thanks"

"What's the deal with Shane?" asked Mckenzey.

"I don't think he ever intended to leave Chadwick's. But now, I don't think he has a choice."

"Seriously?" said Lathisha, unable to hide her grin. "That's going to have some long-term consequences."

"You can say that again," agreed Seyanna.

Karl Middlesex sauntered over, crossing his arms and propping against the stage. "Young man. You've ensured war is coming. Don't mistake my intentions...I'm not sure we had any choice in the matter. With what I've seen today, it has become clear. As incredible as this all was, you've barely scratched the surface regarding the details of the war against the Demon Prince. I will find a way to help, the best I can." The man stepped forward, shook Jet's hand, and disappeared into the crowd.

Jet bid the other leaders farewell as they began to display their tomes to their fellow students. Not a single person looked disappointed. Seyanna and other Elementals followed. Geb and Nana waited for him on the far side of the stage. They smiled reassuringly, but Nana was anxious. Iris sauntered forward, joining Jet.

"That was incredible," said Nana. "I never imagined I would see such a display of magic. Never in all my years."

"I'm glad you were here," said Jet. "I can't believe it worked."

Geb said, "All the effort that went into keeping you unscathed has come to this. Your parents worried about your safety, but they would be proud."

"So proud," agreed Nana.

Nana and Geb joined the group as they headed back to the administrative building. He heard the excitement in almost everyone's voices as they talked about what had happened over the last few hours. Jet was exhausted.

Nana leaned in and whispered, "We're leaving with the Brotherhood tomorrow. I'm not sure when we'll talk again."

"Call me when you get settled." After dropping off Geb and Nana, Jet declined offers to celebrate at the beach or at the top of the CeU building. "I can't. I can barely keep my eyes open. We can talk more tomorrow. I just need sleep."

Seyanna accompanied him, helping him inside his dorm and into bed. His eyelids were as heavy as a rockslide.

As he drifted to sleep, he heard her mutter, "That was too close. Never do that to me again."

Hours later, when he awoke, he instinctively knew the students, principals, and teachers from Cranbrook, Dillon Lake, Valley Sun, and San Mateo had departed. So too had most of the tribesmen and other visitors. But Seyanna hadn't. She slept on the couch, and he heard her snoring softly.

His clock read midnight. He wanted nothing more than to roll over and fall back to his sleep. But his tome had other ideas. He barely had enough energy to turn the page, and he didn't like the title of the description. He wished it had waited until morning or had given him several days to be idle. But there was no idleness for the exalted.

CHAPTER 33

THE RISE OF THE SHADE ZORICAN

To blossom in the dark world forged by Arisol, one must align and fuse one's depravity with the Demon Prince. They can open the folds of atrocities, but he commands your every move. No one can rise without his blessing. Shades are not undead but use the undead to wreak havoc on the living. They choose to die, rather than be killed, only to become something sinister. They can be destroyed by using a level thirteen Shaman weapon. Their workers, the hirelings, can be killed by any level higher than a three, though some require at least a level seven. The foremost concern of killing Zorican is that no level ten or above Shaman weapons are left.

Depacon, the ancient Shaman Oracle, prided himself on attaining knowledge of the unimaginable. He was unsurpassed at using Reapers, special sprites that chose not to pass to the other side, who can search for the whispers of magic in the world. The Light Reapers revealed a scroll from a library on the island of Avalon explaining the Heir of the Myth, someone who could hold all five types of magic at once. Depacon spent years attaining this information and more, and storing it away.

Allowing the Silver Fox to locate him, she warned Depacon about the plan of the Fisador Pact, which would take magic from the earth. Some ancient Oracles believed this could bring Goth Airtha one step closer to birthing the Heir of the Myth. The Silver Fox expected that Depacon and his knowledge were essential in the civil wars in Goth Aritha. No one could envision the potential pitfalls or tasks of trying to bring forth the Heir of the Myth.

Arisol knew a sliver of the truth. He had discovered small details and sent Shade Zorican to uncover what Depacon knew. Zorican tried following and capturing Depacon. Everywhere he turned, there were signs of the Oracle.

It took years for Arisol and Zorican to learn most of what it would take to create someone who could control all five types of magic. When the most crucial piece of information was given to Arisol, he had just emerged as the Demon Prince and craved continuing his progress and becoming the Heir of the Myth. Needing the precise order of the incantation, they laid a trap for when the Silver Fox was to meet Depacon at the Savannah of Fensca.

Depacon was intercepted by Shade Zorican, pretending to be the Silver Fox's emissary. Depacon was tortured and his lifeforce was stolen. This elevated Shade Zorican into one of the most formidable allies of Arisol and made him unbeatable. The Shade unleashed many poisons, mistakes, and setbacks upon Goth Aritha.

If between the Shade Zorian, the Skeleton, and Arisol, they have uncovered the correct incantation in creating the Heir of the Myth, then magic as we know it is as precarious as a rock on ice during a spring thaw. It will break through, and all will be lost forever. The final piece in becoming the Heir could be as simple as the Phoenix.

CHAPTER 34

The following week passed in a blur, and Jet's energy remained muted and lacking until Thursday. By then, he had taken three finals and turned in more homework than he thought possible. Nana and Geb had broken orders and stayed close, taking him out to dinner on Sunday and Tuesday. They brought pizza for some of his close friends last night. The Axenkind and Principal Smuin checked on him as often as possible. The Wednesday after the Lexicon revival, he received a note to visit Marcella. She was unrelenting, and Jet thought he knew why. When the second note arrived Thursday evening, he knew he couldn't continue avoiding her.

After his last final on Friday night, he sent back a note agreeing to visit Marcella on Saturday morning. Classes were over, and the year had finished, and he was still alive. Jayco, Grantham, and dozens of other Elementals intended to join the rest of the school for games, music, and dancing. Jet made it clear, even to Seyanna, that he didn't want to be disturbed.

Seated in his dorm, he mindlessly watched a few of his favorite shows, recalling his conversation with Marcella just weeks ago. She had helped him in a time of need, and it was time to do her bidding. She had first approached him after he was injured in an attack on the football field. He was in a medical room underneath the CeU building, and she knew of his desperation to find the Lagoon of the Arches. A few days later, she provided him with vital information, but only after a deal had been struck. He must consent to find the lost children of the Coven.

Years ago, the witch tribesmen were tricked or manipulated, and the result of their treachery was that they were cursed. Their children became housed in a prison. Elemental magic was required to free them. When magic was lost, that possibility became nonexistent. Marcella made a pact with Shane to steal Elemental magic to set the children free. That arrangement had failed when she got caught trying to strip Elemental magic from Jayco. Jet wondered if that meant that Fire magic was required.

Marcella had once said, "A witch's child is precious in both life and death. A child must take care of the body, the family heirlooms, and the homes of their ancestors. It is a huge responsibility and a privilege. We keep connections through this service. We cannot pretend to do this unless our children are returned to us."

The Coven had attacked the twins after the battle of Darcoff. They were caught attempting to kill the magical leaders. After the battle, the twins were considered elite, and their true deception wasn't known until later. The Coven was punished for their part in the attack. Marcella believed the tomb where the children were located was in Egypt.

Using the remote, he turned off the television. He needed all the energy possible for his encounter with Marcell in the morning. He headed to get washed up when there was a knock at the door. He wasn't surprised. He never really thought that Seyanna would follow his request.

He flung open the door, saying, "Hey girl, why am I…" Jet stopped speaking. Two girls, not one, stood in the hallway, and neither was Seyanna. He managed to say, "Mckenzey. Why aren't you with the others?"

Mckenzey glanced at the second girl. "Well, Faris came to see me this afternoon. Remember, we promised her that we would fix her voice?"

"I do," said Jet. To Faris, he said, "I remember that you and your sisters each had something affecting you. It seems that Gleam found a way to release her problem a week ago."

Faris said, her voice coarse and rough. "I'm hoping for the same thing for myself. I can't wait any longer."

He welcomed both girls into his dorm.

As he closed the door, Mckenzey said, "I tried using my healing ability a few different times this week, but something is acting as a roadblock. I can't get to the actual problem."

"Faunal," Faris hissed.

"I really hate him," agreed Jet.

She retorted, "We all do."

He led them to his couch, and they sat. He placed a chair across from them.

Faris said, "I don't think my sisters and I ever understood completely his hatred for our family and for our kindred. When you told us about what Alces saw, it helped clarify some things, but not quite his desire to torture us."

Mckenzey asked, "You have a voice, how did he injure yours?"

"My voice, and that of our people, have two features. In a way, we have magic, but we can only speak our own words. The Coven have similar voices. The first is what our words sound like. My voice, for example, has always been this harsh and rough. Faunal did not injure this, but secondly, we can use magic in tiny ways. I help our dead pass to the other side. I'm what they call a 'nudger'. Essentially nudging people toward the afterlife. Without my voice, I can't help our tribe. Without Shaman magic, it would have been impossible either way. But I can speak for those who have died, even when a Shaman can't."

"How did Faunal wound your voice?" asked Jet.

"He was able to deceive Gleam and me. Her injury was to her heart, and mine was to my voice. He used one of his weapons to cut the connection between my voice and my intuition, which constitutes my magic."

"Interesting," said Jet.

"I was born with magic, which allows me access to the magic of my tribe, whereas magic must choose you. There is a connection to all tribesmen, even if we can't use their words. Even Faunal has this."

Mckenzey said, "Let's make it a goal to cut his connection as soon as possible."

Faris genuinely smiled. "That's a beautiful goal. I'm in."

"I wonder what the best way to fix your voice is?" asked Jet. Turning to Mckenzey, he asked, "What have you tried?"

"Three different times I tried repairing her vocal cords, with only slight improvement, as if I were stitching a string back together. Some of the fibers realigned, but I couldn't get them to do more than that."

Jet said, "Maybe a Water spell of regeneration would help." Moving closer to Faris, he spoke "Thera," and a surge of power left him through the spell into her. Her skin color improved and small scratches vanished. Keeping the spell engaged, he nodded to Mckenzey.

She came forward, placing both hands on Faris's neck. A faint glow of green encased her as she closed her eyes. The smile vanished in an instant, as did the greenish glow. Mckenzey stumbled back, breathing rapidly. After several seconds, she muttered, "I thought I had it for a few seconds, but it's impossible."

Jet released his spell, and his energy dropped by a third, a greater amount than it should have.

"Let me get all of us a drink." He stood, wobbled slightly, and went to the fridge. He pulled out two bottles of vitamin water, filled with herbs, mud, clay, and drops of liquid minerals. He also grabbed some bottled water and a soda. Some Elementals had been working on different mixtures to rejuvenate and add energy. He handed his own concoction to Mckenzey, and they both drank greedily.

"Okay," said Jet, deep in concentration. "I can't regenerate the connection."

Faris said," It felt like ants crawling on my skin for a second."

"That's what everyone says when I help them," said Mckenzey. "Something must be blocking my ability to heal you."

"Now that's interesting," said Jet. "Is it from inside her neck, or from the outside?"

"It feels…" Mckenzey's voice trailed off. "Like maybe from outside, near the skin."

"I was thinking the same thing," said Faris.

Jet said, more to himself, "Can't do a firewall, but something to block the body or neck might do something. But how? Mckenzey will still need to touch the neck."

Mckenzey said, "Ariana told me about a spell you did to stop Shane from having control over Raul. Would that work here?"

Jet shrugged, putting down his empty glass. "Come to the center of the room."

Mckenzey had finished her drink, and Faris took another sip of water. Once they were situated, he spoke "Gongpae," and an air shield enveloped them.

Placing her hands on Faris's neck as before Mckenzey didn't attempt to heal. She shook her head, and Jet let go of his spell. "I knew right away that nothing had changed."

Jet thought through all the spells he knew. Nothing in Fire, Earth, or Water would help. He ticked off the Spirit spells. Other than causing Faris some pain, fear, happiness, or sleep, they wouldn't help. In his mind, he kept coming back to the air shield. He asked, "Is it possible to heal her from the back of her neck? Or from the side?"

Mckenzey touched the back of her neck and both sides. Closing her eyes, she tried to heal but stopped quickly. "Nope. It's like something is wrapped tightly around the entire area of her neck. I can't get past it."

"Good to know," said Jet.

"It's useless," said Faris, her voice losing strength. "Unless we capture Faunal and torture the remedy from him, I'm stuck."

Jet stared at Faris. After a few moments, he said, "I have an idea. It'll take me a few tries to get it right."

Faris asked, "Don't bother. I can't see how this will work."

"It might not," said Jet. "I'm hoping that it doesn't make it worse."

Faris looked unconvinced and on the verge of retreating. Before starting his spell, he pictured an object in his mind. It was a 3D cylinder with a circle on top and one on the bottom, with some distance between them. He envisioned taking the cylinder, almost like a scarf, and pulling it over her head and down to her neck.

Jet spoke "Gongpae," and pictured the cylinder. He couldn't feel the air shield, but its design was skinnier, closer to what he wanted. He pulled them apart with his hands, as if willing the bottom circle to widen. When it was large enough, he moved it down to start covering the top of her crown.

Mckenzey's eyes shot to Faris's as her hair was mashed against her skin. Soon her eyes were forced shut.

"Am I going to be able to breathe?"

"Not sure."

Faris frowned, but in the next instant her nose was smashed as if against glass.

"Take a deep breath," said Jet, pulling down the scarf shield. He sensed it pass by her mouth and her chin. The next step was to get it down to her neck. He mentally pulled hard, and the spell moved. Suddenly, it hit something so forcefully that Jet's teeth rattled. An unseen barrier. Once, twice, and a third time, it became clear that he could not overpower whatever was attached around her neck.

"She's having trouble breathing," said Mckenzey.

Jet immediately pushed up the spell, so her mouth was uncovered.

"I felt that," she said after she had inhaled some oxygen. "Something is around my neck."

Jet said nothing as he closed his eyes and mentally tried to alter the air shield. He fortified its strength as much as possible while causing the shield itself to thin. Once he finished, he asked, "Ready to try that again?"

"Um..." mumbled Faris. "Try what again? That was pretty convincing that whatever barrier Faunal created, we can't get around it."

"I have a plan."

"Better than the last one?"

Jet winked, but realized her eyes were glued shut. "On three!"

Faris exhaled and took in as much oxygen as she could.

"Three," said Jet, heaving the spell over Faris's mouth and chin. From here, he wrapped it closer to the skin and down the neck. He went slowly, knowing that Faris's ability to hold her breath was limited.

The spell slammed into the barrier once again. This time, he didn't continue to fight it. He willed the shield to encase the skin from every side of the neck, much like a vacuum sealer does. When he believed he had succeeded, he slowly lowered the shield. He mentally crossed his fingers and let out a sigh when the shield passed between the barrier and her skin.

Faris started lifting her foot and slamming it down. She was running out of air.

Mckenzey said, "You've got to stop. She's turning blue."

Jet had placed the shield a good six inches below the barrier. He said, "Put your hands on her chest. When I tell you, you'll move them straight up the neck. You can't go from any other direction than from below."

"What am I supposed to do?"

"Heal her," Jet grunted, and with tremendous effort, he thrust the cylindrical shield to expand outward. He barely moved a few inches, then it slammed into the barrier. The opening and closing of his hands controlled the cylinder, and he forced them apart as hard as he could. When they were six inches apart, his hands, forearms, and shoulders all burned. He pushed and pushed, then released a barbaric scream. Centimeter by centimeter, the distance between his hands expanded. Faris's leg stomping was frantic. He thought she might pass out.

"Now!" Jet screamed.

Mckenzey had been crouching down. Her hands moved up to the neck, her fingernails digging into Faris's skin. Closing her eyes, Jet knew instantly that her ability was working. Faris was healing, but she still couldn't breathe. He feared letting go of the barrier, that it would reattach and take away her voice.

Sweat poured down his face and his back. His entire body shook. Now, he was only expanding his hands by millimeters, but he couldn't do anything about the cylinder covering her mouth. It was wide enough to hold a bowling ball, but only on the underside of the neck. His energy rapidly melted away. Not only was Fais starting to pass out, but so was he. He gathered for one last attempt. With everything he had, he yanked his hands away from each other as hard as he could. There was a tear in his arms, and then there was a release. It was as if a bomb had exploded, and he was thrust to the ground, both arms flailing, landing face-first. Something toppled to the floor next to him. It was Faris.

Mckenzey rushed over and pulled Jet onto his back. He blinked in slow motion, but no air was entering his chest. He was awestruck at the interior of his dorm. Part of the ceiling had a hole, and he was pretty sure something was wrong with a window or two. He faintly focused on Mckenzey's closed fist as it swung down and hit him once, then twice in the center of his chest. Cold air rushed back into his lungs. He lost focus on his entire surroundings.

"Drink this," said Mckenzey into his ear as she jostled his arm. His head was tilted up, and a thick sludge entered his mouth.

"What's wrong with him?" asked Faris.

"Most of his energy is gone," replied Mckenzey.

Jet understood the words, but the meaning was foggy in his head.

"He has two cracked glass windows. His couch is broken."

Mckenzey said, "I know. I'll call Seyanna. She's downstairs."

Jet rolled his head back and forth at the mention of Seyanna. For some reason, he thought he would see her if he moved his head fast enough. Sometime later, she appeared on his right.

"What happened?" Seyanna asked.

"I'll explain later. Help us get him into his bed."

They lifted him, one girl on each arm, and Faris holding his legs.

Seyanna said, "It looks like a tornado crashed through here."

"It kind of did," admitted Faris. "My fault. I had an injury to my neck. Jet and Mckenzey fixed it. It required a lot of energy and a spell."

"You did it in here?"

"We didn't know what would happen," said Mckenzey defensively.

"Did it work?" asked Seyanna as they placed Jet on his bed. "I don't hear a change in your voice." She hurried and found the covers hanging out of the open window. It took longer to find a pillow that was still intact.

"Yes," said Faris. "My pitch is the same, but my voice is free of its imprisonment." It took a few moments to explain what she meant.

Jet lay there, still hearing the words, but too foggy to react.

"What do we do now?" asked Seyanna.

"Does he keep any rings in his dorm?" asked Mckenzey.

"How would I know?"

"Oh," she replied, appearing embarrassed. "I didn't mean it like that. Can you get him some more energy water while Faris and I try to pick things up? We can search the room for any rings."

When Seyanna returned, he tried drinking. He attempted to talk, but it sounded more like a hiccup. Seyanna just smiled and laid him back down. She rubbed his arm, soothing him.

A few minutes later, pounding erupted on his front door. Mckenzey went to the door and opened it. Eric, Jayco, Latisha, Grantham, Maria, and others spilled into the room. Jet noticed Autumn, Ariana, Raul, and Phillip were still in the hall.

Glancing around the room, Jayco screamed, "Why weren't we invited to *this* party?" Jayco started to head toward Jet's bed.

"Stay back," said Seyanna.

Grantham touched his arm, and a commotion of words ensued. The next few minutes were tense. Even with Jet's mind slightly clearer, he could tell something wasn't quite right. Despite his friend's attempts to calm Jayco and explain what had happened, the tall blond was spitting mad that he'd been left out of something important again. Eric eyed Jet as if he had purposely set up a mysterious rendezvous with his girlfriend.

At some point, Faris must've called her sisters, and in walked Gleam and Em, just as Jayco demanded, "What about Seyanna?"

Mckenzey said, "I invited her. But she stayed downstairs while Jet and I helped Faris."

"And you didn't think to call any of us?" bellowed Jayco.

Faris's voice was firm, "You weren't the one we made an arrangement with. We helped Jet, Mckenzey, and Raul, and they promised to do so in return. Mckenzey tried to fix the problem initially, then we came here. Jet didn't even know I was coming."

Em hurried to Faris. "What does this matter? Your voice is fixed."

"Yes," said Gleam. "But how?"

Faris said, "It took both of them, but they did it."

A vicious look fell onto Jayco's face as he glanced at Jet.

Grantham grabbed his arm, saying, "Let's get out of here."

Jayco stepped toward Jet. "If you want my help on something in the near future, don't even ask."

Jet said nothing. A moment later, Jayco was led from the room. The others were caught in the vortex, unsure if they should stay or go. Mckenzey grabbed Eric and ushered the rest of the group from the room.

Faris came to the opposite side of the bed. "I'll never forget this. You'd better make a full recovery. I don't want to hear your complaints. Get some rest. What you did today will help our tribe."

The three Myntra disappeared. Seyanna brought him a second blanket, as if reading his mind. The door closed, and they were alone.

"Well...that was a spectacle. Is it me, or is there something wrong with Jayco?"

Jet nodded.

"That boy has some serious problems. I don't think he's thinking straight after what he said tonight, and back in the English building. He normally doesn't act this foolishly. I'll chat with Grantham and Latisha."

Seyanna seemed to smile at him as if reading his mind. "No. I'm not going right now. I'll stay for a while."

Jet mouthed, "Good. I've missed you."

CHAPTER 35

Intense snoring woke him at nine the next morning. As he sat up, the room spun, but it wasn't hard to regain control of the moment. He felt better, and some of his energy had returned. A full-fledged magic battle was unfeasible, but he could make himself some coffee. The room was still a mess. The couch was partially broken.

I'm so stupid. Woke myself up from a snore in a dream.

A harsh sound shook the room. Jet inched to the end of his bed and stood. He shuffled to the couch and found it had been rigged with some books and duct tape. Seyanna was out cold, lying on torn couch cushions and some extra blankets. She appeared as peaceful as he'd ever seen her. Not wanting to wake her, he headed to the shower.

When he had finished, he found Seyanna preparing breakfast. She had pulled out the toaster and found some bread, butter, and jam. There were some cut-up peaches and apples. She also poured some orange juice for both of them.

"Wow," said Jet. "Who knew I had so much food?"

"It took hours to prepare. I hope you appreciate my hard work."

"I do." He added, "How are things?"

She handed him a paper plate of food. "About as good as things were last night."

"That sounds promising." He sat in a chair as Seyanna sat across from him. "Is that with Jayco, you, or the entire campus?"

"Latisha said three hundred students elected to go home for the summer. A few of them are Runics and Elementals. A dozen Elementals were at the CeU building, trying to convince them not to leave. By everyone's account, eighteen Elementals left, and they will probably be transferring to different boarding schools. Fourteen weren't mad at how things were going here, but they had friends at the other schools. Four were. Two don't like you, and two are upset at us for 'kicking out' the Runics." She added, before he asked, "All of them know the risks of being followed or found by the Chupovanas."

Jet started eating. "Huh. I never imagined that Elementals would leave."

"We heard some whispers. They won't be the last."

He said, "If that's true, we could lose a quarter of the school."

"Nope. I think some of the students who left without magic might end up back here. We have five hundred enrollees from the other schools that have already signed up to start at Chadwick's in the fall."

Jet's eyebrows rose. "Hear anything from Shane? Do we know when they are leaving?"

"They have a deadline to be out of Chadwick's by next Saturday."

"What's going to happen to the Predilectors?"

"They're going to be divided among all five boarding schools, but most will stay at Dillon Lake. They'll help each magical group as best as possible, or join one type of magic or another. I understand that since Kevin died, no one can create new Predilectors. If they choose not to join a magical group, they will still use their powers in a way that helps the school."

"What about Rozene?"

"She told Jayco that she's moving here in a week. She's bringing about fifty Predilectors with her."

"Any news from the other boarding schools?"

"As far as we've been told, the books have chosen a leader but haven't opened yet, other than what we saw the first day. They can't bring in recruits. It doesn't matter; students will flock to the school they want to join. If that doesn't work, they'll transfer repeatedly."

Jet nodded.

Seyanna asked, "What are your plans?"

"Today or in the future?"

"Both. I can see you're thinking about something." She stood, retrieved two cups, and poured coffee into each.

"This morning, I'm meeting with Rufian and Marcella. It's time to fulfill that promise. It will take some planning."

"Oh." She glanced at the floor. "What should I tell the others?"

Jet said, "Tell them where I'm going and that I want to meet them at the hideout afterward. I can fill them in on whatever she says. I doubt I can do this alone."

"Can I go with you to Egypt?" she asked, handing him a cup of coffee.

"I don't see why not."

She smiled and sat back down. They finished eating quickly. Thirty minutes later, they left the dorm. Seyanna showered, but didn't wash her hair. She had some makeup in her bag, but wore the same clothes as yesterday. Jet's mind slipped into thoughts about Marcella and how he needed to protect himself.

They reached a crossroad, and he was headed right. He hesitantly touched her arm. "Just so you know. I appreciate you coming over last night. I had no idea what was going to happen or how hard that was going to be. I was exhausted."

"Tell me about it. I saw you drooling." Seyanna laughed, and she leaned closer.

He had stopped walking. A compulsion had settled over him, like a cloud blocking the sun. Still, he managed to lift both arms and pull her close.

"What's happening?" she asked.

Jet mumbled, "I need help getting back to my dorm?"

"What's wrong?"

"*The Sorcerer's Guide* wants to open."

"Now?"

"It does that."

It took twice as long to backtrack to his dorm. Handing her the keys, the moment they got off the elevator, he turned and vomited into a trash can in the hallway. She sprinted forward, unlocked the door, and helped him back inside.

Making his way to his bed, he whispered, "Bookshelf," and pulled out his tome. Without a second look, he turned the next page, close to the middle of the book.

The page was empty, and Jet feared something had gone wrong. Suddenly, single sentences appeared on the page near the top. When he had finished one, the next appeared below.

No one knows the true nature of the Coven's curse.

For years, they petitioned for the ability to use Elemental magic, but the 10 Kings denied them.

They were supposed to have attacked the Twins to force them to give the Coven access to the magic.

Whether it was a real attack or a diversion remains to be seen.

Later, Elfin and Lalfin, now deemed as traitors, were killed by Vagerside, and some of the confusion evaporated.

They were given a traitor's burial that later became the home of their tribulation.

The deceit from the Coven was made clear, and Lady Gaea bestowed their curse.

The Coven were driven from Goth Airtha and banished to Ciphadore, a city below the waters of the Caribbean.

You have been chosen to remove the curse.

This can only be done by a quadripartite of Elemental magic wielders—The Mikado, A Soothsayer, An Injured Mystic, and the Zesto Pheidippides.

Near the peak presently known as Mount Catherine, you will find the mark of the Scarab.

Follow the trail to the opening of the tomb of the Twins.

Earth magic will unlock the descent to the ocean below.

Plunge under the wall of confusion to the hidden chamber.

You must master the Gebel ritual.

Seize control and release the children.

CHAPTER 36

Shaking his head, Jet tried to gather his bearings. For some reason, the lines from the tome swirled around his head, lurking in the darkness when he closed his eyes. A reassuring hand gripped his and squeezed. However, when he caught sight of Seyanna, she stared at him with a mixture of perplexity and wonderment.

"That seemed more intense than other pages I've watched you read. Are you okay?" she asked.

"It's time to get things ready to go to Egypt."

"Are you still going to meet with Marcella?"

"Not sure. I still need to talk with Rufian. Can you get the others and meet me at the hideout like we planned?"

Her head shifted, and some strawberry blond hair fell, covering the outer portion of her left eye. The look was endearing. "Was it bad?"

Jet shrugged. "Not more than at other times?"

Her eyebrows rose.

"What?" he asked.

Her hands touched his neckline, where the collar met the skin. "You have a new tattoo. I watched it happen."

"What?" He pulled down his collar but couldn't get a good view. Stumbling to the bathroom, he pulled off his shirt to find a necklace tattoo encircling his neck. It was intricate and artistic, with an eighth-of-an-inch band of connecting black beads that went all around. The chain had small pendants attached to different areas of the necklace.

Seyanna stepped into the bathroom. "I see a pyramid, a scarab beetle, a mountain's peak, the horizon, and sunlight."

"It's incredible and a bit concerning," replied Jet. "Check out all these tattoos. I never thought I would get any."

"Do you know why it happened?" asked Seyanna. "Was it something from what you just read?"

Jet grabbed his shirt and placed it back on. "I don't have a clue."

Seyanna grabbed his hand, pulled him close, and kissed him. He kissed her back. For a long time, he explored her neck, lips, and behind her ear. It felt wonderful and freeing. Sometime later, they both stopped, searching each other's eyes, and smiled.

"Finally," she said.

"I second that."

"I'll go find our friends. Meet you at the hideout when you get there."

Jet snatched up *The Sorcerer's Guide* and stored it, and they left his dorm. He felt apprehensive when they went their separate ways. He wanted to call her back, but he was worried he was overreacting. Glancing back twice, he found Seyanna watching him. He took another few steps, then decided to ask her to join him, but when he looked back, she was gone.

Crossing campus, he felt a mixture of emotions. By the time he reached Rufian's door, Jet texted Seyanna to be careful. Lifting his hand, he knocked.

The door swung inward. "About time. Did you get lost?" Rufian was in his human form, wearing jeans and a white cotton shirt, buttoned only at the waist. He was muscular and confident.

"Sorry. The tome opened and instructed me where to go in Egypt."

"Don't tell Marcella that," he warned. "Don't tell anyone else what you're doing."

"Why?"

Rufian said, "The treachery of the Coven, or a limited number of the Coven, affected a great many people. Many lives were lost, and some of those individuals don't think the Coven has suffered enough. They will attempt to impede your designs wherever possible."

"What about you?" asked Jet.

"I would have counted myself as one of those people before coming to California. I've interacted plenty with the Coven and harbor a decent amount of enmity toward them. I despise Marcella, but her words from a few weeks ago affected me. I had forgotten the ceremonial offering that was given. Keeping the children from the tribe has gone on long enough."

"That's what I was thinking," said Jet. "Should I meet with her?"

"I believe we should. She has been frantic ever since you returned to campus. Now that school is out, she expects you to fulfill your promise. This will placate her for a time. She might also have words of wisdom."

Rufian locked his door, and they set off for the beach, the northernmost spot on campus. Her hut was created months ago, allowing her to live on land and be close to the water.

Marcella waited for them near the water's edge. When they were close, she said, "That's far enough." She refused to face them. "Are you here to bring good or bad tidings?"

Jet said, "I intend to leave Chadwick's tomorrow and travel to Egypt. It is time to release the children of the Coven."

"No," Marcella said coldly. "That time was decades ago."

"I was not—"

"That statement was not for you," interrupted Marcella.

"We come in peace," said Rufian.

"Peace has never existed between us and will never again exist."

Jet said, "Any words of wisdom you can share?"

"You should have left days ago. It would have been better for both of us." Marcella finally turned to face them. Jet let out a small gasp. Her face, the left side of it, had been badly burned. There was redness, blisters, and disfiguration.

Rufian said, "That is a magma poison from the tribe Mafic Labes. They haven't been seen in years. We wondered if they were dead."

"They aren't. Yet they know what Jet Black has pledged to do. They came here to punish me. They'll be ready for you in Egypt."

Jet asked, "Do they know where the tomb is located?"

Marcella's head tilted. "How do you know it's a tomb?"

Jet began to panic. Had he just told her too much? He took a few deep breaths. "You told me three Coven witches were caught working with the Skeleton. You asked me to give you Elemental magic. I told you that I couldn't. That was when I promised to help you. I asked if you knew where the children were, and you said a tomb in Egypt, which will kill anyone who tries opening it, except if they have Elemental magic." He paused momentarily, then asked, "Can you tell me where I'm supposed to go?"

She pulled a piece of paper from a pocket of her long flowing black cloak. "These are the coordinates of the valley that leads you to the opening for the tomb. I don't have a specific location, but someone will be there to meet you, if you survive getting there."

"What happens if I die?"

Marcella's face contorted, and pain spread throughout her body. Tears ran down her face.

Jet glanced at Rufian. "What's happening?"

"She's trying to tell a lie. Remember, she is obligated to tell the truth. This is the most defiant I've seen her in months."

Marcella continued to wrestle with the lie, but finally her face relaxed. Blood and a clear fluid seeped from her burns. She spoke, her voice low and angry. "I will find a way to break Jayco. I'll probably have to kill him. I'll find a way."

"Yikes," seethed Jet. "Thanks for the honesty."

Marcella stared at him, her eyes blazing with hatred. The three layers of her eye were divided—the bright blue, yellow, and purple shone brightly. "Don't fail me, and nothing befalls Jayco."

A wave of lavender wafted over him, and he was taken back to the first time he'd met Marcella, in a dark room, wearing a masquerade mask. He'd thought it was a different student. They kissed. She had tried to beguile him, though he didn't know it then. He can never fully trust her.

"Anything else?" he asked.

"Only you can go inside. This is important. Don't die, and bring back our children."

From behind him, there was a cacophony of splashes. Jet turned to find two witches, dressed in stylish robes, ascending from the water. Jet recognized them as did Rufian, who pulled out a small handheld dagger.

The Axenkind said, "I should have known that Marcella was communicating with you, Bigorea, and you, Camora."

Camora spoke, her voice a trill. "We all want the same thing. Release the children and free us from our torment. It has been far too long since we saw our little heks."

Rufian said, "I will never comprehend why you sided with Marcella."

Camora and Marcella shared a look. The Coven woman replied, "We aren't on the same side politically, but we share a common desire. This will help all Coven." Her gaze shifted to Jet. "If you succeed, we will be evermore indebted to you."

"Yes," Bigorea agreed, and he gave a slight bow. "Forevermore."

"I'm going to go," replied Jet. "I'll do my best."

"Have you found a way to touch the ground like Marcella?" asked Rufian.

Camora approached the beach. A semi-transparent protective barrier arose, preventing them from getting too close.

"Toss her your weapon," said Rufian.

Camora unhitched a dagger from a sleeve near her ankle and impaled it into the sand. Marcella bent down to recover the weapon, but couldn't touch it.

"That curse is as strong as ever," said Rufian. "But you need to leave now. We will decide what to do with Marcella once Jet has accomplished his task."

"You'll let me go," demanded Marcella.

"That remains to be seen." Rufian turned to leave.

Bigorea spoke, his voice harsh. "Human. If you find that fear doesn't allow you to free our children, my kin and I will hunt you for the rest of your time. You'll never set foot on water again."

Jet faced Bigorea. "Next time. I'll command Braverly to cut you in half. Don't threaten me."

The witch's face contorted with rage. Jet was about to leave when Camora spoke to him. "Take that dagger as a reminder of your promise."

He glanced at Rufian, who nodded. The handle was ice cold and burned his skin. He pitched it from one hand to the next, then tried to use his shirt to hold it. Camora sighed, then dropped a black sheath onto the sand. "This will allow you to carry it. Next to an enchanted blade, this is the strongest blade ever made. You'll need to find a glove to hold it."

"We can arrange that," said Rufian.

Macella bowed slightly. "A great gift for the greatest quest in the lives of our tribesmen. You honor him."

"I prepare him for the greatest fight he has ever seen."

"Well prepared is Jet," agreed Marcella.

Bigorea and Camora sank into the water as Marcella returned to her hut, never looking back.

Rufian pulled him toward the boardwalk.

Jet asked, "What now?"

"We've got problems."

"What kind?"

"Before you leave, the entire Coven faction will know you're going to Egypt. If Marcella is telling the truth, and the Mafic Labes also know, you are in far greater danger than before we talked to Marcella. I cannot let you go alone, but you can't bring any of your friends."

Jet protested, "*The Sorcerer's Guide* instructed me that other Elementals are required."

"Ehhh." Rufian grunted in frustration. He grabbed the dagger from Jet with fingers unaffected by the cold. "Fine. I was trying to protect all of you. We need to leave this afternoon. I will arrange a plane to be waiting for us. Meet in the CeU parking lot at 3:00 p.m. Be ready for a battle."

"Seriously?" asked Jet, but Rufian sprinted off.

Jet followed the boardwalk south, passing the girls' dorms, the cafeteria, and the library. He kept a watch for anyone following him or paying him close attention. Several kids recognized him and waved or asked him to join them. He quickly declined. It was impossible to take five steps without nodding at someone. Ultimately, he used spells Oblekii and Gongpae to create an air shield and camouflage, with a decent thickness of clouds. Stepping off the boardwalk, he ducked inside the laundry building but continued the clouds as a distraction toward the football field and beyond.

He took the stairs to the lower section and watched as six mice scattered, the instant the door opened, as if they were interrupted during a meeting. Jet spoke "Kali," and hit two of them with a firebolt. He thought he had seen a glint in their eyes as if they were spying on him.

Paranoid much? he thought to himself as he shifted next to the giant laundry machines. It was only after the fact that he realized how lucky he was that no workers were around.

The passageway descended, and he pulled out a key to unlock the door. From there, he followed the long tunnel to the next door. Once outside, he hid in the cave overlooking the picturesque beach. He thought he heard voices. After several minutes, he hoped he had been hearing things. Still, he created a wind explosion that displaced the top layer of sand. He sent it toward the far rock wall and swirled it back to his position. There were no grunts or screams. Before the sand had settled, he tore down the small incline across the beach's backside. He found the crevice and hurried inside. He removed the shark's tooth necklace, put one side in his mouth, and put it into the special spot. He tumbled inside, ready to see who followed him. No one did.

Voices carried from the main chamber, and Jet walked silently in.

When the voices became discernible, he heard Grantham say, "Jayco is refusing to come to this meeting. He's going to spend some time on the phone with Rozene. I've been texting her and asked her to try calming him down."

Seyanna said, "Jet intends to leave soon. He's going to help Marcella."

"Another reason why Jayco's not coming," pointed out Grantham.

Latisha said, "He has no room to complain about Jet never picking him to help. This could be his moment."

"Doubtful," said Eric. "I've never seen Jet and Jayco get along. Why would that change now?"

Jet waited. He wanted to hear what else might be said. He wasn't disappointed.

Mckenzey replied, "No. This is different. Jayco has screwed up several times. There's something else eating at our friend. Making this something between Jayco and Jet is wrong. He needs us."

"How?" asked Keesha. "Seyanna and I tried to get his help to monitor the school's border, and he would rather spend time with Rozene."

"I think he's in love," said Maria's sweet voice. "I've seen this before. Sometimes love can be a distraction. Maybe his problem isn't Jet, but he's feeling guilty because his head is somewhere else."

"He did tell me how much he likes that Rozene will be here soon," noted Grantham.

"In a few days," added Latiasha. "Let's give him some slack. Does anyone know more about this possible adventure?"

"Why is everyone looking at me?" asked Mckenzey.

Eric said, "You never really told us much about when you went with Jet and Raul to meet with Marcella. Maybe you know more than you're letting on."

"She isn't," said Jet, and he stepped into the room. "I alone made a promise to Marcella, and now I've got to go to Egypt to fulfil it."

"What kind of promise?" asked Latisha. "You do remember that she locked up Grantham, me, and Jayco?"

"I do," said Jet, and he sat in the closest empty chair. "When Marcella first came to campus, she formed an alliance with Shane to get Elemental magic."

Keesha said, "For more power?"

"The Coven were once punished for an attempt at a rebellion back in the time of the 10 Kings. They probably got some people killed or worse. As a result, their children were taken and placed in a prison in Egypt. Only Elemental magic can free them. Marcella wanted Elemental magic from Jayco so she could enter this deep cavern of sorts."

"Does it require Fire magic?" asked Grantham.

"That's my guess, at least a part of it."

Maria added, "Seyanna said you'll take some of us with you?"

"*The Sorcerer's Guide* provided information on what it will require for anyone chosen to go."

"And?" asked Mckenzey.

Jet pulled out his tome and read the last several lines on the page:

"The deceit from the Coven was made clear, and Lady Gaea bestowed their curse. The Coven were driven from Goth Airtha and banished to Ciphadore, a city below the waters of the Caribbean.

"You have been chosen to remove the curse. This can only be done by a quadripartite of Elemental magic wielders—The Mikado, A Soothsayer, An Injured Mystic, and The Zesto Pheidippides.

"Near the peak presently known as Mount Catherine, you will find the mark of the Scarab. Follow the trail to the opening of the tomb of the Twins. Earth magic will unlock the descent to the ocean below. Plunge under the wall of confusion to the hidden chamber. You must master the Gebel ritual. Seize control and release the children."

"Okay," said Seyanna. "Back in Svalbard, I saw a scarab. Does that mean anything?"

Jet nodded. "I think so."

"What is a Soothsayer?" asked Maria.

"Someone who can see the future," said Mckenzey promptly.

"I think it's either Seyanna or Mckenzey," said Jet. "But—"

"It's not me," interrupted Mckenzey, the bitterness in her voice. "I interpret dreams. That's something different."

Grantham's eye rose. "Really?"

"I looked it up," continued Mckenzey.

Jet said, "I believe that Seyanna is the Soothsayer."

"Who else of us is going?" asked Keesha.

"I have my own thoughts, but I will let you guys decide. He read the line of the four people again.

"Jayco? Does he fit any of these categories?" asked Grantham.

"I don't think so," said Eric.

It didn't take long for Eric to be eliminated as well.

Latisha said, "That leaves Maria, Keesha, me, and Grantham.

Eric asked, "What is Zesto Pheidippides?"

"According to the internet, Pheidippides was the first person to be connected with the marathon race," said Keesha as she stared at her phone. "Doesn't Grantham run?"

"He does!" said Latisha excitedly.

"If I remember correctly, Grantham runs better the hotter it is," added Jet. "I think he's included in the four."

"Which of us is injured?" asked Mckenzey, suddenly excited.

"All of us," said Maria. "I lost my brother. Mckenzey had her leg broken by Jet. Her boyfriend betrayed Keesha, and Kee-faux injured Latisha, and she nearly lost her magic."

Maria's last words caused the entire group to stare at Latisha.

"It's you," whispered Mckenzey. "Everyone is injured, but you're an injured mystic."

"That's four people," announced Grantham.

Jet said, "We have four hours before the plane leaves. Let's talk about coordination and protection of the school while we're gone. We need to be particularly careful of Shane and the rest of the Runics. They'll burn everything they can before they depart. Be ready for anything."

CHAPTER 37

Nearly twenty-four hours later, Jet, Seyanna, Grantham, and Latisha landed in Egypt. The flight from Cairo to Saint Catherine International Airport took just over thirty hours. The airport was the smallest yet on their travels. The backdrop was Mount Sinai from the bible. The entire ridge of mountains was breathtaking. The plane taxied onto a flat space between jagged peaks. Where they were headed was not far from here.

Stepping off the plane, they were hit with a scorching, dry heat.

"It's 111 degrees," said Grantham. "This feels great."

"Don't rub it in," said Latisha. "I forgot how much you love this."

"It makes me feel alive."

"Can we take a nap?" asked Seyanna, but she was energized and restless. "I don't think I slept on any of our five flights."

"Neither did we," said Jet.

"Why?" asked Seyanna.

"Because you couldn't stop talking," said Grantham. "You're downright wound-up."

"I am not."

"Girl," said Latisha. "You've wanted to come to Egypt since you were little. I remember some of your presentations back in junior high."

Jet added, "Remember when you gave me that long explanation about the cloth, the fable, and that box we took from Switzerland? This is like ten times worse."

Seyanna smiled. "Ha ha. I spent hours researching that cloth and its history. It talked about Pandora, also called Anesidora. I thoroughly enjoyed researching the hieroglyphics."

"Yep. You love Egypt," said Grantham. "I bet you don't sleep the entire time we're here."

"Fine," Seyanna smiled. "I'm totally stoked that we're standing in the land of Kemet."

"What's that?" asked Latisha.

Rufian answered, "That is what the ancients call this land. He and the Professors, Gimshe, Sidewinder, and Fleener, gathered their items. The four Axenkind were both calm and alert for anything unusual. They didn't love flying and slept almost the entire time.

Latisha asked, "Did you bring an ax for me?"

Gimshe smiled and handed her a large plastic box. Within was an ax they had used in Swordplay.

Grantham asked, "Did you guys take some meds to sleep like that?"

Rufian ignored this question. "Our guides will be ready tomorrow. They are getting things packed. There is a vehicle that will take us to Morgenland Hotel."

"What about the plane?" asked Grantham.

"They have to fly back to Cairo. We will contact them once we have finished."

Latisha whispered, "What about the Coven children?"

"I expect several of the Coven are nearby. The Gulf of Suez or Aqaba would be a perfect place to wait."

"We won't need to fly back with them?" asked Grantham.

"No," said Professor Gimshe. "I doubt you will be allowed to talk with them. They won't answer any of your questions."

"Will the witches be able to come onto land once their children are free?" asked Jet.

"We will find out soon enough," replied Rufian.

Two black SUVs entered the parking area and stopped next to the plane. A driver from each vehicle exited, and simple introductions were given in English. After the suitcases were loaded, Jet, Seyanna, Professor Fleener, and Rufian entered one vehicle while the others were in the second. In no time, they were speeding off through the desert.

A two-lane road took them out of the airport's boundaries. The landscape was filled with rocks, dirt, and mountains, both ahead and behind them. An occasional bush or tree was seen in the distance. The reddish sand was impressive and dry. A sophisticated radio tower emerged on their left, followed by a building as large as a warehouse. There were plenty of cars, but no name on the structure.

Five miles later, they reached a small roundabout and went left, heading south. They passed five or six buildings with rock walls. It was more like a village, but he saw no homes. The tiny supermarket they saw down a side street mainly looked deserted. Five minutes later, everything changed as they pulled into a grand hotel with a gigantic pool in the center. The cost of building this hotel likely exceeded the cost of all the buildings they passed on the way from the airport to this location. A dozen buildings dotted the property. Each had pinkish exterior stucco walls with decorative splashes of red. The landscape was magical with cacti, some trees, and several smaller bushes. They parked on the far side of the pool.

Rufian explained, "We have four rooms. Jet and Grantham will share, and the girls will share. The four of us will take up the remaining rooms."

Latisha asked, "Do teachers have to share a room? Is that a rule?"

"The Axenkind often send couples on missions together," replied Rufian. "Professor Fleener and I are married, and Professors Gimshe and Sidewinder are as well. Did you not know?"

Jet stared at Rufian, shocked. Looking around at his friends, they appeared just as surprised as he was. He managed to say, "Honestly, we don't think much about the private lives of our professors. It never crossed my mind."

"Nope," added Latisha. "Didn't see that one coming."

Seyanna said, "Let's drop our stuff off in our rooms and meet at the pool."

"Totally." Grantham yanked out his suitcase and disappeared into one room. Jet grabbed his items and followed.

He stepped into the pool fifteen minutes later and headed toward the girls. The temperature hovered around ninety-nine degrees, but the water was cool and soothing. Seyanna and Latisha were relaxing, and Grantham was throwing something and diving to the bottom. The pool was enormous, but much longer than wide.

Seyanna said, "I know we've been friends for a while, but I think this might be the first time I've seen you at the pool."

Jet smirked. "How often do we actually swim?"

"When we're at the beach, you never take off your shirt."

"You showed us some scars at the beginning of the year," added Latisha, then she stared at him. Her mouth dropped open. "What's that thing around your neck?"

Seyanna answered, "A new tattoo. It happened just a few days ago. I was there when it appeared."

"When what appeared?" asked Grantham.

"Jet got a new tattoo."

"What!" demanded Grantham, and he swam toward them.

"First," said Seyanna. "What scars are we talking about?"

"You've never seen them?" asked Latisha.

Seyanna shrugged, then her face reddened slightly.

Pointing to his left bicep, Jet said quickly, "Glass from my house in Silverton cut me here." Pointing to his back, he added, "I was burned by lava here and on my lower leg." He rolled his left shoulder and said, "I had a plate put in my shoulder when I fell at the beginning of school."

"That's right," added Grantham. "Seyanna hadn't yet come to school."

Latisha asked, "Were you at Chadwick's when he got his back tattoo?"

"No," said Seyanna. "But I have seen that one."

Grantham asked, "I can't remember exactly how you got it."

"A page turned in The Sorcerer's Guide, and when I touched the image, the emblem of a campfire with smoke, a glacier lake, an ancient tree, and a descending sun behind mountains transformed from the page onto my back."

Seyanna said, "Those two black daggers on your forearm were used to fight."

"Yes," answered Jet. "They both ended up breaking, and now they're black." Jet pointed to the tribal band on his arm. "This was when I fought the Demon Kirche at Starbuck Island. It looks better than when it first happened."

"So much has happened since Silverton was destroyed."

Latisha said, "I don't think I ever really understood how you survived Silverton. I was visiting my family in Florida when it happened."

Jet added, "Grantham and Seyanna were gone as well."

Seyanna said, "You woke up with your house on fire, right?"

"Not right away. I got up just before a gully hit my house, then filled with lava. A second one hit, and my house nearly collapsed. That's when the fire started."

Grantham said, "Back when we were first learning about magic, you told us that you survived because of your talents."

"Magic saved me." He added, "I can manipulate my vision, and I can slow time. I can also expand my peripheral vision and focus it. Three separate things."

"I've heard you talking about it before," admitted Seyanna.

"But you forgot what happened," said Grantham. "Because of the tonic your parents gave you."

Jet smiled. "You were listening."

He glanced at Latisha. "She reminded me last week. I totally had forgotten, bro."

They laughed.

Seyanna asked, "Do you hate swimming?"

"No," replied Jet. "It's just a bit of a fear."

She said, "In ten minutes, I'm going to give you a little lesson."

"On how to swim?"

"We'll start with floating."

An hour later, the sun had set, and after enjoying a swimming party, they settled on the south side of the pool. They ordered dinner and drinks, which the hotel staff brought over. The kindness and pure hospitality of the staff were impressive. The food was delicious and unique, and they each tried something they'd never had before.

When their empty plates had been taken away, Grantham asked, "How far from here is Mount Catherine?"

Jet pointed to the east. "Further down that road, we'll reach the town of St. Catherine. It isn't big, and all the streets are dirt. We'll arrive early and park on the south side. We'll have to walk to a trail. This is a very religious area of Egypt. There are mosques, churches, and a monastery. As we travel down a ravine, we'll come to Mount Moses. Mount Catherine is another few hours of hiking. At the bottom, there are some buildings."

"So...it's going to take the full day," said Latisha.

"We'll need to sleep in tents and bring enough food and water for two or three days."

Grantham asked, "The guides better have horses or something?"

Jet laughed. "Rufian hired two people who will help carry some of our things using camels. We won't have the luxury to ride them, unless we get injured."

Latisha asked, "Is where we're looking for close to Mount Catherine?"

"I hope. I think we'll need Seyanna to guide us to the opening."

"No pressure," said Seyanna, smiling. "I hope I don't disappoint all of you."

"We'll get there," encouraged Jet. "Let's just watch each other's backs while we are out there. We don't know what to expect."

"Did you bring the golden pyramids?" asked Seyanna.

"All three of them. I'll let Iris out first, but if we get into a tough spot, we'll release the other two."

Grantham asked, "What about weapons?"

"I have Gravity and a few other items. Assuming you guys brought yours?"

"I have my bow and arrow and a shield," said Seyanna.

Latisha said, "I brought a general golden sword, but I feel more comfortable using the ax."

Grantham asked, "Why do you think we were chosen to come?"

Jet lifted himself out of the water, except for his legs. "Elemental magic is the key, and the four of us are the best equipped to be here. But other than that, you're guess is as good as mine."

Latisha said, "Seyanna can run fast and hear well, right? Grantham can climb and gets energized in the heat. I've lost my ability to see in the dark."

"But you are needed," said Jet. "All of us are."

"We'll be ready," said Grantham.

"Before we head off to bed," said Seyanna. "Jet, can I talk with you for a second?"

"Sure."

Stepping from the pool, they dried off, and he followed her to some outdoor reclining chairs. Thinking they would sit and relax, he went to the closest one, but she grabbed her shoes and continued walking. Scrambling, Jet found his sandals and went after her. She led him between two buildings and onto a dirt path that circled the hotel.

Jet caught up quickly. "Are you okay?"

She smiled at him. "I am." A few moments later, she said, "I didn't want to miss this moment with you. This place is incredible."

"It is."

They walked in silence and turned right, enjoying each other's company. The buildings on this side of the hotel were larger and appeared to be the main lodge, a workout area, and a restaurant. The lights shone on the landscape, creating a drastically exquisite appearance.

"This is quite a change in temperature to Svalbard Island," noted Jet. "We've gone on some pretty sweet adventures together."

"At least I don't have to carry you this time." Her genuine smile sent a shot of warmth through his chest. But her smile faltered slightly, and she asked, "Is something bad going to happen tomorrow?"

Jet spoke slowly. "I don't know. I hope not. Why?"

"Back at school, it seemed you were hesitant to have me here, as if you knew something perilous would happen."

"I don't know of any impending doom. But Marcella knows we're coming, so does the Coven, and some tribesmen. I've never trusted her, but I did make a promise. I just wanted all of us to know of the risks."

She stopped walking and turned to him, but stared at the ground. "Do you remember back when we were on that ship leaving Starbuck Island? I had this weird feeling that you and I would become disconnected if we hadn't won in the maze."

"I do." He remembered back on the ship when she pushed him into the bathroom, on the verge of sobbing. "Are you feeling that again?"

"Not the same thing," she muttered. "But I feel more unsettled. That if we lose, more people than just you and I will be affected. I think my father is part of the problem."

"He's hunting for you and to find a way to punish me."

She finally looked up at him. "You feel that too. He thinks you and my parents kidnapped and brainwashed me. I saw them before we left for Egypt. They've gone into hiding."

"What!" exclaimed Jet.

"He'll find a way to punish those closest to me." There were tears in her eyes.

"He can try," said Jet, stepping closer to her. Reaching out with both of his arms, he wrapped her in a hug and held her tight. She didn't cry but leaned into him, as if gaining strength. "We probably won't win everything, but we will protect each other. I'm glad you're here. You're the strongest person I know, and you've already saved me."

"Damn right," she retorted. After several seconds, she said, "Promise that you won't get lost tomorrow or worse."

"Promise," said Jet without a second thought.

They walked, and talked, and spoke about the past, the present, and the future as freely as someone without pretention or fear that what they said would be ridiculed. Seyanna shared her hopes of becoming a scientist and researching ecosystems and other biospheres. He enjoyed hearing her describe her ambitions. He did the same, but he wasn't as fixated on the final product of a specific job as he was on finding something he was passionate about. Nothing was said about magic, the Rivalry, or the upcoming war for a long time.

Talking, without needing to kiss, felt like it brought them closer. It was a deeper and more emotional connection. That wasn't to say he didn't love kissing her, but it didn't feel right for this moment.

He walked her to her door, and this time, she pulled him into a hug. "Goodnight," she whispered and kissed his cheek. "I expect to see you again in a few hours."

Glancing at his watch, Jet said, "We might get four hours of sleep if we're lucky."

"It was worth it," she said and disappeared inside.

As the outer door closed, Jet retreated to his room. He was both spent and amped up. Sneaking into his room, he found Grantham snoring in one of the two beds. Jet used the restroom, brushed his teeth, and lay down. Complete sleep didn't come for thirty minutes, but he wasn't fully awake either. His mind wandered, failing to connect with anything specific. He thought about his tome, Jayco, killing the Demon Kirche, and Mckenzey's dreams of blue fog. He managed to mutter, "Endor," and a wave of drowsiness overcame him, and he fell deeply asleep.

CHAPTER 38

The room was exceptionally quiet when Jet woke up the next morning. He had barely unpacked, so he showered, dressed, and was out the door ten minutes later. He expected Grantham to be getting things settled for the day's adventure. Leaving his room, he didn't feel rushed or stressed and found the others at an outdoor café.

"Morning," he said as he approached.

Latisha was leaning forward, her face partially blocked, and she was whispering. At the sound of his voice, she jerked back and focused on her food. No one else turned around. They hadn't waited for him to order.

"Everything good?" he asked as he reached the table.

"Sure," said Grantham.

"Have you seen the Axenkind?"

"Yeah," continued Grantham. "A vehicle arrived, and they're getting things packed."

"Good morning, Seyanna." She said nothing but squinted at him, the sun barely over the rise and blinding. Her face was blotched, and her hair tangled. It didn't look like she had gotten any sleep and might've been crying. "What's wrong?"

Her voice was firm. "Nothing that I can't get over in a few minutes."

He asked, "Did something happen?"

Grantham and Latisha both glared at him.

"What?" he asked defensively.

"It's fine," said Seyanna, and she looked away. "And no. It's not anything to do with your actions. I'll fill you in later. Here comes Rufian and the others."

The four Axenkind strode forward, quickly.

"What's up?" asked Grantham.

Professor Sidewinder answered, "Our two guides have seen an increase in activity in St. Catherine with an influx of tourists. More than usual."

"Are the guides with the Brotherhood?" asked Latisha.

"No, they aren't," said Rufian. "They are locals. They are experts who are familiar with this area, and they are trustworthy."

"Why would there be an increase in tourism?" asked Seyanna. "Is that a bad thing?"

"When tourists bring guns to the area, the locals get worried that something is going to happen."

"Could it be the Azurites?" asked Grantham.

Professor Fleener said, "It is impossible to guess. It might be some local gangs and nothing to do with why we are here."

Seyanna asked, "Would Marcella work with the Azurites to cause us problems?"

Rufian replied, "I don't know. The Coven wants the release of their children. Unless she is working for her own designs, I don't see why she would want to obstruct our progress."

Jet said, "There are multiple possibilities. We saw Faunal working with the Azurites at Spruce Knob. We need to be extra careful today."

"That was our conclusion as well. We leave in fifteen minutes," said Gimshe.

"So, Faunal's only loyalty is to Arisol?" said Grantham.

"Precisely," said Rufian. "He can't be trusted and will turn on whomever the moment he can."

"Is Faunal here?" asked Latisha. "In Egypt."

Professor Gimshe said, "The Axenkind tried tracking him after Spruce Knob. He was last seen in Finland. But we lost the trail."

"Finland?" asked Seyanna. "That isn't far from Svalbard."

"Our Island is on high alert," agreed Professor Fleener.

Seyanna let out a long breath.

Rufian explained, "There is a valley south of this hotel that eventually leads us to our destination, but it will add hours to our hike today. If we were on the opposite side of the mountain range, we would have different options, but our current plan remains the best choice. The parking location in St. Catherine has changed. We've needed places to hide our vehicles. It costs extra."

"We're ready," said Jet.

"Meet you in the parking area," said Grantham.

The Axenkind turned to leave. Grantham and the girls finished their food.

Jet said, "I'll be just a minute. I'll find something to go."

Latisha smiled. "No problem."

Jet found some freshly made muffins and some fruit. He grabbed two juices and hurried back to the table. It was empty. They had left without him.

Fine, thought Jet. *I guess it's going to be a really long day.*

Food, tents, and other supplies were already packed, and he spotted Grantham getting introduced to the two guides. Without a word, they got back into the same two vehicles they had taken from the airport the previous day and drove out of the hotel. This time, he was seated next to Latisha while Grantham and Seyanna were in the other vehicle.

Fifteen minutes later, as the dirt roofs of St. Catherine came into view, Jet was awestruck at the simplicity of the town. Buildings were spread out, and small groupings of trees or bushes divided property lines or bordered the dirt paths. Stone walls were seen as often as houses. They drove through open dirt areas, and as they entered the southern part of town, they took a right, driving past the hospital. He spotted panels of reflective glass on the front and a large area of red above them. It was the most modern building they had seen, other than the hotel.

Moments later, they passed a mosque, a school, and a police building. A few people were walking down the roads, but there were even fewer vehicles. The road became bumpier the farther they went. Turning down a small lane, both vehicles came to a sudden stop. Rufian pointed to a grouping of three trees to their left, across a dry ravine, and another group of trees ahead of them. If they chose the one to their left, they would have to turn the car around and backtrack.

Rufian said, "Keep going forward. There are some houses over there. I think that is where we are supposed to start."

One of the guides drove forward slowly. Veering to the right, they avoided a rock in the middle, and a poorly gated community came into view. The guide of the first vehicle ahead of them exited the car and opened a wooden gate, pulling it back on rollers. They immediately turned left, went about fifty feet, and parked on the side of a house, under some trees, out of view.

No one said a word as the gear and other items were removed from the back of both vehicles. Jet focused on zipping his backpack and ensuring he had everything arranged, ignoring the others.

Rufian handed him a tent and a sleeping bag and asked, "Is everything good?"

Jet nodded. Sidewinder handed him food and water.

The two guides came together and strode partly down a small path, eyeing the area. From his hidden compartment, he removed weapons and put them on the ground. Gimshe also had a hidden compartment, and she removed several weapons. He was curious about her hiding spot, but said nothing.

Professor Fleener interrupted his dark thoughts. "Water will be the most important. Don't drink too quickly, but don't save more than you need. It will weigh you down, and if you don't drink enough, your energy will leach out."

Grantham said, "Jet has a spell that can increase the amount that we bring. I think we'll be good."

"Good to know," said Professor Sidewinder, who strapped some weapons to his back. "I was not aware."

Seyanna kept on the far side of Grantham and Latisha.

Rufian announced, "We have to carry everything, for now. The camels are hidden up the trail. It will be hard for the first twenty minutes."

Two minutes later, they slipped out behind the fence surrounding the few houses and trees. The two guides, then Rufian, set the pace. Seyanna was a step behind Rufian. Sidewinder, then Flenner, were followed by Grantham and Latisha. Gimshe and Jet brought up the rear.

A quarter of a mile later, they stepped into a dry and arid valley, nearly single file. The different colored sand and rocks were breathtaking and beautiful. A dry ravine was situated a few hundred feet to their left, along with some additional buildings that were possibly abandoned.

The land was rocky, and it took them longer to cross the gap before the base of the next closest jagged hill. The peak went skyward a few hundred feet.

"What's that?" asked Latisha. She stopped momentarily to catch her breath.

Rufian, breathing hard, said, "Let's go take a look."

As they approached the base of the rocky hill, they moved directly next to it. When everyone had grouped together, they were led around the edge of the first rock cliff and into a side passage. After another fifty feet, they could see an opening off to the right. This pocket didn't go very deep, but two camels were tied to a barren tree.

"Our first rest spot," said Gimshe.

Most of their items were packed on both camels. After getting some water and a snack, they resumed their hike. Fifty feet later, they passed another rock cliff on their right, smaller this time, and the next pocket opened up to the larger valley.

"Was that a shortcut?" asked Grantham.

The guide standing closer to Grantham said, "This valley is one of the most traveled in the region. We know secret places to avoid confrontation or being spotted." The man's accent was foreign, but he spoke English well.

After another half hour of walking, a ravine appeared in the distance. It had smaller rocks, and there was even a path leading to it that made movement easier.

An hour later, they stopped to get a drink. The rock walls, on both sides, were taller than they were five minutes ago. However, up ahead, the wall stopped at a spot where a small rock structure on their left protruded near the path. This one spot was lower than the rest. Sunlight hit the top sections, and it was already warming considerably. Jet knew that once the sun hit them directly, it would be beyond miserable.

"We need to talk," said Seyanna. She had her back against the rock wall. Her strawberry-blonde hair was tied into a ponytail. She wore her white cloak with hiking shoes, and she carried one walking stick. Her cheeks were slightly flushed from the hike. She had just taken a sip of water. Grantham and Latisha were placing some items on a large rock that had broken off years ago and fallen to the valley floor.

Jet asked, "Are we good?"

She nodded. "You and I are fine. Mostly."

"Is it about Grantham and Latisha?"

"No," she said. "But someone saw you and me out walking last night."

A lump formed in his stomach.

"Incoming!" screamed Rufian.

The red fireball passed a foot over Jet's head, crashing into the base of the wall on the opposite side. A section of grass burst into flames.

"Coming from above us," cried Sidewinder.

Looking up, the next fireball was heading straight for the center of Jet's chest.

Seyanna moved so quickly that he didn't realize he was being dragged sideways toward the large rock. His stomach lurched at the movement.

"What's happening?" screamed Latisha.

Professor Gimshe yelled, "We are under attack!"

In quick succession, four fireballs struck the ground in different places. A hot glob collided with Professor Fleener's lower leg, and she screamed in agony. Rufian rushed to her side, pulling her to safety.

Jet spoke "Abzu," and unleashed a volley of ice crystals onto the rocky plateau above them. He had no direct line of sight, so it was a blind attack. He figured his attackers were hiding up there. They had the high ground. The fireballs did not stop, but they appeared less strategically placed.

A sparkle of light caught his eye, and he glimpsed a dozen glass spheres plummeting down. The first few collided with a surface three times before breaking open, releasing a faint mist. Fearing poison, Jet immediately spoke "Aer," and directed the contents of the glass spheres away from their group.

He missed at least two, and the mist passed close to Professor Gimshe as she instantly collapsed to the ground.

"What is that?" demanded Latisha. "Is she hurt?"

A voice spoke from behind them. "I'll check on her." Professor Sidewinder had his sword drawn and vaulted to her side, covering up his mouth with his other arm. He sheathed his sword and checked her pulse. He began dragging her closer to the wall. When he could speak, he said, "She seems fine. Just unconscious."

A fireball rammed Professor Sidewinder's back so forcefully that he was thrust forward, smacking his head into the wall, then falling backward.

"They must've moved," said Grantham, "That came from a different position."

Rufian shouted, "We are pinned down."

The next fireball struck one of the guides as he attempted to flee. The smell of burned skin was sickening. The second guide crouched, covering his head, and began crying. One of the camels had taken a direct hit and was knocked on its side, dead. The other camel was making its way back in the direction they had come from.

Jet spoke "Oblekii," and willed clouds, rain, and fog to fill the valley. This would make targeting them nearly impossible.

From above, he heard someone shout, "Anti-Water," and glancing up, he watched as another volley of crystals shot into the air. He forced his vision to magnify and watched as the crystals exploded ten seconds after release. Anywhere close to where the spheres exploded, his spell began to lose its effect. Two more clusters of crystals were launched. Within two minutes, the fog and clouds had dissipated completely.

He knew instantly what was happening, and he had moved the entire group farther up the valley, keeping close to the wall.

"Did those counteract your spell?" asked Seyanna.

"Seems like it," agreed Jet.

"How's that possible?" asked Latisha.

Jet said, "We're going to find out."

They pulled the injured Sidewinder and the unconscious Gimshe into a crevice. It only went back a few feet, but it had an overhanging ledge that would keep them safe for a few minutes.

"What's the plan?"

Jet said, "I'll create some vines up the side of the rock wall. We'll climb them and face our attackers."

"What if those crystal spheres bypass all your magic?" asked Seyanna.

Grantham answered, "Climb up the rock wall. I can do that without vines."

Jet changed his tactics. "Okay. Tell Rufian that Grantham and I will climb. If the vines are still intact, then you guys can follow us. If not, sprint to a different spot where you can climb."

"What about me?" asked Latisha.

"Stay down here and make sure the other teachers are fine." Spinning, he spoke "Neis," at the section of rock wall to the right of the crevice. He pointed to the opposite side for Grantham to climb. The vines attached to the wall and branched upward as if being sewn into the rock.

"I'm coming," hissed Seyanna behind him.

He wasn't going to argue. Instead, he thrust corn kernels into each of their hands.

Grantham asked, "Do we need to say anything to activate these?"

"Nope. Just drop them."

Grantham and Jet set off up the rock wall. It went straight up, the vines creating places to grip. Jet heard a grunt and knew that Seyanna had started. He refused to look down. While Grantham and Jayco were the most talented climbers at Chadwick's, Jet was one of the worst. Grantham shot ahead, and even Seyanna passed him, but he pushed as quickly as he dared.

With his expanded vision, he watched Latisha crawl towards Rufian and Fleener. The movement elicited two more fireballs, both of which missed.

Partway up, Jet spoke "Oblekii," repeatedly, trying to gain some control over the visibility. More spheres were tossed into the air.

Someone spoke above them, "It's working. Our Anti-spells are ingenious. Get the next attack ready. They're planning something."

Jet thought he recognized the voice.

Rufian pulled out something like a crossbow, unleashing three arrows at once. The instant they became airborne, they glowed a bright red for a dozen feet, then they exploded, blotting out the light.

A male voice yelled, "Axenkind magic. A void arrow. Get ready to drop the Anti-Earth magic next. It'll affect their gravity. Three Axenkind are down...one left."

Jet spoke "Pan," trying to shake the ground above them. He heard screams and hoped this was the right spell, but it was not accompanied by a green aura.

"We're under attack," bellowed someone.

Sounds of fighting erupted. His fear of heights vanished, replaced by a different one, and he bounded up. Grantham was gone, and Seyanna was pulling herself onto an upper ledge. It took another full minute for Jet to reach his hand and grasp the ridge. He pulled himself up and found a chaos of fighting. Two outer groupings were shooting things at two central figures. But beyond, a third group attacked the two groupings. Several people lay on the ground, unconscious.

The Azurites wore red and gray leather armor, including a head cap similar to a beanie. They had breastplates and arm and leg sleeves. They also had red leather shoes. An Elemental spell collided with a tall boy, bounced off the chest plate, and diverted into a rock wall. A frozen expanse covered the face of the rock.

"To me," screamed Mckenzey as she and Eric rushed toward a brunette that Jet recognized. The same voice he had heard giving out commands.

"Brenda," Jet seethed, and he set off in her direction at a sprint.

"My father," cried Seyanna, as she pivoted, fighting next to Grantham.

To his left, Professor Rysen and Charlie Eckenkeep were positioned between two large rocks, aiming the large red bull's head with curved horns directly at Jet. The fireball shot out of its mouth. From this distance, it came toward him at lightning speed. He dropped onto the ground, barely missing the projectile.

From his back, Jet spoke "Gongpae," and hoped his air shield could protect him. The second projectile glanced off the shield and was sent into a rock wall on the other end of the valley.

A voice bellowed, "Capture Rainbow!"

Jet was momentarily unsure where he should go. Help with Brenda or protect Seyanna. He didn't have much choice as the third fireball collided directly with his shield, and he was hammered back to the edge.

Charlie Eckenkeep yelled. "Fire the Astrolators at the air shield."

Five Azurites turned, holding blue and yellow spheres, launching them at him.

Jet yanked out three golden pyramids and tossed them onto the ground. He spoke "Pyramis of Aurum" and Iris transformed. The yellow spheres collided with his shield, wiping it out.

Charlie Echkenkeep smiled. "Now...you're mine."

Dropping his two corn kernels, six perfect duplicates arose. Seyanna did the same as four Azurites stalked toward her. She retreated, trying to get closer to Jet. He willed his replicas to go in different directions. Grantham worked his way toward Mckenzey and Eric, but he became cornered by two Azurites. He dropped his kernels, but the replicas surrounding Grantham stayed close to him. The Azurites charged forward, with nets, intending to trap Grantham.

Suddenly, the golden bear and lion bellowed and charged the two oncoming Azurite attackers, and they both chose to flee instead of getting mauled. Grantham pushed forward to support Mckenzey.

"Duck," cried Seyanna, and she pulled him down as another fireball missed him by inches. Pulling out Gravity, he felt energized to unleash a full Elemental magical attack. Focusing on the stone at the end of his staff, each spell he spoke had more and more power. He knocked several Azurites to the ground and froze two more. Each of his replicas also held a staff. It was impossible to tell which of them his spells were coming from.

A replica to his right was hit by a fireball and vanished. Suddenly, Charlie and Professor Rysen fired at all the images of him, Seyanna, and Grantham. One by one, the replicas were slowly obliterated. Two of Seyanna's vanished when a single net captured them. Jet sent the Azurite a pain spell that forced the girl to slam her own head into the ground, knocking herself out.

Tominiko, Phoebe, Asher, Keesha, Maria, and others began to wear down the Azurites, forcing them to retreat. Iris stayed close to Jet and Seyanna, and the lion and bear took down any stragglers.

Latisha, swinging her axe, joined the fray. She began to shout out commands of her own.

Charlie yelled, "Kill that boy who's kidnapped my daughter and turned her against me."

The fireballs were now directed at Jet and Jet alone. He'd pushed Seyanna away. Three Azurites flanked and protected Charlie and Rysen. He wanted to pursue Brenda for her deceptions and needed to obtain one of the Insidious weapons. His mind was made up for him in the next few seconds.

Long wooden sticks appeared above the heads of eight Azurites, and Jet halted, unsure if this was a form of communication or an attack. The other Elementals became just as confused and cautious. The sticks began to rotate as if an unseen hand spun them.

The eyes of the eight Azurites focused on Grantham, Mckenzey, and several Elementals, and Jet knew the twirling sticks would be used as weapons. Brenda and six other Azurites pulled out different weapons, and two held glass spheres of Anti-magic.

As forcefully as he could, Jet shouted, "Pachamama," and a ten-foot-deep crevice cut dividing the two groups. He knocked down both Azurites and Elementals alike.

The bent-up energy of the sticks missed their intended target and slammed into a rock pillar as thick as a house and twice as tall, knocking it off the ledge and into the valley below.

A fireball slammed into Seyanna as she stepped in to push Jet out of its path. She was struck on the right shoulder and was sent into a twirl. She landed hard and there was a blackened stain in her white cloak.

"Are you hurt?"

"Shoulder... Air out. Fine." Her last two remaining replicas vanished. Jet still had three left.

He put a protective spell around himself and Seyanna, and two of his last three replicas vanished.

The concussive force of the next fireball was intense as it collided with the air shield.

Three Azurites remained standing, including Brenda. She screamed, "Your mom's energy ring gave me the details I needed to create some Anti-magic weapons. This one is called the Drainer." Brenda and the other Azurites produced black, handheld sticks that bent at 90 degrees.

They could crank them to create a rotating motion. "You're such an idiot, Black. Gifting me a ring because you felt sorry for me. I was a lonely little girl. So gullible."

She pointed the sticks at Tominiko and Maria, and Jet watched as their magical strength was slowly pulled from them.

Seyanna stood next to him, protected behind his shield, which probably wouldn't hold up against the Drainers.

"Use that on him," demanded Charlie. "Take away his power and bring me my daughter."

Tominiko and Maria stumbled to the ground. Eric, Nolan, and Allison, nearby, had to steady themselves.

Jet raised his hands as Brenda changed the direction of her attack to focus on him.

Iris, the bear, and the lion crouched, ready to strike.

"This ends now," shouted Brenda. "Keep your pets at bay, and no one else has to suffer. The Azurites will have all the power going forward."

Jet's shield vanished. From the periphery of his vision, he noticed that Em and Gleam stood unseen directly behind Professor Rysen and Charlie. That meant Faris was nearby.

The pull of his energy was like feeling water slip through his fingers. It didn't hurt, but his mind recognized what was happening, a subtle decline. He could no longer access or think about magic.

His animals inched closer, and Brenda screamed, "Tell them to back down." She marched forward, just as Faris silently landed behind Brenda, but she was too focused on Jet to notice. Faris held a mahogany needle sword, and instead of cutting her, Faris used the pommel of her sword and struck Brenda in the head, knocking her unconscious.

"Fire," cried Charlie. Rysen aimed the red bull at Jet. Gleam and Em bounded forward, slamming both men to the ground. The unusual weapon glowed bright red, as if ready to fire, then the glow disappeared as the men toppled over.

Iris and the lion rushed at the remaining two Azurites standing. They were quickly dispatched. The bear crashed into a bush, chasing a boy that Jet recognized. He was an Elemental that Jet had personally trained.

"Corvin," said Jet.

Corvin, a tall boy with bleached-blond hair, said, "They kidnapped me."

Keesha hurried over to the bush and uncovered six canisters of unused anti-magic weapons.

"That seems plausible," replied Jet.

Ariana, Raul, Mckenzey, Grantham, Eric, and others got to their feet, but it was clear they had little energy. Latisha appeared less fatigued.

"Sisters!" cried Faris, standing next to the unconscious Brenda.

"Get back," yelled Rysen, and he stood holding a grenade. "If this device leaves my hands, it will explode within seconds. Non-magical are exempt from the damage they cause. The Azurites have discovered a liquid that melts away magic and certain types of protection, and damages everyone it touches."

Rysen stepped toward the red bull's head weapon, but Iris growled. In the commotion, she had put herself between it and the two men.

Charlie pulled out his own grenade.

"Father," said Seyanna. "This must end. Why are you here?"

Charlie's voice said, "You've been deceived. All of you have. The Brotherhood and the magical are puppets of the Silver Fox. The real danger is those—"

"More lies, Dad?" retorted Seyanna. "Look around. Many of us have been given Elemental magic. Right now, what matters is that we are prepared for the upcoming war. The more we fight among ourselves, the less primed we will be. The Azurites have been fighting with the Brotherhood for years, and you've accomplished nothing. All five magic books are now awake. Magic will be taught in the boarding schools. Arisol or the Silver Fox will be unleashed in a matter of months. But yet, you attack us to stop us from what?"

Rysen hissed, "If you unleash the children of the Coven, we will be on the verge of losing the war. Have you ever considered that? Can you trust the Coven? If we injure a few Elementals in the process, at least we've stopped The Sliver Fox from gaining an advantage. Sacrifice of a few for the good of the rest."

Jet said, "You can't stop us from freeing the children."

"You aren't there yet," hissed Professor Rysen. "We've done a pretty good job so far."

"Do you believe in the magical books we've been given?" asked Jet.

"No," said Professor Rysen. "We know at one time, they were intended to teach you magic. But they've been polluted by the Brotherhood for their own perception. They have keywords within them that open their pages. The Brotherhood picked and chose what should be added."

"But not everything added was by the Brotherhood," said Jet.

Rysen nodded. "Nothing you say can be trusted."

"I find it ironic that your weapon of choice, to kill my parents and attack us, is one of the Insidious Six. I'm assuming that you know about them."

"That's not possible," replied Charlie. "I've discovered scrolls about them. The Insidious Six were people, not weapons. The Silver Fox was the leader of a secret group, which included the Twins, the Skeleton, and the two kings who became Erpofalco. The twins were the only ones killed."

"No," Jet said flatly. Pulling out the black loop

Rysen cried, "I will release this grenade."

"You'll die before you leave this ridge. My golden panther, the lion, the bear, and the three Myntra will kill you even if you take magic from us. We knew the Azurites. We've planned a counterattack for weeks. We had two sets of Elemental groups expecting you. Jayco is leading the other group. Look around, he isn't here, and he's already close to releasing the Coven's children. *We* were the diversion. Elemental magic allows us to communicate. They already know what's happened here." Confidently, he strolled to where Iris stood guard. "Before you remove magic from us, I want you to watch something." He pulled out the black looped emblem.

"What is that?" demanded Rysen. "Are you going to attack us?"

"As the Mikado, this entire diversion was to get this weapon. After you see what happens...you are free to go?"

"Seriously?" hissed Seyanna.

"What?" cried Charlie. "You aren't here to free the children?"

"No," said Jet. "This weapon is why I'm here?"

"You lie," said Charlie.

"Watch and learn." Jet focused on the bull's head. He felt the evilness of the weapon. He presented the Kindred Loop for all to see and spoke "Uovu Vernietik."

The Bull's head quivered as if it were trying to escape its own death while being deathly afraid. Iris retreated two steps to stand next to Seyanna. As before, the loop transformed into a black mamba with silver eyes and silver fangs. The entire red bull's head materialized into a creature as large as a Great Dane, and the head was attached to its entire body. Several screams erupted. Firey breath shot out of its nostrils, but the creature stared at the coiled black mamba, Jet still held. The red bull pawed at the ground aggressively.

The snake rose from Jet's hand, weaving back and forth. The bull, having nowhere to go, lowered its head and prepared to attack. This seemed to be what the snake was expecting and waiting for. The black snake struck so quickly that an instant later, its fangs sank deep into the bull's neck. The same black smoldering overcame the entire bull, and moments later, it was nothing more than ash.

From his hidden compartment, Jet retrieved the Fogle horn and tossed it onto the ground. He knew that Latisha had reached her moment.

"What's that?" asked Professor Rysen.

"The fourth piece of the Insidious Six." He pointed to Latisha, who strolled forward and handed her the Kindred Loop, back in its original form.

He could feel that the horn no longer had its protective barrier. When Latisha took the Kindred Loop from Jet, the Fogle horn transformed into an eagle. The black mamba reappeared just as quickly. The eagle's wings expanded, and Latisha sprinted forward and tossed the snake onto the back of the eagle as it lifted into the air. The snake struck before it had climbed ten feet, and the creature tried spreading its wings to gain some altitude. The eagle's cry was deafening as the snake bit into the bird. It dramatically burst into dust.

Walking forward, Jet caught the looped amulet before it hit the ground. He announced, "That's two more of the Insidious Six. Let's reconvene at the hotel. We've accomplished what we have come for." He turned his back on Charlie and Rysen. Em and Gleam had moved out of their way. "Travel safe."

"What?" demanded Charlie. "This was really a ploy the entire time?"

Seyanna said, "It's not like we could just ask you to hand over the weapon. You would have never believed us."

"And you're serious?" asked Rysen.

His hand clicked the button of the grenade. Jet spun and spoke "Ignisnaeth," and he shot a fire spray at the hands of Professor Rysen and Charlie, hitting both of them. They wore fire-protective gloves, but their grenades were destroyed.

The gas inside, however, spilled free. It rose into the air, orange in color, creating a barrier between them and the two men. They sprinted down a path on the plateau and were soon surrounded by a dozen Quills and the Rufu squad.

Corvin wiggled free and stepped freely into the haze. Jet watched as his Elemental magic power ceased to exist. A smile crossed the boy's face. "Glad I don't have that poison any longer. I think I'll be fine. See you soon."

"Can't wait," replied Jet.

The boy marched to a second hiding place and pulled out a box of anti-magic weapons. He smiled one last time, then ran after the others.

Grantham said, "We need to retreat down to the valley floor."

"Lead the way," said Eric.

The orange mist spread out. Even the Myntra were hesitant to let the particles touch their skin. Brenda and the other eleven Azurites they had captured were zip-tied, and several of their weapons were collected. Brenda swore profusely, but she did so with a smile on her face as if trying to incite him.

There were five Elementals, including Phoebe, Keesha, Nolan, and two others, who were injured. Their wounds were tended to once they reached the safety of the valley floor.

Seyanna, Eric, Grantham, and Latisha spread out and kept guard. Mckenzey, Raul, Phillip, Maria, and Ariana helped tend to the Axenkind.

Phoebe stepped forward, "Hey, can I ask a question?"

"Anything."

"Was what you just said true? Was this entire thing a ploy?"

"Yes and no. You're here because we suspected the Azurites would attack us. But Jayco is not leading a group to free the Coven's children. We're going to be doing that."

"That's what I was afraid of," said Phoebe. "This place is so hot. How far do we have to hike?"

"Only another six hours. Get a drink and restore some of your energy. We've still got a long way to go."

CHAPTER 39

Jet stored the Kindred Loop, and the twelve Azurite prisoners were thoroughly searched for hidden weapons, as their armor was removed. Thirty spheres were confiscated. Bottles of natural energy drinks were handed out to the Elementals, but this did little for those affected by the energy extractors.

Walking over to Gleam, he said, "I don't think you guys were invited. How did you know to follow us?"

"We just had a feeling you might be vacationing in Egypt, and we were overcome by jealousy." She smiled and went to help Sidewinder.

Jet transformed the bear and the lion but kept Iris close to him. He approached Mckenzey, and she looked pale. "How's everyone feeling?"

Mckenzey said, "I was empty and I can't heal anyone. It's not as bad as when it first happened, but man, that was powerful. We've bandaged all the wounds. We should be good to go in the next few minutes."

"I was only minimally affected," said Seyanna, who was suddenly at his side. "I can't imagine what *you're* going through."

There was a slight inflection in her voice, but Jet wasn't sure what it meant. Seyanna asked, "Are you guys thinking of heading back?"

"No," said Mckenzey. "We have the energy to walk but not to fight. Let's stay together."

"*The Sorcerer's Guide* was clear that only the four of us can go in."

"We know."

"Is Eric okay?" asked Seyanna.

"Vomited for the first few minutes. I should go check on him." She smiled, then walked over to the valley wall. Eric and Nolan were hiding the Azurite's weapons in the same crevice Sidewinder had been placed into.

Jet strode towards the captives, both curious and hesitant about what Brenda might say. The brown-haired girl had looked so innocent when he had first seen her in the mail room at Chadwick's. No one in his life had ever tricked him like she had. Faris stood nearby as the last of the prisoners were searched.

Brenda beamed. "That was a marvelous trick you just performed. Maybe the best I've ever seen. You must be so proud. So, this is the infamous Rainbow. Charlie will never stop looking for you. You two make quite the team."

Jet said, "You deserve all the props. Creating Anti-magic weapons. Who would have guessed."

"The Brotherhood gave us the idea."

"Us?" asked Seyanna.

Brenda refused to acknowledge Seyanna more than she already had. "We know they created paint that repels some magic attacks. That is downright brilliant. Maybe the first reasonable thing the Brotherhood has ever done."

"You're quite the character," said Jet. "Who did you give my mother's ring to after you were finished with it?"

"A Brenda," she exclaimed. "It had to be 'a Brenda' for those stupid roommates of yours to get it right. It took three weeks to find the right homeless girl."

Seyanna interrupted, "You took some girl from the streets?"

"Don't judge me. We are on the verge of something unmistakable. We will make magic obsolete."

Jet grabbed Seyanna's arm, and he could see the disbelief across her face. "We won't get anything out of her now. She's deeply immersed in her mindset. She thinks she's won."

"Achievements define winners. You haven't seen anything yet," announced Brenda as they walked away.

Iris growled.

"Nice kitty." Brenda cackled.

Over the next hour, they ate, tried to recover, and spent time chasing down the remaining camel to organize their belongings. Iris stayed close, and Seyanna even closer. The prisoners were fed and given water.

Mckenzey and Eric brought down three donkeys carrying their items. Eric said, "There were five, but two were killed."

They buried three Azurites, including the one Jet knocked off the ledge, in some hills.

Rufian finished cleaning and wrapping Professor Fleener's lower leg. Professor Sidewinder had trouble moving. He spoke quietly with Professor Gimshe, who had mostly recovered, except for a large gash on her head.

Jet said, "I'm glad to see you guys are safe. How bad are the wounds?"

"Dar's leg is burned," said Rufian. "The wound is deep. But she never cried out in agony."

Professor Gimshe added, "Val's injury is serious. He can't walk. I imagine he will need to spend many days in the Vetex to heal partially. We will need to go back to Svalbard as soon as possible."

"You won't come back to campus?" asked Latisha, who, along with several others, was close enough to hear the conversation. "We have the Vetex there."

Professor Gimshe explained, "We Axenkind are not completely comfortable in any location that isn't frozen. We need to return home. They will send two others, very competent, to take over our teaching responsibilities."

"What about my training?" asked Latisha.

"We have informed our replacements on what to expect." Gimshe stared at Latisha, "Yes, things have changed, but you will still learn our ways. We've explained that. Don't worry about a thing."

Latisha bowed her head.

"You've already contacted them?" asked Jet. "How?"

Rufian pulled out a flat, rectangular device the size of a large television remote. "This acts as our emergency beacon. It provides our location as a precaution in case of an emergency. We can also call for help and communicate in the short term."

"Like a telephone," said Grantham.

"More like an iPad," said Professor Gimshe.

Jet asked, "What about you, Rufian?"

"Dar and I will return to Chadwick's. Her injury is not so severe that she can't use the Vetex at the school."

"Our guides are gone," noted Seyanna.

"No," said Jet. "You're our guide. They just helped with our things."

Rufian said, "Be careful. I am sorry that I cannot accompany you further."

"Raul, Ariana, Tominiko, and Phillip are going to stay behind to make sure you're safe."

"Thank you. Be careful. I doubt Marcella doesn't have something else up her sleeve."

"Time to move out," announced Jet. It took some motivation for the prisoners and some of the Elementals to want to move. Though sitting in the blazing heat was its own type of motivation.

They followed the steep rock wall for the next hour. The Myntra refused to remain with the Axenkind. They positioned themselves at the back of the group. It was hot, and much of the excitement of the morning had vanished. They came to an impressive but small stone structure on their right, known as the Church of the Forty Martyrs. There were several openings in the wall where people could enter.

"Are those wooden balconies?" asked Eric. "Can we go see what's inside?"

"We need to keep moving," said Jet, and he eyed the area. "We're behind schedule."

"What schedule?" asked Autumn.

Glancing over, he wasn't sure he'd seen Autumn before now. "Where have you been?"

"Mckenzey assigned me to watch the prisoners. I called your name when you were talking to Brenda."

"I didn't see you."

"No worries."

Nolan announced, "There are more buildings to the left. Should we rest there?" The boy had injured his leg and burned his arm. He was struggling to keep moving.

"No," said Jet. "We need to stay together and keep moving."

The valley widened, as if a crossroad, and much of the area was flat for several hundred feet in all directions. People exited the different buildings but paid them no attention. They carried water or other items, and it seemed as if they were headed somewhere together.

"Who are they?" wondered Phoebe.

"I'm not sure," said Jet.

Grantham answered. "This is a sacred area. That path leads to the base of Mount Sinai. If you go on the other side, there is a way to the top."

"I wish," said Nolan.

Jet announced, "We'll rest in thirty minutes."

Ten minutes later, the group crossed the dry creek bed. The rock fence surrounding the Church of the Forty Martyrs and the adjacent buildings allowed them to cross. Behind the fence was the thickest group of trees they'd seen since leaving their vehicles that morning. Jet steered them away from the trees and onto a path that entered the next portion of the valley. The rock colors were dark, nearly as dark as volcanic rocks. They slowly gained elevation for the next twenty minutes. The walls on both sides narrowed significantly, and they found a shaded area to rest.

Wounds were assessed and rebandaged. The prisoners were demanding and difficult, and they refused to continue. It took time, but Tominiko somehow persuaded them to carry on by promising extra food and water.

The next phase of the hike was slower as they gained the most elevation quickly. As they reached the highest point so far, Jet glanced back from where they had come, then forward as the path dropped into another dry creek bed, before rising on the opposite side of the valley. Two peaks stood out, the right standing taller than the left.

Jet announced, "That's our destination."

"Both peaks are called Mount Catherine," added Grantham. "We have to arrive before it gets dark."

Three and a half hours later, they stepped onto a vast, open space dividing the base of both peaks. The terrain was white sand, resembling the landscape on Mars, but it was flat and empty, with no water, trees, or grass in sight. It was bleak and scorching hot. Everyone was exhausted. The climb had been brutal.

Eric muttered, his lips chapped, "We need to find shelter and water before the sun sets."

Tominiko added, "The prisoners can't go marching around. Send scouts to find something."

At that moment, half the prisoners collapsed, as did some of the injured Elementals. Two volunteer scout groups set off in opposite directions. Some canopy tents were erected to block the sun. Twenty minutes later, Autumn's group, which included Phoebe, Seyanna, Keesha, and Nolan, signaled they had found something.

Phoebe described a crevice large enough for the entire group. The prisoners, most of the Elementals, and the Myntra followed Phoebe and Seyanna towards a slot canyon on the side of the larger mountain. Jet and Nolan waited for the second group.

An Azurite prisoner walked by and hissed, "I'll escape and kill you. This is torture."

Jet retorted, "Maybe you should have thought of that before you attacked us. Decisions, even poor ones, have aftereffects."

The boy stopped, stood to his full height, and said, "You're a thousand steps closer to your demise."

"Aren't we all?"

The second scout group came into view a short time later. They had found something, but not as good as the first group. Jet and Nolan led them back toward the valley they came from but entered a wide offshoot a hundred feet before. After five minutes, they spotted Autumn waiting to show them into the slot canyon.

They entered single file, but the width expanded after a dozen feet. The walls on both sides were twelve feet high. After another fifteen feet, it opened into a large, flat space of ground, with several bushes, a half-dozen trees, and some overhanging ledges. Some of the bushes and two dead trees were uprooted and used as fuel for four fires. Soon, Mckenzey and Eric gave orders to prepare some hot dogs, chili, and canned vegetables.

Jet raised his eyebrows.

"What?" asked Mckenzey. "It was this or boxes of macaroni and cheese."

"Good choice. But how?"

"It pays to be well-prepared," she shot back.

The prisoners eyed daggers at him whenever he walked close enough. That stopped when he poured a bucket of water into a hole in the ground. They thought he was mocking them, but he spent the next ten minutes redoubling the water, and soon, they had enough to drink and wash their hands. Two or three nodded their appreciation.

He did the same thing in two other spots around camp. The water lifted everyone's spirits. They had enough food to feed a small army. After their long hike, his magical expenditure, and the stress of the day, it was some of the best food he had ever eaten.

Seyanna sat next to him, eating her food. After he'd eaten most of his, he asked, "Who saw us?"

"Mckenzey." She didn't look at him. "She sent me a strong text message, telling me her thoughts on what she saw."

Jet shook his head. "I didn't think they would be so close to watching us like that."

"Me neither," said Seyanna. "Any regrets?"

"Nope." He forced a tired smile. "Not a single one regarding last night. I'm sorry if her words hurt you. Today is another story."

"That was intense. Who knew the Azurites had such powerful weapons?"

"Maybe I should stop assuming that magic gives us that much of an advantage."

"Maybe our problem is that we really don't know the advantage magic actually gives us. The Azurites were focused on making sure we couldn't use magic suitably. That tells us something."

"You might be right." Hurt still remained in Seyanna's eyes. His answer hadn't been enough. He asked, "What exactly did Mckenzey say? How did it make you feel?"

It took her a while to answer. "She...she told me that I was stealing you *from* her. It hurt more than it should."

"What?"

Before she could say anything else, Grantham, Eric, Mckenzey, Latisha, Keesha, Maria, and Autumn joined them.

Grantham said, "We need to make a plan on what will happen tomorrow."

"It all depends on whether we find the opening or not," said Jet, trying to recover. He smiled but wasn't sure he had even convinced himself. "Only the four of us can enter, but the others can help."

Mckenzey said, "Let's hope we have more of our magical energy back by then. There is a distinct possibility that we might have to fight someone else tomorrow."

"Or tonight," said Eric.

Seyanna stood abruptly. "I will examine our perimeter and assign lookouts. I assume all of you will be willing to take an hour or two."

"Uh...sure," said Keesha. "You good, Seyanna?"

"Feeling a little exposed right now. I would like to know our vulnerabilities. Anyone willing to help?"

"I will," said Autumn. Maria also stood.

The three of them left Jet and the others in complete silence.

* * *

The next morning, Jet awoke before the sun broke the horizon. The temperature was chilly, but he knew it would change once the sun came up. He hadn't slept well, taking his turn to be on guard duty from two a.m. to four a.m. He couldn't get Seyanna out of his mind, but he didn't cross paths with her all night.

Iris greeted him with a yawn, and he spent a few minutes rubbing her head and neck. She had slept outside the tent as he, Grantham, Eric, Nolan, and Tominiko had slept inside. He had tossed and turned but had regained most of his energy.

Standing, he moved into a side crevice, used the bathroom, and brushed his teeth. Iris accompanied him wherever he went. Feeling unsettled about last night and how things had gone, he set off to find Seyanna.

Instead, he found Grantham, Latisha, Autumn, Phoebe, and Maria moving around camp, preparing breakfast, brewing coffee, and checking on the prisoners. Most of the prisoners slept under canopies or on mats, often with just a few blankets. The Elementals were better prepared with group tents, hammocks, pillows, and blankets, but they hadn't planned on twelve new additions.

Several people, including Seyanna, were unaccounted for.

"Don't worry," said Grantham as he handed Jet some coffee. "They're out exploring and making sure we aren't secretly attacked."

Jet drank several sips of his coffee, enjoying the warmth. Iris's ears perked up as a commotion erupted from the entrance as quick steps approached. Seyanna, Keesha, Nolan, and Tominiko hurried back through the opening. Seyanna caught sight of him and motioned for Grantham and the others to join her near Jet. She was haggard, likely sleep-deprived.

Mckenzey and Eric were the last to arrive. When everyone was together, Seyanna announced, "I found something. We went near both peaks of Mount Catherine." She motioned vaguely back to the slot canyon. "There are buildings on both summits. We didn't climb to the top. At first, we found nothing, but there's a big ravine on the far side of both peaks, almost like a way to send water from one peak to another. I can't explain it more. It was created with purpose rather than through erosion."

"What are you saying?" asked Mckenzey.

"The ravine overlooks a vast valley. The view is spectacular. The ravine goes to the left and right. To the right, there is a scarab carved into the wall of the ravine. It has wings and is more intricate than what I saw in Svalbard."

Jet's heart raced.

Grantham said, "You went…just the four of you?"

Jet had been thinking the same thing.

"We had no visitors all night. I needed to be out doing something." She intentionally avoided looking at Jet.

Latisha asked, "How far is it from here?"

"Fifteen minutes." Before anyone moved, she said, "I did jump into the ravine to look at the Scarab."

"I thought you said you didn't explore," huffed Jet.

"Didn't explore too much," corrected Seyanna.

"And?" questioned Eric.

"I know where we need to go to get inside. But we can't get there through the ravine."

Grantham hesitated. "Let's be ready to leave in thirty minutes. We'll need a few to stay back to guard the prisoners. I won't be surprised if all hell breaks loose the moment we go inside. Everyone needs to be ready."

"Leave me in charge of the prisoners," said Asher, who had overheard their conversation. "You can count on me."

"Tempting," admitted Grantham. "What do you think, Jet?"

"Good luck." He stood, preparing to leave. "I'll be back in fifteen minutes, ready to go."

"Seriously?" said Mckenzey. "Nothing more than that?"

Jet smiled at Asher. "Don't screw up."

Deciding not to return to his tent, he hurried out of camp, needing to get a look at the scarab for himself. His adrenaline was surging. Iris was a step behind. He released the lion and the bear to guard the opening. Turning left, he soon entered the empty field. He stared at the far end, the plateau ended, and he presumed that was where the ravine was. He took no more than ten steps when the feeling of being watched settled over him.

Spinning around, he found no one in the area. He wasted no time getting to the plateau's edge. He was right. Miles and miles of valleys and hills lay before him, just beyond a ravine, three feet deep, that traveled to his left and right, then out of view. The vista was breathtaking, with just enough light to see far in the distance.

A dark cloud of movement caught his attention, coming in from the southwest. Four dozen blackbirds swarmed closer and closer. When they sailed over the open area, they came to perch on a rocky overhang near the ravine. Ignoring this, Jet stepped into the ravine and quickly found the scarab. Iris followed. It was beautifully carved into a rock wall, the size of a small pumpkin. Its back shell was open, transforming into wings, with six legs spread outward. He reached to touch it but jerked his hand back. Something was wrong.

By the time he scrambled back up to the plateau, things had drastically changed. In addition to the blackbirds, dozens of rabbits, equally spaced, were grouped a distance from the blackbirds, who had spread themselves out. Hundreds of snakes poured from holes in the ground on a small knoll at the base of the larger peak, just as dozens of mice poured down from the smaller peak.

Jet turned and sprinted; the animals closing in behind him. The shadows of the morning vanished as the sunlight peeked over the horizon for the first time, bathing the entire field. A cacophony of sounds erupted behind him. His vision expanded, and he watched in horror as the blackbirds became soaring Pepracons, flying beasts larger than a wolf. The snakes turned to Scorepos and half-dug into the ground. The rabbits became Ratas, and the mice became Razors.

Minutes later, he turned into the slot canyon, knowing an army was following him and bellowed, "We're under attack!"

Iris growled at the same time, speaking to the lion and the bear. The three of them sprinted back toward the open area, and Jet followed a few seconds later. Behind him, he could hear screams, shouts, and some fighting. The prisoners were trying to escape.

The landscape before him was monstrous. The sheer number of enemies was jarring, and he knew he couldn't see all of them. Jet set off spells that would entangle those on the ground. Some worked, most didn't. He pulled out Gravity, and his next set of spells had more power and control.

Tominiko, Autumn, Maria, and Eric were the first to arrive. They spread out as Eric tossed several golden maces and swords on the ground. The natural formation on their left and right would protect them from being overrun. Even the flying Pepracons would be limited. The unknown was the Scorepos, who could travel underground.

Keesha screamed, "What's happening?"

"A trap," replied Jet. "It was set to start the instant the sunlight hit the field."

"What are we going to do?" cried Maria. "There are so many."

"Hold them off," said Tominiko. "Until Jet can release the Coven's children."

"Seriously," said Phoebe. "That's the plan."

"I've got bows and arrows," yelled Natalia. She, Allison, and Alivia were bringing over one of the donkeys. In a matter of a few minutes, the Elementals were releasing arrows and spells and attacking with ferocity.

Mckenzey, Eric, Maria, and Keesha arrived, followed by Seyanna, Latisha, and Grantham. They carried bottles of muddy water and lots of rice cakes.

Grantham said, "We're working on a new food source. These are baked from seaweed."

The bear and lion would crush anyone who got too close. They quickly brought down a Razor that had gotten past some of the spells. They followed a Scorepos that tried to dive into the dirt. They latched onto it and dragged it from the ground.

Jet released a spell that caused a geyser of water to erupt from an underground source. Even he was surprised by the amount of water. Several creatures scattered.

Mckenzey pushed his chest. "Nice spell, but this isn't your fight. Go release the Coven's children."

"We can't leave you guys. We can stay and help. The Coven's children can be released tomorrow."

She shook her head. "More enemies will be here by then."

Mckenzey moved as fast as he'd ever seen her. In the next instant, she kissed him hard on the lips. "Just in case one of us doesn't make it back alive. I had to do that one more time."

Jet was disoriented. She pushed him away again and screamed, "Now go!"

Several people rushed past him and into the fray.

Seyanna said, "We need to backtrack. I think I know the way."

Latisha looked as helpless as Jet felt. Finally, reaching a decision, he took Grantham's and Latisha's arms and followed Seyanna. Iris followed. Jet knew that Seyanna had seen the kiss, but right now, he knew they just had to hurry.

Tominiko bellowed, running forward, slashing at two Razors that had broken free.

Jet didn't get to see what happened.

They followed the open ravine, passing the slot canyon and continuing forward. They went for about half a mile and came to a dead end. Seyanna stepped into a narrow ravine hidden behind a second wall of rock. They followed this pathway single file. The walls on the left and right rose so high that the two sides touched, as if they were in a tunnel. Only a sliver of sunlight passed through the tiny opening.

A tenth of a mile later, the light ahead of them brightened dramatically. Something changed. They slowed and found, as before, that the path ended abruptly. This time, a sheer cliff and a fall of a hundred feet lay before them. Iris stopped barely in time before she knocked one of them off the ledge. There was no other way to go.

"If we had done this at night, we would have walked right off the edge," said Latisha.

"What now?" asked Grantham.

"This is the right place," said Seyanna, and her hands touched the wall to their right and to the left. In seconds, she found the most intricate scarab Jet had ever seen. Seyanna traced the remarkable details of the wings, the legs, and the antennae.

The instant she finished tracing the carving, the entire outline of the scarab began to glow, a greenish-yellow. The floor below their feet fell away, casting them into an abyss. It felt like his stomach was shoved into his head as he fell. His friends, on his left and right, toppled down with him as did Iris. After several feet, he hit hard, landing in a pit of sand. Something shifted, a tunnel opened, and they descended a shaft, sliding uncontrollably. They were being whisked deep below Mount Catherine. With the amount of sand around them, they would be lucky to survive.

CHAPTER 40

The shaft below them ended as if the sides of the world vanished, leaving behind only emptiness. Suddenly, they were free-falling. Jet's legs kicked out, and his arms flailed as if he could somehow prevent falling to his death, into the deepest pit in the world. A faint golden glow did nothing to dampen the darkness.

Someone screamed, "Use magic."

The words penetrated his fear, and he screamed, "Aer!"

They slowed, but only a touch.

Thud

They landed hard in a second pile of sand, this one shaped like the tip of a cone upside down. Both of Jet's legs plunged deep into the sand, and more sand fell on top of him. Before he had time to react, he was buried alive.

Jet spoke "Fracterra," and the sand parted for a moment, then covered him again. He bellowed, "Pachamama" hoping to find a way out. Nothing happened.

He screamed, "Gongpae," and an air shield formed above him, creating a barrier for the descending sand. He was covered and had no way of escaping. But he heard others digging near him. He kept his concentration fixated on the shield, but it was becoming heavier and heavier. A hand scraped next to his face.

"He's here," cried Grantham.

The six hands uncovered him, pulling him from the sand. They tumbled down the sand for several steps before Jet released the spell. A small ridge of sand fell onto the pile. Before he'd taken another two steps, Iris bowled him over, licking his face.

"I'm fine," he sputtered.

"Check out where we are," said Latisha

Jet pulled Iris close, hugged her, and tried to stand.

"This is crazy," added Seyanna, turning in a circle. "How far did we fall?"

His mouth gaped open as his eyes adjusted. The room was larger than the cavern back in Silverton. Different shades of green rocks, crystals, and petrified wood were embedded in the walls. They were still three stories above the stone-and-sand floor below. Their access to the room was only a fourth of what it could be. A gigantic, deep green gate and fence, almost black, barred their access to the rest of the room. Two large items were tied to the main entrance.

"What are those?" asked Grantham.

"You don't want to know," replied Jet as he and Iris slid down the sand to the main level. When they all reached the ground floor, he added, "Be ready for anything."

"How in the world are we going to get out of here?" demanded Latisha, pulling out an ax. "I don't get a good feeling about this place."

"A place that's trapped children of the witches," said Grantham, "Can't be good. Pure evil."

"Are we going to have to fight something?" asked Seyanna, jumping around nervously at every sound.

Grantham stepped forward. "Are those two items part of the gate?"

"Those are the last two pieces of the Insidious Six," said Jet.

"What are they?" asked Seyanna.

Jet said, "My guess would be the cobalt blue book of recipes and the jasper blade."

Latisha asked, "What does it mean?"

"Not sure." Jet brushed sand from his hair.

A voice echoed from the darkness behind the gate, "Salam."

Footsteps crunched on the ground, and a four-foot-tall man with a long beard, with what could only be described as dwarf characteristics, stepped into view. His muscles bulged, a sneer was plastered on his face, and he had an exceptional amount of hair. His skin was both pale and light silver, and yet it seemed to glow. His armor, weapon, and hair were silver but far darker.

"I am Ransforth, the bodach, and the fallen overlord of the Arma Arches. I was born in Simigrava, the northern swampland of Goth Airtha. I was swallowed by Catherine the Whale when I failed to recover the Insidious Six. You see, I am their creator, the artifacts, but the Skeleton caused them to become a curse. I am now the warden of the prison for the Coven's Children."

"Are we to fight you?" asked Grantham. "For the ability to free the children."

Ransforth laughed, his voice carrying through the entire cavern. "I could never beat you four in a fair fight. Nor do I have a desire to quarrel with you. I am here purely to warn you that entrance is forbidden. If you would consider waiting a few days, I am sure AmunRe will be more amenable to allowing you to enter. If you wait a few months, AmunRe can be bargained with to join your side. Arriving here today, two days before the first Solstice, you'll find AmunRe the most powerful he has been in a century."

Grantham asked, "What is that symbol in the gate? It looks like the Washington Monument."

"That is Amun. It is the shape of an Egyptian obelisk." Ransforth pulled a silver pouch from within a pocket. "You must choose to leave or enter. Each has its risks."

Jet worried that his friends above might be in serious danger, but waiting, even a few days, could bring more peril. "We must enter."

Ransforth bowed in such a way that neither his waist nor his knees bent, but his ankles did. It was unnatural. When he had returned to an upright position, he reached into the pouch, pulled out amber-colored dust, and blew the fistful into the air. The particles moved directly to the gate, settling on it like gold blasted onto a rock wall. The gate shimmered. They watched as the red jasper blade, without a handle, dislodged itself from the gate, followed by the blue book. Both toppled into the sand. The obelisk symbol on the gate disappeared.

"I may be the creator of these items, but I am not their father," explained Ransforth, his voice quivering. "The Skeleton poisoned them to become what they are."

The two items became interconnected, and Jet pictured the amalgamation process that must've taken place with Leotyton and Erpofalco.

A beast arose before them, its chest marked with the obelisk symbol, burned into its flesh like a brand.

Ransforth spoke, his voice heightened. "I would like to introduce you to AmunRe."

The creature before them was bigger than Siwalik and any land animal on Earth. The scarab beetle with wings was monstrous. It moved, unlike anything Jet had ever seen.

"AmunRe is a distant cousin with some of the most powerful creatures to have ever lived in Goth Airtha. He is deadly beyond comparison. Leave now; this is your last warning. His power surpasses even Angola."

The beetle's tenacity and aptness vibrated around it. It had six long legs. The back shell was blue, like the book, while the rest of the creature was made of red jasper. It had three regions, a head, thorax, and abdomen. Jet was pretty sure the exoskeleton was nearly unbreakable. The head rotated to glare at Jet and his friends.

"What the freak are we supposed to do?" asked Seyanna.

"Step back a few steps," said Jet. "Maybe it will give us time to come up with a plan."

"To kill that thing?" asked Grantham, and they all retreated.

Ransforth, appearing relieved, declared, "You cannot come back here unless the price is paid."

Jet had no idea what that meant but noted that a door materialized in the wall behind them. The falling sand to their left had come to a stop. "We're not leaving," he announced as his mind whirled on the name Angola.

"I've heard that before," he said through gritted teeth. The clarity sprouted in his mind. He'd fought a creature named Angola during his last Trial of Averseen. It was why he'd lost. He had shot magic directly at the creature.

Jet leaned in towards his friends. "If you use magic, make sure it is not directly at AmunRe. We must fight this creature."

"How?" asked Grantham. "I don't know how to use my magic like that."

"Use it the same. Just don't aim at the beetle itself."

Latisha questioned, "No chance in retreating and coming back a different day?"

"None," answered Jet, placing Gravity directly ahead of him.

AmunRe lowered itself to the ground, seeing the weapon and the gate behind it.

"Use all that you have. Your gifts, magic, weapons, and ingenuity. We need to cut down its legs and wings first. Let's spread out." Pointing to the right, Iris scampered off. Jet went to the left.

Ransforth backed away, muttering, "You can't win."

AmunRe faced the bodach, expelling a fine mist of silver through the gate and onto Ransforth, encasing him in a silver cocoon.

"I guess we know why he's all silver," yelled Grantham.

Seyanna sprinted partially up the sand pile while Grantham climbed the back wall near where the exit once was. Within seconds, the hard shell of AmunRe's abdomen opened and fluttered. Seyanna was knocked off her feet, and Grantham slipped. On his way down, Grantham shouted, "Pachamama," and a small gorge opened beneath AmunRe. The creature staggered slightly, and the shaking stopped.

Jet spoke "Aer," pointing to the ground, and he was launched into the air. His next spell was aimed at the floor, intending to explode pieces of the ground like a projectile bomb. A dozen small boulders exploded outward, but AmunRe moved effortlessly away from the debris.

Seyanna unleashed a golden arrow, but the scarab used one of its legs to grab a rock piece and use it as a shield. The arrow glanced away harmlessly. The beetle scuttled forward, unleashing a yellow glow from its underbelly that illuminated the room in an intense brightness.

Jet bellowed, "Vestalia," and a wall of fire encircled AmunRe, but not before pain exploded in his head.

The creature's wings beat swiftly, and it rose a dozen feet, intending to go over the wall. The brightness was a distraction, and AmunRe caught sight of Iris; its mouth opened.

Jet bellowed, "Iris, come!"

Iris, who had passed Seyanna, obeyed immediately.

Something acidic, like a projectile orb, erupted from both eyes of the beetle. The orbs sailed through the air, landing where Iris had been. The stone floor disintegrated. A toxic smell surged around them. Jet tried raising the level of the firewall, but two more orbs were shot in his direction.

The firewall vanished, and Jet spoke "Gongpae," and a protective air shield blocked the attack.

AmunRe dove toward Iris, who was retreating as fast as possible. Iris ducked, turned, and sprinted up the sand pile. Seyanna was forced to retreat as well.

Jet spoke "Urania," repeatedly and aimed the spell behind Iris. A dozen wind bombs exploded, and bits and pieces of sand were thrown into the air. The spell did nothing to slow AmunRe, but it gave Iris a lift, and she reached the top of the pile. It was clear that she could not escape down the backside. She was trapped.

Grantham shot another spell at the ground. The scarab came to a stop, turning to face them. Seyanna unleashed an arrow, but this time, it was at the front pair of wings. These hardened wings, called elytra, blocked the shot, and the arrow glanced away harmlessly. Two globes of acid were unleashed at Grantham halfway up the back wall.

At the same time, Latisha soared out of a shadow and began swinging her axe. She bashed AmunRe off its path, and the two acid balls hit several feet below Grantham. The creature swerved, and Latisha's next swing missed the creature's wing by inches. A leg shot out, kicking Latisha hard in the chest. It wasn't a direct hit, but hard enough to knock her down. The attempts by Latisha, Seyanna, and Grantham only slowed AmunRe. Within seconds, he was closing in on where Iris was cornered.

Jet, pointing Gravity, screamed, "Neis," but his mind pictured the vine as a tool rather than a weapon. A vine exploded from the ground, grabbed Iris's foot, and slung her away from the beetle, down the sand, and into the back wall. Jet wished he had his golden orbs or something to launch at the creature. He remembered what Jayco had done back in Argentina. He hurried over to a pile of rocks that had fallen from the ceiling.

A sound escaped AmunRe, as if it were clattering with its mouth pinchers as it rose into the air. The beetle searched for Iris, who hobbled along the back wall. Jet couldn't understand why the beetle was so fixated on the golden panther.

Jet spoke "Chango," and several small rocks began sizzling. "Enlil,"—the rocks were lifted into the air. "Aer!" and they were unleashed at AmunRe.

The creature knew exactly what Jet was doing, and it folded up its wings and fluttered twenty feet toward the ground. Still, the attack forced AmunRe to crash into the fence, bending it slightly. Jet, Latisha, and Seyanna tore off, hoping the beetle was injured.

AmunRe rolled, attempting to unleash another sunray. Seyanna slowed slightly and unleashed an arrow. It connected with the side of the abdomen, missing the hard outer shell. There was a clear impact.

Grantham leaped from a side wall and swung his half-crescent weapon like a sledgehammer. He struck the back abdomen of AmunRe, and a blistering sound reverberated through the air. Both the scarab beetle and Grantham were affected. The beetle was knocked sideways, into more of the fence, but Grantham's golden weapon shattered into a thousand pieces, and he was flung backward, still holding only a broken handle.

Jet spoke "Artemis," and a layer of mud formed under the beetle. He repeated the spell two more times as he hustled toward AmunRe. All six of its legs became entangled with the sludge as it tried to move or stand. He spoke "Chango," three consecutive times, and the mud solidified into stone, trapping AmunRe.

The beetle lobbed a jet of acid, and Jet was forced to halt his attack as the liquid dissolved two feet of stone floor for several feet just ahead of him. The creature's wings opened, and it fluttered again. This time, Jet dove down to protect himself. The acid, which had mainly been used on the floor, was now propelled at him in tiny droplets. Several hits landed on his lower legs and back. Where it touched his skin, it burned painfully.

Pulling himself off the ground, Jet rushed toward the gap in the ground, his adrenaline pumping. AmunRe legs were breaking free from the cement.

He spoke softly, "Gravitas," and he heard a click and pulled out the majestic sea-blue enchanted blade. Within five strides, he had closed the gap to AmunRe. He swung it with all his might and completely cut through the three legs still encased in rock. Blue liquid spilled from the wounds, but he had unintentionally freed AmunRe.

Its wings unfurled, beat hard twice, and rose into the air. Jet swung twice, missing both times. Grantham lay injured, and Seyanna hurried over to check on him. Latisha scooted away, wounded by the kick to the chest. That was when Jet realized his mistake. Iris was huddled against the back wall, unprotected from AmunRe.

The scarab dove at his golden panther. Jet was frantic. He considered sending a spell directly at AmunRe, but he knew that would only make things worse, yet he couldn't lose Iris. She was family.

"No!" Jet screamed. He spoke "Neis," at the side wall, and a dozen vines shot outward, but they did nothing to slow AmunRe.

The creature was going to kill Iris; he knew it.

A voice spoke into his head, "Ash me."

The words were so foreign, yet he knew they came from Iris. In his mind came a word, a spell he had not attempted before. It was because it had no use "Hai" would create ash, but what good would that do?

Without hesitation and full of trust, he bellowed "Hai!" and a mystic outpouring of fire-ash leaped from Jet and merged with Iris. The golden panther instantly quadrupled in size, and the loss of his energy was mind-blowing. He wasn't sure he had enough energy for two more spells. The glow from her fur coat ignited as if she were on fire.

AmunRe grasped what was happening and extended its wings, attempting to halt its momentum.

Iris attacked. Hurling herself toward the flying scarab, she sprang into the air to meet the beetle. The three unbroken legs kicked at Iris, but she couldn't be slowed.

AmunRe tried closing its wings, which worked momentarily. Iris kicked the creature's back, slamming it into the sand. AmunRe moved quickly, now trying to retreat. Iris clamped down on a back leg, spun, and threw the scarab into the back wall. AmunRe struggled to stand. Iris bound over in a few steps. Opening her jaws, Iris clamped around the neck of the beetle, flipping it over and slamming it onto the ground. The wings and the back shell of AmunRe were broken beyond repair. Jet watched in awe as Iris dragged AmunRe toward him.

"Kill it," screamed Grantham, speaking to Iris.

Jet desired nothing more than to see the creature killed. But Iris did not attempt to break its neck. AmunRe was beaten. Iris towed the creature closer, and it thrashed back and forth. Its mouth pinchers opened and closed as if trying to bite.

"Break his head off," added Latisha, who had shifted to one knee, trying to catch her breath.

"Why hasn't she killed it?" asked Seyanna. "I don't think I can watch."

Tilting his head, Jet wondered if Iris was bringing AmunRe to him like a gift.

Her voice filled his mind again, "Only she can finish him."

Jet was confused. He lifted his enchanted blade, and Iris stopped moving instantly. "That can't kill him." As if to confirm this statement, the beetle's three injured legs began to heal on their own. He also thought he saw a crack in the shell that was knitting itself together. Into his mind came the image of the Kindred Loop. It finally dawned on Jet what she wanted.

Placing the enchanted blade back into Gravity, he pulled out the Kindred Loop and spoke "Uovu Vernietik." The item mutated into the black mamba with silver eyes and silver fangs. The beetle began to thrash back and forth. Iris could barely hold onto it. The snake slithered and grew in size until it reached where Iris had pinned the beetle to the ground. AmunRe bucked one last time, his head breaking free, but Iris quickly placed a paw on the under chin of the creature.

The black mamba struck, sinking its fangs into the neck of AmunRe. The creature screeched out its last breath, then began to vibrate as its eyes rolled up, and a black smoldering spread through its entire body. Moments later, Iris released AmunRe, and it was nothing more than a pile of ash.

The Kindred Loop began to transform itself. This time, the black mamba did not revert to the amulet. A tall, aged lady, thin and gaunt, with midnight black skin, curly black hair, silver teeth, and silver eyes, hunched before them. Her legs were unsteady, and she brushed aside a few silver strands of hair. A silver necklace hung around her neck, and she wore a silver knee-length dress.

"Thank you, my friends," she mumbled softly. "That was the worst exile I could have ever dreamed up."

"Who are you?" Jet asked tentatively, and he heard his friends coming close.

With effort, she stood up to her full height, a few inches taller than Jayco. "I am Queen Lom Doost, and the queen of the Wind Whispers. The oldest Khalicaan, and she who was sacrificed by her tribe to forge the connection with the Chupovanas. I was nothing more than a puppet vassal for many years. After the creation of the Insidious Six, by the Skeleton, I was rescued by Alces and brought to Queen Aurora. I gave my lifeforce, along with other tribal magic, to become the Kindred Loop and fight what the Insidious Six had become. You have freed me."

Jet stepped closer. "Does that mean the curse of the Insidious Six is gone?"

"I believe so. I can no longer feel their evil."

"You can feel the weapons?" asked Latisha.

"Indeed. My life was connected to them." She faced the four of them. "You brought back the three missing magic groups, but on a limited basis. No person could be chosen by magic for those three factions until the Insidious Six were destroyed. Without the six, you've ensured that magic cannot be corrupted as in times before. Magic has the protection now granted by the Fisador pact. No one can lie about their intentions when they receive the magic. If deceit is in their mind, magic will not choose them. This does not mean that evil can't later enter their hearts, but this is a wonderful gift."

"Will you help us release the Coven's children?" asked Grantham.

"No." She glanced around the spacious cavern. "This is my final resting place."

Seyanna asked, "Are you dying?"

A hollow laugh escaped her. "No. I died a long time ago. My time has already come to an end." She reached up to grasp the silver necklace.

"What are you doing?" asked Jet.

"This is for you."

For the first time, Jet focused on the necklace with six diamonds. "Is that one of the lost Chalua weapons? Maybe, Confusion?"

"It was foreseen that you would need this and Gravity to fight those who align themselves with Arisol."

"Is it keeping you animated or alive?" asked Latisha through gritted teeth, holding her side and looking pale.

"It has, how should I say, the power to release me. Thank you for allowing me to fulfill my promise to Queen Aurora." Pulling off Confusion, she handed it to Jet. "I will always be watching you."

Her legs began to dissolve into black, smoldering dust. She glanced at Latisha and said, "You have the hardest choice you'll ever make ahead of you."

Queen Lom Doost became a pile of ash before another sound was uttered.

But Jet wasn't sure how much Latisha had heard of the warning, as she collapsed to the ground, unconscious, barely breathing.

CHAPTER 41

Grantham pulled Latisha into his lap. He watched her chest slowly rise, then he felt for a pulse. "She's barely breathing, but her heart is racing."

"What do we do?" asked Seyanna.

Grantham's face paled, and his head frantically searched all the shadows in the room, as if the solution to Lathisha's injuries lay hidden just out of reach. "Please," he pleaded.

Jet remembered vividly when he had sustained an injury after fighting Lucretius, and it had been impossible to suck in a breath. The world had spun and gone black. Mckenzey had healed him, but she was outside, far away. There was no way he could find her and bring her back here in time.

"Do something," Grantham shouted angrily.

Jet bent down, knowing it was unlikely he would have enough strength or knowledge to heal her. Closing his eyes, he spoke "Thera." His spell lasted thirty seconds, then his control over it floated away.

"I saw the tiniest of improvement," insisted Grantham. "Do it again."

Seyanna said, "Jet can't. His energy is gone."

"What?" cried Grantham. "That can't be."

There was a nudge on his shoulder, and Iris nestled into him, still towering over him. She pawed the ground, decreasing in size right before him. It took but a few seconds, and she was back to her normal size. More importantly, though, she had given him some of her energy.

Bending over Latisha, he spoke "Thera," again. He knew that she was dying, and his senses detected a broken rib that had ruptured her lung. It was filling with blood. His spell was able to remove the blood and return oxygen, but what he had done was only temporary.

When he opened his eyes, color had returned to Latisha, and she was breathing shallowly.

"You did it," said Grantham.

Jet shook his head once. "It's only temporary. We need to get her out of here."

"How?" asked Grantham.

"We can't go back; we can only go forward."

Seyanna added softly, "If we need to fight anything, I don't think she'll make it."

"Let's go." Jet stood, and Iris came to prod his hand. He rubbed her and spoke softly about what she had done.

Grantham lifted Latisha carefully. She was barely hanging on, but she was breathing. Jet and Iris led the group. They came upon a space in the broken fence where they could cross. Darkness lessened a little with the slight glow from Iris, which was nothing compared to what it had been when she was supersized. A silver cocoon stood in the main path.

Scanning as far back as he could see, he noticed a portion of the ceiling in one corner, as if an extra room had been attached to the cavern.

Jet pointed to the back wall. "We need to go over there."

The silver cocoon cracked, then broke open with a hiss. The bodach stepped out, shook his head, and silver dust showered the floor. "How did you survive?"

"By killing AmunRe," said Seyanna, nocking a golden arrow. "Do we fight you next?"

"No," he cried out as if injured. "I was a prisoner. I want nothing more than to escape this place."

Jet wasn't sure if he believed him, but they had to keep moving. Without saying a word, Jet pushed through. Ransforth followed. It took ten minutes to cross the open space. They passed mounds of broken bones, spires, drip stalagmites, and dozens of water pools, some frozen and others releasing steam. Scratches on the stone told them they weren't alone. Danger lurked beyond the path, as cave creatures patrolled the darkness.

Ten feet from the back wall, he spotted a set of intricate carvings down a short hallway leading to a back room. Blue torches shone dimly, but they were enough to see. The images reminded Jet of what he and Seyanna had seen in Svalbard, where he had been healed. The alcove was a hollowed-out room in the side of the mountain. It was twenty feet long and wide, with eight-foot ceilings. Eight stone sarcophaguses were positioned evenly a few feet away from the far wall.

"What is this place?" asked Seyanna.

Jet studied the carvings. "This is the story of the imprisonment of the Coven's children." He pointed to the first image in the pathway. The woman kneeling in shackles had eyes that went from bright blue to yellow to purple.

"Is that Marcella?" asked Grantham as he placed Latisha on the floor.

"I think so," muttered Jet.

Seyanna said, "She is kneeling before a tribunal? Is she being punished?"

"No," said Jet, pointing to the next painting. "She is the reason the Coven's children were confined. Look."

A hundred male and female witches were wailing as many hundred children were being marched into the mouth of an enormous room. The gate was in the far back. The third image showed two items being brought forward to help guard the prison.

"They didn't know those items were evil," said Seyanna. "They willingly gave them to help defend this area. Look. They brought Marcella to be a witness to the punishment of her crimes."

The fourth image was a close-up of Marcella. The gleam on her face told a different story.

"She knew," said Jet. "She must've known all along that two of the Insidious Six were here."

"She never wanted us to succeed," said Seyanna, her voice full of awe and horror.

"She didn't know we had the Kindred Loop," said Jet. "We could have never beaten AmunRe without it."

Seyanna spat on the ground. "That freaking witch."

Iris came and nudged Jet's leg. Kneeling down, she pawed at him as if trying to communicate. She no longer spoke into his mind, but what she wanted became clear as she lay down, exhausted. He petted her twice, then transformed her into a pyramid and placed her inside his hidden compartment.

"What now?" asked Grantham, turning in a circle, surveying the room. "There isn't a way out."

Jet stared at the fifth image in disbelief. It was a perfect depiction of this room, the one they stood in. Five people were depicted here. Him, Seyanna, Grantham, an unconscious Latisha, and Ransforth. He stared at himself in a carving.

Words in English were written on the wall of the carving, but were not there in real life. Stepping closer, he read them.

Even Prior to the Legendary Battle
Eight Sentinels stood the Test of Time.
They were Lost but Reborn of Magic Design.
Two Records became the Gatekeepers.
And the Sentinels were Remade and Hidden.
One has Come to Rest at Mount Catherine.
He is the Regeneration of the Soul.
Now Choose which Tomb to Enter.

Jet inspected each sarcophagus. At first, he noticed no differences, but subtle variations emerged. He had no idea what it meant.

Grantham checked on Latisha. "Her breathing is slowing. Whatever we're going to do...we need to hurry."

"We're trapped. There isn't a way out from here," said Ransforth.

"There must be," grunted Grantham as he stood.

"Is there a greater meaning with those words in the carving?" asked Seyanna.

Jet considered what he had read. "The Legendary Battle...is the fable inside *The Sorcerer's Guide*. It talks about the books teaching Elemental magic and Runic magic as being the gatekeepers. There were also eight

Sentinels." He finished exploring the room but found nothing. "I just don't know what the last part of the riddle or poem means."

"Which part?" asked Grantham.

"There are five elements, but only four Elemental sentinels were released. The key phrase is the next to last—'He is the Regeneration of the Soul.' Does that mean Water magic or Spirit magic, or am I missing something completely?"

"Why water?" questioned Seyanna.

"Water is rebirth. And the Soul is like Spirit magic."

"Even if it is," said Grantham, "what are we supposed to do with it?" Leaning closer to Latisha, he cried, "Her breathing is bad! Can you try healing her again?"

"Heal," said Jet absentmindedly. "My spell doesn't heal, but it regenerates." He strode quickly past each sarcophagus and spoke "Thera." Without the energy from Iris, it would have been impossible to perform any additional magic. The lid of the sixth sarcophagus disappeared, replaced by a green, cloudy, enchanted water.

An ancient voice spoke from the darkness, "This is the Well of Reawakening. Each of you has been called here to receive a healing. But you must speak your choice to your friends and slumber inside the tomb. Once all four of you have complied, the children will be freed, and the bodach will be allowed to leave."

Seyanna asked, "Does that voice mean what I think it does?"

"Can I pick Latisha?" asked Grantham. The answer seemed to come to only Grantham. He held up the Rivalry weapon. "I want this healed."

"I want my magic back," Latisha whispered, catching everyone off guard so much that several embarrassing screams followed.

"Babe," said Grantham, bending down. "You okay?"

She was awake but somehow looked worse. Jet and Seyanna inched closer.

"Wait," said Seyanna.

"What?" demanded Grantham.

Seyanna said, "Remember Queen Lom Doost's warning? You have the hardest choice you'll ever make ahead of you."

"So?" hissed Grantham.

"Something has changed for Latisha. That choice might have once been the correct choice, but it is no longer."

"What is?" demanded Grantham.

"To live," said Jet. "I can't heal your wound. If it isn't healed, I think you're going to die. Even having your magic back won't save you."

"What about Mckenzey?" whimpered Latisha.

"That's the risk," said Jet.

There was a long pause as Latisha considered her injuries. Her eyes fell closed, and Jet worried they might not open.

"Babe," said Grantham kindly. "It's your choice."

Latisha shivered, then smiled, but her eyes remained closed. "My choice is to be healed physically."

"What about you?" asked Grantham to Jet.

"I want my cloak repaired."

They both turned to Seyanna, "And you?"

Seyanna stared directly at Jet. "I need my heart to be healed so I can love without darkness."

A look of puzzlement crossed Grantham's face, but he said nothing as he lifted Latisha and walked to the edge of the sarcophagus. Seyanna's hand slid into Jet's as they stood across from Grantham.

"Here we go." Grantham carefully laid Latisha into the water. She sank instantly from view.

Grantham climbed in next and vanished.

Seyanna squeezed his hand hard. "I hope this works."

"Me too," said Jet, and his thoughts had nothing to do with his own wish.

An instant later, she was gone.

"Don't forget me," said Ransforth.

Jet glanced up, having forgotten about the dwarf creature. "After we are gone, you'll be free."

He got into the water and leaned back, feeling a coolness over every inch of his body. When he was flat, he sank deeper into the water. He suddenly remembered the Lagoon of Arches and prayed this would be different. The water settled over his body, then forced its way into his mouth and lungs. Every ounce of oxygen was sponged from his body. He drifted off to sleep, then his body shifted so forcefully that he found himself standing in a room that was dim and murky.

The air on his face was icy cold, but his body felt warm and protected. Peering down, he found he was wearing the brown cloak. Grantham and Latisha hugged as if nothing had happened. Seyanna had the most peculiar look on her face. Jet took a step toward her when the entire cavern brightened, forcing him to close his eyes.

When his eyes adjusted, he found a large underground river dividing their small platform with a bank on the other side. Hundreds of stalagmites and stalactites littered the space across the water. But other than them, there were no other voices, sounds, or inkling that anyone alive was down there or had ever been.

"Hello," called our Latisha, and her words echoed around the cavern.

"This makes no sense," said Seyanna.

Behind them was the rock wall. To their left and right were shadows, dust, and debris, but all natural. Jet strode to the water as the others began their own search. He put his hands in the fast-moving, deep, warm water. He wasn't sure he could reach the opposite side safely if he took even a single step. The water at the bottom sparkled with golden sand.

"What's this?" asked Latisha.

Jet retreated and met Seyanna partway there. Her hand fell into his. They smiled but said nothing. When they reached Latisha's side, Grantham was already there. Together, they stared at a stone box, partly buried and nestled next to a small cleft. The box was similar to the boxes found inside the caverns for the Rivalry holding piece of the Phoenix.

"What should I do?" asked Latisha.

"Open it and see what is inside," said Grantham.

She did. Her eyes widened in surprise. Reaching in, she grasped something. Pulling it out, Jet was shocked to see that she held an ancient and large skeleton key. It was silver, the same color as Jet's new necklace. It was ten inches long and featured the traditional blade with numerous notches and ridges. However, Jet couldn't take his eye off the skull opposite the blade. This key dwarfed the one they had found in Congo.

Her voice shook when Latisha asked, "What now?"

The question answered itself. A green box began to glow, not five feet from where they stood, and on a mantle in the same wall. The keyhole was a softer green.

"I'm not putting that in there," said Latisha.

"It should be me," said Jet. He took it and climbed up three feet to reach the spot. Without a second thought, he inserted the key into the hole and turned it. Like a comet shooting through the nighttime sky, the green light refracted through the wall, floor, and around every pillar, crevice, and hole until the whole room was emblazoned with green.

"It's a chain reaction," said Seyanna.

She was right.

A hundred loud clicks all happened at once. Every protrusion or outcropping transformed into a huddling child. There were hundreds of them. Their bonds were broken. The green light dissipated, except near where the water met the wall. The children's screams were full of delight, and a wave of emotion passed through Jet.

A deafening cracking sound turned the cries of joy into cries of fear. The cave wall, still bathed in green, began to crumble away, and sunlight shone through.

Seyanna's voice, tear-choked, managed to say, "They're free."

The cries returned to joy, and Jet had never seen such happiness. Latisha and Seyanna squealed with delight, and a broad smile formed on Grantham's face. The river hastened as if these vestiges of water would be its last. The children instinctively sprang into the river, allowing themselves to be taken home. The moment when the final child, waving enthusiastically at them, exited the cave, the water dried up as if it had never been there.

"We did it," said Seyanna. "I can't believe we freed them."

"Absa-freaking fantastic," exclaimed Latisha, and there was only a trace of forlornness in her voice.

"I'm ready to go home," said Grantham. "But I have no idea how we are going to fly home with five hundred children."

"We don't have to," said Jet. "That river will lead them to their parents."

Jet put an arm around Seyanna and began marching toward the opening. Halfway to the entrance, a second wave of green lights snapped through the cave, then faded away, except for a flattened wall several feet to the left of the opening.

An earthquake shook the cavern, sending fragments of the ceiling and walls crashing to the floor. Instinctively, they pulled out their weapons as prepared for an attack. The green wall fell, and a second prison became distinguishable. The creature was the most hideous and evil thing Jet had ever seen. He let loose a scream that matched his friends.

A figure, twenty feet tall, stepped out into the hollow, staring at them. The beast was made of bones and tendons, thick and strong, of a yellowish-gray color. A dark purple, torn cloak hung over its shoulders and down to its legs. Purplish flames emitted from its hands. The creature bent the wrong way, arching its back opposite, and allowing its hands to touch the ground. Suddenly, its feet were in the air, and it righted itself. Jet's eyes were focused on the three horns, cutting through the hood, on the top of its head. Two of the horns were thicker and slightly angled forward. The third horn went skyward.

"Hello, Mikado and friends," said the Skeleton in a voice that grated on their senses. "To get here, you defeated the Insidious Six, which was no small feat. But your deaths will be pointless. Freeing the Coven's children will do nothing to stop my master from escaping. Now I am free to wreak havoc like you've never witnessed." Its voice was deep, harsh, and exotic. "I am not weak like Faunal and cannot attack you. I choose to be here, to imprison myself, to end the conflict before it can go any further. A maestro beguiled you. Now die." The Skeleton crept forward on all four legs and moved so fast it would have killed them before they had time to react.

Jet cried, "Spread—"

Before he finished, a flash of yellow light startled them, as it knocked the Skeleton back several feet. A bird dropped from an opening in the ceiling, landing on the ground before them, directly in the path of the Skeleton, which let loose a snarl. The flying creature had a stork's head, a long beak, and elongated legs that bent backward. Blue flames surrounded the creature.

"A Rhoenix," said Jet.

The Skeleton mocked, its words dripping with contempt, "Hello, Sarcoff. I half hoped you had been scared away by Elfin and Lalfin, but I should have known better. Your protection of the Mikado is noteworthy, but it cannot last when Arisol is released. You have but a few months until the demise of magic carries on. This isn't 'goodbye'... but 'till we meet again.'"

The Skeleton hurled itself at a different cavern wall. The wall stood no chance, and it exploded outward. Sarcoff swept after the Skeleton through the open hole and out of view.

"What just happened?" demanded Grantham.

"Something terrible, I fear." Jet looked from one to another. "I would've *never* freed the Coven's children had I known what was truly hidden down here. The Skelton will continue and continue until we fail. One wrong step and all will be lost. What have we unleashed on the world?"

THE ŒND

Thanks for your support and I hope you enjoyed *Insidious Six*. I ask that you consider leaving a review on Amazon or Goodreads (or both). This is an incredible way to support authors, and we appreciate each and every review. I read the reviews with an open mind, and equally important, they help new readers discover my books.

Additionally, you can sign up for my Newsletter at my Author Website https://lscottclark.com/. This will give you the chance to stay up to date on the latest book news, promos, and other awesome opportunities that might come down the line. It will also give me the opportunity to get to know you better. I update my readers at least once a month.

ABOUT THE AUTHOR

L. Scott Clark is intrigued by the magical world surrounding each of us. He writes young adult novels influenced by the incredible beauty of nature, the vastness of our world, and the psychological complexities between each of us.

Born and raised in Colorado, L. Scott deeply loves nature, mountains, oceans, and the sense of adventure that awaits us each time we step outside.

He is the author of **The Sorcerer's Guide** YA Fantasy series and hopes to expand his writing capabilities. He has written two books in the series – *Path of the Phoenix, Soul of Anesidora, Gravity of Deceit, Pool of Sorrows, and Insidious Six*. This is a seven-book series, and there are more surprises to come. He has written stories in YA, mystery, Short Stories, and more.

His path to becoming an author began in high school, fueled by his love of reading and writing. Initially, he pursued a degree in Physician Assistant Studies and has worked for many years in the medical field, correctional medicine.

L. Scott Clark began writing shortly after graduation, and it has been his own adventure to become a published author.

You can visit him online at www.LScottClark.com or on Twitter (@LScottClark) or Instagram (@lscottclarkauthor)